Praise for The Sleuth of Blackfriars Lane

No one writes action scenes like [...] it, and a cast of colorful characters for [...] re through the streets of Victorian London, as Kit struggles to find her place in the world. . .and the shadowy mastermind behind a string of mysterious crimes.

—Julie Klassen, author of *Shadows of Swanford Abbey*
and *The Sisters of Sea View*

Once again Michelle Griep crafts a tale that will keep readers flipping the pages to learn more about the adventures that these characters who have become friends get themselves into. Fans of the series will be hooked from page one!

—Roseanna M. White, Christy Award–winning author

Griep takes the reader deep into the gritty underworld of Victorian London, but they don't go alone. Always the light of hope, love, and justice goes along. Readers will relish the puzzle, the banter, and the smash-bang heart-pounding conclusion to this rollicking good series!

—Erica Vetsch, author of the Thorndike
and Swann Regency Mysteries

No author grabs my attention quite like Michelle Griep. I have loved and devoured each book in this series and couldn't wait to see more of Kit and Jackson! Oh, but now the stakes are even higher. It gutted me, then I found myself holding my breath, and finally cheering with tears in my eyes for this incredible couple.

—Kimberley Woodhouse, bestselling and award-winning
author of *The Secrets Beneath* and *A Mark of Grace*

The Sleuth of Blackfriars Lane is a phenomenal, heart-pumping ride through the streets of London, complete with danger, intrigue, and a dash of romance. My favorite Blackfriars story yet!

—Tara Johnson, author of *Engraved on the Heart*,
Where Dandelions Bloom, and *All Through the Night*

Mystery, suspense, and romance bundled up in a well-written story full of fun and interesting characters, shocking plot twists, and edge-of-your seat suspense. All found in *The Sleuth of Blackfriars Lane*, along with incredible scenery and language that will put you right there on the streets of London in 1887. Another raving hit for Michelle Griep!

—MaryLu Tyndall, author of bestselling
Guardians of the Saints series

Tender, heartwarming, sometimes madcap and never dull—Kit and Jackson are back, both growing into new roles. With a new season of life, they might be older and wiser, both shouldering responsibility that stretches them to their limits, but they are still the Kit and Jackson we know and love, always trying to save the world—or just the next person who happens to be in need. Fans of Griep will not want to miss this one!

—Shannon McNear, 2014 RITA® finalist,
2021 SELAH winner, and author of *Elinor*, *Mary*,
and *Rebecca* (Daughters of the Lost Colony)

Michelle Griep at her best! *The Sleuth of Blackfriars Lane* straps you into an emotional rollercoaster, so hang on for a wild ride!

—Ane Mulligan, award-winning author
of the Georgia Magnolias series

Kit and Jackson are at it again! With humor, heart, and a case as twisted as the back alleys of London, this intrepid pair once more thrills and delights with their madcap mayhem that will keep pages turning long into the night.

—Chawna Schroeder, author of *The Vault Between Spaces*

THE SLEUTH OF BLACKFRIARS LANE

MICHELLE GRIEP

BARBOUR
PUBLISHING

© 2024 by Michelle Griep

Print ISBN 978-1-63609-794-7

Adobe Digital Edition (.epub) 978-1-63609-795-4

Cover Design: Kirk DouPonce, DogEared Design

Published in association with the Books & Such Literary Management, 52 Mission Circle, Suite 122, PMB 170, Santa Rosa, CA 95409-5370, www.booksandsuch.com.

Published by Barbour Publishing, Inc., 1810 Barbour Drive, Uhrichsville, Ohio 44683, www.barbourbooks.com.

Our mission is to inspire the world with the life-changing message of the Bible.

 Member of the
Evangelical Christian
Publishers Association

Printed in the United States of America.

Dedication

To Katie Griep
because, my dear, I suspect there is a little bit of Kit in you.
And as always to my long-suffering, ever-patient Savior
because there is a whole lot of Kit in me.

Chapter One

London 1887

Three years ago, Kit Turner had been skiffing marks. Gaming dupes. Looking over her shoulder to stay one step ahead of the law. She ran with ruffians, consorted with cutthroats, swam in the bilgewater of London society. Just thinking of it twisted her lips into a smirk. No one would believe it of her now, not standing next to a retired police sergeant in a smart blue suit and married to the chief inspector of one of the city's busiest stations. Her gaze lifted to the freshly painted golden letters above the one-room office front. THE BLACKFRIARS LANE ENQUIRY AGENCY. Her agency. Well, to be fair, hers and her father's. The smirk bloomed into a full-fledged grin.

God surely did have a sense of humour.

"You can still back out, you know." Her father shot her a sideways glance. "I am more than capable of handling this on my own. I don't see how you are going to manage a baby and—"

She shot up her hand. "We have been over this a hundred times, Father. You know Jackson has given me his blessing on our new business."

"Foolish man," he mumbled. Maybe. Hard to tell with the rumbling wheels from a passing dray behind them.

"What was that?" She narrowed her eyes on him.

He narrowed his right back. "You have been wearing the same gown now for the past week, Daughter."

She glanced down at the green poplin. Sure enough, a few milk stains darkened the fabric of her bodice, and was that a smear of gunpowder at her waist? She swiped it away and awarded her father a sheepish smile.

"Well, it is mostly clean. Leastwise more than the rest of the laundry."

"See what I mean?" He lowered his voice as an eagle-eyed matron skirted them on the pavement. "You can barely keep your head above your household duties as it is."

His shot hit true, but it didn't sting. Household duties—as he put it—were a waste of time. Was it not far better to bring justice to the streets than to have a cupboard full of washed dishes?

"If Jackson doesn't mind, then I don't know why you should. Now"—she hooked her arm through his—"how about we start our first day at the Blackfriars Lane Enquiry Agency?"

Her father heaved a sigh. "I hope we know what we're doing."

"Of course we do." She tugged him towards the door. "With your history of tracking down scofflaws and my street smarts, we shall be the best investigators this city has ever seen."

Once inside, her father hung his hat on the coat-tree then eased his big frame into an old wooden chair behind the larger of two desks. Untucking the newspaper from beneath his arm, he shook it out and disappeared behind the headlines.

Kit opened her mouth to comment but just as quickly clamped her lips. Let him enjoy his peace and quiet. When clients started rolling in, neither of them would have time for such niceties—and speaking of which, she pulled out a cloth-wrapped bundle from her bag. "Here, Father, I brought you a little something for this auspicious day."

Lowering the paper, he retrieved her offering. "A brick?"

"No," she huffed. "A loaf of bread. I made it myself and thought we could share it along with some cheese at lunch today."

"Bread, eh? Very thoughtful of you." He set the bundle on the desktop, and she winced when it thwunked. "A valiant effort, at any rate."

At least he was being generous. The bread had turned out heavier than she'd intended. She was much better at hunting down crime-bent streeters than following a silly recipe.

Once again her father's paper unfurled. Kit strolled over to her desk. For a while she fiddled around with the inkstand, contemplating if it looked better at the center of the tabletop or on one of the corners. She opted for the top left. Pulling a notepad from the drawer, she set it in front of her, ready for the details from their very first client. And to be on the safe side, she even dipped her pen and wrote Case 001 at the top of the page along with today's date, for surely any minute now someone would stroll through the door seeking their help.

Yet the clock ticked on.

And on.

And on.

And still no one called.

Kit blew a curl off her brow. "Looks like we wasted our money on those newspaper advertisements."

"Give it time." The words crept around the side of her father's paper.

Kit drummed her fingers on her desk. "The handbills don't appear to be working either."

"Rome wasn't built in a day."

It would have been if I'd had any say in the matter. Biting back the retort, she crossed to the window. Beyond the glass, life bustled about. Across the street a pickle seller stood behind a large barrel, hawking green whoppers. A broken-springed hack lumbered down the lane at a rakish angle. Pedestrians of all sorts scuttled by: a ragman, two washerwomen, and a frizzle-haired fellow with an orange neckcloth clutching a messenger bag to his chest. Not one of them so much as glanced at the agency's door. Where were all the poor souls in need of excellent sleuthhounds?

She paced the outside track of the braided rug. "I bet if I went trolling down at the docks I'd find someone who could use our services. There's always some sort of crime in want of investigating around there."

Her father arched a brow over the top of his paper. "I will not have you traipsing amongst stevedores and sailors."

"Pish. I've done worse."

"Don't I know it. Sit down." Once again he disappeared behind the newspaper. "Let the work come to us."

She stifled a snort. That didn't sound like a viable business practice.

Heaving a long sigh, she strolled to the picture hanging on the wall and straightened it—though it didn't need it. A sepia-toned print of her and her father stared back, his bushy beard the focal point. She'd asked him to go clean shaven, suggested that average citizens would find his bear-like appearance intimidating. After all, they wanted to attract clients, not frighten them off. But he'd simply chuckled, saying, "Many a case has been solved by the simple act of the stroke of a beard or the twist of a moustache."

And yet, whiskers or not, they still didn't have a case!

Kit reached for her hat. "Maybe I'll just poke about the backstreets of Whitechapel. No doubt I can scare up a victim or two who'll pay to see justice done on their behalf."

"Jackson would not thank me if you were to become a victim yourself." At last her father folded up his paper. "So, the answer is no."

No? She popped her fists onto her hips. "You cannot tell your business partner what to do or what not to do."

"I just did." He folded his arms, the gleam in his dark eyes a gauntlet thrown to the ground.

"We have to do something to drum up business." It was churlish of her, but she couldn't resist flailing her hands. "At the very least I could shake out a swindler or two on Threadneedle Street. The businesses over there would be happy to rid themselves of the vermin preying on their customers."

"Have you not yet learned to trust in God's timing instead of your own?"

Oof. That was a low blow. She rehung her hat and set about making a pot of tea on the small hearth. While it steeped, she returned to her desk, and for a long while she sat tapping one finger against her lower lip. She had learned to trust in God's timing. . .but even so, weren't idle hands the devil's playground? She ought to at least—yes! That was just the thing. She grabbed her pen and started writing.

"What on earth are you doing?" her father asked.

"Jotting down a few notes," she murmured as she redipped her pen.

"Notes?" Footsteps thudded on the floorboards, her father's shadow soon looming over her page. "About what?"

She glanced up. "How to increase our business."

"Kit, what did I just say about trusting—"

The bell over the door jingled. In walked a bird-framed lady in a deep blue day dress with an accompanying peacock feather in her hat. She clutched her reticule in front of her as if it were a shield. There was something familiar about her cat-like eyes, but when she spoke, so silky was her voice that Kit had surely never before heard such a mesmerizing tone.

"Pardon me, but I am in need of a private enquiry agent. I hope I have come to the right place."

"See, Daughter?" Kit's father muttered under his breath. "Sometimes all it takes is a little faith."

Sure, faith could move mountains, but it would take more than that to sort through this mess of paperwork. Many hours would be required, not to mention a fair number of paper cuts. Yet there was nothing to be done but to dig in. Jackson Forge grabbed a handful of files and whumped them onto his desk. No wonder the former chief inspector had been so cross all the time.

But that didn't mean he had to be. No, indeed. He would face this challenge with a smile and be glad for the honour of serving in his new position. Becoming chief inspector was nothing to sneeze at, and he would make his sponsor—the Earl of March—proud he'd recommended him. He owed him that much and more for all his kindnesses in showering Bella with gifts when she was born and for becoming an ongoing patron for the soup kitchen.

Cracking his knuckles, Jackson geared up for the job. The sooner he got this over with, the sooner he'd get back to serving justice on London's streets. He flipped open the cover of the first file just as a knock rapped on his door.

And there went his brilliant beginning.

He shoved the stack aside and folded his hands on the desktop, striking a quintessential chief inspector pose. . .at least he hoped it was. "Enter."

A round ball of a man rolled in, his spectacles so thick the eyes behind them popped like an owl's. "Inspector Ira Harvey reporting for duty, sir." He yanked out a handkerchief and swiped it across his sweaty brow—which did nothing to relieve the darkened circles of perspiration spreading out from his armpits. The man didn't look capable of finding a child's stolen lollipop, let alone hauling in a ruthless criminal. Why the deuce had former Chief Inspector Ridley hired this soft fellow?

Then again, perhaps there was more to the man than first glance credited. Jackson gave him a crisp nod. "Excellent, Harvey. I understand this is your first day of service as an inspector."

"It is, sir."

"Very good, then I shall find you something to ease you into the swing of things." He shuffled through a few of the open cases, his gaze settling on one in particular. "Looks like there's a rat pit running over on Old Pye." He glanced up. "We can't have that, can we?"

"Oh, no sir." With a flourish, Harvey tucked away his handkerchief. "Absolutely not, sir."

"Good." He shoved the file across his desk. "Then shut it down."

"Mmm. . .I cannot, sir." The man shook his head, an amazing feat considering it didn't appear he had a neck.

Jackson frowned. "Why not?"

Harvey sniffed, his puffy cheeks jiggling with the action. "Rat fur makes me swell, sir."

Looks like you already have. Jackson swallowed the retort. The fellow could hardly be blamed for a physical deficiency. "Fine. I'll send someone else on that one." Once again he fingered through a few files, then flopped another atop the rat pit case. "How about you go over to Seven Dials and investigate who roughed up the owner of the gin shop on Queen Street? Sulkies is the name. Find the villain who committed the act and bring him in."

"Oh, I do not think so, sir." Harvey lifted his nose as if he smelled a fresh pile of manure.

Which, of course, was not to be borne. Jackson slapped his hands on the desk. "Why the devil not?"

"It is too far, sir. Perhaps you ought to enquire if the Charing Cross or Covent Garden stations might take on that case?"

Was this fellow seriously trying to tell him his business? Jackson lowered his voice to a growl lest he blast the man with a few oaths. "It is not for you to deem the boundaries of our jurisdiction."

"Naturally not, sir. But even so, I personally cannot travel such a distance." He whipped out his cloth once more, this time pulling off his spectacles and wiping away the fog. "You see, sir, I get terribly road sick when inside a coach."

"Then hoof it, man!"

"I have a bunion on my left foot, a real stallion of a bulge." Replacing his glasses, he honked into the cloth then stuffed it back in his pocket. "I do not think it in my best interest to inflame the thing any further."

And it is definitely not in my best interest to have you serve as an inspector!

Jackson sucked air through his teeth. It was either that or jump over the desk and throttle the man for insubordination. "Listen, Harvey, assignments are not up for debate. If you are not able to perform as commanded, then—"

A great scuffle from the corridor burst into the room. His old friend, Inspector Charles Baggett, clutched the collar of a wild-haired collection of rags that smelled little better than the Aldersgate Sewer.

"Oh, dear." Harvey edged to the far side of the office.

"Look what I found slinking around Spitalfields." The grin on Baggett's face shone particularly white-toothed against the backdrop of his soot-smeared face. "Been after this kipper for nigh on three weeks now."

The thug in his grasp struggled to free himself, an impossible feat with his wrists handcuffed behind him and Baggett's unrelenting grasp about his neck. "Ye got the wrong man, I tell ye." He choked. "Why, I'm a regular saint, tha's what. Ye've no right to treat me so poorly. Ye hear?"

"Shut yer gob, Pinge." Baggett gave him a good shake then faced Jackson with a gleam in his brown eyes. "You'd have loved the chase. This cully thought he'd give me the slip by going topside, but after scrabbling over three roofs, skimming down a drainpipe, then mucking through Nuckbuckle Alley, I—"

Jackson held up a finger, cutting him off. This story would be better told over a pint after hours. "Well done, Baggett, but perhaps you ought to first lock the man up before you regale me with the whole story?"

"Oh, right, I—"

"Chief Inspector Forge!" In barreled Sergeant Doyle, a steamroller with his broad shoulders, practically flattening Harvey against the wall. Even Baggett and his captive stepped aside, and no wonder. The sergeant held a bloody rag to his head, looking more like a monster than a police officer.

"Something's got to be done, Chief. This station is falling apart. My lamp fixture just broke loose from the ceiling and beaned me on the skull with no warning a'tall! We need more funding before someone gets seriously hurt, and as chief inspector, you're the man to make the request."

Jackson blew out a long breath. This was the sort of trouble the former chief had to deal with? No wonder the man had gone to an early grave. Rising, Jackson squared his shoulders. "Yes, Sergeant, I am fully aware of the need and my responsibilities, but—"

"I'm the one what's wronged here!" The thug wriggled in Baggett's grip.

"Pipe down." Baggett cuffed him in the head.

"About my assignment, sir." Harvey squawked from his corner, his voice rising above the curses spewing out of Pinge. "Is there any case less, em. . .suffice it to say I feel I would be a better fit for catching accounting errors or clerical espionage. Paperwork is the thing for me."

"This is all a moot point if this building crashes down around our ears!" Sergeant Doyle roared.

And at that very moment, the worst possible time for a long-legged, flint-faced superior to enter, Superintendent Hammerhead elbowed his way into the room.

"What sort of three-ring circus is this, Forge?"

Chapter Two

"You have come to the right place." Kit ushered the agency's very first client to one of the overstuffed chairs in front of the desks. The woman was a strange mix of rosewater and steel—an odd impression that Kit couldn't quite shake, nor could she account for it. Clearly there was nothing strong about the lady. In her fashionable blue gown, feathered hat, and silk gloves, she was likely more adept at attending dinner parties than besting some ruffian in a dark alley.

"I am Mrs. Forge, and this is Mr. Graybone." Kit swept her hand towards her father. "And at the risk of sounding pretentious, allow me to put your mind at ease that between us, we have years of experience investigating crime."

"Oh, I am so happy to hear it, for you see I. . ." The lady's lower lip quivered, and she pulled a lacy handkerchief from her reticule. "I need the best. The *very* best." A few delicate sniffles escaped, and she dabbed the corners of her eyes, the tail of lace bobbing just above a distinct mole near her mouth.

Oh dear. Whatever she'd come here about was clearly a heart-breaker. Kit rose. "Can I get you a cup of tea, Miss—?"

"Mrs., actually. Mrs. Charlotte Coleman. And yes, please. A spot of tea might help calm my nerves." She drew in a shaky breath.

Kit flew to the kettle while her father took over.

"Well then, Mrs. Coleman, how can we be of service?"

"She is gone. Oh, she is gone!" The last words came out on a wail.

Kit rushed back to the woman with a stout cup of Assam. "Here, now. Steady on."

"Thank you." Gratitude shone in Mrs. Coleman's eyes as she took a sip.

"Why don't you start at the beginning, Mrs. Coleman." Kit's father pulled out his pad of paper and a lead pencil. "If we are to help you, we must know all the details, such as who exactly is gone and what the circumstances are."

"Yes, yes. Of course. Forgive me." She set down her cup on the small table between the chairs, then squared her shoulders. "It is my husband, you see."

Hmm. Kit frowned. That didn't add up. "Yet you said *she* is gone."

"Indeed." The lady nodded. "So she is. But I'm getting ahead of myself. Everything started last year when Mr. Coleman began working late hours. I did not think much of it as I was in confinement and admittedly did not provide very good companionship. Yet his odd hours did not change even after our sweet little Lillibeth arrived. My husband became more snappish. Furtive. And these last few months"—she shuddered—"even violent." She pressed a hand to her cheek, a giveaway she'd been struck in the face at some time in the past.

What a cad! Anger flared in Kit's belly. "And you say this is unusual behaviour?"

"Yes. Mr. Coleman was ever the gentleman up to this point, but now. . ." The lady leaned forward in her seat, veins straining on her swanlike neck. "I fear for Lillibeth. You must get her back!"

"Aha." Kit's father tapped his pencil on the paper. "So, it is your child who is missing?"

"My child *and* my husband. He took her out of her crib and fled in the night."

"How awful!" Kit huffed. Good thing she wasn't holding a pencil or it would've been snapped in half.

"Please." Tears glimmered in Mrs. Coleman's green eyes. "You must find Mr. Coleman and get my child back."

"Without doubt! A babe should be in its mother's arms." Kit gripped the chair to keep from barreling out of the office this very minute and hunting down the bully with her boot knife.

"Yet," her father drawled, "the girl is with her father, who has every right to take the child, for she is his."

Kit's jaw dropped. "What about Mrs. Coleman's rights?"

Mrs. Coleman shifted uneasily on her seat. "You will take my case, will you not?"

What a question. She might not even charge the woman, so egregious was Mr. Coleman's act. It would be a pleasure to see him brought to heel. Kit lifted her chin. "Of course we—"

"A word, Mrs. Forge." Her father stood.

"But—"

He tipped his head towards the far corner of the room, the granite set to his jaw indicating he'd brook no argument.

Kit followed, barely reaching his side before she whispered, "What is the problem, Father? This woman's child has been stolen."

"Not stolen. Taken, and by the child's father no less."

"But that's not right!" She clamped her mouth shut and glanced over her shoulder. Thankfully, Mrs. Coleman sat with her back to them, apparently unaware of her outburst—or politely ignoring it.

"The twist in my gut tells me something isn't quite right about Mrs. Coleman either." Her father scrubbed a hand over his beard, his dark gaze meeting hers. "I think it would be a mistake to take on this case."

"How absurd. We cannot turn down our first paying job simply because the eggs you ate for breakfast are rebelling."

"After thirty years on the force, I've learned to trust my instinct." He dipped his head, a sure sign his heels were digging in. "If you'll remember, our policy is not to take on a case unless we are both in agreement. And I am not in this instance."

Kit stared at her shoes, preferring to study the scuff on her left toe than swallow that hard truth. "And you will not reconsider?"

"No." Her father's big hand rested gently on her shoulder. "I know this hits close to home, but we cannot let emotion run our business or we will not have a business to run."

A sigh deflated her. "Fine." She lifted her face, jaw clenching. "But I don't like it."

"Neither do I." Sincerity darkened the brown of his eyes. "We will pray God brings His conviction upon Mr. Coleman, aye?"

"And comforts Mrs. Coleman in the meantime."

"That's my girl." He squeezed her shoulder then broke their huddle.

Mrs. Coleman spoke before they reached their desks. "So, you will take my case? I shall pay whatever fee is required. Funding is not a problem."

Easing into her seat, Kit cut her father a sideways glance, begging with her eyes for him to field this one. Her throat was too tight to answer, her heart too sore to turn the woman down.

"I am sorry, Mrs. Coleman." And he was. Kit could tell by the gruffness in his voice. "My colleague and I shall have to decline, no matter how much you are willing to pay."

"But you do not understand. My child is in the hands of a fiend!" Rising, she closed in on Kit's desk, gaze locked on to hers. "Please, Mrs. Forge. From one woman to another, you must know how desperate I am."

"I do. Believe me, I truly do. No woman deserves such ill treatment." Nor did the helpless babe. Kit rubbed her eyes.

Oh God, protect that little one.

It felt wrong helping the woman by prayer alone, yet her father was right. They had agreed not to field a case unless they were both of one accord.

Tearing off a bottom portion of paper, she quickly wrote down the address of the Old Jewry Police Station and handed it over. "You may find some help by going to the police and opening a missing person's file. My husband is the chief inspector, and I know he shall do everything in his power to locate your husband and daughter. I cannot promise Mr. Coleman will return the child to you, but still, it might afford you an opportunity to speak to him with an officer present."

Lips tight, Mrs. Coleman tucked the paper into her reticule. So much sorrow weighed on her that the petite woman looked even smaller than when she'd arrived. "Thank you, Mrs. Forge."

Heart bleeding, Kit rose. Her father was right. This case did hit too close to home. "Allow me to see you to the door."

The lady rummaged in the small bag on her wrist and pulled out a calling card, then pressed it into Kit's hand. "If you change your mind, please contact me anytime. Day or night. I shall do anything to get back my baby girl. *Anything.*" Pain roughened her silky voice.

And stabbed Kit in the chest. Why was this so hard? Couldn't their first client have been a simple background check on a potential employee or an open-and-shut case of insurance fraud?

She patted the woman's arm. "God be with you, Mrs. Coleman."

Valiantly fighting another round of tears, the lady nodded then scurried into the flow of pedestrians. Kit shut the door behind her, tucking the card into her pocket. With heavy steps, she sank into her chair, the shine of her first day as an enquiry agent dulled to an ugly grey.

"Now, now. Chin up." Balling up his page of notes, her father arced it into the dustbin in the corner. "We're off to a rough start, but there will be other cases. I promise."

"I know." She blew out a long breath. "Just a little bit of faith, eh?"

White teeth flashed in his dark beard. "That's more like it." He stood and retrieved her hat. "How about you call it a day? I'll stay a bit longer and manage anything else that comes along."

Though it felt like defeat, even so, she nodded. "I suppose Martha wouldn't mind if I stopped by earlier."

"No, she wouldn't. Now off with you." He handed over her bonnet.

Kit fumbled with pinning her hat in place, then arched a brow at her father. "But you will let me know if we have a potential client?"

"I'll send a note should that happen." He slapped his hand to his heart. "I vow it."

"Drama? From you?"

"I learned from the best." He bopped her nose.

"You are as incorrigible as Jackson. Good day, Father." Rising to her toes, she buffed a kiss on his cheek, his whiskers tickling her mouth.

"Until tomorrow." He steered her out.

Midday in Blackfriars was a bubbling cauldron of life. Skippers, hawkers, beggars, and even the occasional smartly buttoned gent filled the streets. For some, such bustle annoyed. Not Kit. She welcomed the chaos with open arms. She belonged here in this throng of humanity, and thankfully Jackson had agreed...though their town house was several neighbourhoods over in a more civilized part of the city.

After only a five-minute stroll, she swung into a narrow back lane and pushed open the rear door to the soup kitchen. Standing at a stove, a willowy woman in an apron two sizes too large stirred a huge pot of deliciousness. The aroma of rich beef broth filled the air. Three pairs of eyes glanced up from peeling potatoes and chopping greens.

"Miss Kit!" the three girls said in unison.

Kit grinned. It was always a treat to be greeted with such enthusiasm. "Afternoon, girls, Martha."

Her friend turned from the stove, her blue eyes darkening with concern. "Yer back early. Everything a'right?"

It was for her, but not for poor Mrs. Coleman. Better, though, to leave that sorry business in the hands of God. She gained her friend's side and leaned over the pot, breathing in the meaty scent of the hearty stew. "Just a slow day, being the first one and all. Besides, better to catch you before the dinner hour." She waggled her eyebrows at Martha. "And before Inspector Baggett stops by, eh?"

"Flit." Martha's lips pursed. "What would ye know about that?"

"I'm not blind, my friend. He's sweet on you—and you're sweet on him."

"Don't be daft." Martha waved her spoon in the air, droplets of broth flying out in a spray. "He stops by for a meal, that's all. And who's to blame him, what with being a bachelor. My soup is better than a cold crust o' bread, can't anyone quarrel about that."

"You'll get no argument from me. Your soup is divine. But it's more than a belly filling the handsome inspector is after, for he could as easily take his meals at his boardinghouse." She elbowed the woman.

"Off with ye." Martha gave her a playful shove to the arm. "Who'd want a worn-out woman with seven mouths to feed besides?"

"Charles Baggett would, that's who."

Behind her, the three girls giggled.

"Hope all ye like, all of ye." She eyed her daughters then narrowed her gaze on Kit. "But hoping won't make it so. Now then, would ye like to collect a certain little bundle o' love?"

Kit grinned. "I'd like nothing better."

Leaving behind the heat of the kitchen, Kit strolled into the public room, quiet save for the soft breaths coming from a bundle of blankets in a makeshift crib. Kit leaned over the railing, heart swelling as she gazed at the dark-haired cherub sleeping sweetly. "Come to Mama, sweetums."

Bella's eyes popped open as Kit lifted her. "Ba-ba!"

"Mama," Kit corrected her. Everyone and everything was ba-ba to Bella, and yet Kit would have the girl's first word be *mama* despite Jackson's efforts to get her to say *papa*. She nuzzled her face against her little girl's neck, breathing in the warm-milk scent.

Bella cooed.

"That's my darling," Kit murmured.

And that's when it hit, right in the gut. If anyone—even Jackson—tried to pull this child from her arms, she'd fight to the death to get her back. . .just as Mrs. Coleman was trying to do. Frowning, she squeezed Bella tighter. Mrs. Coleman deserved to hold her own child.

And Kit would see that she did.

There was a noose swinging in the wind with his name on it—one fashioned by Superintendent Aloysius Hammerhead. Jackson tugged at his collar as he trotted up the few steps to home. He'd endured quite a bloody tongue-lashing from his superior today and, worse, suffered it in front of Harvey, Baggett, and Doyle. It would take time to rebuild the respect he'd surely lost from those men. Even more time to regain the confidence of Hammerhead.

Oy. What a day.

He unlocked the door and stepped into a dark entryway, immediately hitting his shin against the console table leg. Blast! Why hadn't Kit left the sconce on? Granted, it was late, but she always kept the light turned to dim whenever he worked long hours.

After a good rubdown of the offense, he hung up his hat to the sound of claws skritching along the floorboards. Kit and Bella may be a'bed but leave it to good ol' Brooks to greet him. Crouching, Jackson patted the armadillo on his rock-hard head.

"There's a good fellow."

He had hardly finished praising the animal before Brooks continued on his way, snuffling about the baseboards for any tasty spiders or other unsuspecting insects. Not a very conventional pet, but better than the tiger kit they'd rescued from an unscrupulous exotic animal dealer in Africa last year. Naturally the big cat was more at home in the London Zoo than in their modest town house, but he'd have preferred to trade the tiger for a Persian or a Pekingese instead of an elderly armadillo.

He'd learned, however, to carefully choose which battles to fight to the teeth with Kit and which to let go.

He loosened his collar as he bumped his way along the shadowy corridor. Two steps later, he stubbed his toe on a bucket of coal that had not yet made its way to the sitting room. Blast! Stifling a groan, he steadied himself against the wall, his gaze landing on a crooked picture frame. He straightened the thing with a smirk. Kit had many virtues, but housekeeping did not make the list.

Near the end of the passageway, pale yellow light eased softly out the dining room door. Odd, that. Instantly on alert, he covered his gun, ready for a draw as he crept down the carpet runner, listening intently. Brooks' claws clicked in the dark behind him. Outside, a horse clip-clopped by. But there was no sound whatsoever in the dining room. Jackson peered around the doorframe.

Then dropped his jaw.

Candlelight painted Kit in a golden glow where she sat across a table laden with platters of food. Her raven hair cascaded over her shoulders—bare shoulders, at that. A scandalous dressing gown hugged her curves in all the right places and the gleam in her eye made his mouth go dry. Sweet heavens. Was it warm in here? How could a woman he'd seen every day for the past two years still look so heart-stopping gorgeous?

And that's when it hit him. Those painted lips and blushing cheeks weren't just accidentally tempting. The little schemer. Either his wife had done something very bad or she wanted something.

He strolled into the room, his stomach growling at the scent of roast beef and buttered potatoes. "So, did you forget to pay the gas bill?"

She arched a brow. "You know, most husbands would say, 'Oh darling! How thoughtful of you to prepare a candlelit dinner.'"

He bent to give her a greeting kiss, but Lord have mercy! The moment their lips touched, she snaked her hand behind his head and kissed him senseless. Ahh, but he'd never tire of this woman's passion.

"Darling," he whispered, his mouth trailing down the arch of her neck. "How thoughtful of you to—"

Pulling away, she put a finger on his lips. "Let's just leave it at a kiss, shall we?"

He grabbed her hand and pressed his mouth to her wrist. "You, madam, are an enchantress."

"I haven't even tried yet." A mischievous twinkle gleamed in her eye. "But first, you must be famished. How about we eat before...?"

"Mmm. I like the sound of that." Waggling his eyebrows, he sat opposite her and shook out his napkin, marveling that for once there was not only a napkin but a full set of flatware beside a clean plate. He glanced at Kit as he served up heaps of meat, potatoes, bread, and even a perfectly moulded Gâteau de Pommes. How could she have possibly whipped up this much food? "I presume Bella is asleep?"

"Soundly." Kit licked one of her fingers.

Jackson leaned over his full plate and took a moment to inhale the savory scent. It smelled like heaven, looked like it too, but would the taste live up to his expectations? He took a tentative bite, chewed thoughtfully, then leaned back in his chair and eyed Kit. "All right, who are you and what have you done with my wife?"

"Very funny." She angled her head. "How was your first day as chief inspector?"

He shoved in another bite of beef before giving her a tight smile. Definitely a topic he'd rather not think about until tomorrow. "How about you tell me of your day, it being the grand opening and all. Did things go well for you and your father?"

"As well as can be expected, I suppose." She pushed a potato around the plate with her fork. "So far no clients, which is a bit disappointing."

"You know what they say, Rome wasn't—"

"Built in a day." She narrowed her eyes. "Which seems a case of gross mismanagement, if you ask me."

He grinned. No doubt had Kit been there, those men in togas would have fallen over themselves to do her bidding. He sopped his bread through a puddle of brown gravy and filled his mouth. "This is really very good," he mumbled between bites.

"Thank you. Speaking of Bella..."

His fork paused midway to his mouth. "Were we?"

"At one point." She fluttered her fingers in the air. "Hypothetically, I wonder what your reaction would be if someone were to take her."

He set down his fork, bite uneaten. That was no offhand comment. "What do you mean, 'take her'?"

"As in steal her away from you."

"What blackguard has threatened such a thing?" he roared as he shot to his feet. Armadillo claws scrambled out the room at high speed. "I'll make short work of anyone who dares touch my little girl."

"Calm down, Husband. No one has threatened her, so you don't need to break open anyone's head tonight." She dabbed her mouth with her napkin then folded it on the table, taking care to smooth the creases with her fingers. "I merely wondered what your response would be."

Jackson eased into his seat, no longer interested in the meal. "I would defend Bella—or you—with my life."

"Nothing would stop you?" Kit's gaze burned into his.

"All the powers of hell couldn't stop me. You and Bella are my world. But you know this." He cocked his head. "What did happen today? I would have all of it, so don't leave anything out."

Kit leaned forward, blue eyes shimmering in the candlelight. A lock of hair flopped over her brow, and she shoved it back. "Shortly before noon, a woman came into the agency who wished to hire my father and me to find her baby. Her husband took the child, and apparently the man has violent tendencies, leastwise towards her. I'm not sure about the daughter. At any rate, she charged us with bringing her back."

Jackson rubbed the tip of his moustache between his forefinger and thumb. No wonder Kit had gone to such dramatics this evening. Such a tale must have hit her hard, for though this former swindler knew her way around the roughest of London's streets, beneath that gunmetal exterior beat a soft heart. "I thought you said you had no clients?" he murmured.

"We don't." She slumped in her chair, knotting her neatly folded napkin into oblivion. "My father refused to take the case."

"Why?"

Kit slammed the wadded-up ball onto the table, rattling the glassware. "He claims he didn't have a good feeling about Mrs. Coleman. Something about his gut."

"Mmm. He does have good instincts. I think you should trust him in this."

"I do trust him, but..." She folded her arms, lips twisting. "Did Mrs. Coleman stop by the station? I told her to ask for you."

He shook his head. "Even if she had, I wouldn't have had time for her, not the way today went."

With a sigh, Kit rose and swept out of the room. Could be she was pouting, but no. That wasn't really her modus operandi. More like her fretting had driven her to heat up a pot of tea.

What she returned with, however, was a blanket bundle, one which she gently handed to him. He gazed upon the precious face of his little Bella, and once again his heart melted, just as it had the day the midwife had first given into his arms his newborn daughter. Bella's long lashes fanned against cheeks rosied by sleep. She smelled of warm milk and fresh bread, and for a moment, her lips worked as if she sucked her thumb. Pressing a light kiss against her brow, he took care not to wake her, and relished the velvety softness of her skin. He'd never stop marveling at what a miracle his union with Kit had wrought.

He glanced up at his wife as she took her seat. "You're not playing fair, you know."

She shook her head, fire in her eyes. "There is nothing fair about this."

"Perhaps the man had good reason to take his daughter, one neither his wife nor you know about."

"Possibly. Though unless someone looks into it, no one will ever know."

And there it was. The entire reason for the lengths his wife had gone to tonight.

"So that's what this is about." He nodded towards the table. "The candlelight, the meal you ordered out. You wish me to override your father and give you my blessing to take on this case, don't you?"

She frowned. "How do you know I didn't make this meal?"

"Because I didn't break a tooth on the bread, and the meat"—he lowered his voice as Bella stirred in his arms—"doesn't taste like an old boot."

Kit's frown folded into a scowl. "I can hardly be expected to excel out on the streets *and* in the kitchen." She lifted her chin. "But yes, if you must know, I would not like to be at odds with you over this case."

A smirk twisted his lips. "Since when do you need my consent?"

"I am your wife, Jackson." She looked down her nose at him. "I would not take on any venture without your agreement."

He snorted. What a whopper. Bella squirmed in his arms, her little face squinching up into what could be a rather magnificent wail.

"Shh," he soothed, rubbing his finger across her brow again and again. Slowly she relaxed in his arms, her face smoothing back into peaceful slumber. Such a sweet little blessing. He could only imagine the hole in his chest—in his soul—were she to be taken from him. Was that what was bothering his father-in-law? Was he remembering that his own daughter had been lost to him and this was simply too personal a case to manage?

"Very well." Jackson sighed. "Find that woman's baby and assess the danger, but you must let your father know that's what you're about. You're a team, remember? And I said *assess*, not rescue, mind? If the child is in peril, you will come to me for help, understood?"

"Yes!" she whisper-screamed then tore around the table and kissed him on the cheek. "Thank you, Husband."

He reached for her hand and entwined his fingers through hers, his jaw clenched rock tight. Hopefully that woman's child wasn't in harm's way, for as it was, he wouldn't really be able to help Kit with her investigation, not personally. The superintendent had made it abundantly clear he was to unsnarl the paperwork fiasco left behind by the former chief, and he was to "do so bloody well as soon as possible!"

Or he'd be let go.

Chapter Three

Darkness owned the streets at night. Not so much the mere blackness of sky or the sinister shadows hiding God knew what. No, this sort of insidiousness ran far deeper than that. Evil burrowed into men's hearts and sprang out on the unsuspecting. Sharpers. Bludgers. Killers and thieves. Charles Baggett understood that singular truth more than most.

But that didn't stop him from whistling as he strode along Blackfriars Lane. Let 'em try to take him down. He guaranteed he'd be the last man standing—on wobbly legs perhaps, but standing nonetheless.

He upped his pace, eager to see a certain golden-haired beauty. Indeed, fear was no way to live. Caution, however, was a whole different tale, which was why he kept his Webley revolver loaded and good to go.

No merry light shone out of the dining room's windows. He peeked inside as he approached the door. Dark, save for the glow coming from the kitchen at the far side of the room, making the empty tables look like hulking bully boys about to launch. Blast. He was later than he'd thought.

He tried the doorknob, a strange mix of relief and irritation churning in his empty belly. Martha should know better than to leave the thing unlocked. Any number of malcontents could bust in here and harm her and her children. His annoyance quickly faded, though, as he swung through the kitchen door and spied the graceful figure of Martha Jones and her four older girls working together to wash the dishes.

"Need some help cleaning up, ladies?"

Five heads turned his way. "Evenin', Mr. Baggett," two of the girls said in unison. The eldest, Harriet, frowned, but ten-year-old Jane broke rank and raced over to him, her face shining up into his. "I knew ye'd come! The others din't, but I knew it."

"You can't keep me away so easily." He swung her up into the air until she giggled, then set her down.

"Back to work, Jane." Martha arched a brow at the girl as she reached for a bowl. Despite her soiled apron and loosened strands of hair trailing from beneath her white cap, the woman's allure never failed to make Charles forget to breathe.

"What I be needin' help with, Inspector," she said, grinning, "is someone to eat this last dish o' stew. Be ye up for the task?"

And that right there was what he admired most about Martha Jones. She always thought of others, sometimes to her own detriment. Charles leaned against the doorframe, unable to pull his gaze from her. "I'll do my best."

"I thought ye might." She winked. "Mind the cleanup girls. I won't be a minute."

A chorus of "Yes, Mum"s blended with some giggles and a few giddy whispers. Harriet merely gave him a sour side-eye as he and Martha strolled out to the shadowy public room.

"Sit yerself down and dig in." Martha set the bowl on the table then retrieved a candlestick and lit it while he shoveled in his first bite.

Rich broth filled his mouth, the meat so tender it melted on his tongue. "Mmm," he moaned. "Delicious as always. Thank you, Mrs. Jones."

"Ye sound like a starving man." She sat across from him, a frown bending her brow. "And ye're late tonight. Rough go of it today?"

"More so for Forge than me. Actually—" He shoved in another bite, manners be hanged for food this good. "I had rather a banner day. Finally hauled in that sharper I told you about. After a little convincing, he ratted on his handler and gave me a lead on a bonneting gang troubling Regent's Park."

Martha bit her lip. "Sounds dangerous."

"It is—for them." He smirked.

"Don't be takin' any chances now, Mr. Baggett." She wagged her finger at him. "Who would eat the leftovers should anything happen to ye?"

He picked up his bowl and drained it dry, then set it down with a satisfied sigh. "I suspect, m'lady, any number of men would be happy to fill this chair. I do not take this privilege lightly. Rather, it is an honour."

"Go on with ye." A brilliant smile lit her face as she cut her hand through the air. The movement lifted her sleeve, revealing a small bruise on the inside of her wrist.

A mark the size of a man's thumb.

All his good humour vanished. He reached for her hand and turned her arm over for inspection. "How did this happen?"

She pulled back, tugging her sleeve into place with a lighthearted "Pish! 'Tis nothin'. Caught my arm on the corner of the table. I suppose you should know what a clumsy sheep I can be."

Could be. And actually, he ought to be grateful she'd suffered naught but a bruise instead of a burn, for kitchens were notoriously dangerous. But still. . .he studied the depths of her blue eyes. Was she lying? And if so, to what purpose?

"Now don't go sizing me up like one o' yer bounders off the street. There is no crime in being a namby-footed blunderer, and I'll thank ye not to embarrass me further."

Heat flashed up his neck. Thunder and turf! He'd never meant to shame her. "I beg your pardon, Mrs. Jones. I wouldn't ever wish to discomfit—"

She held up her palm with a grin. "Enough o' such talk. Now then, ye were sayin' Kit's man had a spot o' trouble."

"More than that, I'm afraid." He blew out a long breath. Poor Forge. He'd have done anything to help his old friend, but instead he'd done the opposite. "And I didn't help matters."

Martha patted his hand. "But ye'd ne'er willingly harm yer friend. Everyone knows that."

"No. Not intentionally." Martha's touch soothed, yet not nearly enough to take away the remorse that still tightened in his chest. "I should have known better than to haul my suspect up to Forge's office no matter how eager I was to deliver the man to justice. Horrible timing on my part because the new inspector Harvey and the sergeant piled in there as well. And of course, that's when the superintendent chose to grace the place with an impromptu visit. Quite the ugly tongue-lashing ol' Jackson received. He'll be smarting from that for days."

"Kit will see to him, don't ye worry none on that account." Martha squeezed his hand then pulled away. "Besides, ye had no way of knowing the boss man would pop in like that."

"You know, Mrs. Jones, sometimes I think you should join the force. I could use a partner with your loyalty, especially now that Forge is chained to a desk."

"Me, a bobby? Imagine that." Laughter as warm as an August day filled the room. "Why, I'll ne'er be anything more than a soup slinger. But don't get me wrong. I am glad fer it. Had Kit not purchased this kitchen and funded this mission to begin with, I daresay I'd be on the streets with my girls and my Frankie. T'aint much else fer a widow to do. Flit. E'en when ol' Olly were alive, we were barely a step above the gutter."

Rage clenched Charles' gut. Martha's former husband hadn't provided much for her save for a rough hand in life and even less in his death, leaving her nothing but some gambling debts he'd incurred while off on his fishing stints. Unbidden, Charles' hands curled into fists. The man hadn't deserved her.

"I would never see you in such straits, you must know that." His words came out huskier than he would've liked, but so be it.

"Yer a good man, Mr. Baggett." A smile curved her lips. "A very fine man."

"And you have a big heart, Mrs. Jones."

She blinked, her blue eyes filling with an emotion he couldn't name. He was about to ask her about it when the front door burst open.

"I did it. I did it!" Twelve-year-old Frankie dashed in and slammed a handful of coins onto the table. Martha's boy was at that awkward age between colt and stallion, all arms and legs and not grown into his skin quite yet.

"Such manners, Frankie!" Martha scolded. "Apologize to the inspector at once."

"Sorry, sir." He flashed a rakish grin.

"All's well, lad, yet in the future do as your mother says and don't go tearing into a room like a bookie's runner." Charles cuffed him on the shoulder. "But if I may ask, how did you acquire so much money?"

Frankie thumped his thumb against his chest. "Got me a job."

"Oh dear." Martha grimaced. "What sort this time?"

"Don't worry, Mum. 'Tis on the up and up. Why, e'en Miss Kit would bust a button o'er the fish I landed." He wrapped his fingers around the lapels of his raggedy coat. "Yer lookin' at the new stock boy fer Bellow's Glassworks."

Charles let out a low whistle. Quite the position for one so young. "How did you manage to accomplish that?"

Frankie leaned towards them both, eyebrows waggling. "Let's just say ol' man Bellow felt beholden to me."

"In what way?" Martha popped her fists onto her hips. "What sort o' tomfoolery have ye been up to, Franklin Oliver?"

Charles stifled a snort. The boy had to know if his mother used his full and formal given name, she'd take the truth and nothing less.

"Nothin' a shade too dark, Mum. I just happened to save Mr. Bellow from breaking his head when a runaway horse near to trampled the blighter."

"Mind your language, young man," Charles warned.

"Pardon." This time a genuine contrition actually dipped the lad's head. "Meant to say the horse nearly trampled the gent."

Martha shot Charles a grateful look before facing her son. "That's better. But how did ye manage to be in the right place at the right time?"

"Em. . .er. . ." He scuffed his toe against the floorboard, a telltale sign it wasn't only his foot that scrambled for traction. A moment later his face brightened. "God's providence, that's what! When Mr. Bellow learned I could read and cipher—thanks to Miss Kit—he took me on with an advance." He poked the money with his finger. "That's what he called it."

This time Charles did snort. "That is highly irregular, lad. No businessman hands out coins like peppermint drops."

Frankie slapped his hand to his heart. "God's truth." He pecked his mother's cheek then wheeled about. "I'll be off to bed now. Got to work tomorrow." He waved a hand in the air as he dashed to the stairs. "G'night, Mr. Baggett."

Silence reigned in the absence of the young tempest. Charles stared at Martha. She stared back—worry pinching her lips. That didn't sit well. Up till now her life had been nothing but worries. He'd gladly take this one from her.

"Don't fret." Reaching across the table, he squeezed her hand. "I will check into the validity of your son's story tomorrow and make sure Frankie is not in harm's way."

Her face softened, candlelight dancing lovely in her blue eyes. "I do believe, Inspector, that ye would save the very world if ye could."

"I do what I can, though I don't think there's anything I can do for poor ol' Forge. He's going to have to sink or swim on his own. And if he doesn't get that paperwork snarl untangled soon, he and his family will be in deep waters."

"Then we'll give 'em our prayers, eh? And by God's grace they'll manage. After all, 'tis not the job that provides their needs but the gracious God above what does."

Warmth swelled in his chest. She grounded him, this woman, always circling back to remind him that God was—and is—ever in charge.

He cracked a smile. "I think you are a saint in disguise, Mrs. Jones."

"Stuff and nonsense! Off with ye now a'fore my head swells too big fer my bonnet." Rising, she rounded the table and bent close to collect his bowl, her scent of warm bread and sweet butter leaving him hungry for more of her.

"Ye might not want to be late tomorrow evenin'. Fish chowder and sourdough. Won't last long, I suspect." She straightened.

He stood, one brow arching. "But no doubt a magical bowl will appear even were I to come after hours."

"Ack. Think ye're onto me, do ye?" She angled her head, loosing another strand of wavy blond hair.

He shoved his hands into his pockets lest he give in to the temptation to rub that silkiness between his fingers. "It is my job as an inspector to read people."

"That so?" She stepped close, face lifted, nothing but an empty soup bowl between them. "And what sort of story do I tell?"

"The most beautiful sort."

The words flew from the cage before he could recall them, and though he'd given his best effort for restraint, his hand snaked out of his pocket, and he brushed back that wave of hair. Just as he suspected, the downy feel of it nearly drove him to his knees. She was all softness and light, this woman. Someone he might pledge his heart to.

Suddenly sobered, he stepped back and gave her a sharp nod. "Good night, Mrs. Jones. Oh, and be sure to lock the door this time."

He stalked out without looking back, not even when she said, "G'night, Inspector."

Cool night air slapped him in the face as he pulled the door shut behind him. What was he doing? Flirting with a woman he had no business pursuing! There could be nothing between them. Martha Jones deserved better than a lawman who could be taken out by a bullet any day. She had already suffered the death of a husband, and he would not put her through that again. He was a good several years older than her, so that didn't work in his favour either. Besides—more importantly—he was a confirmed bachelor, one who'd vowed never to drop the guard around his heart.

Indeed, Edwina Draper had made sure of that.

Chapter Four

Strolling the rows of white stucco terrace houses in the Pimlico neighbourhood always made Kit toss back her shoulders in defiance. Here lived
the middle class, looking down their noses at those with less wealth, less
status, less humanity—leastwise according to many who resided here.
The funny thing is that those who inhabited Cavendish or Grosvenor
Square would do the same thing to the tenants of Pimlico.

And it would serve them right.

Kit smirked at the thought as she climbed the stairs to number
thirty-seven and rapped the door knocker.

Moments later, a housekeeper in a freshly starched apron answered,
her hair tucked neatly beneath her white cap. The tips of her shoes
peeking beneath her hem were polished to a fine sheen. Nary a wrinkle
marred her skirt. My. This quintessential servant had to be the envy of
every household on the street.

"May I help you, miss?" Even her voice carried dulcet tones.

"Yes." Kit held the woman's gaze. "I am here to see Mrs. Coleman,
following up on a visit she made to me yesterday."

"Ahh, yes. Right this way, please." She opened the door wider, and
after Kit passed through, she led her to a sitting room just off the side
of the front hall. "Whom may I say is calling?"

"Mrs. Forge. Your mistress will know who I am."

"Very good, Mrs. Forge." She dipped her head then pivoted with
military perfection.

Kit wandered the room. A lot could be learned about a person from the furnishings of his home. For the most part the space was sparsely furnished, indicating the Colemans felt no need to flaunt their money—and they must have a fair amount to live in Pimlico. A silver cigarette box adorned the mantel, as did a clock inlaid with gold filigree, indicating a fashionable taste and a desire for punctuality, or at least they were sticklers for timing the length of their visitor's stay. Nor were they the sentimental sort. Not one family picture or portrait graced the walls. Two overstuffed wingbacks and a sofa sat in a cozy collection in front of the hearth, none of which bore so much as a smudge from soot. Everything looked new. Unused. How unusual. Perhaps the Colemans didn't have many visitors.

"Mrs. Forge. I am delighted to see you."

Kit turned as Mrs. Coleman rushed in and clasped Kit's hands. Hopeful eyes locked on to hers, and a queer pang struck Kit's belly. She'd swear she'd seen that green gaze before, but she just couldn't place the face surrounding those eyes. Had they met sometime in the past? But. . .of course. No doubt this green-eyed woman—for such a hue was a rarity—reminded her of the wily Jade Swanson, a sharper who'd cheated her years ago when she hadn't known any better, or perhaps Carky Smathers. A shiver rippled through Kit. She hadn't given Carky a thought in years, not since she was shipped out to Australia.

"I hope this means. . . ?" Mrs. Coleman's fine neck strained.

"It does." Kit squeezed the woman's fingers. "I have decided to take on your case after all." A slight pang of guilt squeezed her chest for going against her father's wishes. But she would tell him of her decision and beg him to reconsider his. That had to count for something, didn't it? Perhaps he would change his mind.

"Oh!" Mrs. Coleman's hand flew to her chest, and she sank into one of the chairs. "I have been praying all night for just such an outcome. You have no idea how relieved I am. Please, have a seat."

Kit took one corner of the sofa and pulled out a notepad and pencil from her reticule. The devil was in the details, and if the devil who'd stolen his own child were to be found, she'd best take copious notes. "I will need a few particulars to get me going, starting with your husband's full name."

"Harold V Coleman, though the V does not stand for anything.

His mother thought it lent an air of mystery to her son." She blew a delicate snort. "I never suspected that mystique would play out in the disappearance of my baby daughter."

Kit jotted down the name. "Can you give me a physical description of your husband?"

"Nut-brown hair, normally slicked back. Brown eyes, rather intense. A full mouth, some might say overwide, and a square jaw." Kit's pencil flew, and she was grateful when Mrs. Coleman paused for a few beats before continuing. "Oh yes, and there is a hump on his nose from having been broken as a younger man. You know how schoolboys can be."

Hah! She didn't know much about schoolboys, but street-rat lads could certainly bust a face or two with their flying fists. She penciled down the defect then glanced up at Mrs. Coleman. "Age?"

"Thirty-two."

"And when was the last time you saw Mr. Coleman?"

"It has been three weeks now. I know I should have sought you out sooner, but I had hoped—" She choked. Pulling a finely embroidered handkerchief from her sleeve, she pressed the white fabric to her lips.

Such emotion was to be expected. Had someone taken Bella from her, she'd be a raging lunatic. Three weeks would be an eternity to be parted from her little love. It was hard enough to leave her behind at Martha's each morn.

She copied the information then angled her head at Mrs. Coleman. "You did the right thing in seeking me out, but I think the best course of action will be for me to accompany you to my husband's station to file a report. I would then be able to work alongside an officer to find your husband and child."

Kit smiled. She wouldn't be breaking her promise not to rescue the child if she had an officer along to do it for her.

Mrs. Coleman shook her head violently. "No police. There is a reason I sought a private investigator."

"Such as?"

The woman's lips pinched, the large mole near her mouth flattening somewhat. "My family."

The thin woman crossed to the window, sunshine blessing her auburn hair with glints of gold. Though she stared out the pane of glass, Kit got the distinct impression she didn't see a thing. "You have no idea the pressure my mother puts on me for social perfection, how my father values the sanctity of his good name. Were word to slip into the papers, linking me to either of them, the shame would be too much to bear." She whirled back, hugging herself. "Please, it is of the utmost importance this matter be kept out of the public eye, or I will be ostracized from society and my family. I would have nothing left. *Nothing.*"

Kit couldn't begin to understand the push and pull of such strangling family ties, but she did know desperation when she heard it. "I understand, Mrs. Coleman. Please be at ease. I don't see any reason why this cannot be kept discreet. In fact, I have a successful history of keeping to the shadows when need be."

Relief sagged her slim shoulders. "Thank you. I knew I came to the right person." She resumed her seat, posture once again erect. "You have my eternal gratitude for your prudence and your kindness."

"Think nothing of it." Kit flipped to a fresh page in her notebook. "Now then, pardon my prying, but were there issues between you and Mr. Coleman? Any infidelities, gambling habits, drinking problems?"

"Heavens, no. None I know of, or I suppose I should say *knew* of." She tucked away her handkerchief, jaw hardening. "I suspect my husband has recently fallen in with a bad crowd. He might even be involved in something illegal."

Kit narrowed her eyes. "What makes you say such a thing?"

"The last few months he has been so secretive, coming home late, leaving early, cagey, tense, angry—so unlike the man I married."

"Interesting." She tapped the pencil against the paper. Men didn't usually change for no reason. "How do you account for such an alteration?"

"I do not. I tried time and again to discuss the matter with him, but whenever I asked questions about his behaviour, he threatened me with violence." She rubbed her forearm lightly. Were that sleeve to rise, how many fading bruises might there be? Or worse, burn scars from cigarettes. An ugly truth but one Kit had seen on the abused women who frequented the soup kitchen.

"Oh, Mrs. Forge." The woman scooted to the edge of her seat. "I fear for my Lillibeth with the state my husband is in. He is so volatile. Even the smallest trifle sends him into a rage. Were little Lilli to cry overmuch, wailing as only a baby can, there is no telling to what he might resort."

Kit sucked in a breath. She knew exactly the desperation a crying baby could instill. Even sweet little Bella had moments of making her and Jackson fairly mad with frustration. But never—*ever*—had either of them even so much as thought of harming such an innocent babe. If that bully Mr. Coleman had dared lift a hand against the missing Lillibeth, he'd have more than the devil to pay. He'd have Kit Forge to answer to. "Believe me," she said through clenched teeth, "I shall do everything in my power to retrieve your little one unscathed."

"I trust you will." Mrs. Coleman breathed deeply several times, then brightened as her fingers fluttered to her necklace. "Would you like to see a portrait of my little darling?"

Kit smiled. Who could refuse a baby picture? "I would."

Mrs. Coleman closed the distance between them, sinking next to Kit on the sofa. She opened the locket and held the ornament out as far as the gold chain allowed.

Instantly Kit's heart melted. Large dark eyes—so much like Bella's—smiled out above a toothless grin. The child was several months younger than Bella—who was nearing her first birthday already—which only made the stab in her heart twist. Was little Lilli crying even now? Was she frightened? Cold? Hungry? This baby needed the arms of her mother!

Fighting her own well of emotion, Kit gently closed the locket. "She is a lovely child."

Mrs. Coleman wrapped her fingers around the golden oval and clutched it to her breast. "She is my heart."

"And I will get her back. I vow it." Once again she put pencil to paper, prepared to capture anything and everything that might be of help. "Tell me where your husband frequents, where he is employed, clubs he belongs to, the location of his family, favourite haunts such as pubs or coffeehouses. Nothing is too insignificant to mention."

Mrs. Coleman settled against the sofa cushion. "Mr. Coleman is—or was, I should say—a financial officer for Willis, Percival & Company. He has been with them for the past ten years."

"What do you mean *was*?"

"Well, naturally I stopped by his office. Several times, actually." Picking up a pillow, she toyed with the fringe. "On my last visit, Mr.

Percival informed me my husband had not been in for work since the very day my Lillibeth went missing. He also told me my husband's employment had been terminated for failure to attend his duties."

"Not surprising." Kit wrote it down then glanced up. "What about Mr. Coleman's family? Are your in-laws able to shed any light as to where your husband might be?"

The woman shook her head. "Mr. Coleman has no living relatives."

"How about friends, then? Acquaintances? Anyone who could be harbouring him?"

"Mr. Coleman led a very solitary life, which makes finding him all the more difficult. This is why I came to you."

"I see." Kit rolled the pencil in her fingers. A lone wolf was always harder to capture than someone who traveled in a pack. "Is there any other information you can give me? Obviously I'll check with his former employer, but have you no idea of where your husband may have gone when he was out for such irregular hours?"

"I do not. It is as if. . ." The woman's voice trailed off for a moment before hardening diamond sharp. "Why, it is as if my husband has disappeared off the face of the earth!"

Kit set down her pencil. What a fine bucket of fish guts this was turning out to be. She'd hoped for an intriguing first case to solve—

Not an impossible one.

Some mornings the universe conspired against you, and this was one of them. Jackson upped his pace as he approached Blackfriars Bridge. He'd been forced to take time to change into a new shirt and waistcoat when Bella had soiled through her nappy, which made him late to catch the omnibus, which forced him to hire a hack. All might have been well at that point had the coach not broken an axle. . .and if he'd not discovered the hole in his pocket where his money had fallen out. So, here he was, hoofing it to the Old Jewry station, later than he ought to be. A smirk twisted his lips.

Just like old times.

Traffic rolled by, cart and carriage wheels grinding in a higher pitch on the bridge deck than on the road. Ahead, several people clogged the walkway. Jackson's gaze skimmed past them, attracted by the flash of scarlet coattails flapping in the breeze. A stick figure of a man, more fence post than human, balanced precariously on the railing, arms outstretched. If the wind gusted, the fellow would set sail and plummet to his death. Jackson scowled. The lengths buskers would go with their theatrics, all for the passing of a hat and a few coins. He ought to haul the man in for being a nuisance, but that would take time he didn't have. A simple hand down and a warning would have to suffice.

As he drew nearer, though, silence complicated the situation. The man wasn't thrilling the onlookers with an engaging monologue. He wasn't singing a captivating ditty or extorting any coins by threatening to jump. He wasn't even looking at them. Jackson's blood ran cold. This was no macabre entertainment. Either the fellow was mad or he wished to die.

Jackson sprinted, shoving through gawkers, annoyed at their inaction. Humanity, of late, seemed incapable of taking any risk to self-preservation, which pumped his legs all the harder. If he didn't reach this man, no one else would save him.

Wind gusted.

The man swayed.

And the top half of his body fell forward.

Jackson lunged, wrapping an arm like a great hook around the fellow's legs as he flew through the air. Yanking him sideways. Tugging him back.

They hit hard. Ribs and hips smacking against bricks. Skulls skidding. For a long moment, Jackson lay dazed. Everything sounded muffled, as if he were underwater. And then it all roared back.

"Look a' that! He killed him!"

"Shoulda let the fellow take his own dive 'stead o' finishing off the sod hisself."

"Mebbe they're both dead."

Maybe—except a corpse wouldn't have such a banger of a headache and shooting pains in his side. Jackson pushed to all fours, testing his strength, then rolled over to sit. Five pairs of eyeballs gaped, and suddenly he understood how a freak at a sideshow felt.

Shaking it all off, he leaned over the body next to him. The man in the scarlet coat lay back towards him, deathly still. Blast! Had he killed him?

God, no. Please! I wished to save the fellow, not harm him.

With a firm yet gentle touch, Jackson rolled the man flat on his back. Morning sun glinted off gold paint embellishing a black mask that covered the top half of his face, from hairline to just above his lips. Had the fellow perchance been to a masquerade the night before and forgotten to remove the covering?

And still, he didn't move.

"He did kill 'im!" A bushy-bearded onlooker pointed a thick finger at Jackson. A collective "oohhh" whooshed like an unholy wind as the rest of the gawpers closed in.

"Back off!" Jackson barked. "Give the man some breathing space." Pressing a light touch to the fellow's neck, he felt for a pulse. Weak, but there. Thank God!

Jackson nudged him in the arm. "Are you all right, mate?"

Through the holes in the mask, the man's lids fluttered as if his eyes were flickering back and forth. A good sign, that.

"Hey!" Jackson slapped his cheek. "There's a good fellow. Talk to me."

A moan rumbled in the man's throat. His lips parted. Air rushed in and gushed out several times. His eyelashes quivered momentarily, and then eyes dark as bootblack flicked open.

"That's it." Jackson grinned. "Take some more deep breaths."

"What—" The man's voice squeaked. "What happened?"

"That devil nearly kilt ye, tha's what!" Once again Mr. Bushy Beard stabbed a finger at Jackson.

He stiffened. Of all the inane accusations. "Show's over," he snapped as he flipped up his lapel, flashing the badge he kept hidden. "Be off, all of you, before I lug you in for failure to act in saving a life."

A bogus charge, but the sudden fleeing of feet testified the morbid spectators didn't know any better.

He wrapped an arm around the man's bony shoulders. "How about we get you sitting up, eh? Might be easier to gather your wits when the world isn't upside down."

He gave the man a heave-ho, though he needn't have put so much force into it. The fellow couldn't have weighed any more than

Kit, so effortless was it to ease him against the railings. "There now, feeling better?"

Ebony eyes blinked behind the gaudy mask, yet the fellow said nothing. Was the face covering hindering his breathing? Jackson reached for the black ribbon. "Perhaps if we removed this—"

"No!" The man batted away his hand with surprising strength. Great tears welled, breaking loose in a stream behind the mask. "No, no, no," he wailed, folding at the waist.

Jackson rubbed his hands along his trousers, unsure what to do. Had hitting the pavement so hard unhinged the man completely so that he could no longer cope? But no. Clearly he'd already been disturbed—and greatly at that—or he'd have not been on the bridge railing in the first place. This fellow needed help, the sort of which he wasn't trained to give. And yet he had to do something.

"Come now." Jackson patted him lightly on the back, bones sharp against his palm despite the padding of his thick suit coat. The man's garments were of the finest quality, so lack of money couldn't be the thing that drove him to end it all. . .unless the fellow had recently lost his wealth. "It cannot be all that bad. There is no problem too great that our good and gracious Lord cannot help us with."

"You do not understand," he yowled.

"So enlighten me."

A great shudder shook his shoulders, then he jerked upright and stared at Jackson with red-rimmed eyes. "I should be dead!"

He'd not argue that point. "Clearly God has other things in mind for you."

The man's thin lips pulled into a line. "I do not believe in God."

"He believes in you." Jackson shrugged. "Enough to have sent me your way at this very moment in time." Aha! Now that could explain the odd set of circumstances that had delayed him thus far.

"Because of you. . ." The man slowly shook his head, lips parting in wonderment. "It is because of you I am not dead."

"Indeed, you are far from it. Already your colour is returning." With a final clap on the fellow's back, Jackson rose and offered a hand. "Let's get you on your feet before an overladen manure dray rolls by and dirties you with roll-off."

After a quick adjustment to straighten the elaborate mask, the man's pencil-thin fingers clasped his. This time Jackson didn't put quite so much muscle into lifting the man lest he fly into the road and be crushed beneath a wheel. Once standing, Jackson released his grip and studied the fellow. If he'd had a hat, he'd lost it to the breeze, his stringy brown hair peeling back from an angular face—leastwise what could be seen below the masquerade covering. He didn't wobble. Didn't clasp the rail for support. He stood on his own bird legs without aid, seemingly steady enough. Physically, anyway. There was no way of telling how broken the man's mind was.

Jackson rubbed away the grit on the left half of his face, thinking fast. He couldn't very well drop the man off on an asylum doorstep, not morally, at any rate. If the fellow were simply a bit off form from some recent tragedy in his life, locking him away with lunatics was unjust. Still, diagnosing if he was mad or merely eccentric was far beyond Jackson's expertise...that's it! There was a doctor's office just down the street from the station. He could bring the fellow there for a good go-over and let the doctor decide just what sort of help he needed.

Jackson swept out his hand. "How about you tell me your story as I am on my way to work."

The man's head jerked back. "You...you wish to listen to me?"

"Of course. Clearly there is something troubling you or you'd not have...well, you know." He swallowed. No sense in revisiting the near-death experience.

The man's mouth gaped into a large O, and without any warning whatsoever, he flung himself at Jackson, embracing him in a killer of a hug. "Oh, thank you. Thank you, my good man!"

Jackson peeled him off, not wishing to attract another group of gawkers. "No thanks needed. Shall we?" He angled his head. "I cannot afford to be any later than I am."

"Oh! Far be it from me to hinder you. I owe you my life, sir, so in no way shall I cause you to be even a minute—nay, one second—late to your job." He hooked his arm through Jackson's, tugging him into motion with surprising vigour.

"I think we shall do better unattached." He pulled away, uncomfortable with the man's excessive gratitude. "What is your name?"

"Ezra Catchpole, at your service." He dipped a bow as he walked. "And you are?"

"Jackson Forge."

"Oh, Mr. Forge, I cannot tell you how obliged I am to you, how your act of bravery has buoyed my very spirit, has restored my hope in mankind." His voice squeaked into a wistful pitch. "Perhaps life may be worth living after all."

Leaving behind the bridge, Jackson turned right at the next crossroad and gave Catchpole a sideways glance. The man didn't sound quite as insane as he'd first credited, for Jackson knew exactly the despair lost hope could bring. He'd been there before after witnessing ugly crime upon crime, all the injustice of the London streets, the downright evil he'd seen, felt. Always, though, God had reminded him to look past the darkness to see the light that yet remained in the world. And if Ezra Catchpole didn't believe in God, as he claimed, then no wonder he'd been ready to end it all at the bottom of the Thames.

"What happened that caused you to be so low, Mr. Catchpole?"

The lips below the mask twisted into a bitter line. "Loss. Unspeakable loss."

"Such as?"

Catchpole eyed him as if he were the crazy one. "I said it was unspeakable, sir."

Jackson's brows rose. Apparently the man literally meant what he'd said.

"Tut-tut. Take no offense." Catchpole skirted a loose chicken, then dodged the lad chasing after it before rejoining Jackson's side. "Rather, take heart you have completely refurbished my bleak outlook, and I shall spend the rest of my days repaying the debt I owe you."

"You owe me nothing, Mr. Catchpole."

"Oh, but I most emphatically do!"

That could be a problem. He had enough troubles to deal with without having to evade an overly clinging scarecrow bent on compensating him for some imagined obligation.

"Truly, I insist there is no duty on your part whatsoever." He stopped in front of Dr. Stapler's door and pushed it open. "Here now, be a good fellow and tend to that scrape on your jaw. Let a medical examiner assess you fully. Will you do that?"

Catchpole gazed up at him. Not only was the man thin, but the top of his head barely came to Jackson's chin. "Do you really think it necessary?"

Jackson nodded sharply. "Without a doubt."

"But what about you? There is already a bruise darkening your cheek."

"I am a police officer, Mr. Catchpole." He smirked. "Believe me, I have seen worse." Hah! Being a lawman had nothing to do with the aches he'd suffered the past few years. He had Kit to thank for those.

"An officer? Outstanding!" A mouthful of crooked teeth spread in a grin. "You really shall need my assistance."

"Yes, well. . .off with you now." Jackson flicked his fingers towards the doctor's office. "Get yourself a thorough go-over, eh?"

"Upon your word, yes, I shall. Absolutely." He stiffened to a ramrod, one skinny arm snapping a salute. "Good day, Mr. Forge. I will be seeing you."

The odd little man darted inside, ribbon strings from the mask flying behind him.

Jackson pulled the door shut and re-entered the flow of pedestrians, his gut clenching. Was he wrong to hope the doctor would deem Catchpole mad enough to warrant confinement, or at least to provide some tonic to set his mind straight?

Because otherwise, his already-complicated life was just about to gain another twist.

Chapter Five

Kit strode through the enquiry agency's door, mind whirring as she mapped out a plan of attack for the Coleman case...and the first battle would be with her big bear of a father, who eyed her from his desk. She'd have a much easier time of finding the missing man and child if she could sway him to join her in the search.

"Good morning, Father," she said sweetly as she hung her hat on the coat-tree.

"Mmm," he rumbled. "Taking after your husband, are you?"

Repinning a loose strand of hair, she frowned. "In what way?"

"It is no longer morning." His thick index finger pointed at the wall clock.

Bother! Half past twelve already? She never should have stopped by the launderer's to pick up Jackson's shirts after leaving Mrs. Coleman's house. But it was either that or ask her husband to go yet another day in the same shirt—the one he'd been relegated to for the past week. He didn't complain, though. In fact, she doubted he even noticed the increasing odour, so preoccupied had he been with work. But wrinkles and stink aside, it was the washerwoman who had forced her hand, threatening to sell his garments if Kit didn't retrieve them.

"I had a stop to make first." Two, actually, if she counted Mrs. Coleman's. As she took the chair in front of her father's desk, she glanced at the ceiling.

A little favour here please, Lord?

Smoothing out her skirt, she faced her father, still not quite sure how to tell him she'd taken on the Coleman case without his agreement. "I should like to speak with you." Eyes narrowing on the open file in front of him, she scooted to the edge of her chair and stretched her neck. What was he up to? "That is, if you aren't already occupied."

He slammed the folder shut, his ham-sized hand fixed firmly atop it. "I always have time for you."

True, but a clear deflection...one she could use to her benefit, perhaps.

"I should hope so, being I am your partner." She sank against the cushion, pausing for a beat. Just like reeling in a large fish, it never paid to be overly hasty. "And speaking as your business partner, I hope you will hear me out with an open mind."

His bushy brows gathered like thunderclouds, an accusing gleam in his dark eyes. "You didn't."

Annoyance flared in her belly. How could he possibly know she'd taken on Mrs. Coleman's case before she told him? The man was far too canny—a trait she enjoyed in herself but would prefer if others didn't possess quite so much. "As a matter of fact, I did."

"Kit." Disgust sullied her name. "I believe I made myself more than clear on that Coleman business."

"Yes, but Father—"

"Uh-uh." He wagged his big finger. "Partner, you mean, for you cannot have it both ways. Either we keep our relationship outside the door or we do not. And up to this point you have made it abundantly clear you wish to be treated as a professional associate, not as my daughter. Therefore, it is not right that you play upon my sympathies in order to wheedle me into doing your bidding. That is not how a business is run."

Scads! She'd used the wrong bait. She hefted a great sigh. "You're right."

"What's this?" His head reared back. "Humility?"

"Pish!" She cut her hand through the air. "Can we get back on topic please?"

A chuckle rumbled in his throat. "You know, your nose—"

"Yes, yes, my nose scrunches when I am incensed, so Jackson has told me time and again." She'd always heard a woman would marry a man most like her father, but it didn't seem fair she'd met Jackson *before* she knew this man.

She shifted on the chair, angling for a better position and new line of attack. "Now then, about Mrs. Coleman. As you already assumed, I have taken the case, but if you would only listen to the details I have discovered this morning, I think you might change your mind on the matter—or your stomach, as the case may be."

His nostrils flared as he folded his arms. "I highly doubt it."

Bullheaded man. A great quality for a police sergeant. Now, not so much. Rising, she planted her palms on his desktop. "But Father, just think if Jackson stole your very own granddaughter."

He arched a single brow.

Blast. Once again she'd veered into the ditch of playing the family card. She straightened, annoyed at her mistake. "Imagine, then, if the baby you know as Isabella Jane Forge were abducted by a violent man. Would you not do everything in your power to return said baby to her rightful mother?"

"We don't know if Mr. Coleman is violent. It's Mrs. Coleman's word against her husband. You don't even know his side of the story."

He spoke truth, but that didn't mean she had to like it—and she most emphatically did not. "Which is why I should find him, don't you see? Allow him to explain what's going on. Doing such will either prove or disprove your gut feeling about Mrs. Coleman, so will you please reconsider this case?"

Unfolding his arms, he laced his fingers on the tabletop, gaze never once straying from hers. "At the moment, no."

"Fine." The word snipped out sharper than she intended, as petulant a sound as the stamp of her feet as she clipped to her desk. A churlish reaction, one that irritated her as much as it likely did her father. Perhaps she was a bit too emotionally attached to the case.

Pull yourself together, girl.

"If it makes you feel any better about the situation, Father, I did discuss the matter with Jackson. He gave his blessing as long as I only locate the father and baby—which is in no way illegal—then turn the case over to him if there appears to be any wrongdoing." She lifted her chin. "And he charged me to let you know that's what I am about, which I just did. So, there you have it."

He arched a brow, his opposite eye narrowing. "You may be fooling yourself, but I don't believe a word of that drivel. If you see a child in harm's way, you will dive in headfirst to rescue it whether it is safe for you to do so or not. Whatever promise you made to your husband will be null and void."

Drats. There was no point arguing over that.

So she ignored him, sliding out her notepad to organize her next steps. First a visit to Mr. Coleman's former employer was in order. Then a cursory check with nearby hospitals to make sure no injured baby girls had been admitted, and after that—

Movement caught at the corner of her eye. She glanced up as her father strode to the coat-tree and retrieved his hat, folder tucked beneath his arm. "Where are you going?"

"I have a lead on another case." He continued on to the door.

So, that explained the earlier deflection, but not completely. She set down her pencil. "Who? What? When did you acquire it?"

"I don't have all the details yet, so I have not officially taken it on, but perhaps when you're finished with your own case"—he flashed her a wink over his shoulder—"I shall tell you about this one."

Charles Baggett doffed his hat as he strolled through the open door of Mr. Royden Bellow's office suite. Then frowned. Why was it business offices were all the same? A stuffy anteroom, usually with a window and a nearby potted plant, a sturdy desk, a closed door with the name of a bigwig flourished in gold paint on a glass pane, and a clerk to keep out the riffraff. Bellow's Glassworks was no different—save for a beagle sitting at attention by Bellow's office door. A *stuffed* beagle. Dead as a corpse on a slab at the deadhouse yet preserved and posed to look as if the dog might trot over and sniff his trousers. Apparently Mr. Bellow had a soft spot for this former pet and his wife didn't, hence the hound in the office instead of the owner's mansion.

Pulling his gaze from the dog's glassy eyes, Charles faced the clerk. "I should like to see Mr. Bellow, please."

The clerk peered up at him, both cheeks as abnormally red as if he'd been freshly slapped. "Have you an appointment?"

"No."

"Then I am afraid that is impossible." He tapped an open ledger with his finger. "Mr. Bellow is booked for the day."

Charles glanced past the clerk's shoulder. Behind the glass in the mahogany-paneled office sat the president himself—or so he assumed—ensconced behind a massive desk and eating some sort of pie. Clearly Mr. Bellow wasn't booked at the moment.

Charles' gaze drifted back to the cherry-faced clerk. "I do beg your pardon, but I suddenly realize that my name might be on today's diary. How about you look? Baggett. Charles Baggett."

"You might have said so to begin with," the clerk grumbled.

The instant the fellow began running his finger down the day's appointments, Charles dashed around the desk and rapped on Bellow's door, ignoring the clerk's ragged cries of "Stop! Stop this very minute! You are not allowed to—"

Charles cracked open the president's door. "Might I have a word with you, Mr. Bellow? I vow I shall be brief."

The president's fork stopped midair. "Who are you? And how did you make it past my clerk?"

"I am sorry, Mr. Bellow!" The clerk's voice stabbed Charles between the shoulder blades. Fingers bit into his upper arm. "Off with you, now!"

Charles stifled a chuckle. He outweighed the man by at least two stone and was an entire head taller. The small clerk was no more threatening than the dead dog outside. He certainly had pluck, though. Charles would give him that. Still, Bellow really ought to employ a larger man as his gatekeeper.

In one swift movement, Charles shrugged off the clerk and flipped up his lapel, flashing his badge—a trick he'd picked up from Jackson. "Your clerk is not to be blamed, sir, just educated in evasion tactics. I am Inspector Baggett, and I reassure you, I need but a moment of your time."

Mr. Bellow set down his fork. Meat pie, not fruit—kidney, judging by the savory scent and richness of the filling colour. "That will be all, Mr. Popkin."

"Yes, sir."

Footsteps retreated as Mr. Bellow leaned back in his seat, perfectly framed by the panes of glass behind him that overlooked the glassworks. He was a fit man, his bespoke suit moulding neatly over his trim physique.

A sharp tack, both in figure and intelligence, his silvery-blue eyes keen as they swept over Charles. "Have a seat, Inspector. Am I under some sort of investigation?"

"Nothing of the sort, sir." He perched on one of the leather chairs in front of the desk. "I am here on a personal matter."

Bellow cocked his head like a spring robin on the hunt. "Such as?"

"The boy you hired yesterday, Frankie Jones. He returned home with a handful of coins, supposedly an advance from you. I'm merely checking on the validity of his story." He held up a finger. "Not that the lad is untrustworthy, mind, it just seemed a bit suspect. I promised the lad's mother I'd look into the truth of it."

"I suppose in your line of work you see ill intent behind every act, be it kind or not."

Charles dissected the man's words with lightning speed. Much could be gleaned when tossing up a statement and allowing the chaff to blow away. "So, am I to understand kindness motivated your generosity?"

"Obligation, actually."

Ahh. Perhaps Frankie had been forthright, though just how much remained to be discovered. Charles shifted on the chair, angling for answers and comfort on the hard cushion. "Has this anything to do with a horse?"

One grey brow lifted slightly. "He told you, then."

"He did, but I would still like to hear your side of the story."

The sudden dip of that same brow indicted in ways Charles couldn't understand. "Brief, eh?"

Oh. That. A good reminder never to make such a promise. He flashed Bellow a grin. "I realize I am interrupting your meal, and for that I beg your pardon, but for the peace of a mother's heart—as your own dear mother would surely have requested the same—would you relate a short account of yesterday's happenings?"

Bellow laughed, the foghorn richness of it surprising for such a compact fellow. "Very shrewd, Inspector. I daresay the force is happy with your performance." He rose and strolled to the big window overlooking the work floor, then swung back around. "Normally I engage in a short constitutional immediately following my lunch. Not far, merely a leg stretcher the length of the factory wall, across the lane, along the opposite side of the road, then return to finish off my day in the office. But yesterday. . ."

Absently, he rubbed his shoulder, a slight wince tightening his jaw. "As fate would have it, when I stepped off the pavement, a runaway horse nearly took me out, and would have, had not young Jones launched his full weight into me. We both took a tumble, yet because of the lad's brave act, I came away with nothing but a suit coat in need of repair and a bit of an ache."

Dropping his hand, he returned to his chair. "I felt I owed the boy for such a daring feat of courage, hence the handful of coins. A reward, if you will."

So, Frankie's story had been true—mostly. No doubt the little scofflaw had cased the area, learned Bellow's schedule, and arranged for a loose horse at just the right time when he could play the hero. Cunning—something he'd expect from one of Kit's protégés. A smirk twitched his lips. Poor Martha had her hands full managing Frankie every bit as much as Jackson did reining in Kit.

He met Mr. Bellow's gaze. "Thank you for the information, sir. By all you've shared, it sounds to me like your obligation was fulfilled. You needn't have hired the lad as your stock boy."

"That was more of a favour than an obligation." He spread his hands, a thick gold ring on his pinkie flashing his wealth. "I took pity on him, you see. Judging by the patches on the boy's coat, I figured he could use the employment. And when I learned Jones was literate, he seemed a natural fit to take on the job of my former stock boy. So, I hired him on the spot."

Charles narrowed his eyes. That didn't add up. "How did you discover the boy could read?"

"A document must have fallen from my pocket. Jones collected it and—quite forthrightly, I must add—returned it with the admonition that I ought not lose a paper from Greaves and Grunkle." Bellow held up the paper in question, pointing at the top of the wrinkled page. "There was no way he could have known that's who this was from unless he read the letterhead."

Jackson shoved down a snort. More like the boy had pickpocketed the thing to make a grand show of his intelligence. "Is that so?" he drawled.

"Yes, so you see, Inspector, all is on the up-and-up. My other stock boy happens to be out of commission, and young Jones fits the bill." He reached for his fork. "Have you any further questions?"

"Just one. Might I stop by and check on how Jones is doing on his first day?"

"As you wish." He speared a piece of pie. "But you should know this is a hot and sooty industry. Rarely have I visited the floor and left without at least one cinder burn on my suit. You'll find him in the glassery." He hitched a thumb towards the large panes behind him, indicating the swarm of gritty workers below. A rather macabre scene lit by the orange glow of fire when small doors opened and glass entered the flames. And a surprisingly good view it was. How much did Bellow pay to have that grand window kept clean?

Charles rubbed the back of his neck, something yet niggling. Frankie had told him he worked in the warehouse, not the blazing work floor. "I thought the lad served as a stock boy."

"He does." Bellow shoveled in a bite of pie and chewed. "Jones keeps a fresh stock of soda ash and limestone handy for the blowers. It is imperative he keep an eye on their supplies and replenish as needed. If the furnace temperature dips, production is hindered."

"Oh, my misunderstanding." He rose and extended his arm. "Thank you for all your help, Mr. Bellow."

He shook his hand with a wink. "I only did so for the sake of my dear mother, God rest her."

"Indeed." Charles grinned. "Good day."

He strode from the office only to be met with daggers shooting out of Mr. Popkin's dark gaze. Charles leaned over his desk, one brow arched. "A piece of advice, sir. Never trust words alone to stop a man. I suggest you invest in a truncheon."

"Why, I never—"

Charles whistled as he strode from the room, ignoring the clerk's slurs. He'd expect no less from the fellow after suffering such an embarrassment in front of his superior.

His merriment soon faded as he descended several flights of stairs to the maw of hell. It was a black world down here, full of red sparks and glowing hot orbs. The glassery. Hah. More like Hades.

Heat blasted his face, and he tugged at his collar. How did the sweat-streaked men and boys—for yes, lads in aprons two sizes too big were everywhere—stand the heat?

"Mind yer step!"

He ducked as a rod with a tip as fiery as a branding iron nearly clouted him in the head. Even without making connection, the intensity of it seared across his cheek. He pressed his fingers to the burn and edged to a wall, then jumped away from it. That was no mere wall but the side of a furnace, singeing his backside.

Thunder and turf! This was no place for a lanky-limbed boy who hadn't yet grown peach fuzz on his chin. No wonder the former stock boy had been put out of commission. This was Dante's Inferno where accidents were just waiting to happen—nay—*begging* to happen! Charles scowled. Bellow hadn't been doing Frankie a favour. He'd doomed the boy to possible injury.

Or death.

Chapter Six

It was the little things that destined a day to greatness, and Jackson had a hunch deep in his gut that this would be a spectacular day. How could it not be? Not so much as a dab of baby drool marred his suit coat *and* he wore a sweet-smelling shirt. For once. The passionate kiss Kit had sent him out the door with still burned on his lips, and he'd even gotten a full night's sleep. Well, five hours anyway, which was practically a miracle considering Bella's habit of babbling in her sleep. No doubt his little angel would be an orator when she grew up—though as of yet he'd not gotten her to say *papa*. He grinned as he turned onto Blackfriars Lane. Isabella Jane was every bit as fiery as her mother, and he loved them both so much his heart swelled to a sweet ache in his chest.

A flash of red lurched out in front of him. Morning sunshine glinted off golden paint on a black masquerade mask. Jackson barely stopped before bowling over the stick figure of Ezra Catchpole. Evidently the man wasn't certifiably mad, for here he was in all his unconventional glory.

"Good morning, Mr. Forge! On your way to work, I see, which is exactly where I had hoped to cross your path." He shot out an arm thin as a rake handle, a paper sack clutched in his hand. Grease stains soaked through in splotches. "I have brought you some fortification for all the important criminals you must wrangle today."

Jackson shook his head. "I appreciate the gesture, but you really needn't have."

"I insist, though you deserve more than this mean gift." He shoved the bag into Jackson's hand.

Jackson had no choice but to grab the thing lest it fall to the pavement. Inside sat a jumble of squished pastries, apple and mincemeat fillings smeared against the paper. One roll had already been sampled, hopefully broken off and not bitten, but hard to tell. What a contradiction the man was. Dressed in fine garments—albeit garish with that red frock coat—and able to purchase food to share. Yet that stringy hair could use a good washing, and his shoes, while shined to a fine gleam, had paper-thin soles as if he roamed the streets day and night.

"Thank you for your thoughtfulness, Mr. Catchpole." Jackson scanned the man's face, what he could see of it, anyway. The scrape on his jaw from yesterday's tumble bloomed a darker shade of purple and shimmered with some sort of salve that'd been applied atop it.

Jackson angled his head. "Say, how did your doctor visit go?"

"Absolutely capital!" Catchpole's lips parted in a grin, teeth like crooked fence posts popping out. "Other than a blister on my left toe—which was a foreknown condition—he could find nothing at all of concern."

"Nothing? Not even. . .mentally?"

Catchpole tapped his temple. "You will be happy to know I am in a far better state of mind than yesterday, and all because of you. Why, Dr. Stapler declared me as fit as the queen herself. Is that not spectacular news?"

"Er. . .yes. Of course. I am happy for you."

"As I knew you would be! So"—he leaned close, dark eyes gleaming behind his mask—"now my health need be no hindrance whatsoever in serving you."

Jackson's gut clenched. No doubt the man meant well, but he didn't have time for this. He ought to be at the station this very minute instead of nattering over a bag of crushed pastries. "I assure you, Mr. Catchpole, I require no service whatsoever other than that you go on and live your life to the fullest."

"Yes, yes! That I will." He nudged his shoulder against Jackson's. "Once I have sufficiently repaid my debt to you."

"There is no debt."

"Oh, humble man!" he cried, attracting the stare of a passing nurse and her young charge. "You, sir, are a veritable temple of modesty and decorum. I daresay there is no one more unpretentious than you, Inspector."

"Mr. Catchpole," he upped his voice to compete with the bonging of St. Andrew's bells, "I really must insist—"

"Dear me! Pardon the interruption, but I must dash. I have completely lost track of the hour. Until next time, Mr. Forge."

"There will not be a next time," he muttered after the fleeing legs of the red-coated scarecrow, then gritted his teeth as the bells finished tolling—all nine of them. Blast. He should have been in his office by now.

He set off at a fast pace, weaving through street hawkers and pedestrians, and finally arrived at the station winded and sweaty. He barely tipped his hat at Smitty, the front desk clerk, as he hastened to the stairs.

"Hold on there, Chief." Smitty's raspy voice lassoed him from behind. "I've a note for you."

Jackson circled back, hand extended to simply grab the message and continue on his way. A good plan. . .but one that hitched as Smitty ducked behind the counter and began rummaging while mumbling, "I know the little badger is here somewhere. Kipes! What a snarl."

Jackson gritted his teeth. He knew exactly how the man felt. His own rat's nest of paperwork awaited him upstairs.

"Aha! Here's the rotter." Rising, the beefy constable held out an envelope.

With a seal.

Heart sinking, Jackson handed Smitty the bag of pastries then snatched the envelope. "For your trouble," he said as he turned away and slid his finger to break the wax insignia.

> *Forge,*
>
> *I need the complete tally of cases, including names, dates, and sentences within a fortnight to hand in to the commissioner. Failure to supply such information by then will result in your termination.*
>
> *I am,*
> *Superintendent Aloysius Hammerhead*

Bah. Jackson crushed the paper into a ball as he mounted the steps, wishing beyond reason the former chief were still around so he could interrogate the man as to his filing system. The information required by the super was waiting in the many file drawers, but not in any sort of order that a normal human being would have catalogued. It had taken him the past two days just to figure out how to gather the names of all the offenders—let alone copy them down on one document—and he had yet to match the dates and sentences to those names. For some reason known only to God and the dead Chief Inspector Theodore Ridley, the man had encrypted all his files not only in code words but in separate folders.

Two steps from reaching the landing, movement from below snagged his attention. He leaned over the railing. A round ball of a man bounced to a stop. Jackson narrowed his eyes. What on God's green earth was Inspector Harvey doing there, squatting in the corridor like a fat frog, when he'd assigned the man to investigate the suspected arson at the fishmonger on Charles Street?

Hefting a huge sigh, Jackson trotted back down the stairs, shoving the super's balled-up note into his pocket. "What, may I ask, are you doing, Inspector?"

Light glinted off the man's spectacles as he glanced up, a momentary blinding flash. "I can hardly be expected to walk another step without first fixing my stocking. It twisted just so, you see. Never could stand things out of order, not even a stocking."

"You and your stocking are not supposed to be here at the station."

After a final yank to his infernal stocking, Harvey resettled his trouser hem then rose. "But I work here, sir. Where did you expect me to be?"

"Your work is at the fishmonger on Charles Street." Surely the man hadn't hauled in the firebug this early in the investigation.

"About that." He smoothed each side of his moustache with his podgy fingers. "I did as you asked, sir, and tried to examine the arson matter, but the smoke damage lingering on the walls proved too much for my lungs. I am of a rather delicate constitution."

Delicate! Jackson clenched his hands lest he throttle Harvey's neck—if he could even find it, so thick was the rookie inspector. "Are you telling me the case remains unsolved?"

Harvey bobbed his head as if they discussed nothing more pressing than an undisputed score in a cricket game. "Naturally."

"And how do you intend to resolve it?" The words barely made it past the tightness of his jaw.

"Why, by returning the case to you, of course."

Jackson planted his feet. It was either that or lunge at the worthless excuse of an inspector. "Consider yourself dismissed, Mr. Harvey. Effective immediately."

"I am afraid that will not do, sir." He shook his head, his jowls swaying against his collar. "That will not do at all."

Anger flooded Jackson's veins, hot enough that he might blow at any moment. "Are you presuming to stand there and tell me I cannot dismiss you?"

"I am, without a doubt, sir."

That did it.

Jackson sucked in a breath, preparing to spew fire, when the stuffed goose of a fellow lifted to his toes. "I am the commissioner's nephew. Did you not know?"

By all that was right and just! *That* was how Harvey had come to be on the payroll of one of the busiest stations in the city? And now Jackson would be the one saddled with this useless inspector who would be of no help whatsoever, and in fact would prevent the hiring of a competent man to take his place. Closing his eyes, Jackson counted to ten.

Then twenty.

And it took until sixty-four before he could safely face the man without mowing him down. In truth, it wasn't Harvey's fault he'd been propped up as an officer. The blame lay on the commissioner, who knew exactly the sort of strain Harvey would put on the justice system.

Taking a deep breath, Jackson mentally riffled through the cases awaiting him on his desk upstairs, searching for one that would require no physical effort. "Very well, Harvey. Do you think you can manage a simple case of—"

"Oh, no need to assign me anything else quite yet, sir." He pulled out a handkerchief and dabbed at the ever-present beads of sweat decorating his brow. "Smitty has requested my service for an internal office matter."

Jackson cocked his head. "What matter?"

"Revamping the front desk. His paperwork is woefully unorganized. I shall report to you once it is cleared up, sir." Tipping his hat, Harvey strode off, seemingly unaware of the damage he'd done to Jackson's blood pressure.

Growling, Jackson took the stairs two at a time. Perhaps he'd been wrong about how this day would be—

"Chief! A moment, please."

He cast a longing gaze at his office door at the top of the stairs before turning back. The urgency in his friend Baggett's voice could not be denied, nor would he refuse the request even were it not urgent. He owed Charles Baggett that much and more.

Doubling back, he stopped at the bottom of the stairs, where the wide-shouldered inspector stood with a folder in his hand. "What have you got for me? But mind, I don't think I can take another station problem right now."

"Rough morning already, old man?" Baggett cuffed him on the shoulder. "But you're in luck." He handed over the folder. "That is the finished—and well-documented—Meagle case, all wrapped up sans bow. And furthermore, yes, I do have a personal matter to discuss."

Jackson tucked the folder beneath his arm. Would that all the men under his management were this efficient. "Shall we speak in my office?"

Baggett grinned. "It's not that personal."

"Very well. Let's have it."

"Have you ever heard of any investigations into Bellow's Glassworks?"

Jackson rubbed the back of his neck, trying to recall if he had come across the name. "None I know of," he murmured. "Though if it's documented in that unholy mess of a file cabinet in my office, good luck finding it. Why?"

"Mmm." Baggett looked past him, but Jackson got the distinct impression he wasn't focused on the bluecoats pouring out of the roster room. "Just wondering."

"No, you're not. Spill it."

"It's Martha—" Red rose up his friend's neck, stark against his collar. "I mean Mrs. Jones, of course. Well, actually it's about her boy, Frankie. The lad's taken on a position at that hellhole of a glassery. He'll be lucky to make it home every night without some sort of injury. Bellow ought to be fined for endangering children."

Ahh. This was more than personal. This was a matter of the

heart—whether Baggett admitted to it or not. And he most certainly wouldn't. Why the stubborn fellow didn't just marry the woman was beyond him, for clearly his friend cared deeply about Martha Jones and her children. Still, that didn't mean he ought to step in and tell his friend what to do or stop Frankie from working at a place Baggett didn't like. Granted, factories were notoriously dangerous, especially for the underage, and he himself would hate to see young Frankie harmed in any way. So would Kit.

But there was nothing he could do about it. The lad was a free agent.

He stepped aside as a constable strode past with a wriggling felon in tow, then faced Baggett. "As hard as it is, sometimes you must let go of things such as this. The boy has every right to work there if he chooses."

"I know." Baggett scowled. "But I don't like it. Mrs. Jones won't either."

"So talk Frankie out of his decision. Problem solved."

Baggett shook his head. "I'm not so sure he'd listen to me."

"He was one of Kit's crew. Shall I get her involved?"

"No." The lines on Baggett's face softened. "I suspect your wife has enough to manage. I don't want to burden her, but I wouldn't mind if you looked into finding any wrongdoings on Bellow's part."

Jackson snorted. "You want me to find dirt on the man to shut down the whole company for the protection of one boy?"

"Could you?"

He blew out a long breath. Scraping up charges on a well-connected business owner was like looking for a particular piece of gravel in a quarry. And yet. . .well, he never would have made it past his first year on the force had it not been for Baggett's friendship. "Very well. I will investigate on one condition."

Hope burned bright in his friend's dark eyes. "Which is?"

"That you find the arsonist responsible for the fire at the fishmonger on Charles Street."

Baggett's brows gathered. "I thought Harvey was on that."

"Don't ask."

"Harvey strikes again, eh?" He chuckled. "No matter. I'm on it. And thanks for poking about the glassworks. I'd hate to see anything happen to the boy. Martha—Mrs. Jones would be devastated."

And again with the name slip. Jackson cuffed his friend on the back. "You know, Baggett, the better solution to the whole Frankie problem might be to simply marry Mrs. Jones and pool your resources. Then young Frankie wouldn't have to work."

A deep flush spread over Baggett's face. "We are not...I mean...We are merely acquaintances. Marriage is far beyond the scope of things."

"That's not what Kit tells me." He winked and stalked off, once again climbing the stairs.

"What is that supposed to mean? Jackson! You cannot just walk off like that."

Grinning broadly, Jackson ignored his friend.

But when he reached his office, that grin vanished.

Sergeant Doyle stood at his door, blood oozing from his nose, uniform torn at the sleeve, and with a glower fierce enough to make a lion back down.

Jackson tipped his head. "Sergeant? Please don't tell me your entire ceiling caved in."

"Would that were it. I'm afraid you're needed immediately below stairs, Chief. That cully Scarther hauled in is a cornered rat. We need all hands available."

Blast. He wheeled about, bellowing for all officers to muster with truncheons in the cell block, then he raced down the stairs without a backwards glance at his office. How was he to get paperwork done with so many other fires to put out? He'd been wrong. Horribly—almost grotesquely—wrong. This was not going to be a good day after all.

In fact, it was turning out to be spectacularly awful.

Kit sat as still as a snake on a rock, nothing but her gaze sweeping the opulent office of Mr. Ives Percival. As a supposed member of the Mayfair Ladies Aide Society, it wouldn't do to physically poke about in the man's private belongings. But she didn't need to. Language wasn't merely written words or air across the vocal cords, and this room spoke volumes about the senior partner in Willis, Percival & Company...namely that he loved expensive cigars, preferred scotch over brandy, and had an interest in hot air balloons, if the collection of titles on the shelf was his and not merely an ornamentation. And he loved his wife. Dearly. Excessively. To the point of idolization, apparently, for there wasn't a horizontal surface that didn't sport one of her photographs. Perfect.

Kit's lips curved. All those tip-offs she'd gathered about the woman would surely be a boon.

"Good morning, Mrs. Forge." In strode a giraffe of a man, his long legs carrying him in front of her before she could rise. He held out his palm, staying her further. "No need to stand on my account; in fact if you don't mind, I shall take my seat straightaway. It's been a dashed busy morning already."

He sank into the tall-backed wooden chair behind a massive cherrywood desk. Lower back trouble, no doubt, for such a mean form of seat. He winced before softening his jaw and awarding her a pleasant smile. "I hope you didn't mind the wait."

"Think nothing of it, Mr. Percival." She returned his smile. "I am only glad to have a minute of your time."

"Yes, about that...my clerk informs me you belong to the same club as my wife, but I am unclear as to how I may be of service. Matilda"—he cast a loving glance at one of the many picture frames on his desk—"didn't mention anything to me this morning at breakfast about your visit."

"Oh, you know women." Kit waggled her fingers in the air. "I am hoping you can tell me about one of your employees."

Mr. Percival pursed his lips, the pull of skin making his nose look all the longer. "What has that to do with the Mayfair Ladies Aide Society?"

She leaned forward as if taking him into her confidence. Rule number one of gaining information was to appear as if you were supplying it. "I shall fill you in on that after you tell me about Mr. Coleman, your former financial officer."

"Officer?" Mr. Percival laughed, a squawky sort of sound that ended with a slight whistle. "Coleman was a staff accountant, nothing more."

"You must pay very good wages, then. Pimlico is not for paupers."

Mr. Percival shook his head. "You are misinformed, Mrs. Forge. In no way could Mr. Coleman have afforded to live in such a fashionable neighbourhood."

Interesting. Had the home she'd visited yesterday been funded by Mrs. Coleman's family? That would explain why the woman was so skittish about alienating herself from her mother and father.

Kit tugged down her bodice as she shifted on the chair. Dressing the part of a high-society woman never did make sitting an easy pastime. "What sort of employee was Mr. Coleman? Were you happy with his work?"

Mr. Percival angled his head; any farther and it might roll off that long neck of his. "Really, Mrs. Forge, such enquiries cannot possibly be related to—"

"Now, now, Mr. Percival. You must allow a lady to have her intrigues." She wagged her finger. "Your wife certainly has hers."

His spine stiffened. "What would you know of that?"

"Enough that if you do not answer my questions, I just may have to let the editor of the society page in on her recent faux pas."

And there was rule number two—information acquired before skiffing a mark was like bullets in a gun, only she need never pull the trigger. The threat would be fatal enough.

Deep red crawled up Mr. Percival's giraffe neck. "Are you black-mailing me, Mrs. Forge?"

"Nothing of the sort." She tapped his desk with a light finger. "I prefer to think of it as encouragement to do the right thing."

His dark eyes narrowed to slits. "Who are you really?"

Phew. At last, she could drop the high-society image. She loosened the pin that'd been grazing her scalp and allowed the tight bun at the back of her head to fall into a tail. "I am a detective, sir, on the hunt for the missing Mr. Coleman."

"Is this what the world has come to? Women taking on men's roles? A detective, of all things." His upper lip curled.

The slurs rolled right off her back, for she still held the best hand. She started to rise. "I suppose I shall bid you good day, then. I ought to make the *Times'* editorial offices before the final pages head to press."

Mr. Percival's face twisted. "Take your seat, Detective." He spat out the word like an unexpected olive pit. "Though you won't need it for much longer. As for Mr. Coleman, he is no longer an employee here, so I can have nothing to say on the matter."

"Oh, but remember I have plenty to say to the newspaper. Imagine if word gets out that just last week your wife was seen sneaking into the back door of the Kitsch Street Gin House." She lowered her voice to a conspiratorial whisper. "And that it wasn't the first time she'd frequented such a vulgar establishment."

"How would you—?" Purple bloomed across his cheeks, and it took him several deep breaths before the shade lightened to a mere murderous red. "What exactly do you wish to know about Mr. Coleman?" It was a wonder the question even made it past the clench of the man's jaw.

It was naughty of her, truly, to put Mr. Percival through such anguish, yet very necessary if she were to find poor little Lillibeth. Kit pulled out her notebook, then removed the small silver pencil attached to it. "You said his position here was as a staff accountant. How many of those do you employ?"

"Only one. Coleman was directly overseen by Mr. Blade, our chief financial officer."

She jotted down the name then looked up. "Did you have any concerns about Mr. Coleman's work performance? Were there any irregularities in his schedule? Did he ever show up late for work or leave early?"

"As far as I know the man was punctual and methodical, as those who work with numbers so often are."

Kit made a note of it. Evidently Mr. Coleman only kept odd hours at home, then, which begged the question. . . "Are you aware of any troubles with his personal life?"

"No. I make it a point to keep out of other people's business." Mr. Percival's dark eyes hardened to embers, his gaze burning into hers. "A lesson you would do well to learn."

She grinned. "Ahh, but then I would not be a very good detective, would I?"

"Are you quite finished, Mrs. Forge?" He swept his hand towards a stack of documents on his desk. "I have business to attend."

"Nearly." She flipped to a clean page. "Did Mr. Coleman have any violent tendencies? Argumentative, perhaps? Was he quick to take offense?"

"Coleman?" A snort puffed out of his nose. "The man was a timid rabbit. The few times I had reason to stop by his desk, he spoke so quietly I strained my back leaning to hear him. He was an amiable enough fellow, I suppose, but rather a lone wolf, more comfortable with ledgers than people. Again, the trait of a good numbers man."

Kit bit her lip. A clear discrepancy from what Mrs. Coleman had told her. Either Mr. Percival was lying or Mr. Coleman's anger only flared at home—which wasn't beyond the realm of possibility. Still. . .

She tapped her pencil against the page a long moment before glancing up. "What do you think happened to him?" Edging forward on the chair, she met the man's gaze head-on. Rule number three when reeling in a mark was to make them part of the process, provide a bit of perceived ownership in the conversation. "Where do you think Mr. Coleman went, Mr. Percival?"

"Who knows?" He spread his hands. "Perhaps he reached the stage in life that breaks a man. At some point everyone realizes they'll never be anything more than what they are. There was no chance for advancement for Coleman, so maybe he chucked his life into the dustbin."

Her brows shot sky-high. "Are you suggesting Mr. Coleman may have committed suicide?"

Mr. Percival shrugged his sharp shoulders. "Wouldn't be the first time a man succumbed to disillusion."

Maybe, but that did nothing to explain the disappearance of little Lillibeth. Kit tucked away her notebook and stood. "Thank you, Mr. Percival. You have been most helpful."

"Not by choice." He glowered.

Kit stifled a smile. No sense irritating the poor fellow any further. "Oh, one more thing. Where is Mr. Blade's office? I should like a quick word with him."

Mr. Percival shook his head. "I'm afraid that is impossible."

"Why?"

"Mr. Blade is recently deceased."

Instantly alert, she felt the hairs at the nape of her neck stick out like pins in a cushion. "By what cause?"

Mr. Percival's dark eyes bored into hers. "Murder."

Chapter Seven

Who'd have thought a large office complete with prestigious title was the same thing as a millstone hanging from one's neck? Jackson tugged at his collar as he turned his back on the bank of file cabinets that had yet to be sorted for the report Hammerhead expected in two weeks. No, make that thirteen days. He'd slaved away until midnight yesterday and hardly made any progress. Thunder and turf! It would take a miracle to hit that deadline—especially since the folder he now held in his hand had nothing to do with the paperwork fiasco.

He dropped to his chair and flipped open the records Smitty had pulled on Bellow's Glassworks. At least this wouldn't take long. The folder was woefully thin. He scanned the first page, a complaint filed by a disgruntled glassblower who'd been severely burned. Hard to say if his claim of negligence was born of anger over the injury or was truly from disregard for safety on Bellow's part, for the case never went to court. The man had died.

Jackson flipped to the next page, this one from a neighbouring business. Apparently some stray embers had started a fire on the roof of one of the neighbour's sheds. The court had ordered Bellow to pay, which he had, and that was the end of it.

He turned to the next—and last—report, submitted by proxy for a Mr. Tippins. Hmm. Odd, that. In all his time on the force, he could think of only one case that had been proposed by proxy. He leaned closer, intrigued by who filed it and why.

And was promptly interrupted by a rap on his door.

"Come back later," he grumbled. Probably Harvey mewling about eyestrain or some other nonsense.

The door swished open anyway. Blast. Did no one in this station respect his word? "I said—!" He swallowed the rebuke as he glanced up. "Well, this is a surprise."

Kit strolled in, lovelier than a summer morn. Oh, her hair flopped in a lopsided ponytail and baby drool marred her left shoulder, but that did nothing to quell the stirring of desire deep in his belly whenever she walked into a room.

She sashayed over to him, one brow arched. "I always like to keep you on your toes, Husband."

"You didn't last night. As I recall, you kept me pinned to the matt—"

Her lips came down hard, warm, and the same thrill that always heated his blood from her kiss made him hunger for more.

But this was definitely not the time or place.

He set her from him with a grin. "You really can't get enough of me, can you?"

She laughed as she rounded his desk and took the chair. "Actually, this is a business call."

He smoothed his moustache, ruffled from her sweet attack. "I sincerely hope you do not conduct your business in such a manner with anyone else, or there will be the devil to pay."

"I adore it when you are jealous, you know." Planting her elbows on his desk, she propped her chin on her hands. "Makes your nostrils flare in a most endearing fashion."

He narrowed his eyes. Flattery—even of such a ridiculous sort— always meant she was up to something. "I hardly think a discussion of my nose is grounds for this visit. What do you want, Wife? And why did you not simply ask me at home over breakfast?" He coughed to cover a snort. That square piece of carbon she'd served him on a plate could hardly be called breakfast even though she'd smeared it with a liberal amount of strawberry jam.

"I wanted to exhaust my contacts first without bothering you, which is how I spent my day yesterday and a good part of this morning. Turns out, though, that there is precious little information on the street about the murder of Mr. Blade."

"Blade?" The name didn't sound familiar in the least. "Is this a recent homicide?"

"Relatively." She shrugged. "Within the past few weeks."

That was news. Why had he not heard of it? He steepled his fingers. "What do you know?"

"Mr. Blade was the chief financial officer at Willis, Percival & Company, the same employer as the missing fellow I'm looking for. His boss, actually. I had hoped to question Mr. Blade, but turns out he's gone as well. Permanently, that is."

"Mmm," he drawled. "And you think the two are connected. Do you suppose your missing man is responsible for Mr. Blade's death?"

"Could be. Too soon to tell." She leaned back in her chair. "I need more information, and that's where you come in. Would you work your magic and see what you can find out?"

Pah! He didn't have time to dig into another case, but how to refuse those hopeful blue eyes blinking at him? "Where was he murdered?"

"Near Westminster."

Perfect, leastwise to legitimately turn her down. "Sorry, love." He spread his hands. "You know that's out of my jurisdiction."

"That's never stopped one of your investigations before."

"This isn't my investigation."

"True, but it is your wife's, and are we not one?" She tipped her chin to a rakish angle.

Saucy wench.

A lung-deflating sigh ripped out of him. "Very well. But I'm not promising anything soon. As you know, I'm in over my head here."

"I know." She rounded the desk and leaned in close, her breath soft against his brow as she whispered, "But you, my sweet, are a champion swimmer."

Hang the time and place! He pulled her into his lap and kissed her long and hard enough that she pulled away breathless.

"Well, if this is how you conduct business, sir, there will be more than the devil to pay."

He quirked one brow. "Is that my cue to talk about your adorable nostrils?"

"I should hope you find more than my nose to appreciate." She smirked as she rose. "See you at supper."

He admired her fine form all the way to the door, then cherished the memory of her lips against his for a moment longer before digging back into the Bellow file.

Now then, where was he? Ahh yes, the anomaly of a grievance filed by a proxy. Turns out the woman who brought the charges bore the same last name of the deceased man in the case. Wife? Mother, perhaps? A relative, at any rate, one who claimed the dead employee had warned of mismanagement in the storage of supplies, some of which were volatile. She accused Bellow for the accident that resulted in the man's death—a direct result of exposure to those very same chemicals.

Jackson rubbed little circles on his temple, thinking hard. Bellow couldn't be blamed for an accident, for in essence the very word implied no one was to be liable, but improperly stored dangerous supplies? Now that was something he could check into. Maybe stop by the place. Make a few enquiries. And if he did turn up anything, file for an investigation with the factory inspector overseeing that district.

Lacing his fingers behind his neck, he leaned back in his chair, already devising the best way to nose about that warehouse without raising any hackles—when he spied the file cabinets. Twin towers of doom, more like. Thunderation. He couldn't tackle the glassworks for Baggett and reorganize the years of files at the same time. Still, he did owe his friend for saving his hide so many times, when—as a rookie—it was Baggett alone who'd believed in him. And yet he also owed allegiance to his new superior, to completing the task Hammerhead had assigned, due in a fortnight.

He closed his eyes beneath the weight of it all. And if that weren't enough, there was Kit and the murder she wished him to investigate…in a jurisdiction not his own.

Blast.

He wasn't merely stuck between a rock and a hard place. He was slowly being buried alive, boulder by boulder.

Days like these, when she spun about like a crazed marble in a boy's pickup game, Kit couldn't help but wonder if she was doing the right thing by working so many hours. As much as she loved the thrill of working on a case, she missed cuddling her sweet babe. She yearned to kiss Bella's chubby cheeks and breathe in her warm, yeasty scent. . .which would be a definite improvement over the stink of blood and offal wafting from the butcher next to their new agency. Kit held her breath as she shoved open the office door.

But it didn't smell much better in here. Had her father even bathed in the last several days? She doffed her bonnet then crossed the room to where he stood with his back towards her, staring at a mess of cards and strings tacked to the wall. Whatever he was working on surely mesmerized him.

She pursed her lips as she studied the geometric pattern. "Very pretty."

He speared her with a scowl, his bushy brows gathering like a storm. "You're late this morning. I thought we were to be partners."

"I had a few stops to make first, none of which were very fruitful. Say, speaking of partners, I wonder if you wouldn't mind looking into something for me, that is, if you're not too busy working on this art project." She circled her hand at the makeshift case board on the wall.

"Actually, I *am* too preoccupied." He pulled a push pin from his coat pocket and tacked up one more card at the end of an empty string.

She puffed her cheeks. It seemed as if the whole world were too busy. Curiosity mingled with her disappointment, though, and she stepped closer to the wall. "I assume this is your preoccupation."

He grunted.

She touched the farthest card on the left. "This man here, Mr. X, has hired you. You've taken on the case you've told me about, then? The one you didn't have any details on? Or scant details, as I recall. Why didn't you tell me?"

"I am now—and I think you will agree it is a viable project that will interest you as well. I don't think you'll have any qualms whatsoever about taking it on."

Slowly, lest she snag the whole string from the wall, she followed the length of it to the next card. "Clearly he is connected to Company A. Employee, perhaps?" She scanned the other name cards—only two. Mr. X's was a size larger. "No, he is one of the owners, maybe the sole proprietor even."

"Easy enough to deduce," her father grumbled.

She traced the string that connected the company to the next name, which had many lines attached—too many to make him an innocent. "Mr. Y is who you're investigating."

For a long beat, her father said nothing, then he shot her a sideways glance. "Go on."

She tracked another length of twine to a different name. "A woman? Ahh, the plot thickens." She waggled her eyebrows. "But is Mrs. Y an accomplice to her husband's devilries or not?"

Air snorted out his nose as he folded his arms. "I haven't decided yet."

Well, good to know he struggled for information every bit as much as she did. She skimmed the next piece of string, which ended at a card that read *Glyn Mills*.

"A bank? Well, if money is involved, naturally Mrs. Y must have something to do with—wait a minute." She shoved her nose closer to the card. Clearly her father had scrawled this one in haste. "No, I take that back. Mrs. Y is not implicated, not if your man is tangled up with the Old Pye rat pit." She glanced over her shoulder at her father. "I didn't know that was in operation."

"Neither did I until this morning."

She swiveled her head back to the wall, gaze traveling to the next card. "And the law has already been called upon, eh? Barrister Featherstone." *Featherstone.* Mentally she held the name up to an imaginary lamp, examining it until recognition dawned. "He's a counsel for the wealthy...which clearly is not Mr. Y, not if he's hanging about Old Pye." She snapped her fingers and whirled to face her father. "I've got it!"

He eyed her. "And that is...?"

"Your client, Mr. X, here"—she tapped his name card—"hired you to find a particular employee of his, one who has information on an embezzlement scandal or is maybe even in on the embezzling himself."

Admiration flared in his dark gaze. "Very good. But for the record, I don't think Mr. X is the culprit. I suspect it to be Mr. Y, though that's a stretch at this point. He is a well-to-do gent and would bet on horses instead of rodents, so the pit connection doesn't ring true."

"Don't be too sure about that. You'd be surprised at how much coin a pit draws in, especially if you're the one running the ring."

Her father stroked his beard. Judging by the purse of his lips, gears turned in his head, ones that may be missing a sprocket or two since his bushy brows knit together as well. "Kit, I think you should know this case intersects with yours."

"Oh?" She tipped her head. "How so?"

"I was hired by Mr. X—or Mr. Willis, I should say."

Her eyes widened. "Of Willis and Percival?"

"The very same. He's charged me to investigate an employee of his—this Mr. Y—for possible embezzlement, which is rather difficult being the man has inconveniently turned up dead."

Kit gasped. "Let me guess. . .Mr. Blade?"

Her father nodded. "Somehow he's entangled with the rat pit and Featherstone, though I don't think his wife—Mrs. Blade—has any knowledge of either. I have a meeting with Featherstone in half an hour that will hopefully shed some light on this."

Kit couldn't help but grin. "So we are working on the same case despite your gut feeling!"

He scowled. "Yes, we are, which is why I didn't think you'd have any problem with me taking this one on. We can work from different angles."

"We can, but you do know that the details of Mr. Blade's death are still hazy, don't you?"

Her father nodded his big head. "Yet that does not stop my—or your—investigation. Neither does it mean my instinct about Mrs. Coleman was incorrect."

The bell above the door jingled. In dashed a lad in a cherry-red cap, his cheeks every bit as rosy. "Message for Mrs. Forge." He waved a letter in the air.

"That's me." She strolled over to the boy and exchanged a coin for the missive. "Thank you."

"Kipes!" He stared at the money in his hand then lifted his face, gaping. "A whole bob?"

"Yes, I may have need in the future of a stalwart young man such as yourself to deliver messages for me."

"Oh, I'm yer man, miss!" He thumped his thumb against his puffed-out chest. "Just holler for ol' Toffy."

"Very good, Toffy. And mind you don't spend that all in one place."

"No, miss. I've a sister to care for and this'll buy her some milk." He darted to the door. "G'day!"

Kit smiled to herself as she sat at her desk and reached for the letter opener, all the while lifting a prayer for Toffy and his sister. Far too many children lived hat in hand. At least he'd found reputable work. She sliced open the seal and unfolded the page to Jackson's strong penmanship.

> *My Love,*
>
>   *Turns out your request took me no time at all to check into, since I was able to skirt jurisdiction politics by messaging the coroner directly. Mr. Blade was the victim of a simple mugging, as was recently confirmed at the St. James Mortuary. If you hurry, you may be able to view the body before it is taken away.*
>
> *Hope that helps,*
Your Loving Husband

Perfect! If she made haste, she could learn another clue and might also be able to pick up Bella early to cook a special supper to thank Jackson for the information. She flew to the coat-tree to grab her hat but then thought better of her plan. If she really wanted to show her appreciation to Jackson, it might be better to ask Martha to cook something. Burnt kippers weren't exactly the best way to show gratitude.

"Where are you off to?" her father rumbled at her back. "I wasn't finished telling you about the case."

"No time now, Father." She winked at him over her shoulder. "I'm off to the deadhouse to see about your—and my—Mr. Blade."

Chapter Eight

Charles pounded his fist against his chest as he waited outside the soup kitchen. That spiced kidney pie he'd snagged off a street cart probably wasn't the wisest choice for lunch. But it had been tasty and timely. Frankie Jones ought to be rolling out the door for his afternoon shift at the glassworks right about—

The door flew open. A gangly lad in an oversized flatcap tore out, a supper pail swinging in one hand. He darted down the pavement like a cat-chased dormouse, not even noticing Charles as he scurried past. Evidently he was running late.

But that didn't stop Charles from grasping the boy's collar. The lad may not listen to him, but he had to give it a try. "Hold on, young man. I'd like a word with you."

Frankie wriggled loose, his spray of freckles riding the wave of a huge glower. "I ain't done nothin', Mr. Baggett. I swear it!"

Charles smiled. "I didn't say you did."

His brow wrinkled in confusion. "Then why ye nippin' me?"

"Like I said, just a word." He swept his hand towards two upturned crates sitting against the building. "Shall we?"

The boy shook his head, resetting his cap low over his eyes. "Don't have time, gotta get to work."

"That is exactly what I wish to discuss. Shouldn't take long."

"Can't it wait till later?"

Charles pulled a coin from his pocket and held it out. "I might not have this shilling later."

Frankie's muddy-brown eyes brightened a few shades a second before he snatched the money and whumped onto one of the crates so quickly, the wood wobbled. "Must be pretty important to be bribin' the likes o' me."

Cheeky monkey. The boy was far too street smart for a twelve-year-old, though if his memory served, he'd be thirteen in no time.

"It is important, or I'd not be here." Charles sat next to him, sorting through what to say. Like a hand of cards, he'd have to play this the right way if he wanted to win the boy over to his line of thinking—namely that he ought to quit the glassworks immediately. "The way I see it, you're the man of the house now, what with your father having passed."

The lad's thin chest swelled. "Tha's right. Tha's what I am."

For one so young, he definitely had a well-aged ego. Charles stifled a laugh. "And as man of the house, it is your responsibility to care for your mother and sisters."

"Aye, Mr. Baggett. That I do."

"Agreed, and a fine job you're making of it. You are a conscientious young man, one of the most reliable I know."

Instantly Frankie's big brown eyes narrowed. "What do you want, Mr. Baggett?"

Blast. He'd overplayed the flattery. He should've known a kid trained by Kit would be on his toes mentally. Now what to say? He glanced at the overcast sky, praying for some inspiration. None came. And by the way Frankie was banging his foot against the crate, his time was running out.

Charles scrubbed a hand over his face. Nothing for it then but the truth. "I want you to reconsider your employment at Bellow's Glassworks. More simply put, I want you to quit your job."

Frankie's head reared back, his hat nearly sliding down his back. "Why?"

"It's not a safe environment. If your mother knew the dangers you face, she'd swoon dead away."

Frankie snickered. "Women."

Charles couldn't help but smile, yet it didn't last long. This arrogant young lad was clearly having none of this conversation. Still, for Frankie's sake and his mother's, he had to keep trying. "You know, Frankie, you could do better. Delivery boys make fat tips in the right neighbourhoods. I'd be happy to be your reference."

"Thanks, Mr. Baggett, but I can't quit. I'm kinda beholden to Mr. Bellow after I—I mean, he offered me the job as a sort of reward, so I ought not let him down."

Well. That was quite the noble way to describe how he'd cast a net for the unsuspecting factory owner. The boy's tongue was as silver as Kit's!

"Look, Frankie, I know it was a setup, fair and square. You planned that little accident and now you feel remorse for it, don't you?"

The boy sucked air through his teeth as if he'd been hit in the gut. He shot to his feet, lunch pail once again taking a wild swing. "I gotta be goin' now."

Charles grabbed him by the sleeve. "It was wrong of you to snag a job that way as much as it is wrong of Mr. Bellow to allow his workers to labour under such unsafe conditions. You're old enough and smart enough to know two wrongs never make a right." Charles shoved his face close to the boy's, lowering his voice. "If you're injured—or worse—your mother and sisters will have no one to fend for them."

"Now there yer wrong, Mr. Baggett. They've got you." Frankie laughed as he wrenched away and tore down the pavement. "G'day!"

Charles' shoulders sagged as the boy swerved around a lump of pedestrians and disappeared. That hadn't gone at all as he'd hoped.

"Isn't it a little early for ye to be here?" Martha's sweet voice curled over his shoulder.

He turned, caught off guard by the woman who usually heightened his senses. A good surprise, though, her enticing scent of warm bread and sweet butter wrapping around him like an embrace. She may run a soup kitchen, but there was a certain refinement to her posture. An elegance to the way she carried the basket on her arm. Why, as far as he was concerned, she could hold her own against a Portman Square lady any day.

"I was just stopping by to. . .em. . ." He sputtered to a stop. He couldn't very well tell her he'd been trying to convince her son to stop going to a factory that might maim or kill him.

So he snatched the basket off her arm and held it up, hopefully making a believable point, or at the very least a distraction. "I came to walk you to market."

"Is that so?" Suspicion sparked silver in her blue eyes. "Ye never have before."

"Yes, well, there is an upsurge of crime in the area. Just wanted to make sure you arrive unharmed." A lie—sort of. There were increased cutpurses roaming about.

"How. . .thoughtful."

That slight hesitation shouted clear as day she didn't believe him. Undaunted, he offered his arm, and with a single arched brow, she rested her fingers on his sleeve. He set off, overwhelmingly aware of her touch.

"I hope seeing me to market doesn't interfere with yer job, Mr. Baggett."

He glanced at her sideways. "Keeping the citizens of Blackfriars safe is my job, so no need to fret."

"I never fret when yer around." A lovely shade of pink washed over her cheeks.

Which pleased him to no end. For a while they walked in companionable silence, more of necessity than desire due to the clamour of drays, horses, and carriages.

"How are the girls?" he finally asked as he led her to the other side of Blackfriars Bridge.

"The younglings are fine enough. 'Tis Harriet what vexes me. She's at that age between kit and cat, sometimes sharpening her claws, other times purring."

Well. That was promising. He glanced sideways at Martha. "So it's not just me she hisses at?"

"No." She chuckled. "The girl wars with herself as much as any."

That was a relief, somewhat, anyway. "I am happy to hear that for the most part all is well with your family. How goes it at the kitchen, then?"

"Busy." She tucked away a loose piece of dark golden hair beneath her bonnet. "I think little Bella is cutting a tooth, which makes it all the harder to cook, what with a babe a-swingin' on my hip."

He pressed his lips tight, straining not to glance down at those hips.

"Or could be Bella just misses her mum," she continued without missing a beat. "I suspect when Kit is with her, she's not really present. Once that woman gets a puzzle in her head, 'tis hard for her to think of anythin' else." Martha heaved a sigh. "I daresay she doesn't recognize how good she's got it, with a lovely home and a faithful husband. I'd trade places with her in a heartbeat."

Charles cut her a wicked grin. "Have a thing for Jackson, do you?"

"Pish!" She nudged him with her shoulder. "Ye know what I meant."

He chuckled, admiring her spirit. But then as quickly, he sobered. She'd been serious about trading places with Kit, and it would be callous of him to laugh it off. He guided her to the side of the pavement and collected her hands in his. "Jesting aside, you deserve all that and more, and I hope someday your dream comes true. I can think of no woman who more deserves to have the comfort of a house and a man who loves you fiercely."

Like I do.

He let go of her hands as if they seared his flesh. Where on God's green earth had that wild thought come from?

Martha's luminous eyes blinked at him. "Thank ye. I hope it comes true as well. In fact, Mr. Baggett, if I may be so bold, I hope that maybe ye might someday consider—"

She flew sideways, knocked by a boy too large to be running pell-mell down the pavement. Charles lunged, barely getting his arm beneath Martha before she hit the cobbles. He swung her up and held her close, yelling over her shoulder at the little blighter. "Hey! Mind your step! There are ladies present."

The lad's pace didn't so much as hitch as he vanished into the throng of Borough Market. Scowling, Charles searched Martha's face. "Are you hurt?"

"Hah! Not in the least. Yer strong arm kept me from quite the tumble, though I have lost my shawl." Pulling away, she bent to sweep up the plaid wrap.

And that's when he noticed the back of her neck, now bare. Red prints marred her porcelain flesh, almost as if someone had tried to choke her. A knife twisted in his chest, as sharp and real as if a bludger had planted a blade hilt-deep into his heart. When she straightened, he clasped her jaw gently and tipped her head to the side for a better look.

She jerked away and tugged her shawl tight at the neck.

"Who did that to you?" he bellowed.

"What?" She tipped her chin to a defiant angle.

"You know very well what. That mark on your neck. Someone tried to harm you."

"Don't be silly." She grabbed her basket off his arm and tossed back her shoulders. "The market is just across the road. No need to see me any further. I'll have yer supper ready at seven tonight, so for now, I bid you g'day, Mr. Baggett." She whirled.

He grabbed her arm and pulled her back. "Tell me the truth. All of it."

For a long while she said nothing, merely sized him up and down with a keen eye. That hurt. After the past year of looking out for her and expecting nothing in return, did she really think she couldn't trust him?

"Very well," she said at length. "If ye must know, though I hate to admit it, I burnt myself."

Of all the flaming lies. He'd heard better clankers in the interrogation room down at the station. "There is no way a pot or pan could have seared you on the neck. Not even steam would land such a mark." His brow sank with a fierce glower. "Who are you protecting?"

She merely rolled her eyes. "La, sir! Such imaginings. Ye ought to try yer hand at writing penny dreadfuls."

"I am no author. What I am is a police inspector, one who knows all the possible ways of skirting the truth, and though you do it very prettily, I will have the facts of how you came about those marks now, madam."

"But—"

"Now, Martha!"

Her head dipped. Regret rose to his throat, as real as the burn of that spiced kidney pie.

"Yer right," she murmured. "It weren't a pot or pan. Pardon the delicate topic, but. . .well. . .I ne'er shoulda put on my nightgown so soon after ironing the high collar last night." She lifted her face, her blue gaze meeting his. "But it didn't blister, and I should be right as rain by the end of the day."

As much as he didn't want to, he studied her, trying to detect deception—the pinch of her lips, a wayward gaze, eye blocking—but he spied nothing of import. Either she was as accomplished as Kit or she really was telling the truth. And what did he know of women's nightwear anyway? Maybe such a gown really did have a high collar. He opened his lips to ask, then clamped them shut. Asking this woman about such an intimate garment hefted another log onto the fire in his gut.

"Now, then." She peeled away from his hold and straightened her bonnet. "Thank ye for the escort, Mr. Baggett. Don't be late tonight. Ham and beans is yer favourite. See you then."

She strolled off. He didn't. He stood like a dazed badger having been whapped over the head with a stick, wondering if he ought to trust her story or the police instinct screaming in his head. More than anything he wanted to believe her. He *needed* to believe her.

Because if he didn't and someone really had tried to choke her, he'd be the one locked behind bars for murder.

The stink of London in the summer could be surpassed only by the stench of a deadhouse—even with corpses preserved on ice. And on this August afternoon, the parish mortuary of Westminster was a real belly turner. But Kit was too enthralled with the body in front of her to bother with pressing her handkerchief to her nose. The coroner, Mr. Mortis, was far too entertaining.

He was a whippet of a fellow, with his abnormally small head and long snout. A distinct curvature of the spine swelled out the back of his lab coat, which might be a defect from birth but was more likely from spending hours on end bent over cadavers on slabs. How his spindly legs continued to hold him up was anybody's guess.

But looks aside, the man's theatrics were the true attraction. He swept up the grey arm of the dead Mr. Blade, flourishing his free hand in the air just above as if pointing out the merits of a Degas painting. "As you see by the lacerations on the palms and wrists, thus and thus"—he made a stabbing motion towards the brownish-black lines sliced into the skin—"Mr. Blade tried to fight off his attackers. Yes, I say attackers because I believe there were two involved. Clearly one of them committed a frontal assault with a very sharp—yet small—blade from close range. Likely lured the poor soul into the alley immediately after he exited the pub. Probably concocted some tale of woe or another."

Perhaps. Or could be Mr. Blade somehow knew the brigands. Either way, he'd made a fatal error of trust. She glanced at Mr. Mortis. "And you say this alley is just 'round the corner from the Two Chairmen's pub?"

He dropped the dead man's arm and held out both of his own as wide as they'd go. His lips twisted as he looked from finger to finger and back again, several times. "Yes, yes, I should think three times this distance plus the measure of a long-legged stride." He flopped his hands back to his sides, a satisfied grin stretching his mouth. "Twenty-five paces at most, Mrs. Forge. I'd say that qualifies as *just 'round the corner*, wouldn't you?"

"Indeed, but what makes you think he was lured? Maybe Mr. Blade was merely drunk and stumbled in there to relieve himself, becoming a victim of chance instead of something premeditated. A pickled mind loses all possibility of keen thinking, as you well know."

"Could have done. But that is neither here nor there as the fact remains that for whatever reason he did indeed go into the alley, for that is where he was found. Now if you will notice here on his skull—" He stepped to the head of the table then whipped a comb out of his pocket. Ever so gently, he parted Mr. Blade's hair, snagging it now and then on flakes of dried blood.

Taking care to keep her hem lifted lest the putrid liquids on the floor soak into the fabric, Kit joined the coroner's side—the side not next to the flick of his comb as he shook it out.

He tapped the utensil against the man's cranium. "There is breakage of skin here and fracture of bone. It is my belief this gentleman suffered a cerebral hemorrhage induced by blunt force, delivered from an assailant he may never have seen closing in behind him, being so distracted by the knife-wielding villain. This is why I conclude there were two brigands involved. And it is this very head wound that is the true cause of death, though I own it does not account for the discoloration of his organs."

No doubt. That sort of head basher could take down a horse. Still, something in her gut warned that such a simple solution might be too good to be true. She peered at Mr. Mortis. "Mind if I examine him?"

"Oh, Mrs. Forge! You are a woman after my own heart. Yes, yes, dear lady." He stepped back and dipped a formal bow. "Please, be my guest."

Holding her breath, she crouched eye level with the corpse. There was no denying that caved-in depression had broken bone. A mighty swipe with a stocking full of rocks could do such damage. So could a lead pipe. But who knew? Could've been just about anything. "What were you saying about his organs, Mr. Mortis?" she murmured.

"Ahh, yes. A bluish tinge to them all, liver, lungs, kidneys. . .almost as if his air had been cut off, yet there are no other indications of asphyxiation. I suspect he may have suffered from malaria and recently been treated with the new remedy on the market. . .methylene blue."

Ever so gingerly, she pressed her fingers to the cold head and lifted it to see if any more swipes had caused damage or if that one strike had done the trick. Nothing more marred the man's head. In fact, he must've recently been to a barber—unless Mr. Mortis spent his time dressing every corpse's hair—for the dark locks were closely shorn at the nape. Well, maybe this was a simple mugging after all. Unusual for that particular neighbourhood, but still—hold on.

She leaned closer. There, just at the hairline slightly behind the ear, was a small puncture wound, the size of a sharp pencil lead or a very thick needle. Odd, that. She glanced over her shoulder. "Look here, Mr. Mortis. Did you notice this?" She leaned aside so he could stoop next to her. "Or did you by chance happen to inject the body with anything?"

"By Jove, Mrs. Forge. What a find!" He shoved her out of the way as he went nose to neck with the dead man.

Kit grabbed on to the table to keep from tumbling into the nastiness on the floor. "This methylene blue you spoke of, could that be the injection site?"

"No, it is administered orally as a pill or dissolved in water. I've not seen such a wound as this since my time as an army surgeon. The Labbai Muhammadans in southern India left such a mark when using their blow darts to take down an enemy."

Her eyes widened. "Do you think there's a chance Mr. Blade may have been poisoned before he was mugged?"

"Why, I. . .I will have to reexamine. Such a folly!" he wailed. "Such a great and grand debacle."

Pulling back, he made a sweeping motion towards the door. "I shall have to ask you to leave now, Mrs. Forge. There is much to be done. This body will have to be reassessed. I can hardly believe I have committed such a grievous error."

"Please calm yourself." She pressed her hand to his sleeve. "I'd have not noticed it myself had I not been so close."

"You are a true saint, dear lady, but now make haste. I've not a moment to spare if I'm to reexamine Mr. Blade by closing time."

"I understand, Mr. Mortis. If you discover anything more, please send word to Chief Inspector Jackson Forge. Thank you, and good day." She picked her way to the basin of water near the door and quickly washed her hands, then once again collected her skirt hem and left behind the chill of the morgue for the front office. All the while she thought on what she'd seen and heard. That mark on Mr. Blade's neck had to have happened before the mugging, for there was no sense in doing so afterwards. If he had been injected with some sort of poison, that may have accounted for his lack of discretion in allowing a mugger to lure him into an alley, but why take the trouble of attacking someone who was about to die anyway? Unless the assailants hadn't known.

She stopped in her tracks, conspiracies galore whirling in her head. What if the assault had been a cover-up, a great puff of smoke to hide the true cause of death? To conceal who the real killer was? And if—*if*—that were true, such skulduggery and level of craft hinted at one thing.

An assassin.

She stepped out into the grey afternoon, mulling over that possibility. Mr. Blade may not have been killed by a bash to the head but by a trained killer who'd bumped against him with a poison-laced needle at the ready. It would be easy enough for someone to feign a tipsy step in a pub. Or perhaps someone had employed a blow dart as Mr. Mortis mentioned. Granted, this could be a leap of logic, but nonetheless something that ought to be considered.

Her heart raced with the thought. After all, were an assassin involved, that could very well be why her missing Mr. Coleman went into hiding. He just may fear for his life and the life of his child. But if that were true, then why didn't he care about his wife as well? It didn't add up unless Mrs. Coleman had left out some important facts about her husband. . .or herself.

Kit flattened her lips. Perhaps instead of only digging into the missing man, she ought to scour Mrs. Coleman's past.

Chapter Nine

The chaos of London's streets paled in comparison to the bedlam of an average morning inside Jackson's own kitchen. Bella whaled a wooden spoon against her high-chair tray, ear-piercing laughter burbling out at a pitch that ought not to be heard by the human ear. Kit fanned away a cloud of black smoke from a plate of toast while calling down oaths that would make a sailor blush. The dairyman banged his fist at the back door with a bellowed "Fresh milk!" All of it combined to quite the swell, and it took every bit of Jackson's willpower not to stop up his ears as he poured a cup of coffee. Such a cacophony wasn't exactly how he'd imagined family life.

"That cannot be the time!" Kit flew from the sideboard to the high chair, scrubbing Bella's cheeks with a cloth. "I'm going to be late again in getting you to Martha's, little one."

Bella threw the spoon, nearly taking out the armadillo snuffling in the corner. Her whole face reddened with what promised to be a screeching howl.

Stifling a smile, he saluted Kit with his cup. "Oh, for a lazy morning, eh?"

"What I wouldn't give." She swung Bella up in her arms, making a game of the flight to thwart the child's cries.

"I'd pay a queen's ransom," he muttered, then took a swig of coffee and immediately spat it into a bucket. Foul brew. Had Kit forgotten to use fresh grounds again?

"Are you so unhappy with our life?" Kit frowned. "I realize it's a bit hectic at the moment, but it's only the first week at the enquiry agency. Things are sure to simmer down once I get the hang of balancing it all."

He set down the cup then closed in on his girls, wrapping them both in a bear hug. "I could never be unhappy with you two."

"Ba-ba!" Bella smacked her little palm against his face repeatedly.

"Papa," he urged as he grabbed her chubby little hand and planted a kiss on it. "Now off with you, tiny beast. Your mama has work to accomplish, as do I."

"Ba-ba!" she cried again and nuzzled her face against Kit's neck.

Kit's frown merely grew. Odd, that. Usually she tried to coax a *ma-ma* from the girl.

"Hey," Jackson said softly as he brushed loose hair from his wife's brow. "What's going on in that head of yours?"

"Sometimes. . ." A huge sigh deflated her chest, taking Bella along for the ride. "Well, I can't help but wonder if I'm doing the right thing in leaving our precious girl every day." This time she did nuzzle the top of Bella's head—and quite forcefully at that. Almost as if she were trying to imprint the memory in her mind. Clearly something troubled her.

"Kit?" He nudged her chin with the crook of his finger, forcing her gaze to his. "Do you want to quit your job?"

"No. I love what I do, but I also love our sweet little dear. Oh, Jackson. *Am* I doing the right thing?" Conflict obliterated the silver flecks in her blue eyes, turning them into murky pools.

His chest tightened. He'd do anything to erase that confusion and remove that angst. . .anything but tell her what to do. Such a move would be worse than handing a gun to an assailant.

"Tell you what." Leaning over Bella, he kissed the tip of his wife's nose. "How about when you wrap up this missing-man case—for I know you will not rest until you find him—you reevaluate then if you should continue working with your father or not."

"That could take a very long time. My case is a muddy mess. It was far easier to sort through the one my father is working on." She pulled the bib off Bella's neck and laid it over the back of the high chair. "I thought I had a brilliant lead from the coroner's yesterday, but now I'm not so sure, and I have exhausted all my resources."

"Well, at least you know one place he is not." Jackson winked as he strode from the room to retrieve his hat. He'd have to grab coffee from a street seller on the way to work, so there wasn't a moment to waste.

"Yes, but I don't know where he *is*." Kit followed close behind. "If you wanted to hide where no one could find you, where would you hole up?"

"That's easy." He pulled his hat from the coat-tree then faced her. "Somewhere no one could find me."

"Such as?" Shifting Bella to one hip, she straightened his collar with her free hand, her rosewater scent slightly smoky from the burnt-toast affair. She really did try to be the quintessential wife—God love her—even though deep down he knew she still keened to bring justice to the streets.

His gaze bounced between Kit's luminous eyes and Bella's, a fierce love for both squeezing his heart. "If—God forbid—I needed to tuck the two of you away for a time, I would take you where we could blend into a crowd and not be singled out. A place where no one would take notice of me because they'd be too busy trying to lay low themselves. A place like—"

"A rookery, but no good." Kit shook her head. "I already checked with my contacts in St. Giles, Whitechapel, and even so far as Frying Pan Alley."

He thought for a beat, then said, "What about the Devil's Acre, what's left of it anyway? Not a huge area for a hidey-hole, but that might make it all the more plausible, being that no one much thinks of it anymore."

"Of course!" She smacked her palm against her brow and Bella laughed. "How did I overlook that one? I shall enquire there straightaway. You, Husband, are a genius." Rising to her toes, she planted a loud kiss on his lips, which Bella immediately mimicked, over and over again.

"Hold on." He stayed Kit from snatching her bonnet with a touch to her arm. "I didn't say you should go poking about there on your own. In fact, I forbid it."

She pulled away with a grin. "That's easy enough to remedy. Come with me, and then I won't be on my own."

"You know I cannot. I'm down to twelve days to get that paperwork finished for Hammerhead, and I'll need every minute of that time if I am to save my job. And—"he pressed a finger to her lips—"no amount of cajoling will get me to change my mind. Though, I suppose, I could allow you to go to the Devil's Acre with your father at your side. He'd keep you safe enough."

"He would, but he is occupied as well. Please, Jackson. Can't you just take an hour or two? We could drop Bella off with Martha then swing by that rookery. It'll be like old times." She bounced like a little girl and Bella squealed with delight. "Why, there might even be a sewer we could dive into just for memory's sake."

Despite how adorable they both were, he shook his head. "A capital idea were I to fancy a brush with death today, but the answer is an emphatic—"

A rap on the front door drowned out his *no*. Of all the timing. He swung open the door to Baggett, a Cheshire grin splitting the man's face even though he looked like a burning building had collapsed around his ears.

"Mornin' Forge, Mrs. Forge." He dipped his head at them, flakes of ash falling like snowflakes. "Thought you'd like to know, my friend, that the Charles Street arsonist is locked tight at the station, which is why I won't be in to work this morning." Sniffling, he swiped his hand beneath his nose, jiggling loose some soot darkening his moustache. "Just on my way home after a rollicking night. I'll catch a few hours then see you for a new case, if that's all right."

"Well done, Baggett!" He clapped his friend on the shoulder. "Of course you have my approv—"

"All caught up on your work, are you, Mr. Baggett?" Kit wheedled her way in front of him, Bella ba-baing all the way. "How lovely. Naturally you shall need some rest, but first I wonder if you might accompany me to the Devil's Acre? Shouldn't take long at all. We'll just pip in and out, and you'll be no worse for the wear."

Baggett blinked.

Jackson raged. Of all the bold requests! "Look at the man, Kit! He's got a bloodied jaw, his waistcoat is ripped, and his hat is burnt on one side. No offense intended, but Charles looks as if he dove headfirst into a meat grinder before landing in a dustbin. He deserves to go home for a good scrub down and some sleep, not a romp through a slum."

She tossed a saucy look over her shoulder. "Is that your only objection?"

"Do you need more?"

"Listen," Baggett cut in, "if you two need a moment—"

"No," they said in unison.

"Please, Jackson." She laid a hand on his sleeve. "It is my only lead and you said yourself you're too busy to go with me. Surely you trust your best man here to keep me safe."

"Without question, but—"

"Then it's settled." She turned back to Baggett. "Would you mind swinging by Devil's Acre on your way home? We'll have to stop at the soup kitchen first to leave off little Bella, but I'm sure Martha can fortify you with a bite of breakfast. What do you say, sir?"

Jackson's stomach grumbled. He hadn't known some of Martha's cooking would be involved in this excursion. Maybe he should have accompanied her himself.

"I'd say that's up to your husband." Baggett met Jackson's gaze head-on. "I am willing, ol' man."

Certainly he was. A truer friend didn't walk the face of the earth. Jackson scowled. "You don't have to do this."

White teeth flashed in a grin, quite the contrast to the dark smudges on his face. "You know your wife will traipse into that rookery alone if I don't go with her."

Kit arched a brow over her shoulder, a distinct smugness in the lift of her nose.

Bah! Jackson's hands clenched at his sides.

Once again he'd been outgunned by the pixie in the blue dress.

Sore. Tired. Hungry and grimy. Charles second-guessed his agreement to accompany Kit the moment she joined his side and all the way to the soup kitchen, especially every time his left foot hit the pavement. That boot and sock had been drenched in last night's chase when he'd shimmied down a drain spout and tipped over a rain barrel. Thankfully that's all that had been doused or more than just his ankle would be chafing.

But as soon as they entered the kitchen and Martha turned from a pot at the stove, all his discomfort vanished. The concern scrunching her brow immediately straightened his shoulders, surging new life through his veins. She cared about him, that much was certain, and he relished the feeling.

Which was probably a mistake.

"Mr. Baggett!" She rushed over to him, tipping his head to peer at the cut on his jaw. "Ye've been through a real wringer."

"Morning to you too, Martha." Kit smirked as she worked to remove little Bella's bonnet.

Martha whirled on her. "What's in that head o' yers, Kit Forge, to be draggin' this poor man about when he needs tending?"

Kit tipped her head in defiance, a look he'd seen Jackson suffer many a time. "Don't blame me for his condition. And besides, I brought him to the right place, didn't I?"

"I s'pose I can't fault ye fer that." Martha huffed then turned to the two oldest girls kneading dough at the big table. "Harriet, fetch a basin of warm water and a few rags. Alice, I'll be needin' me sewing kit." Swinging about, she tugged him from the room. "This way, Mr. Baggett. The light's better near the front window should I need to be doin' some needlework on ye."

"There hasn't been any fresh blood for a while, so I doubt I'll need stitches." His heart, now? That could use some lashing down as her fingers entwined with his, palm to palm, skin to skin.

"I'll be the judge of that." She eked out a bench with her foot, close to the large, mullioned glass. "Sit ye down and tell me what happened."

"Just chasing a ruffian, that's all. Nothing out of the ordinary." He sank onto the wood and pulled off his hat, raining down a snowfall of dust and ash. Quickly he swiped the mess off the tabletop. "Sorry."

"Hsst! Once I open those doors there'll be more than a smidgen o' dust a'decoratin' these slabs. Jane needs to sweep in here anyway."

The two older girls entered. Harriet, the picture of her mother, carried a porcelain basin, and Alice, two steps ahead of her, set down the sewing kit without a word. She was a shy redhead, a contradiction to the fire atop her head and to her feisty mother.

As soon as Harriet safely delivered the large bowl, Martha nodded at them both. "Thank ye, girls. Help Mrs. Forge settle Bella in, aye?"

"Yes, Mum," Alice said as she turned on her heel, dashing off in an unladylike fashion.

Harriet lingered, her lips twitching like she had something to say but couldn't quite figure out what. Of all Martha's children, she distrusted him the most, and rightfully so. She'd seen and remembered best the heavy hand her father had used against her mother—against her. It was only natural she employed caution around men.

Martha glanced at her. "Yes, child?"

"I. . .em. . .should I not stay here with you and help tend to Mr. Baggett? Ye ought not be alone with a man." Her cheeks pinked but she held her ground.

"Thank ye, but I can manage, girl. Off with ye, now. See that Mrs. Forge takes a bite to eat, and set aside a crust o' bread and cheese fer Mr. Baggett."

The girl dipped her head, but just before she turned away, Charles caught the challenge in her eyes as she gazed at him. He hid a smile. She'd make a fine mother herself some day with her protective ways.

Martha sighed as she reached for a cloth. "That girl. Don't take no offense from 'er. She nurses a general distrust of men."

"Well, then." He smiled. "I shall have to win her over, show her that not all men are angry brutes."

"If anyone can do so, Mr. Baggett, it'd be ye." She wrung out the cloth then closed in on him. "This might hurt."

He chuckled. She had no idea the sorts of hurts he'd endured in the line of service. "I won't feel a thing, I promise."

That promise, however, was instantly broken the moment she lifted his face to the light and began swabbing away the grit and grime with a soft touch. He felt all sorts of things he ought not to as he breathed in her fresh-baked scent. And when she leaned closer to rub away a particularly stubborn smudge, the tickle of a loose hank of her hair brushed against his neck, nearly driving him mad. He could no more stop his fingers from grabbing that golden piece of silk than he could stop the earth from turning.

"You're nearly as disheveled as I," he quipped as he tucked away the curl—then stiffened. At the top of her ear, the lobe of flesh swelled in an angry shade of red, looking as if she'd been pinched unreasonably hard. Instant anger flared in his gut. He reared away from her ministrations. "What happened to your ear?"

"'Tis nothin'." She readjusted her mobcap, pulling it low over the offense. "Hit it with my curling iron, is all."

"That is not a burn," he growled. Did she really think him so naive?

"Din't say it were." She wrung out the cloth, a rebellious tilt to her chin. "Ye can bet I jerked the iron away as soon as I felt heat. But I'm not the one what needs doctorin', now am I?"

Stubborn woman. Who was she protecting? Then again, she had no cause to lie, not to him. Were she in trouble, she knew he could—and would—protect her. And what did he know of curling irons anyway? Perhaps she really had injured herself. At the first convenient time, he'd ask her girls about these recent injuries. Maybe she wasn't feeling well and was refusing to see a doctor. Maybe she truly was overworked. It seemed right to give her the benefit of the doubt. After all, had he not read only just yesterday how love believed all things, hoped all things?

Whoa.

Wait a minute.

Again with the idea of love?

He tipped his head, shoving the thought far, far away. "Let's get this over with, then."

Her cloth came down more firmly this time, directly dabbing where his jaw had caught on a shingle nail as he'd slid down a roof headfirst.

"Ye'll be lucky if this don't harbour infection. Scamperin' after brigands takes a toll on a body. Ye're as reckless as Frankie." Martha shook her head as if he were one of her own. "I don't like to think of ye on the streets at night. T'aint safe."

"That's the whole reason I'm out there, to keep you and yours from harm's way."

"And I do appreciate it, Mr. Baggett, truly." She wrung out the rag once more, the water increasingly murky with dirt and blood. "But I still fear for ye."

"Don't fret on my account." He winced as she rubbed a bit too hard. "I can hold my own."

"La, sir!" Her hand froze, instant remorse clouding the blue in her eyes. "I meant no disrespect. A strappin' fellow like ye, o' course ye know how to handle yerself."

Truly, he ought not to grin, but the praise tasted too sweet to keep his lips from curving. "I took no offense, Mrs. Jones. You've never been anything but kind to me."

"Yer an easy one to be kind to," she whispered, her breath warm against his cheek.

This was dangerous ground. Far too dangerous. He should pull back, end this banter, but he was trapped between the window, the woman, and his own desire. There was no good way out of this.

Other than humour, perhaps. "I'm sure you say that to all the fellows who cross your threshold."

"No." She shook her head slowly, her gaze never once leaving his. "Only you."

"I am happy to hear it." Blast. Did that husky voice belong to him? The roughed-up hand that suddenly stroked her face, was that really his? How could he—a hardened officer used to composing himself in any and all situations—lose self-control like this?

Footsteps tapped into the room. Martha whirled like a top, splashing water from the basin as she dropped the cloth into it.

Kit raised a knowing brow. "Hope I'm not interrupting anything, but is Mr. Baggett all patched up yet? We've a rookery to shake down."

Martha retreated several steps from him, though the starch in her spine didn't wilt. "He's a bit worse for the wear but no stitches required, and I'll thank ye to keep it that way, Kit Forge."

Charles grabbed his hat and rose, admiring Martha's spirit. "It's Mrs. Forge you ought to worry about. If I bring her back to Jackson with so much as a scrape, he'll have my head."

Kit popped a fist onto her hip. "And you don't think Martha would do the same and more to me if you get banged up? I suspect we'd better both stay on our toes." She swaggered over to the front door and yanked it open. "G'day, Martha. I should be back around four to fetch Bella."

Charles tipped his hat at Martha. "Thank you, Mrs. Jones. Your ministrations have made me a new man."

Her cheeks bloomed dusky rose, then she held up a finger. "Hold on." She dashed out of the room. He exchanged a glance with Kit, who merely shrugged her shoulders.

"Perhaps she is—" Kit began but was cut off by Martha's green skirts swishing back into the room.

"Here." Martha handed him a cloth bundle. "Can't have ye runnin' about on an empty stomach. 'Tis only bread and cheese, though, so I'll feed ye a proper meal at supper, eh?"

"I look forward to it. Good day." He wheeled about and followed Kit outside, where she abruptly stopped and faced him.

"Why don't you just marry the woman and be done with it?"

"I don't know what you're talking about, Mrs. Forge." He strode off, unwrapping the cloth and shoving a huge bite of warm bread into his mouth. Better that than to talk himself into a hole he'd never climb out of.

Her footsteps caught up to him in record time. "Liars will burn in a lake of fire, you know."

He swallowed his bread without so much as looking at her. "Takes one to know one, I'd say."

"So you *do* love her!"

Thunderation! The woman could trip up a straight-talking saint. Jackson really ought to install her as the station's lead interrogator. He upped his pace. "I didn't say that."

"You don't need to, Mr. Baggett," she hollered after him, once again scurrying to gain his side. "It was written all over your face—and hers—when I stepped into the front room. Had I not intruded, I daresay you'd have kissed her. Wouldn't have taken much, for you were practically nose to nose."

He scowled as he shoved a chunk of cheddar into his mouth. Kit Forge was far too canny. Perfect for Jackson—not for him.

"Well?" she persisted. "When are you going to admit it?"

He dodged around an organ-grinder setting up for a performance, the nattering of the man's monkey as irritating as Kit. "I admit nothing, for you have read the situation entirely wrong. Mrs. Jones tended to my injury and, in doing so, was forced into close proximity, nothing more. Nothing less. And that's the end of it."

"But—"

"I said that's the end," he growled. "I am out here for your sake, not to discuss my personal matters. Is that clear?"

Her head bowed; even her shoulders sagged. A precious sight, and very uncommon. "I beg your pardon, Mr. Baggett. You are right. I have overstepped a boundary, one that I will not cross again." She peeked up at him, sunshine casting an angelic glow on her pixie face. "Forgive me?"

And that, right there, was Jackson's downfall. His as well. It would take a cold, cold heart to ignore such contrition. "Forgiven and forgotten."

For some time, then, they strode the bustling streets in companionable silence, but the closer they drew to what remained of the Devil's Acre, the more his curiosity blossomed. "This jaunt we're on, what's it about? Who or what are we looking for?"

"A man who's gone missing." Kit hiked her skirt as she stepped over a pile of manure, the bane of every London road. "Mr. Harold Coleman's wife came to me with a tale of woe about him stealing her daughter. Lately, however, I've come to suspect he might be in hiding not for nefarious reasons but in fear of his own life and that of his child's. I could be wrong, though."

"Kit Forge *wrong*?" He slapped his hand over his heart. "Say it is not so."

"I know." She grinned up at him. "'Tis a rarity, eh?"

He chuckled. "What makes you think this Coleman is holed up in the Devil's Acre?"

"It's the one place I haven't yet looked. Have you been there before?"

He turned onto Old Pye Street, Kit at his side, the stink of what was left of the slum greeting them before they even set foot in it. "I have been here, but not often. Folks in these parts aren't keen to fess up to anything, so it's usually a waste of time. Blind, deaf, and dumb, the lot of them, or so they'd lead you to believe."

He edged ahead of Kit, scanning from one ramshackle building to another. The addition of Victoria Street had cut the heart right out of this rookery. Most residents had scattered like rodents from an upturned nest, settling in St. Giles or Whitechapel. A few though, those with roots too deep to yank out, had merely dug in. . .which made this stretch of road particularly dangerous. Somehow they could always sniff out a lawman.

"Hold a moment." Facing a brick wall, he withdrew his pistol from his coat, then dug in his pocket for fresh lead. His fingers met but one bullet. Blast! He'd used far more than he'd credited last night.

Kit laughed behind him. "You won't have time to pull off a shot."

He shoved in the bullet, then turned back to her as he tucked the weapon away. "You never know."

"Actually, I do." With an arch to her brow, she slid out a knife from her boot and tucked it up her sleeve. "In tight quarters, I'll take a blade any day."

He glanced down the lane where shadows skulked in doorways from buildings that practically shook hands over the road, so far did they lean on their crumbling foundations. She was right. He'd take a shiv to the back before he even twitched his trigger finger, which would leave Kit wide open for attack. And if anything happened to her, Jackson would never forgive him. Nor would he forgive himself.

For he'd never yet pardoned his part in that fateful day Edwina Draper had died.

Chapter Ten

Squalor felt like home. A sad fact, that; leastwise that's what people would say. But people be hanged! Kit tossed back her hair and marched along Old Pye, grateful for the fish bones, the broken glass, and who knew what else littering the pavement. She'd spent her childhood on streets such as these, knew them as well as the mole on the top of her forearm. Want and need had been harsh taskmasters but had taught her well to be thankful for the little things in life.

She scanned from door to door, window to window, never making direct eye contact with the suspicious faces peering back. Such an affront wouldn't go unmet in this part of town. There had to be a bawdy house in this mix, which would be the best place to start looking for a man. And using a man for bait would render a fat fish much sooner than her gawking about for one.

She turned to Mr. Baggett. "How about you stroll five or six paces ahead of me? Put your hands in your pockets, elbows out, and add a bit of swagger to your step. Oh, and pardon me but—" With deft fingers, she loosened his necktie and pulled his collar apart, showing a bit of skin.

He batted her away. "What do you think you're doing?"

"We need to attract a loose skirt."

"Are you mad?" The horrified look on his face was priceless.

"I didn't say we'd hire one, Mr. Baggett. Besides, you're here to help me, aren't you?"

"Fine," he hissed. "But for the record, I don't like it."

"Don't worry. I won't breathe a word of this to Martha."

A growl ripped out of him, but the jab got him moving. He wheeled about so quickly the breeze of it flapped a row of handbills nailed into the rickety boards of the nearest building. Ten paces later, a red scarf dangled out an open window, held firmly in the fingers of a woman whose lily-white bosom half spilled out the top of her bodice as she leaned over the sill.

A shrill whistle passed her painted lips. "Up here, handsome."

Kit gained his side and faced the ladybird, holding up a coin as she did so. "I'm looking for a man. This shiner is yours if you can tell me where he is."

"Looks like ye got one. A right fine one." She finally pulled her gaze from Mr. Baggett and arched a kohl-black brow at Kit. "How 'bout ye leave this 'un here with me while ye find yerself another?"

"Don't even think about it," Charles huffed in a harsh whisper.

Kit ignored him. "The fellow I want has a hump on his nose, an overwide mouth, square jaw, and brown hair. Have you seen him?"

Coarse laughter rained down from the window. "I don't pay no never mind to those parts of a body, ducky."

Well. This was getting them exactly nowhere. She spun on her heel. It didn't take any convincing to get Charles to join her side, where his fingers flew to straighten his collar and tie.

Two doors down she stopped in front of an open door with a signboard hanging catawampus from one chain above it. The Black Sheep. She smirked. Appropriate name for a flash house.

"I'll handle it this time." Charles held out his hand. "Give me your knife."

"You cannot be serious."

"You said yourself I'm here to help you, and to do so, I require the use of your knife." His palm didn't waver.

Evidently this was to be quite the show, then. Curious, she handed it over and followed him inside.

The stink of sour ale and sweat punched her in the nose. The low drone of men's voices didn't stop, but it did quiet quite a bit. From the shadows in the murky taproom, the whites of several sets of eyeballs tracked their steps all the way to the counter.

An ox of a barkeep lumbered over to them, his bald head glistening with a sheen of perspiration. The man was so large, should tending bar not pay off, he could easily nab employment as a workhorse.

"Well?" He eyed them.

Charles lifted his chin. "Two mugs."

While the barkeep grabbed two filthy steins, Kit's gaze roamed the perimeter. Six drinkers, by the looks of it, keeping to the corners. Even in here, handbills hung stark from a few posts that propped up a sagging ceiling. Advertising for a circus, from the looks of it, though she doubted very much they were fishing for customers. More like for workers.

The barkeep slapped down the mugs on the counter, foam sloshing over the rims. "Two bob."

Charles pulled out a pound note and laid it down.

Kit choked. What on all of God's green earth was the man thinking? Flashing such an amount in this wicked denizen was a good way to get them both killed.

"New here, eh?" A slow grin split the barkeep's face into a sharp-toothed grin. "We don't do change in these parts." He made a grab for the bill.

"And I don't give something for nothing." With a quick stab of the knife, Charles pinned the man's hand to the counter, the thwack of it digging through the barkeep's sleeve and wood alike. Any closer to the fellow's forearm and he'd have hit skin.

The barkeep growled, but before he could yank back his arm, Charles pulled out his gun and aimed it square at the man's forehead. "Not another move from you, aye?"

Murder flared in the barkeep's black eyes. "What do ye want, cuffin?"

"Information," Charles said as breezily as a summer day. "A man, hook nose, slasher of a mouth, dirt-brown hair, and square jaw. Seen him?"

Kit clamped her mouth lest she gape. No wonder Jackson kept this man at his side.

"Mebbe I've seen him." The man's voice was kicked gravel. "Mebbe not."

"Maybe I've put too much money on the counter, then." Charles twisted the knife, the blade nicking against the man's skin and blooming blood on the fabric.

Sweat ran down the barkeep's temples in rivulets. "Maybe you've not put enough."

"Need a hand, Paunch?" A voice shot out of the darkness, accompanied by the scrape of a few chairs.

Kit pulled out the rest of her coins and smacked them down before this spiraled out of control. "You gonna answer the man or not?"

The barkeep's gaze flicked between the money and her, then slid to Charles. "See Sissy Boggs. Next door down. Don't know if she's housin' yer game or not, but she's got an extra jingle in her pocket from some new boarder."

Charles lowered his gun and yanked out the knife. "Nice doing business with you." He nodded at the money. "That oughtta cover a bandage and then some."

He pivoted. Kit tagged his heels. A grumble of "Don't let me see yer faces again" hit them square between the shoulder blades as they left.

Once past the door, Kit shot out her hand. "While I appreciate the lead, I'd like my blade back now. And I'll be taking this next one. Can't have you mauling a defenseless woman."

Charles flashed a grin as he laid the hilt in her palm. "I highly doubt Sissy Boggs is a frail flower."

And he was right. After Kit's knock on her door, the woman in question appeared with a thick club clutched in her beefy hand, and judging by the thickness of her arms, one swing of the thing could take a man's head clear off his neck.

"Penny a night." Her cancerous gaze drifted to Charles and back again. "Two fer yer man. And ye'll be sharin' with ten others."

Ten? Not bad for these parts. But all the same, good thing she wasn't in the market. "I don't need a room," Kit explained. "I need to know if you're renting to a man with a crooked nose, square jaw, wide mouth, brown hair and eyes. He might have a baby with him."

The woman's lips pinched. "I'm no squealer."

Drat. She'd given her last penny to the ox behind the bar. She lifted a pleading glance to Charles, and though he shook his head slightly, he produced a shilling and handed it over.

Sissy bit the coin with teeth that looked as if they'd been coated in mouse fur. Apparently satisfied, she shoved the money into a grimy apron pocket and flung the door open wide. "Second floor, last door."

She disappeared into her quarters, leaving them alone in a narrow hall with holes in the plaster. After exchanging a glance with Charles, Kit began scaling the rickety staircase. One flight up, she nearly gagged on a stench that rivaled the morgue. Behind her, Charles coughed into his sleeve, and they both upped their pace. It didn't smell much better on the second flight, nor was the lighting any brighter. A poorly boarded hole at the end of the long stretch of corridor leaked in the only light available. Thankfully, that's where the last door—hopefully Mr. Coleman's—was located.

Kit stopped in front of it and peered up at Charles. "Follow my lead."

Charles shook his head. "Not again."

She banged on the door before he could complain any further. "Aye-oh Neddy boy! Got a cone o' fish to share wit' ya, lovey."

"I thought you said his name was Harold?" Charles whispered.

"You think he'd answer to that?" she whispered back, then with another thump-thump-thump on the door, shouted, "Neddy! Open up, luv."

"Looks like he's not answering to anything," Charles quipped. "Want I should kick it down?"

She reached for the knob, and surprisingly it turned with ease. "Save the brawn for now. Though it could be a trap." She pulled her knife.

He pulled his gun and nudged her aside. "Then I'm going first."

Save for some sparse furnishings, the room was empty. Seedy, decrepit, and filthy, but completely void of human life. Disappointment sank like sour milk to Kit's belly. "Whoever rented this room has flown, *if* it was Mr. Coleman."

Charles tucked away his pistol. "Maybe we can find out who was here and where he's gone. A man always leaves something behind he didn't intend to."

Her lips twitched at Charles' truth. Jackson always left an unintentional trail of destruction behind him at home. She approached a table while Charles rummaged through a washstand drawer near a pallet on the floor.

"Sissy didn't lie." He held up a broken razor. "There was a man in this room."

Kit joined him, squinting at a half-empty bottle of. . .too hard to read the smudged label. She picked it up and sniffed the contents, the sharp tang of chemicals jerking her head back at once. "Or could be the bearded woman from the circus was in here bleaching her hair."

He chuckled as he wandered to the wardrobe. Kit crossed the warped floorboards to the small hearth. An astonishing amount of ashes for August heaped in a pile. She poked about with her finger, displacing a cloud of dust and revealing a small collection of burnt bone buttons, enough for a man's shirt. . .but no one in this neighbourhood would intentionally ruin a good set of garments.

She glanced over her shoulder at Charles. "If Mr. Coleman was here, looks like he's gone incognito. New hair and new clothing."

"Then he did so a few days ago." He pointed at the mattress. "That pallet isn't as flattened as it ought to be had a body laid on it last night and the night before." He swiped up a stack of papers. "Also, the man took the news, though yesterday and today's aren't here. Clearly whoever stayed here wasn't hurting for coins to have paid for a single room, purchased papers and a whole new look, so why stay in this rathole?"

"Those on the run don't often have a lot of choices."

Charles flopped the newspapers back to the table, and a ripped paper fluttered to the floor. He swept it up with a frown. "Thunderation. Those bloody circus handbills are everywhere."

But she couldn't care less about that slip of garbage when she spied a balled-up wad of paper wedged against the baseboard. She stretched her arm, fingers grasping to snatch the wayward piece of trash. Victory. She rose, and the instant she unfolded the wrinkled ball, a smile curved her lips. "He was here!"

"How do you know?"

"This letterhead. It's the company he worked for." She squinted at the numbers arranged in odd squares covering the paper. Orderly, yet with no rhyme or reason. She held it out to Charles. "What do you make of this?"

He studied the thing for some time, turning it one way then another as he did so. Eventually he handed it back. "I don't know. But that is definitely ledger paper."

"Makes sense. Mr. Coleman was an accountant, but this doesn't look like any kind of bookkeeping I've ever seen." She frowned at the grids of numbers, each of them sporting exactly nine digits. "Some sort of code, perhaps?"

Charles snapped his fingers. "A betting sheet. Maybe this Coleman of yours is on the run from a bookie with a grudge."

"This is beyond the brains of a bookie, though I suppose this could be a complicated parlay calculation." She frowned at the mysterious paper, once again trying to make sense of the nine 3x3 grids scattered over the page. "No. Parlays would be only two columns and use more than single digits."

Far below, angry voices drifted up the stairs. Must be loud to be heard clear up here. She shoved the paper in her pocket as she padded over to it and craned her head into the corridor to better hear what was going on below stairs.

"Out of our way, woman!" was followed by a sharp, feminine yip. Boots stamped up the stairs, as did a man's grumble. "If he's not alone, we take 'em all out."

Kit slammed the door shut. "We've got company. Help me move the wardrobe."

Oof, but the hulking thing was heavy—a boon and a curse. They barely got it shoved in front of the door as something slammed against it from the outside. "Open up, Coleman! We know yer in there."

"That's not gonna hold," Charles warned with a wild glance about the room.

Kit ran to the single window, only to see a gunman aiming up at her. A shot cracked. She ducked. Glass shattered, hundreds of tiny shards showering her hair and shoulders.

"Back away!" Charles shouted.

"Open this door!" the men outside bellowed.

Of all the pickles. Jackson would kill her if she came home maimed and bloodied—*if* she came home, that was.

God, a little help here, please. She lifted the prayer as her eyes landed on the chimney. She could probably shimmy up that narrow throat, but Mr. Baggett's broad shoulders would never fit. Her gaze drifted along the wall, towards the corner, where a hole in the plaster revealed some rotted wattle and daub. Not ideal, but it would have to do.

"Well, Mr. Baggett"—her voice competed with the incessant banging on the door—"I'll take you up on that offer of a kick right now."

He followed her gaze to the weak spot on the wall. "It'll be quite a drop from second floor."

"At least there won't be an armed bruiser waiting for us on that side of the building. And besides, it's an outside corner. There's sure to be a drainpipe to slip down."

"You've got to be jesting."

"I don't think they're in the jesting mood." She hitched her thumb over her shoulder as a huge thud hit the door. The wardrobe gave several inches of ground.

A few more rams like that and the blackguards would be in.

Jackson pounded his chest with his fist as he swung into the station, fighting back a slight burn near his heart. That greasy pork pie he'd nabbed off a street seller would likely stay with him for the rest of the day.

"Afternoon, Inspector. Sergeant left a note for you." Smitty waved a paper over the counter. Behind him, inside a glassed-in anteroom filled with shelves of ledgers, hunched the round lump of Mr. Harvey, engrossed in rearranging portfolios on a lower shelf.

Jackson retrieved the folded slip and shook it out. Sergeant Doyle's sweeping strokes requested an inquest into a Mr. Bigham Willowbee for possible insurance fraud. Wonderful. Such scams were notorious for the killer amount of paperwork it took to prove wrongdoing in a court of law. . .paperwork he didn't have time to fuss with. He tucked the note into his pocket. "How long do you intend to keep Harvey tied up back there?"

"He ought to finish by the end of the shift, sir." The hefty clerk leaned over the counter, the edge cutting into his big belly. "The man's a miracle worker, I tell ya," he whispered.

Jackson's gaze roved past Smitty's shoulder to the rookie inspector. Harvey looked like an oversized turtle the way he crouched, all round backed, no neck, great sweat stains darkening the deep green of his coat to black circles beneath his arms. Apparently miracle working induced quite the perspiration.

"Whether the shift is over or not, Smitty, send him up as soon as he's done."

Smitty nodded sharply. "Aye, sir."

Jackson trotted up the stairs. No doubt Harvey would have some sort of excuse as to why he couldn't manage the Willowbee case. A strain on the eyes, perhaps. Or maybe the ink used on insurance documents gave him hives. Either way, the man would see to this inquest or Jackson would have to let him go, commissioner's nephew or not. This was a police station, not a nursery to care for childish whiners.

As soon as he shut his office door, the great load of unfinished paperwork taunted him from his desk. Stacks of folders towered on one side; hastily created piles of paper filled the rest. He'd made a minuscule amount of headway this morning, finally matching several criminals to their subsequent offenses and then to a date and outcome of their respective court case. But there were hundreds to go. The former chief ought to be flogged for such an unnecessarily complicated system.

Jackson dropped into his chair and once again pounded his chest, the burn working its way up to his throat. With any luck he'd succumb to the pain and keel over dead, effectively escaping the nightmare on his desktop.

A knock rapped on the door. Before he could open his mouth to tell whoever it was to go away, in strolled Ezra Catchpole, a huge fish draped over his outstretched arms. It was a wonder the skinny man remained upright with such a fat load.

"A very wonderful afternoon to you, Chief Inspector Forge, for yes, I now know that you are not a mere inspector but the very tip-top of this station. How grand! Such a stupendous achievement." A crooked-toothed grin flashed beneath the absurd mask.

Jackson clenched his hands to keep from burying his face in them. "What are you doing here at the station, Mr. Catchpole?"

"Why, I have brought you your supper." He flopped the flounder onto the desk. Papers flew, some drifting to the floor, others merely scattering. Most were dampened with a healthy dose of fish slime.

"This has to stop, Mr. Catchpole." Jackson groaned. "There is no need for you to continue bringing me gifts."

"There is every need, my good man. You saved my life!" Pulling an enormous handkerchief from his pocket, Catchpole rubbed furiously at the gooey remnants on his coat sleeves—the same garish red coat he'd been wearing since that fateful day on Blackfriars Bridge.

Jackson hefted a sigh. Patience was a virtue in which he'd grown considerably since being married to Kit. . .yet apparently not enough, judging by the urge to shoo the man out of here. "At what point will you consider that debt paid?"

Catchpole tucked away his cloth, flipped out his coattails, then sat on the chair directly in front of Jackson's desk. "When I can help you in a life-or-death situation, then the universe will right itself. Until such, I shall do everything in my power to enrich and enhance the drudgery of your day-to-day existence."

Unbidden, Jackson's gaze drifted to the disaster on his desk. Drudgery was right. . .but the only enhancement he needed was a burst of brilliance to crack the former chief's absurd filing code or a raging fire to burn down the whole building. He scrubbed a hand over his face, shaking off the wild thought. Even though he hadn't voiced it, he was no better than Harvey mewling about his work.

"Mr. Catchpole"—he faced the man—"surely you have other matters to attend. A job, family ties, maybe even a cat or a canary to see to?"

"Oh, blessed fellow!" He clapped his bony hands together, the sharp report of it loud in the small office. "How very thoughtful of you to consider that which might require my attention. Putting others first is highly commendable. But"—he lifted a finger in the air—"I assure you my commitments, while important, are few, which enables me to ponder and procure these little delights for your pleasure."

Delight? That was a stretch for the milky fish eye staring up at him. He collected the cold flounder and rounded the desk, depositing the thing on the wooden chair next to Catchpole. Better it should decompose there than on his files.

Rubbing the stickiness from his hands, he angled his head at Catchpole. "What are your commitments exactly? Have you a home? A job? Any family to care for or care for you?"

"You. . .you ask this of *me*?" Behind the mask, great tears shimmered in the man's dark eyes. "Your benevolence is unequaled," he whispered as he laid a hand on Jackson's sleeve. "I have never met with such true compassion. May the good Lord—yes, I am now on speaking terms with the Almighty thanks to you—break open the heavens and rain down blessings upon your head, Chief Inspector Forge."

Pity welled in Jackson's gut, a bad combination with that pork pie. All he'd done was ask about the man's connections. Why such an emotional response? What sort of life had Catchpole led that left him so desperate for attention?

Whatever, he surely didn't have time to sort through the man's past or present. Jackson reclaimed his chair. "I appreciate your kind words, Mr. Catchpole, but I am certain there are others who care for you. I don't know what you've suffered in your past, but perhaps it is time to reconnect with whoever those people are. Reconciliation is always worth a try. Now, if you'll excuse me. . ." He swept his hand towards the piles on his desk. "As you can see I have an inordinate amount of—"

Catchpole shot to his feet. "You are right, my fine fellow. Absolutely and without any shadow of a doubt right! You have given me such inspiration." He flew to the door, then paused, the sides of his mouth falling practically to the floorboards. His chin quivered slightly. "I might require your assistance should I get hauled out, though. I do not fancy another ride in a Black Maria."

Jackson cocked his head. "Hauled out of where?"

"Parliament, of course," he drawled, then winked. "So it is very fortuitous that I now know a chief inspector. Until later, my justice-seeking friend." The door opened and closed so quickly, the accompanying gust of air fluttered several more papers off Jackson's desk.

Oh mercy. Sweet unadulterated mercy! Jackson could only pray to God that whatever Catchpole was involved in, it wouldn't involve Parliament.

Chapter Eleven

Charles' shirt stuck to his skin, moist with sweat, as irritating as his still-damp sock from last night's dodgy criminal chase. Using all his muscle, he kicked again at the wattle-and-daub wall, this time his foot going straight through to air. He yanked back his boot, and the hem of his trousers caught on a dagger-sharp piece of wood, shredding the fabric. Well. At least now that side matched the other ruined leg.

He reared back for another whopper of a boot bash, and an accompanying crash hit the door. What a race. Those cullies in the corridor would soon be in. If they didn't kill him, then Jackson would if anything should happen to Kit.

"We've got to hurry, Mr. Baggett." Kit grabbed a chipped chamber pot and began whacking it against the opening in the wall.

"Stand back." He shooed her away with a swipe of his arm. "Just one"—he punched his heel into the crumbling daub—"more"—he grunted as he landed another strike that juddered up his backbone—"kick!"

Wood snapped. Centuries-old mud crumbled. Daylight poured through a jagged circle roughly two feet in diameter. Charles shoved his head through, assessing. Five feet down was a roof, flat, poorly tarred, and beyond that yet another roof about waist-high above it. Taller buildings towered on each side. They'd be rats in a sky-high maze. Fabulous. He'd hardly recovered from last evening's mad rooftop dash, now this?

"Mr. Baggett!" Kit's voice crackled with urgency. "They're just about through."

Judging by the next chest-rattling thump, she was right.

He dove through the hole, slicing his jaw on a sharp piece of wattle before landing on his shoulder. Hard. Blast it! He'd give his left kidney for a paperwork assignment like Jackson's right about now. Staggering to his feet, he wheeled around to catch Kit.

Too late.

She'd already flown through the void, hat gone, hair wild. Her skirts billowed as she rolled to her feet like a cat.

"Well done, Mr. Baggett!" Kit's blue eyes glimmered, her cheeks radiating an excited flush. Saints above! Clearly the woman loved this sort of thing. He couldn't imagine Martha scrabbling through a hole in the wall and being pleased about it, as any decent female ought not to be. Occasions such as these made him appreciate the hearth-and-home heart of Martha.

Something boomed inside—the wardrobe hitting the floor, most likely.

He grabbed Kit's hand. "Time to go."

She wrenched from his hold. "Don't work harder, Mr. Baggett; think smarter. Your gun. This is the perfect ambush site." She circled her hand at the ragged gap.

He shook his head. "I've only got one shot, and there's more than one man that'll breach that hole. I guarantee it."

"Then I'll whack the other one on the head as he emerges." She pulled out her knife, hilt at the ready.

"Don't be daft. We have no idea how many men are going to pour out that wall. I will not have you endangered in a bloody brawl on a roof."

Kit jutted her jaw. "I'll take the risk."

"I won't." Lunging, he dug his fingers into her arm and yanked her along as he tore off. Wood creaked beneath the layers of felt and tar, all of which was slick with a coating of green slime. It took his years of footwork in the boxing ring to keep from flipping head over behind.

At his side, Kit yipped like an angry pup until they reached the next ridge. Releasing her, he scrambled up then gave her a hand, and as he did so, he glanced over to the maw he'd created. One man had already dropped and was staggering to his feet. Another shimmied through the hole, working to free his broad shoulders. Both were bruisers.

"They're onto us. Let's go." The instant he righted Kit, they sprinted, barely stopping in time as they reached the edge of the roof. A thirty-foot drop—give or take—gaped in front of them. No windowsills to cling to. No awnings to break a fall. Nothing but a sheer plummet to a narrow passage between buildings. . .and the next building was at least several hands higher than this one.

He snapped a glance over his shoulder, breathing hard. The men's heads—two, not three—were already crowning over the top of the ridge. He could shoot one then take out the other hand-to-hand; but if he missed his aim, there'd be two raging bulls to manage and he and Kit would lose their distance advantage.

He faced her, and though he hated to ask such a thing, there was no choice. "If I help you, do you think you can leap such a distance?"

Chest heaving, she rolled her eyes. "Who do you think you're talking to, Mr. Baggett?" She tucked her skirt hem into her waistband as she backtracked several steps, a strange gleam in her eyes. Great heavens! She couldn't seriously be thinking of trying this on her own.

"Kit!" he yelled as she galloped past him, terrified to let her go yet even more petrified to yank her back lest they both plummet to their deaths.

His blood drained to his feet as her blue gown went airborne.

And he died several times over when she didn't quite make it.

God, no! Please—

She stretched her arms.

He held his breath.

Her hands barely made purchase on the next rooftop, but they held, thank God. They held! The bottom half of her swung like a crazed pendulum as she worked her way up to her forearms then her elbows, and with a loud guttural grunt, she finally heaved herself up onto the next roof.

Charles swiped sweat off his brow. Never again. He'd *never* go solo with this wildcat if he had anything to say about it. Jackson could mind his own insane wife.

Boots pounded the roof at his back. The sooner he and Kit were on solid ground, the better. Rearing back, he lifted a prayer then shot off like a sixty-four pounder from a Mark II canon.

Unlike Kit, he overshot. His legs collapsed and he skidded to a stop chin first on a layer of bird droppings and gravel from a nearby crumbling chimney. He barely made it to his feet when Kit snatched a broken brick and clambered up the back side of that chimney.

"What are you doing?" he growled. "Those men will catch up to us."

"Divide and conquer, Mr. Baggett." She hefted one leg over the smokestack's edge. "Lead them on a merry chase, and when they speed by here, I'll pop out and clobber the fellow in the rear with this brick." She waved the weapon in the air.

"Are you mad? I'm not leaving you!"

"It's a brilliant idea." She cocked her head, dark hair flying in the breeze. "Have you a better one?"

"I said I'll not leave you, woman." The words, his tone, both harsh, but wholly called for. Jackson would have his head if he left Kit defenseless. Then again, she wasn't completely vulnerable. She did have a brick. And a knife. Not to mention her dangerous wits and reckless courage.

"You also said you have one shot, Mr. Baggett. Use it to your advantage. There are only two of them. We can do this." With a final defiant arch to her brow, she flung her other leg over and disappeared into the chimney.

"Kit!" Mule-headed, irritating woman. Why had he ever sung her praises to Jackson and encouraged him to wed such a rebellious skirt?

He spun towards the roof's edge. Just as he'd predicted, the scrappers were already belly-crawling over the wall. Nothing for it, then.

Trotting backwards as fast as he dared, he held a straight line—hopefully—while flailing his arms. "Fancy a fight, do you, fellows? Over here, you worthless tubs of guts."

The lead man lowered his head and charged like a bull. The other sped ahead as well but wasn't nearly as fast as the first. There'd be no time to see if Kit's aim met its mark, not if he hoped to somehow get the drop on the man-sized freight train barreling his way.

He pivoted and whizzed ahead, tired, winded, desperate. He would run out of roof in about forty more paces, and the next building looked too far of a distance to gain with a wild leap. Everything inside screamed for him to stop and shoot, but if Kit had managed to whack the other fellow on the head and was already climbing out of that chimney, a poorly aimed shot could hit her. There was nothing else to do but pray.

Spare Kit's life, Lord. . .and mine.

Then plunge.

He flew over the edge, this one with a gutter, and grabbed so tightly to it that the metal cut into his flesh. He'd never been so glad in all his life to spy a drainpipe two meters to his left. Arms shaking, he scrambled hand over hand as fast as he could without losing hold, then wrapped his leg around the pipe and slid. Another button flew off his waistcoat as it snagged against a metal cuff securing the rainspout to the building. The next cuff ripped his coat.

This time when he landed, he'd be ready for that rain barrel and use it to his advantage instead of his detriment.

His feet hit gravel. His knees buckled, and he flung out a hand to stay upright. Thunder and turf! Where was a barrel when he needed it? No choice, then.

He pulled out his gun and cocked the hammer, aiming for the man's legs as the thug skimmed down the drain. Fingering the trigger, he steadied his arm, gauged the distance, and—

A brick careened out of nowhere, cracking into the skull of the brigand. Charles barely stepped aside before the body whumped at his feet. He blinked at the unconscious man. What the devil?

He jerked his head up to see the brilliant grin of a pixie in a blue dress peering over the roof. "Handcuff that one, Mr. Baggett, then climb back up here and slap another pair of darbies on the other fellow I took down."

Charles shook his head. The woman was completely unstoppable. "I hate to disappoint you, Mrs. Forge, but there is a slight problem with that plan."

She shoved back the hair hanging in her face. "Come on, sir. Surely you can find no fault with my idea this time."

"Ahh, but I can." Though he really shouldn't, he grinned back at her, satisfaction at thwarting her followed hard by the current problem at hand. "I used my handcuffs on the blackguard I lugged in last night."

Which begged the question. . . How exactly was he to haul in these two?

Kit rubbed the tender spot on her aching hip as she aimlessly ran a finger along the edge of Jackson's desk—what could be seen of it, anyway. So many papers cluttered the top that not much wood showed through. What a mess.

Then again, she and Charles had made quite a mess of their own. Not only had the brigand she'd left on the roof gotten away, the one they'd dragged in had hardly been coherent after her thwack with the brick. . .not to mention the struggle that'd ensued when Charles had tried to hog-tie him with his braces. Thank heavens for Mr. Baggett's quick fists. She glanced at the wall clock, then narrowed her eyes. That'd been a good two hours ago, though. Surely the man ought to have come 'round enough by now to have spilled a morsel or two of information.

Behind her the door opened. Kit whirled. In strode a haggard-looking Jackson—and no wonder. Bella had squawked on and off all night the previous evening, working on teeth, so he'd not gotten much sleep. Then there was the guillotine of paperwork threatening to cut off his head. . .or more like a superintendent who would if he didn't get it finished in time. Her chest squeezed that she'd added to his weariness by the impromptu interrogation he'd been foisted into when she and Charles had brought in their man.

But that didn't stop her from peppering her husband with questions as soon as his long legs crossed the threshold. "Did he squeal? What did you find out? Where's Mr. Baggett?"

Jackson closed the door behind him, deep lines carved into his brow. "I bid him go home. Baggett deserves a mug, a good scrubbing, and a pillow." He shook his head like a disgusted fishwife. "I still cannot believe the pair of you. You were supposed to be on a simple reconnaissance mission, not a rooftop scramble for your lives."

"Flit. It's not like I haven't done that before."

"You're a mother now, Kit!" The words were thunder, as forbidding as the dark flash in her husband's eyes. "It is high time you put a stop to such risky behaviour. In fact," he said, lifting his chin, "I demand it."

If she'd had hackles, they'd immediately be raised on end. Husband or not, Jackson ought not to act so imperious. She advanced, toe to toe, poking one finger against his broad chest for emphasis. "All I did was ask around for my missing man and search a flat where he'd been reported to be living. And with Mr. Baggett at my side the entire time, nonetheless. How is that risky?"

Without a word, Jackson whipped out his white handkerchief with one hand and pinched her chin with the other. After a few swipes that left her wincing, he held up the cloth, now marred with dirt and blood. "Clearly it was no tea party the two of you attended."

A sigh ripped out of her. Maybe she was taking too many risks—not that she'd admit it to him, though. "There is more at stake here than a few scrapes and bruises. A child is out there somewhere, Jackson, a babe as helpless and innocent as our sweet little Bella. She deserves to be with her mother every bit as much as Bella deserves to be with me."

"True, but I am second-guessing my consent for you to scrabble about the streets. It's not safe." He tucked away his cloth and pulled her into his arms, his tone softening. "I will not have you getting hurt, Wife. Bella needs you. *I* need you." He pressed a kiss to the top of her head.

She grinned up at him. "Looks like you need a secretary as well." Pulling away, she swept her hand towards the chair near his desk, where a great fat fish sat at center. "Or maybe a chef."

A long breath leaked out of him. "No. What I need is a miracle."

He circled his desk and sank into his seat.

Kit smoothed her skirts as she took the only other empty chair, the crinkle of paper in her pocket a reminder of evidence that Jackson might have an idea about. She pulled it out, about to set the ripped paper on his desk, then thought better of it and stood, placing it into his hand directly. "What do you make of this? I found it in Coleman's flat."

His lips pursed as his eyes skimmed over the number grids on the page, a slight shake to his head. "I don't know. I've never seen anything like it."

"All those numbers have to mean something. Maybe a clue as to where Coleman might have run off to or others he is involved with. A code, so to speak. Or perhaps it's a key to a new and intricate gaming swindle."

"Could be any of those things," he drawled as he refolded the paper and tucked it into his pocket. "Or none of them. I'll see what I can find out."

"Thank you." She shifted on the chair, the bruise on her hip tender. "What did you and Mr. Baggett find out from that bloomin' cully we hauled in?"

He aimed a finger at her. "Mind your language, Wife."

"Fine. What did you find out from that *criminal*?"

White teeth flashed beneath his moustache. Truly she ought to be incensed at such an obvious show of satisfaction for her acquiescence, but sweet heavens! He was more handsome than a man had a right to be when he grinned.

Lacing his fingers behind his head, Jackson leaned back in his chair. "Apparently the fellow—and the one that got away—was hired by someone to watch the flat in order to snag the man residing there."

"Who hired him?"

"He won't say."

"Let me have a go at him, then." She shot to her feet, but before she could reach the door, a strong grip on her arm pulled her back.

"He won't tell me *yet*, but trust me, I will find out." A muscle ticked on his jaw. "This is my job, Wife, not yours."

The words hit her like a sledgehammer. He was right. This was his job. If she marched down to the holding cell and began questioning that cully—criminal—the very act would belittle Jackson in the eyes of his coworkers. She pressed her hand lightly to his cheek. "That was a bit rash of me. Of course I trust you. Besides, I have my own sweet little *job* to pick up from Martha."

"And a delicious dinner to prepare for your husband." He bopped her on the nose with his finger.

She arched a brow. "Then I'd best be sure to pick up some soup from Martha as well."

"You're incorrigible, you know th—"

Rising to her toes, she cut him off with a series of fierce kisses that trailed all the way to his ear. "Would you have me any other way?" she whispered.

"I would have you here and now, did I not have a man to interrogate." He guided her mouth back to his.

She pulled away with a grin. "Until tonight, then."

"I shall hold you to that promise." The blue of his eyes smouldered dusky—a look that never failed to heat her belly.

She fled before she gave in to the desire to once again press her body against his. The rest of that craving was squelched as she braved the chaos of the late afternoon streets, especially when she was forced to dodge an overly zealous ginger-beer seller and slipped in a puddle of what appeared to be day-old porridge. At least she hoped it was that.

She flicked back her loose hair and soldiered her way onward, Jackson's words haunting her at every step. He did have a point about the hazards she faced as a sleuth. La! She'd only been at it five days now and already she'd managed to scuff up not only herself but Charles as well. It was important to seek justice for others...but what sort of justice was it for little Bella to daily deprive her of her mother? Granted, Martha was as loving as she could be in respect to her sweet girl, but was that truly the same as caring for the babe herself? She arm wrestled such questions all the way to the soup kitchen, and by the time she reached it, her already ragged skirt had added a new tear in the hem and a thick layer of grime towards the bottom.

Avoiding the long line of eager eaters, she swung around to the back door. Inside, just as much hubbub buzzed. One girl stacked bread slices on platters. Another hustled out to the dining room with a basket of spoons. The youngest dashed after her with a handful of cloths, and Martha directed it all with a wave of her ladle from where she stood near the range.

"Good afternoon, ladies. Looks like I came just in time. You surely don't need Bella added to this mix." With a wave, Kit headed towards the room off to the side where her sweet little dear ought to be just about finished up with her second nap.

"Yer right, ye are just in time. I feared ye'd not get here before I must open the door to the hungry mob." Martha nodded towards the dining room. "Someone's waitin' for ye."

Odd, that. "Who?"

Martha shrugged. "Din't have time to drag out a name. The poor soul was upset enough as is. Jane!" She aimed the ladle like a spear at the ten-year-old. "Get yer lazy behind to work helpin' yer sister with that pot o' beans. Anna, see that ye mind Hazel and—"

Kit turned on her heel. It would be faster—and kinder to Martha—to simply find out who called on her. Ducking around the two girls returning from the dining room, she strode into the large space, then gasped when Mrs. Coleman turned to face her.

With a black eye, a split lip, and tearstains glistening on her cheeks.

Chapter Twelve

She'd seen wallopings before. Knew the metallic twang of blood in her own mouth after a good whack of a backhand. But this? Kit forced her breathing to steady even though rage licked white-hot along every nerve and vein. The lady in front of her was no scrapper, pinching about for a fight. Mrs. Coleman was a proper lady. A decent woman. One who ought not to be sporting a purpled eye and bloodied lip.

This was a violation of the most heinous sort.

Skirting tables and benches, Kit rushed across the dining hall and collected the woman's hands in her own. "What happened? No, wait. First, please be seated." She guided Mrs. Coleman to a bench away from the front windows. No sense allowing the eager faces waiting for a meal to peer in at the woman's distress.

"Oh, Mrs. Forge. It was so dreadful." Tears shimmered in the woman's cat-like eyes.

And once again an odd feeling of recognition tingled through her. How many times during her years on the streets had she stared into a face such as this, brimming with fear and despair?

Mrs. Coleman gripped Kit's hands as if she dangled over a cliff's edge. "I beg your pardon to have called upon you here, but your office was closed, and I—I simply did not know what to do."

"Think nothing of it." But Kit did. . .how had this woman tracked her down to a Blackfriars soup kitchen? She angled her head. "How did you find—"

"Oh, my baby!" Mrs. Coleman wailed. "I fear for her so!" Releasing her death grip, Mrs. Coleman sobbed into her hands.

Kit dug out her handkerchief and pressed it into the woman's fingers. "Please, take this."

Sniffles ensued, followed by the most ladylike honk of a nose Kit had ever witnessed.

"Thank you, Mrs. Forge." After a final dab at her eyes—and wincing when the cloth met the bruise—Mrs. Coleman lifted her face. "Everything happened so quickly, I. . .well, I can scarce believe such a dreadful encounter happened. And yet, here I am, as you see."

Two of Martha's girls scurried into the dining room, setting down bowls with such a clatter that she waited until they vanished into the kitchen before plying the distraught woman with questions. "Who did this to you?"

Her dainty brow pulled into a scowl. "Two men. Two great, hairy beasts, I should say." A shudder rippled across her shoulders. "I never should have gone out unattended. Oh, why was I so injudicious?"

"You cannot blame yourself for harm that others inflicted." She patted the woman's knee. "Now then, how about you tell me the whole story?"

For a moment, Mrs. Coleman didn't say a word, just stared to the far corner of the room, clearly tormented. At length, she shifted her gaze back to Kit. "The truth is I could not bear the emptiness of the house anymore. The vacant nursery. The rattle left on the rug where little Lillibeth last played." She inhaled a shaky breath. "So, I thought to stop by the milliner's to put my mind on something else. Not to make a purchase, you must understand, for nothing holds appeal to me anymore, not until I once again hold my child."

Rising, Mrs. Coleman folded her arms across her chest, swaying slightly. A pitiful sight, for surely she was reliving the feel of her babe.

Then just as suddenly, she dropped her hands, eyes sparking. "But as I strolled down Straight Street, a man strode up on my right side, keeping perfect pace. Out of nowhere, another appeared on my left. Before I knew what was happening, they steered me off the pavement and into an alcove."

Typical. Such a flanking maneuver was common among dragsmen and dippers. Kit twisted her lips. "So, you were mugged."

"No. Threatened."

Kit peered up at her. "About what?"

She began pacing in a tight circle, hands clenched in front of her. "Somehow—and I have no idea how—my husband knows I have hired you. And in retaliation, he employed those—those *animals* to deliver a message, that if I do not immediately cut ties with you and stop trying to find him, next time I shall be more than marked up, as they called it." She stopped, her skirts swishing from the abrupt change of pace. Mrs. Coleman's face went sheet white. "They told me I would be killed."

Of all the coercion! Kit clenched her jaw, stifling a flinch as the movement tugged at a cut near her ear. Men's wickedness truly knew no bounds, for she had no doubt if Mr. Coleman were desperate enough to have retained such mercenaries, he would have no trouble whatsoever in asking them to do his dirty work for him. But there was the hitch. *If.* Had Mr. Coleman actually hired some thugs? Yet what other explanation could there be for the sight before her? No woman, even a desperate one, would intentionally get herself roughed up so.

"Oh, Mrs. Forge." Mrs. Coleman sank to her side on the bench. "If those men have done such terrible violence to me, what of my helpless little Lillibeth? You must find my monster of a husband and my defenseless babe. Please—*please.*" She squeezed Kit's arm, gentle yet fervent. "Tell me you have located them."

"I have, or that is, I have found where he has recently been, at least up to a few days ago."

"Truly?" The woman fairly squealed with delight. An odd transformation, but then again, a woman so emotional already could hardly be expected to maintain composure no matter the swing of her feelings. "Does this lead you to believe you know his whereabouts, Mrs. Forge? Where is he?"

"I don't know—not yet. But I do have a man in custody, whom my husband is even now interrogating. It is my hope that information from him will provide more avenues to investigate, so please take heart."

The hope on her face fell away as she clutched her hands to her breast. "My heart has been stolen from me, so I am afraid that is impossible."

The hollow tone of her voice struck a chord deep inside Kit's chest. A minor chord. The sort that vibrated with horrifying anguish. Were

Bella to be taken from her, why. . . Her throat closed. Tight. Clogged. Burning. Just thinking of her baby girl being ripped from her life opened a cavern of ache in her soul. She'd go to her grave with that pain, for such a fissure could never be breached. Not on this side of heaven.

Footsteps clipped in from the kitchen. Pink-cheeked Martha, perspiration glistening on her brow, held a squirmy Bella who bounced against her hip. "Sorry to be interruptin', but—"

"Ba-ba!" Bella leapt, flying into Kit's arms, and nuzzled her warm cheek against her neck.

Tears burned in Kit's eyes.

Oh, dear God, please don't ever let my little one be taken from me. I couldn't bear it!

Martha shoved a hank of hair into her mobcap. "As I was sayin', I needs be openin' the dining room. If you ladies would like to take yer business up to my quarters, ye're more than welcome."

"No need. I think we are finished." Kit turned to Mrs. Coleman. "I promise you, Mrs. Coleman, by week's end I will return your child to your arms no matter the cost."

As soon as the words flew from her mouth, she grimaced. Jackson would have her head if she put herself into any more risky situations. She hugged Bella all the tighter.

Hopefully the cost she spoke of wouldn't be too high.

Dodge Gruver squealed like a branded Berkshire hog whenever Constable Snagg let loose a fist—which was far too often for Jackson's liking. Such violence was getting him nowhere with this interrogation. Not that he'd expected it would, nor did he condone it. Snagg ought to be locked up himself for such abuse.

With a sigh, Jackson ran a hand over his face, the wooden chair beneath him creaking. Which tack to take now? He'd exhausted most—all, truth be told—honest ways of pulling information from the man who'd so ruthlessly chased down Kit and Charles.

Standing within striking distance, the constable flexed his fingers, his knuckles the colour of bruises. "Just gimme five minutes with 'im, Chief, and ol' Gruver here'll be singin' any tune ya want 'im to."

"Once and for all, stand down, Mr. Snagg." Jackson ruffled his own hair, weary beyond measure. He never should've allowed this overzealous brawler in a constable uniform to accompany him inside Gruver's cell. "He'll talk soon enough."

Gruver rolled out a long string of curses. "There. That enuff talk for ye?" He howled with laughter at his own coarse jesting.

Jackson stared at the man. Heaven above, but he was ugly. Sharp bones poked out over concave cheeks, one riding higher than the other, like a mad sculptor had taken a chisel to a piece of marble and carved away too much in spots. Except for his lips. Those pieces of meat had swollen to soft pillows from Constable Snagg's jabs, bloodied and raw now.

Once again, Jackson scrubbed his face. There was nothing for it. He'd have to pull some sort of swindle to tease out the information he needed. Straddling the chair, he folded his arms nonchalantly over the top of it. "I was hoping not to be forced to tell you this, as it is classified information, but unlike Constable Snagg here, I am not without mercy. You should know, Gruver, that we've snagged your partner. Holding him topside right now in the interview room. And the first one who gives me the name of the man who hired you will be let go. Free as a child's kite. I vow it. The other can spend some quality time with Constable Snagg until a hearing can be arranged. And if I somehow misplace the paperwork on your case, well. . ." He shrugged. "That could be quite a long stay indeed."

As if on cue, Snagg smacked his fist into his own palm over and over, the sound slapping against the walls. "Now yer talkin,' Chief."

Gruver merely spat a bloodied wad onto the stone floor. "Yer lyin'."

"Could be." Jackson leaned over his arms. "Or maybe I'm not. Do you really want to take that chance?"

"Don't matter no netherway. Blackjack'll never squeal."

Ahh. At least now he had a name for the other offender—even if it was a nickname. A small boon, but a boon, nonetheless. He pulled out the paper Kit had given him, gave it a good shake, and held it up for Gruver to see. "What do you know about this?"

Gruver squinted for a moment then let out a rip-roaring laugh. "Looks to me ye don't know how to count properly, tha's what."

Bah. Clearly Gruver didn't have any idea what the puzzling numbers meant. Jackson shoved the paper into his pocket. He'd have better luck running the thing down to the Foreign Office or perhaps the army's cryptanalysis department.

Rising, Jackson grabbed his chair. "Freedom is a siren's call, Mr. Gruver. A call few men resist, especially after a night in here. Perhaps tomorrow your tongue will loosen." He tipped his head towards the door. "Mr. Snagg, if you please."

The constable let fly one last strike, jerking Gruver's head sideways, before pulling out a key and opening the door. Jackson gritted his teeth as he passed the man. Such brutality was uncalled for. He'd have to make it a point to talk to Sergeant Doyle as soon as possible tomorrow to see about toning down the overzealous Snagg. Or better yet, moving him to a different role in the department. Then again, with his willingness to bend the rules, he could be just the man to sniff out Blackjack.

After locking the door, the constable reached for the chair. "I'll take that for ya, Chief."

"Thank you, Mr. Snagg." He leaned close, speaking for Snagg's ears alone. "We need Blackjack in custody straightaway. Can you manage that?"

A grin twitched his moustache. "My pleasure."

No doubt it would be, but God have mercy, hopefully the man wouldn't employ too much *pleasure* in apprehending ol' Blackjack.

"Carry on, then, Mr. Snagg, but be sure to bring the man in whole, not in pieces." Jackson strode away, anxious for the workday to be over. Then again, the thought of dinner with Kit caused a certain amount of angst to settle in his gut. His feisty wife would not be pleased with his lack of intelligence concerning Gruver.

He trotted up the back stairwell, circled 'round to his office to snatch his hat, then left via the main staircase, all while wondering how he'd explain Gruver's reticence to a woman who'd like nothing better than to have a go at the man herself.

Passing by the front desk, Jackson did a double take. Behind the counter, a round ball of a man was donning his hat. Jackson cocked his head. "Inspector Harvey? You're here quite late."

"Indeed." With a pinch of his podgy fingers, Harvey straightened his bow tie, the fabric the only indication he had a neck at all. "I strained to the finish line, sir, and am happy to report that victory has been achieved."

Jackson glanced past the man's shoulders to the glassed in records room behind. Sure enough, ledger upon ledger lined up like little soldiers ready for battle on the shelves. "So, you've put an end to Smitty's administration woes, have you?"

Harvey yanked a cloth from his pocket and swiped it over his sweaty brow. "I have, sir, and it was quite the fight."

Jackson stifled a snort. The rosy-faced fellow looked as if he'd barely survived the Bhutan War instead of simply rearranging some record books. "I am happy to hear of your success, Mr. Harvey. And now that you are finished, I have an insurance fraud case that needs tending."

"Oh, I don't know about that, sir. Sounds like a lot of legwork." He rubbed his hip with an exaggerated flourish. "My physician has informed me that my sciatica is given to flare-ups. Tender hips are the bane of my mother's family, you know."

Stars above. The man was softer than a pudding. Jackson clapped on his own hat. "Not to worry, Mr. Harvey. The only footwork involved in a fraud of such nature is that of climbing a mountain of paperwork. I daresay the project would keep you chained to a desk for a good three or four weeks. Maybe more."

And what excuse would the man have for that? A tender bottom to go along with those precious hips of his?

Surprisingly, Harvey tucked away his cloth with a fervor never before seen, his glasses skewing sideways from the violence of it. "Does eight o'clock tomorrow morning suit, sir?"

"Em. . .for what?"

Harvey shoved his glasses up the bridge of his nose. "To brief me on the case, sir. Or perhaps we ought to make it half past seven. I should like to get an early start. Unless you would prefer to explain it to me now."

Jackson blinked. Seriously? The man was finally taking a job? Wonders truly never did cease. "No, Mr. Harvey, eight o'clock is fine enough. Good evening."

"Until tomorrow, sir."

Still marveling, Jackson strode out of the station, into the summer night—where a gangly lad, cradling his arm and whimpering like a beat pup, nearly plowed him over. "Here now, boy. What's the great hurry?"

As soon as Jackson caught his footing and a good look at the boy's tearstained face, a brick sank to the pit of his gut.

"Frankie? For pity's sake, what has happened?"

Chapter Thirteen

Sleep always came easy for Charles—especially after putting in an all-nighter and half the next day chasing criminals. Waking up was the dodgy part. Near to impossible some mornings, when the mattress moulded exactly to his body and his head nested just so on the pillow. Times like this he could lie there for hour upon—

He shot up, springs squeaking, bare feet slapping cold on the floor, and dashed to the window. Someone had knocked on the glass, and so help him, it had better not be a jokester looking to pull a prank or he'd shove up the sash and throttle the dim-witted mischief maker.

In a trice, he whipped back the curtain and peered out on a street barely lit by a sun that hadn't fully left its bed. A willowy figure stood poised to knock again, bonnet shading a face he didn't need to see, for the catch of his breath identified the woman even without a good view. Martha. Here. Pounding on his bedroom window in a world not yet entirely awash with dawn's light.

What the deuce?

He pointed to the front door, and the moment she turned away, he snatched his trousers off the chair. He shoved in one leg so quickly he wobbled for balance a moment before he could jam in the other. His nightshirt would have to suffice for now, but cramming so much fabric into the waistband proved a trick. He snapped each brace over a shoulder as he dashed to the front hall. Thank God he'd stood his ground in demanding the street-level chamber of the boardinghouse for an emergency just such as this. . .but what exactly was this? By the time he yanked open the front door, his pulse soared with all the possibilities of why Martha might have come.

"Mrs. Jones! What's happened? Are you hurt? Is it the children?" He swept her with a quick gaze. Though it was hard to assess anything in such poor light, she appeared to be whole, which gave him some relief.

She held up a hand. "No, no, Mr. Baggett. 'Tis not me. I know callin' on ye like this 'tis highly improper, but I've hardly slept a wink what with tending Frankie all night, and I'm that furious! I've nowhere else to turn, and ye've always said to come to ye should I ever be in need."

The tension in his shoulders eased—but not all, not until he determined exactly why she'd traveled all this way. "Yes, of course. You've come to the right place. Do come in, and pardon my state of dress." Hah! State of undress, more like. He smirked while stepping aside, fastening the top buttons on his nightshirt. "First door on the left there, if you please."

She swung into the shadowy room, stopping just inside the threshold.

As he passed by her, his step hitched when he inhaled her fresh-bread scent. It was enough to make a man mad! For the briefest of moments, he considered pulling her to him and burying his face in her neck, breathing deep and long.

Bah! What was he thinking? He indicated the sofa with a sweep of his hand. "Have a seat while I light the lamps, but as I do so, please explain what's gotten you so fired up."

"That fiend at the glassworks, that's what!" Fire licked at the edges of her voice, an angry passion he'd never heard from her before. Not surprising, though. God help anyone who came between a mother and her cub. "I knew no good would come 'o that place. Din't I tell ye so? Kit's man, Mr. Jackson, brought my Frankie home last night. Poor lad was frightened to face me with a burnt arm, and no wonder! I was half out o' my mind seein' my boy's blistered skin."

Thinking on her words, he reached for the matchbox on the mantel. Empty. Of all the inconsiderate moves. No doubt Stubby Parker, one of his housemates, had used the last one and not thought to refill the thing.

"So," he said, crossing to the desk in the corner, "you're saying Frankie was harmed at his job yesterday. Is that what happened?"

"Aye. That firehole t'aint fit fer naught but demons. The place oughtta be shut down. Chained. Locked. Ooh! That snake in the grass Mr. Bellow!" Her voice shook, and he couldn't help but grin at the vinegar in her words. "I'll not be lettin' my boy step foot in there again, ye can be sure of that."

Hopefully Frankie would now be of the same mind. Swiping to the back of the top drawer with his fingers, Charles snagged another matchbox. A distinct rattle indicated a few matchsticks resided within. "And what exactly is it you wish me to do about the situation, Mrs. Jones?"

"I'd like ye to pop Mr. Bellow a good one right in the nose fer allowin' my boy to get hurt!"

Suppressing a chuckle, he arched a brow and pulled out a match.

"Oh, I know I must sound mad, but what with seein' Frankie in such pain and all. . ." She flopped back against the cushion, completely deflated. "I suppose there is naught to be done. I just. . .well. I couldn't sit still another minute after finally getting Frankie to sleep. It weren't right, what happened to my little man. And I—I guess I needed someone to talk to. Bish-bosh. Listen to me. Such a blatherin' ninny. It were foolish o' me to come here, and I beg yer pardon for it, Mr. Baggett."

Warmth flared in his chest. She'd come here to seek solace. From him. Of all men. What an honour. Turning his back on her—and the burning in his chest—he pulled the gas supply chain and struck the match. Fire flared, and as he stuck the flame into the hole in the bottom of the globe, a small pop smacked the air. The mantel glowed, and he adjusted the brightness with the other chain. "I do not accept your apology," he murmured. "For there is nothing to apologize for. Rather, I am pleased you thought to come to me." He shook out the match then turned to her. "As I've said before, I am always available for—"

The words caught in his throat as the light and his gaze landed on an angry purple lump above her right eyebrow. "Merciful heavens! What is this?" He dropped to her side, and before she could shy away, he tipped up her face with a firm grip. Sure enough, a welt the size of a farthing marred her lovely skin, and that, added to all the other injuries he'd witnessed in recent days, stiffened every muscle he owned.

"Who did this to you?" It was more of a growl than a question. "And do not try to tell me you bumped into something."

Fear flashed in her eyes, but only for half an instant before resolve flared her nostrils. "It is nothing." She pulled away and shot to her feet. "Truly, I should be going."

As gently yet firmly as possible, he tugged her back down to his side. "I will have the truth and I will have it now, Mrs. Jones."

Tears welled in her eyes. Instant regret for his harsh tone rose like bile. What a bully he was. What a cad! He clenched his jaw, remorse warring with resolve. He would not see this woman meet the same violent end as had Edwina Draper. He wouldn't fail her. He wouldn't fail ever again.

"Who is hurting you?"

She directed a pointed look at his grip on her wrist. "Currently, you."

Blast. Loosening his hold, he collected her hand between both of his and rubbed light circles against her palm, softening his tone as well. "Forgive me. I would never willingly harm you, nor will I allow anyone else to do the same. And so I must ask—nay, demand—that you tell me who it is that's been harassing you."

A fat tear broke loose, skimming over her cheek. "I cannot."

"Martha, please." He swallowed against the tightness in his throat. If she broke into full-blown weeping, they'd both be undone. "I cannot help you if you do not trust me." He paused a beat, then sucked in a breath as a brick of an idea hit him in the head. "Do you not trust me?"

"O' course I do!" She squeezed his hand, sorrow etching fine lines on her brow. "I would trust ye with my life."

Blessed relief washed over him. . .mostly. He wouldn't completely rest until he knew the name of her tormentor and put a stop to the brutalization. "Then prove your trust. Tell me who's been pushing you around."

Her lips clamped into a tight line, then ever so slowly, opened to allow a ragged whisper. "My brother."

Of all the low blows. A family member did this? It took every bit of his strength to keep from jumping up and ripping the city apart stone by stone until he uncovered the rogue.

"Why?" The question barely made it past his clenched teeth.

"He needs money." Martha pulled her hand away and shifted on the cushion. By now morning light eased through the front window, highlighting the grief bending her shoulders. And then out of nowhere, she threw those shoulders back, regaining her pluck. "But I'll not give him a coin! Not even a ha'penny if it's to be used fer drinkin' or gamblin'. I can't abide either. I won't!"

He narrowed his eyes, hardly believing his ears. "Your brother raises his hand against you because you will not support his vices?"

"It do sound worse when ye fancy it all up like that, but aye. That's the gist o' it." She paced a small circle on the parlour rug then stopped in front of him, hands out. "But ye must understand, Mr. Baggett, Roy don' mean anything by it. He don' know no better. Our father was the same way. I can manage him. And a'sides, he'll move on soon enough, then that'll be the end of that."

His hands curled into fists at the excuse he'd heard time and again from battered women. They all thought they could *manage* their abuser...right up until the time Charles was the one called to fish them out of the river, neck snapped or chest stabbed. He'd seen far too much of that sort of ugliness in his time on the streets.

He sprang to his feet, sofa springs creaking from such a sudden departure. "Where is he?"

Martha retreated a step. "Why ye wantin' to know?"

"I have a few words for him." Hah! He had far more than that. He flexed his fists.

"Like I said, I should be going. I've a kitchen to run." Whirling, she pressed one hand to her hat lest it fly off.

Once again he pulled her back, this time taking far more liberty by holding both of her shoulders. Her lips parted—as astonished as he at his bold move—but even so, he stared deeply into her eyes, hopefully driving home that which he must say. "Martha, listen to me. What Roy is doing to you is not any more right than how Mr. Bellow mismanages his glassworks. That anger you feel about Frankie's injury? That sense of injustice and urge to set things straight so that no one else gets hurt? You're not the only one who's ever felt that way—who feels that way even now, as I do about you. So please, give me your brother's location."

"Ye..." Her lower lip quivered. "Ye won't harm him, will ye?"

In truth? Nothing would feel more satisfying than to pummel the man into a bloody heap. But for the sake of this blue-eyed saint, that urge would have to be curbed. Slowly, he shook his head. "I will not. You have my word. But I shall make it very clear to him that he's not to harm you ever again."

"I dunno. . ." She bit that lip, putting a stop to the quivering.

"Where is he, Martha?"

Her chest heaved with a great sigh. "Gilliam's Circus Royal."

Broadside posters flashed in his mind. The handbills at the Devil's Acre. All had advertised for that same circus. He dropped his hands. "Thank you. I'll see you to the door now."

He strode across the room.

But footsteps did not follow.

"I'll wait here," Martha said.

He pivoted, brows lifting to the rafters. "You cannot wait alone in a men's boardinghouse, Mrs. Jones. This could take me some time."

"Pish. I'm only waitin' long enough fer ye to grab yer coat, ye daft man. I'll not have ye talkin' to my brother alone."

He frowned. "But I gave you my word I won't harm him."

"And I believe ye, yet there's no tellin' what Roy might do to ye."

Until she became a mother, Kit had no idea that bones could actually be tired, but hers were. Deep down. Dog beat. Oh, but she was knuckle-dragging weary. If only there was a way to do this job that allowed her to sit around more on days like this. Shifting Bella to her hip, she yawned large and loud as she pulled open the enquiry agency's door. With any luck, her father would have a hot mug of stout tea on his desk that she could pinch. And with any more luck, he'd be in a pleasant mood—

Pleasant enough to agree to care for Bella while she skipped down to the station.

Mustering as much vim and vigour as possible, she strolled into the office and approached her father's desk. "Good morning, Father. Bella, say hello to your grandpapa."

"Ba-ba!" Bella cooed, straining nearly out of Kit's arms.

"What's this? Two lovely ladies in the office at once?" He rounded the desk and pulled the girl from her arms, much to the delight of Bella and relief of Kit. "There now, come to Grandpa."

While he swung the babe around, inducing a wave of shriek-laughter, Kit swiped up the mug she'd hoped for, and after a few swallows, she felt somewhat more human.

"I see how it is." With one big reach, her father settled Bella atop his shoulders. She straddled the back of his neck, grabbing handfuls of his thick hair to keep from toppling. "Distract me with my granddaughter while you steal my tea, eh? Once a swindler, always a swindler."

"You should have known better." She winked.

He chuckled, then abruptly cut it off as his eyes narrowed on her. "There's a scuff on your cheek. What have you been up to, Daughter?"

More like once a sergeant, always a sergeant. Leave it to him to notice yesterday's injury despite her liberal application of stage makeup. Her lips twisted into a smirk. "I had a bit of a chase, that's all. Nothing too dramatic, really. It's only a scrape and well worth it." She drained the rest of his tea. "Mr. Baggett and I hauled in one of the fleet-foots after Mr. Coleman. Hopefully Jackson is even now getting him to squeal on who hired him. It could be the breakthrough I need, leastwise I hope it is. I'm on my way to the station to find out."

"And what about this one?" He squeezed one of Bella's chubby legs, prompting another scream-laugh from her. "You cannot seriously be thinking of bringing her down there."

"I'm not." She waggled her eyebrows.

"Oh, no you don't. I love Bella, but I am currently tied up working my own dead end. Featherstone wasn't much help." He stabbed a finger towards a file on the tabletop.

Kit glanced at the wall where a few leftover strings dangled, the only remains of his earlier crime diagram. "What happened? You seemed to be making such progress."

"I was—" He gently batted away Bella's fingers that were busily exploring his ear. "Until I wasn't."

"That is rough." Another yawn overtook her, and though she probably didn't appear very sympathetic, she had no choice but to clap her hand to her mouth and ride it out. "Truly, Father, I would help you were I not hip deep into my side of the investigation."

"Mmm," he rumbled. "Perhaps we should work more closely together on all sides of this case. Either we are a team"—he peered down his nose—"or we are not."

"You're right. . .which is exactly why you should watch Bella for me while I nip on down to the station. Thanks, Father. You're a dear." Rising to her toes, she pecked him on the cheek, gave Bella a squeeze to her leg, and took off.

"Hold it right there, young lady."

The words were steel, leaving no quarter for refusal. Curving her lips to an innocent smile, she turned back. "Yes?"

"I am no nanny." Her father slid Bella off his shoulders and held her out—which she thought a great game with her kicking legs and ba-ba-ba giggle.

"No, but you are her grandpapa, and—" *Drat these yawns!* She covered yet another. "I should think you'd be glad of some time with your granddaughter."

Her father's bushy brows gathered into a thundercloud as he studied her. "You're weary."

Wasn't every mother with a babe? Then again, not every mother was also scamping about town trying to unearth a missing man. "Bella didn't sleep well last night, did you, darling?" She stepped near enough to run her finger along her girl's cheek yet did not take her into her arms. "Every time I tried to put you down, you turned into a red-faced badger, aye little one?"

Bella laughed.

Her father shifted his hold on her, cradling her in one big arm. "Can you blame her?"

Kit angled her head. "What do you mean?"

"She's parted from you all day. A babe needs its mother."

"Don't be silly. She's got Martha. Well, except for today. Martha's got her own boy to tend."

Bella made a grab for his beard, and he captured her fingers in his big hand. "Martha is not a replacement for you, Daughter."

Oh boy. Here came the being-a-housewife-is-a-virtue lecture. And yet. . .Well. Not only was she lacking at home but she was failing to solve her first case as well, leaving her virtuous at exactly nothing. She rolled her shoulders, vainly trying to work out some of the strain. "You think I should trade my detective hat for a white-sashed apron and stay home?"

"Would you listen to me?" He chuckled. "But since you asked, what I think is that you should do some soul-searching. There is no shame in trying something new, and then when finding out it doesn't work, admitting it."

That struck a chord, one that vibrated all the way through her. She bit her lip, pondering it for a moment. Maybe it was time to see if there was another way she could put her skills to use, one that didn't involve being away from Bella so much. "Perhaps you are right. But first I've got to check on a criminal who by now has hopefully ratted on the one who hired him. Please, Father." She laid a hand on his free arm. "Will you care for Bella just until I return? You'll be a good girl, won't you, sweetums?" Bending close, she rubbed her face into Bella's tummy then pulled back. "It shouldn't take me long. And you said yourself I ought not bring her to the station."

"Stabbing me in the back with my own words, eh?" He frowned.

"That's a harsh way of putting it, but. . ." She grinned. "Is it working?"

"Fine," he huffed. "Hie yourself out of here but make every haste to return."

"Of course, Father. It's just a quick pop in to ask Jackson the results of his interrogation, and I'll be back in a trice."

She dashed away before Bella realized she was leaving and turned on the tears—which was sure to make her father change his mind. But as soon as she closed the door, she immediately regretted her words. This could take quite a bit longer than a trice.

For Mrs. Coleman strode her way.

Chapter Fourteen

Charles wasn't sure what he expected when he and Martha stepped past the Gilliam's Circus Royal perimeter rope, but this chaos wasn't it. Not this early in the day. Didn't these performers need their sleep for tonight's exhibition?

As they strode the narrow lanes of the workers' tents behind the big top, he kept a sharp eye out for a man with a strawberry-sized birthmark on his cheek—the best way to identify Martha's brother, according to her. The man had been born Elroy Charles Blandin, but who knew if he went by his given name. Like as not, he didn't. Didn't seem as if anyone here did, judging by the names painted above the tent doors. Hemmy Manchu, fire breather. Lulu Begonia, snake charmer. Greenzie Gabon, monkey man.

Charles steered Martha around a peacock and nearly rammed into a rack of machetes. No matter where you turned, dangers abounded. Why, this maze was no different than a back-alley jaunt through Spitalfields. Same freak shows. Same noxious smells. Even the catcalls, the whistles, and the din of so many people in such a small area was the same...though Charles did do a double take as a bearded woman passed by. Now that was something he didn't see every day.

Martha stopped suddenly, eyes narrowed. Several tents down, a rake-thin man was about to strap on a garishly painted sandwich board.

"Is that your brother?" he asked.

She nodded, her lips flattening. Her big blue eyes peered up at him, along with a light touch to his sleeve. "Ye don't have to do this,

Mr. Baggett. The circus will be moving on next week, and so will Roy."

"That doesn't mean he won't return or try to harm you again before he leaves." He patted her hand. "Don't fret. I can handle this. Why don't you wait here? Only not so close to that rack of knives."

She pulled back her hand and lifted her chin. "No. I'd rather come along."

He really wished she wouldn't, but how to refuse that adorable set of her jaw? Bah! But he was far too soft when it came to this woman. Even so, he stopped her a good ten paces out of reach from the man. "Roy?" he called.

"Aye?" The man turned from his signboard. Sure enough, a red mark marred his right cheek close to his eye. The same dark golden hair as Martha's framed his gaunt face, albeit chopped short and slicked down. His eyes were a darker shade of blue, the colour of twilight, hiding secrets. Charles knew the type. This man drifted through life from one shadow to the next.

When Roy's gaze slid to Martha, his whole face hardened to flint. "What ye doin' here, Sister?"

Charles tucked her behind him. So instant was the dislike burning in his gut, he already regretted the promise he'd made not to harm this man. "I'd like a few words with you."

"That so?" He widened his stance, a scrapper of a move. "And who are ye, then?"

"Inspector Charles Baggett, Old Jewry Precinct."

A vein pulsed on his skinny neck. Fear? Contempt? Probably both. He jerked his chin, stubble dark against the morning light. "I ain't done nothin'."

"You've done more than any man should. I've seen your sister's face."

He craned his neck, peering around Charles at Martha. "Ye ratted on me? Ye worthless piece of—"

That did it.

Despite Martha's protests, Charles grabbed great handfuls of the man's shirt and hoisted him up, feet dangling, wishing more than anything to choke the breath out of him. "Mind your tongue," he growled. "Or I know where there's a whole rack of knives to take care of the problem."

Roy's face twisted into a sneer, but such bravado did nothing to disguise the fear flashing in his eyes.

"Mr. Baggett!" Martha stepped up to his side. "Ye said ye'd not harm him."

"So I did." He released the man with a little shove.

Catching his balance, Roy straightened his wrinkled shirt, a scowl tugging at his brow. "I've got work to do, so drop yer load, bobby, then be off."

Charles folded his arms, jutting his jaw at the same time, an intimidating position he'd perfected over the years. "Martha tells me you've been trying to get money off her. That stops now."

Roy's gaze roved from him to her, the curl of his upper lip looking as if he sucked on lemons. "Aye. She weren't givin' me none anyway."

"Ye know I cannot abide gamblin' or carousin', Brother."

"Weren't for that, which ye'd know"—he stabbed his finger towards her—"if ye'd have given me two shakes of a listen."

"Ye came at the worst times!" Martha flailed her arms, her fingers batting against Charles' side. "I've not a minute to spare when there's food to be a'plated. I've a kitchen to manage."

"Oh, ye're that important now, are ye, princess? Got ye a regular range and all such fancies? Well pardon me, yer royal highness." He folded into an exaggerated bow.

"I oughtta swat ye a good one myself." Martha lunged towards him.

Charles shot out his arm, holding her back. "Don't let your anger get the best of you." He spoke for her alone, then louder, "What exactly was the money for, Roy? Why are you in such need?"

"Cain't say." Defiant words, but underneath, buried deep, there might be a note of desperation.

"Told ye, Mr. Baggett." Martha popped her fists onto her hips. "'Twere for no good purpose, just as I suspected."

"Oh, aye! My life ain't worth a rat's tail to ye, that it? Ne'er were to that scoundrel what spawned us neither."

Martha puffed a snort out her nose. "Don't go draggin' the past into this. Ye've got to own up to yer own sins 'stead o' blamin' it all on Father. The man's been dead and gone these past twenty years! Ye've been in yer cups again, that's what, and I won't be party to it."

The two continued bickering, but Charles' mind still snagged on that desperate tone in Roy's voice. Something didn't add up. Why would he insist Martha didn't care about his life? A cornered rat didn't fight for a scrap of bread—or gin, as she accused—but for his very existence.

Ahh. And there it was.

He stepped between the siblings. "Who is threatening your life? Name him, and I'll see that he's stopped."

Roy spat a wad on the ground along with a few ear-blistering curses. "I don't need no bullyboy comin' to my rescue! Now I tol' ye I won't trouble my sister no more, so get yerselves gone. I've got work to do." He pivoted.

"What? Is this true? Your life is in danger?" Martha darted aside and pulled Roy around to face her. "Brother, please. I'm listenin' now, and Mr. Baggett here means nothin' but the best fer us both. What sort o' black kettle are ye stewin' in? I'll not leave till ye tell me, and ye know it."

Roy's gaze darted between her and Charles, a fierce battle waging in those stormy eyes. At length, he wrenched from her grasp. "Fie! Come inside, then. I'll not speak o' it out here." He jerked open the flap of his tent.

Charles followed Martha inside, indicating she ought to take the end of a cot with a rumpled blanket while he perched on a nearby wooden chest. The space was surprisingly larger than it looked from the outside, tall enough for a grown man to stand upright, leastwise in the middle. A change of clothes hung over a wooden chair, next to a crate used as a desk if the papers, inkwell, and lantern atop it were any indication. A spare pair of boots—one with a hole in the toe—lay in one corner. And that was it. Sparse but livable, despite the stink of manure, corn whisky, and stale popped corn.

Roy fastened the door flap with a quick knot to the ties. Odd, that. Why take such a precaution for a simple chat? It wasn't as if anyone couldn't hear with their ear pressed against the canvas. Paranoid behaviour. . .but why?

Spare light seeping in added a few years onto Roy's face as he sank onto the chair. Charles almost felt sorry for the man. Circus life was harsh, and it sounded as though their father had been even more severe. But as Martha leaned forward on the cot and he spied the bump on her sweet face, that inkling of sympathy for her brother disappeared.

"Well, Brother?" she asked.

He propped his forearms on his thighs, shoulders sagging. "Ye were right, partially. One night I did take too many nips and passed out behind the ringmaster's tent, face mashed against the canvas. Woke in the wee hours to overhear ol' Gilliam making a deal with a fella by the name of Spaddy."

Charles' head shot up. "*Bootblade* Spaddy?"

"Aye, figgered ye'd know that scoundrel. He was workin' a deal with Gilliam fer safe harbour and passage to the next town. Ain't the first time, neither. This circus is a bust without a'shufflin' thems that need to go from town to town unnoticed."

Charles blinked. Traveling with a circus surely didn't sound like a good way to go unobserved. Then again, all the swirl, the fanfare and revelry, could make a fine masquerade.

Martha reached out, resting her hand lightly on Roy's arm. "But surely ye're not caught up in that mess?"

"I weren't, till the gin decided to belch out o' me and I were nicked fer overhearin'. Gilliam and Spaddy were none too pleased. Tha's why I need the money. I only got 'til the circus moves on in a week to show my loyalty by payin' my dues."

"Or Gilliam will kill you?" Charles rubbed the back of his neck, thinking hard. "Seems a bit over the top. Then again, Spaddy has been known to carve up a body or two if he's crossed."

Roy shook his head. "'Tis neither of them I fear. The thing is if I don't get Gilliam the money, he'll go spillin' my secret and the ox man'll hammer me into the ground. Now that's a man to dodge or die."

"I don't understand. What secret?" Martha shifted on the thin mattress, angling towards her brother. "What has this ox man to do with anything?"

"I had a little. . .em. . ." Red crept up the man's neck. "His wife is the trapeze artist."

"And you—?" Martha slapped her fingers to her mouth, cheeks far more scarlet than Roy's skinny neck.

That didn't make sense. If Roy had taken liberties with the ox man's wife, then why not just walk away? Leave the circus. Find another life.

No, there had to be some other hold here. He stabbed Martha's brother with a pointed stare. "Why not simply go to the authorities with the information you overheard and remove both Gilliam and Spaddy from the equation? The ox man would never know of your indiscretion if they were taken out of the picture."

"Authorities." He spewed the word like a mouthful of soured milk. "Hah! Gilliam said he'd lay the blame at my doorstep if I breathed a word to police. He'd tell 'em I were the one safeguardin' Spaddy, not him. So tell me, lawman, would ye believe a barker's word over an upstanding circus owner?"

Martha frowned. "Don't sound so upstandin' to me."

But sound and appearance were two different things. As ugly as the truth was, a business owner's word always held more sway than a menial's, often merely by credit of fine clothes and a banknote or two slipped beneath the counter. Charles scrubbed a hand over his face, weary of the unending cycle of injustice. If Gilliam hadn't leaned on Roy, Roy wouldn't have pressed so hard on Martha.

He dropped his hand. "And what did Spaddy have to say about your eavesdropping? I can't imagine he'd let something like that slip by."

"He didn't. He waved that blade o' his around, making sure I knew that if I went squealin' on him, he'd go after my family." A visible lump traveled down his thin neck as he slid his gaze to Martha. "And ye're the only family what I've got. Couldn't let that happen to ye, Sister, which was why I got a little overzealous when askin' fer money. I. . .I couldn't see anything bad happen to ye, not as bad as what Spaddy woulda done." He reached for her hand, wincing as his gaze landed on the bruise above her eye. "I'm powerful sorry fer any pain I caused ye. I din't know what else to do. Where else to turn."

"Oh Roy." The words shivered out of her, and after a shaky breath, she peered at Charles, eyes swimming. "Can ye help him, Mr. Baggett? Can ye get my brother out o' this snarl?"

He could—but the damage left behind would affect far more than Gilliam or Bootblade. Even so, now that he knew of the corruption—and of Spaddy's location—he had no choice in the matter. Slowly, he nodded. "A good shakedown ought to put an end to such trafficking."

"Put an end to the circus as well." Roy kicked at the edge of a rug dirtier than the ground it lay upon. "Hate to see all my friends thrown to the street and scrabblin' fer a meal."

"I'll feed them, Brother." Martha set her jaw. "I won't let one belly go without."

"Ye—" Roy's voice broke, and even in the dim light of the tent Charles could see his chin quiver. "Ye'd do that even after the way I treated ye?"

Of course she would. Charles' heart squeezed. The woman was gold.

"Like ye said, we're family." Her smile shamed the sun.

And shamed him as well. She'd pardoned her brother without hitch, without qualm, while he still nursed a blister of rage every time he chanced a look at the growing bruise above her eye. It had been wrong of Roy to rough her up, but did holding on to unforgiveness make him any more virtuous? He gritted his teeth, eking out a silent prayer that was hard in coming.

God, forgive me even as I forgive this troubled man.

"I thank ye for the offer, Sister." He gave her a sideways hug. "I won't have me a job, but least 'twill have a mouthful o' food."

Charles blew out a long breath, hardly believing what he was about to offer—yet hadn't Jesus offered far more than a few gold coins to those who'd wronged him? "For the information you've given me, Roy, I'll see you get the money that's on Spaddy's head. It's a good sum, ought to hold you over until you can find another job. But—" He sprang upward, hauling the man to his feet as well. He may have forgiven the bully, but he'd not forget nor so easily trust. He shoved his face into Roy's. "If I ever hear that you have so much as wrinkled the sleeve of your sister's gown, I will not be as lenient. I shall hunt you down, and trust me. . ." He lowered his voice to a death growl. "The wrath of the ox man is nothing compared to mine. Understood?"

Roy nodded, slow and deliberate.

"Good." He loosened his grasp and offered Martha a hand. "Then let's be off. I've a squad to pull together."

Her fingers wrapped around his, and as he fumbled with unloosing the door ties, she glanced back at her brother. "Remember what I said, Roy. Send yer hungry friends my way, and yer always welcome to a bowl as well."

"Thank ye." His blue eyes sought out Charles'. "Thank ye both."

With a single dip of his head, Charles pulled Martha out into the morning sunshine, where surprisingly, instead of letting go, she entwined her fingers more firmly with his.

"Yer a gem, Mr. Baggett." Admiration gleamed in her eyes.

Grace and mercy, but he could live in that look. Pack up his belongings from the boardinghouse and dwell right here in this moment until he died. He turned his face lest she see the pleasure that was sure to be pasted like a broadsheet on his face. "Think nothing of it, Mrs. Jones," he murmured.

He walked on a cloud all the way through the tents and halfway past the big top—where a man pushing a broom caught his attention. The hair that stuck out of his flatcap was poorly dyed to an orangish hue. His jaw was cartoonishly square below an overwide mouth. And that hump on his nose was a definite leftover from a skirmish that'd broken it years ago. Intense brown eyes drilled holes into him as the man returned his stare.

Martha squeezed his hand. "What is it?"

"Hmm?" He pulled his gaze away from the fellow who perfectly fit Kit's missing man. "Oh, nothing. Just thought I saw someone."

And if he had—were he right about that being Kit's man—perhaps the squad he was about to organize would shake out more than just ol' Bootblade.

Kit paused at the base of the police station's stairs, her earlier fatigue faded now that she'd engaged in a brisk walk—one that Mrs. Coleman had matched step for step. Flit. She never should have let slip where she was going, not to Mrs. Coleman, for that dogged woman had kept pace with her all the way from the enquiry agency to here. For a pampered lady, she surely was headstrong and surprisingly fleet of foot. Then again, were her own sweet babe taken from her, she'd not only move heaven and earth to get her back; she'd rip apart the whole universe.

Kit sidestepped the woman, blocking her path. "I think it better, Mrs. Coleman, if you wait out here. I shan't be long, and the station isn't fit for a lady such as yourself. It's a rough lot in there, harried lawmen, perpetrators of the most unsavoury sort, language that would make a stevedore blush—you get the idea."

"I am made of sterner stuff than you imagine, Mrs. Forge. I shall be fine." She dodged past her with a wink, then called over her shoulder, "I am keen to speak to the man your husband is interrogating. His information could be vitally important."

Kit rolled her eyes. Jackson hadn't even allowed her to question the man, let alone a lady of standing. What did the woman think this place was? Some frilly-nilly tea shop where one indulged in cucumber dainties and miniature cakes with the inmates? Pish! She darted ahead, catching up to the woman and guiding her over to the front desk. Hopefully Jackson was in his office, already finished with the task of pulling words out of Gruver—which would satisfy her and hopefully Mrs. Coleman as well.

"Morning, Smitty." She rap-tap-tapped on the counter.

The big clerk turned away from a spindle of receipts he'd been wrestling with, a grin appearing when his gaze landed on her. "Mornin', Mrs. Forge. Didn't know you were stopping by today. The chief didn't say."

"My husband has a lot on his mind, I'm afraid. Is he in his office?"

Beside her Mrs. Coleman quit her incessant gawking about and spoke before Smitty could answer. "Are the holding cells upstairs or down?"

Smitty pursed his lips, glancing between them, clearly unsure who to answer first.

Kit frowned at Mrs. Coleman. "The holding cells are below stairs, but there is no need to trouble ourselves with a visit to that dank hole if my husband is in his office." She glanced back at Smitty. "Is he?"

"Aye." He nodded. "But he's—"

"Thanks!" Kit waved her hand in the air as she linked arms with Mrs. Coleman. "This way."

She led the woman up the stairway, at one point having to release her hold of Mrs. Coleman to go single file when two big officers trotted down. At the top, Jackson's office door was shut, so she gave a cursory knock before twisting the handle and poking in her head. "Jackson, I hope you don't mind, but. . ."

What in the world?

A broomstick of a man in a brilliant red coat whirled on tiptoe in front of Jackson's desk, arms sweeping wide. Had he been engaged in a wild round of charades or performing a dance? For clearly he must be an entertainer. He could be nothing but, with that garish black-and-gold masquerade mask covering most of his face.

Jackson sprang from his chair, cornering his desk with the utmost look of relief on his face. He motioned for the strange man to follow him. "I must bid you good day now, Mr. Catchpole. It appears my wife has some business with me."

The man's dark button eyes widened behind his mask. He pranced over to her and Mrs. Coleman and dipped a magnificent bow. "Good morning, fair ladies. And which of you, may I ask, is the other half of this gallant gentleman to whom I owe every breath in my lungs? Nay, the very beat of my heart?"

Kit studied him from the tip of the ostrich feather in his green felt hat, along a red woolen frock coat clearly tailored to his form, and on down to the point of his Italian leather shoes—which appeared to be new. Expensive garments for one who could use a good scrubbing, especially those strings of greasy hair dangling to his shoulders. The man was a contradiction, one that instantly put her on alert. What sort of swindle was this "gentleman of four outs" trying to run on her husband?

She lifted her chin. "I am Mrs. Forge."

"Oh!" He squeaked, then snatched her hand and planted a delicate kiss atop it. "I count myself blessed, dear woman, to have made your acquaintance."

Jackson pulled him away. "And with that, Mr. Catchpole, I'm afraid I must ask you to leave."

"Naturally you must!" Slipping from Jackson's hold, he slapped his hand against his chest. "Far be it from me not to know when to depart. Besides, I trust you will think on all I have related to you this morn, and I look forward to your most astute counsel as to how you think I should proceed. So, I say a very, very good day to you, sir." He tipped his feathered hat at Kit and Mrs. Coleman. "And a particularly merry day to you as well, dear ladies."

As his skinny legs waltzed out the open door, Kit arched a brow at Jackson. He merely shrugged. A deflection—for now. She'd ask about Mr. Catchpole later.

Mrs. Coleman took a step towards Jackson. "Pardon our intrusion,

Chief Inspector, but your wife has taken on my case, and it is of the utmost importance to know if you have found out anything from the vile man in your custody. I should like a word with him myself."

"I'm sorry I cannot comply. Any intelligence I receive is privileged information." Though he spoke to Mrs. Coleman, he frowned at Kit. "Which my wife here ought to have told you."

Did he seriously think she hadn't? She'd pulled every trick from her swindler bag to persuade the woman to simply go home. She turned to Mrs. Coleman. "Why don't you give my husband and I a moment alone. There is a chair down by the receiving desk where we first came in. Smitty the clerk will see to any need you may have."

"That is not necessary. I—"

"Jackson!" In dashed Charles Baggett, breathing hard, smelling of sawdust and sweat. He'd been running, that much was evident, but through what? A carpentry shop? A zoo? "You'll never believe it. We've got to pull a squad together right away. Guess who's holed up at the Gilliam Royal Circus. Oh, I beg your pardon, ladies!" He gasped as his gaze landed on her and Mrs. Coleman. Pulling off his hat, he tipped his head.

Jackson huffed an annoyed sigh. "That's right, just barge right in, Baggett. In fact, let all of God's great creation plow through my door. What have I to do other than host every blessed man and woman who is dying to have a word with me. It's not like I have a prisoner to interrogate and a load of paperwork to shovel through."

"Jackson"—Kit pinched his arm—"don't be pettish. Clearly Mr. Baggett has something important to say." She angled her head towards Charles. "Who did you find?"

"Spaddy." Though he said it nonchalantly, his chest puffed out a full inch.

"Bootblade?" Jackson whistled. "That is a find."

"And that's not all." He faced Kit. "I'm reasonably certain I found your man there as well."

Mrs. Coleman pressed both hands to her belly, leaning towards him. "You found Mr. Coleman?"

Charles' eyes narrowed almost imperceptibly, but enough so that Kit noted the bewilderment. "I'm sorry, but who are you?"

Kit advanced, trailing a hand at the woman as a sort of makeshift introduction. "This is Mr. Coleman's wife, my client who is looking for him. Did you happen to see a baby with the man? Think hard." She peered up at him. "It's very important."

But he didn't think at all, not if the quick shake of his head were any indication. "No. The man was busy sweeping the big top, but I did get a good look at him, and he matches the description you gave me to a tee. Remember that torn handbill I found in the flat? It's my guess the man ripped off the address and applied to be a broom pusher. Perfect place to hide while waiting for the show to move on."

"True." Kit tapped her lip. She should have thought of that. . .and she would have were her brain not so deuced tired from sleepless nights.

"But," Charles continued, "that doesn't mean the man hasn't left the child to be cared for by someone else while he works. I'll let you know when we turn the place upside down. I'm sure to find him and the babe." He pivoted to Jackson. "That is if I have your permission to organize a squad immediately."

"Mmm," Jackson grumbled, absently smoothing his moustache. Kit hid a smirk. She knew that action intimately well. Hundreds of calculations were going on in his mind, too fast for him to explain, all weighing the risks and benefits of the proposal. At least this time she wasn't on the receiving end of the final outcome. . .for rarely did a positive answer come without conditions.

Jackson hooked his thumbs beneath his lapels. "Did you see Spaddy with your own eyes?"

"No," Charles said. "The snake's hiding in the grass, but I have it on good authority."

"How good?"

"*Very* good."

"I see. . ." He thought a beat longer before clapping Charles on the back. "Then Godspeed."

Kit's jaw dropped as Charles raced away. Why did her husband never give her such wholehearted approval whenever she made requests? Granted, hers didn't usually involve asking for backup before dashing into trouble, but this time it did, so he had no reason whatsoever to deny her now.

"Grab your hat, Husband." She bounced on her toes. "We've not a minute to spare if you're to help me find my man at the circus."

"The only thing I'm grabbing is this." He doubled 'round to the back side of his desk and picked up a large coil of rope, then swung it over his shoulder. "I have a prisoner to interrogate. Two, actually. Gruver's partner Blackjack was hauled in early this morning, and I've got something special planned for the pair."

Her brow bunched. Who cared about them now that she knew where Coleman was?

"But Jackson—"

He held up a palm, cutting her off. "When you barreled in here, you were quite keen on me gathering information about who hired those enforcers that chased you and Baggett. . .and that's what I intend to do. So, step aside, please."

Ooh. Stubborn man. She planted her feet lest she stamp one. "That was before Mr. Baggett spotted Mr. Coleman."

"Baggett is more than capable of rounding up your man along with Spaddy. He knows who you're looking for. In fact. . ." He ran his thumb over the curve of her cheek. "All you need do is check back here this afternoon and I'm sure you'll find both Mr. Coleman and hopefully the child. I'll send word to your office the moment he shows up. In the meantime, I have business to attend."

She turned her face away from his touch. "You know as well as I that the second those bluecoats set foot inside that circus, my man will take a dive—*and* take the child right along with him."

"Trust the process, Wife. Trust Baggett. These are trained men who know what they're about, and I believe you already gave me your word you would do no rescuing of your own. Now, I really must be going. I'm late enough as is." He brushed a kiss to her brow and darted around her.

Kit stood motionless, debating if she ought to trust Mr. Baggett to haul in Mr. Coleman or not. She should, she supposed. He was a fine officer who kept a calm head yet strong arm in the midst of chaos. Mr. Baggett would catch her man. Besides, she had not only promised her father she'd be back in a trice but she'd also vowed to Jackson she'd merely locate Lillibeth, not rescue her. She really ought to honour her husband's wishes. Mind made up, she whirled to tell Mrs. Coleman the plan.

But there was no woman waiting near the door.

For a moment, Kit stood stunned. All the doubts she'd been storing away about Mrs. Coleman roared back with a vengeance. What if—and it was a wickedly horrible if—Mr. Coleman was protecting Lillibeth from Mrs. Coleman, not the other way around? The thought washed over her like ice water.

Then she tore out the door. She had to warn Mr. Coleman.

Chapter Fifteen

Jackson jogged down the stairs to the holding cells, the morning's chaos settling in his gut about as well as the burnt porridge Kit had served for breakfast. Catchpole had told him the most fantastical tale about how he'd tried to reconcile with his estranged brother only to be humiliated by the man in front of the entire House of Lords. It was a hard story to swallow, for the guard on duty would have never let a lunatic in a masquerade mask inside the palace. More than likely the man was delusional. Or—giving Catchpole the benefit of the doubt—perhaps he had tried to make amends with his brother and the event was so traumatic, he'd merely felt like he'd been dressed down in front of Parliament. He did have a flair for the dramatic. He really should have become an actor or at least a solicitor.

Jackson plowed his fingers through his hair. Whatever the case, he had no idea how to counsel the man to proceed. What did he know of such family matters? He barely understood his relationship with Kit. No, this was a problem better addressed by a clergyman, and he would suggest the idea next time Catchpole showed up.

"Mornin', Chief." Constable Barrycloth's baritone voice cut into his thoughts as Jackson left the stairwell. The big bear of a man held out a swinging pair of darbies, chains clinking. "Here ye be."

"Thank you." He grabbed the irons. "I trust Constable Snagg has made the preparations I requested?"

"Aye, sir, far as I know. Leastwise he had plenty of time to carry out your wishes."

"Very good, Barrycloth." Jackson snatched a ring of keys off the wall. Gruver sneered at him as he unlocked the cell. "Up you go, Gruver. Hands behind your back, please."

"Well, ain't we just a plate o' manners today?" He rose from his cot, surprisingly compliant. Anxious for a move or eager to try an escape?

Jackson approached him on edge, ready for anything.

Gruver merely pivoted and held out his wrists near the small of his back. "Where we going?"

Jackson snapped on one cuff then the other. "I didn't think it was right keeping you from your friend and all."

"Together or apart don't make no never mind." Gruver rasped a chuckle. "Ye won't crack ol' Blackjack or me."

"We'll see about that." Grabbing hold of Gruver's upper arm, he steered the man out of the cell and up the back stairs. Then up another flight. And another. All the while he breathed out the side of his mouth, trying desperately to ignore the man's eye-watering stench. When was the last time that skin of his had crossed paths with a bar of soap?

The stairwell ended at a door that ought to be locked, but Jackson shoved it open without a hitch. While he hadn't been pleased the only constable the sergeant could spare this morning was yet again Constable Snagg, at least the fellow followed orders, even if a little too exuberantly.

Jackson tugged Gruver onto the roof. Across the flat expanse stood Snagg next to two chairs positioned dangerously close to the edge, facing outward. A black-haired man was tied to one, his back to them. Blackjack, Gruver's partner in crime.

The constable met him partway, his boots crunching the gravel-coated tar paper. "He give you any trouble, Chief?"

"No, I'm just running late from other matters. You are all set, I assume?"

"Couldn't be more ready, sir. Done everything as you asked."

"Excellent." Upping his pace, Jackson yanked Gruver to the end of the ledge. Four stories below, a passing rider looked as small as a child on a hobbyhorse. "Long way down, wouldn't you say?"

"Don't say anythin', Gruver." Blackjack rumbled the warning from his chair.

Challenge sparked in Gruver's dark gaze. "No need to tell me."

Jackson shoved him into the chair, taking care he didn't lose his balance in the process. Unwrapping the coil of rope from his shoulder, he glanced at Gruver's neighbour. Blackjack sported a freshly purpled eye and blood snaked out both his nostrils. A growl rumbled in Jackson's throat as he tied Gruver to the chair. "Was that really necessary, Constable?"

Gruver barked a laugh. "Ye can beat ol' Blackie all ye like, but I tol' ye he'd never squeal."

"Yet ye can be sure I makes the ladies do." Blackjack threw back his head and guffawed.

Jackson gave a jerk to the knot, irritated at the man's crude jest. Such obscene banter wasn't anything out of the ordinary for this line of work, but that didn't mean he had to like it.

For surely God did not.

Straightening, he faced the constable. "Blind him, Mr. Snagg."

"Ye can't be serious!" Gruver bellowed.

"Oh? Are you ready to talk, then?"

Gruver and Blackjack exchanged glances, Blackjack shaking his head a little, then both stared ahead, faces set as stone.

Standing at the men's backs, Jackson yanked a long strip of dark cloth from his pocket, as did Snagg. They both tied the blindfolds tight against the cullies' eyes.

"And now we are ready for a little game I like to call who-will-talk-first." Jackson tipped his head at the constable, signaling for him to leave the roof. As Snagg strode away, Jackson continued with the rules, calm and deliberate, as if he were explaining a round of marbles to a gaggle of lads. "The first one to tell me who hired you to keep an eye on that room and collar the man who lived there gets to walk free."

"We ain't playin'." Insolence ran thick in Blackjack's gruff voice.

Gruver laughed. "You tell 'im, Blackie."

Jackson merely smirked. "I have yet to see a player who didn't finish the game one way or another."

And with that he gave a kick to Gruver's chair, rocking it on the front two legs, tilting the man closer to the edge.

"Hey!" Panic pinched the word and the subsequent oaths gushing out of Gruver.

"Who hired you?" Jackson made sure to keep his tone serene yet loud enough to be heard over a sudden gust of wind.

"Cram it! I ain't talkin'."

A smile twitched Jackson's lips. "Correction. You aren't talking *yet*." He strolled the few steps over to Blackjack and leaned close to his ear. "But maybe you are. Who is it, Blackie? Who hired you and Gruver?"

Silence, save for the faint *clip-clop* of horse hooves far below.

Jackson's boot connected with the back of the man's chair in a mighty kick. Blackjack teetered at a precarious angle, yelping like a whipped pup.

"Blackie!" Gruver cried, his face turned towards his friend though he could see nothing.

Heat poured off Blackjack, sweat caking his dark hair to his scalp as the chair thwumped back to solid ground. "Keep yer bone box shut, Gruver! He ain't gonna kill us. It's a scam, sure as anythin'."

"Oh," Jackson murmured as if they discussed nothing more important than the current price of rye. "Did I mention that as chief here, there is no one I must answer to at the station? No one to question me. No one to so much as bat an eyelash. That means I do as I please, and if it pleases me to blame your deaths on Constable Snagg, well. . ." In three strides he planted his boot on Gruver's chair.

It flew forward.

Gruver shrieked like a girl.

At the last moment, Jackson grabbed the back rail and thumped the rear legs onto the tar paper.

"Who hired you?" This time his question was a lion's roar.

"Shut up, Gruver!" Blackjack ordered.

Gruver whimpered. Pitiful, really.

Jackson stamped over to Blackjack, each footfall exaggerated. "My patience is at an end. Tell me now, or it's time to say goodbye."

"Ye wouldn't dare," Blackjack challenged.

"Wouldn't I?" He kicked.

The chair tipped.

Blackjack plummeted over the edge of the roof, his screams an offense to the ear.

Immediately Jackson dropped to his rear, bracing his feet against what little ridge there was between building and thin air, prepared to grab the chain Snagg had secured to the roof should it not hold.

But it did. The chain jerked to a stop, piercing screams covering the sound.

And then silence—leastwise from Blackjack. Gruver was still crying out his bloody lungs.

Jackson peeked over the edge to see Snagg hauling Blackjack in through a window on the next floor down, the edges of a gag flapping from the thug's mouth. It was a terrifying deception, yet necessary, and one he'd considered only as a last resort.

He pivoted back to Gruver. Manhandling his chair, Jackson turned the fellow away from the edge and yanked off the blindfold. "You ready to talk now?"

"Ye kilt him!" Tears and snot and spittle all leaked out. "Ye kilt Blackie!"

Jackson clenched his jaw. It turned his stomach to allow this man to believe his friend was dead, but the ruse could end up saving lives. "I prefer to think your friend has gone to a better place. And unless you wish to join him, tell me who it was that hired you."

The man's knobby Adam's apple traveled up and down his throat as if he swallowed a rat. "It were Carky. Carky Smathers."

Outside the circus, people queued up in a great long snake of thrill seekers eager for the noon showing. And that wasn't for another hour. Pacing near the back of the throng, Kit frowned. Even if she could sweet-talk the ticket seller into allowing her early entrance or tried to skip beneath the rope, she'd be pummeled by the crowd as a queue jumper.

"Out o' the way, missy!" a dray driver bellowed.

She whirled, then immediately retreated as two workhorses plodded by. A narrow miss, one she chided herself for. She ought to have heard such a big old wagon coming at her, and she would have, were her brain not so fogged from lack of sleep.

Snap out of it, girl. You've got a man to find.

A flurry of little white curls snowed over her as the wagon passed, the load of wood shavings shifting beneath the canvas cover as the dray began to turn into the delivery entrance.

And there she had it. Her way in.

Working fast lest the driver glance over his shoulder, she pulled out a broom from the implements rattling about on a rack at the back. As the wagon lumbered along, she followed close behind, busily sweeping the falling flakes—a moot exercise that any circus hand ought rightfully to question.

Thankfully, none did.

By God's good grace, the wagon rumbled all the way to the big top. A fresh load of shavings for the upcoming performance, no doubt, but she'd not stick around to find out, not when she was this close to finding Mr. Coleman. She chucked the broom back into the rack then ducked inside the huge tent.

Just past a series of stacked board benches, a huge center ring filled most of the tent, the edges of the circle defined by brightly painted red timbers. Inside that circle, a man in a green long-coat cracked a whip, urging a black bear to continue its trek across a slack rope tied between two platforms. Above, a woman in a scandalous blue satin doublet that ended at the top of her thighs dangled upside down by her knees as she flew through the air on a trapeze. At the far side of the tent, a group of men in what appeared to be bathing costumes jockeyed one over the other until they formed a perfect pyramid. A few other men dressed all in white conversed next to a tiger on a leash—blessedly not close to where she stood. Of all the people under the big top, not one fit Mr. Coleman's description, though truly it would have been a miracle if he were still in here after Charles' sighting of hours before.

She clenched her hands, squeezing away defeat, then set her jaw and approached a nearby juggler tossing machetes into the air. She couldn't help but admire his skill, especially when he didn't so much as break his trance as she drew near. "Pardon me, but I'm looking for a Mr. Coleman. He was in here an hour or so ago."

The man shook his head without missing a beat—or a knife. "Don't know 'im, luv."

Of course he didn't. That would've been far too easy. After a final glance around the tent, she worked her way over to the performer's entrance and strode out the back. Here rows of cages, some on wheels, others small enough to be carried with a handle, lined the side of the lane. Past the menagerie, a huge enclosure housed two lions and a man who was attempting to put his head into one of the beasts' mouths.

Kit stared for a moment, mesmerized. She'd faced plenty of danger in her day, but this? Though Jackson might argue otherwise, she'd never willingly tempt death so wholeheartedly.

Turning away from the sight, she stepped into the path of a tall man carrying a wicker hamper. "Excuse me, I'm looking for a Mr. Coleman. Do you know who he is?"

"Coleman?" The man rolled the name around on his tongue, leastwise it sounded as if he did so. What sort of accent was that? "And zees man, you tell me of him, no?"

"Dark eyes, rather intense." She parroted back Mrs. Coleman's description. "A mouth wider than normal set in a very square jaw. He's got a hump on his nose from a previous bad break, and his hair used to be dark, though I have reason to believe he's recently dyed it. He could now be towheaded, or he might carry a slight orange tint if the colour didn't set well."

"Is zis so?" Surprisingly white teeth flashed in a huge grin as the man held up a finger. "Zis! Zis I can do."

Kit's heart skipped a beat at the fellow's exuberance.

He set down the hamper and flipped up the lid. In a flurry, he rummaged through fabrics and furs and Lord knew what else buried at the bottom. Then he whipped off his hat, shoved a poorly dyed flaxen wig on his head, and poked something into his eyes. Running a hand over his nose, he left behind a lump, then proceeded to push his jawbone and tug at his mouth. When it was all said and done, she'd swear to a magistrate that Mr. Coleman stood before her.

"Zis ze man?" He circled his face with his hand.

Kit gaped. "Are you Mr. Coleman?"

He laughed long and loud. "No, leetle miss. I hate to dizapoint you, but I am not zis Coleman nor do I know heem." He dipped an exaggerated bow. "I am Rubberface Lorenzo, at your service, madam."

"Amazing," she breathed, wide-eyed.

"Ha-ha!" He burst into activity, tugging, pulling, packing. He closed the hamper lid and grasped the handle, straightening to his full height, once again the tall man instead of the faux Mr. Coleman. "Eet ees a surprise what a clever disguise artist can do, no?" He winked then pointed at a woman nearby who braided the mane of a white horse.

"Ask Rimma. If zis man you seek ees here, she will know."

"Thank you so much, Mr. Lorenzo. It's been a delight meeting you." Though she'd love to linger and ask him about the art of disguise, she dodged around him, set on questioning the horsewoman, Rimma.

"Sorry to interrupt," she said as she pulled alongside the lady—then momentarily lost her train of thought. That wasn't just any braid the woman worked with her nimble fingers. That sort of weaving was a piece of art, as intricate as a square of Honiton lace.

Rimma paused, glancing sideways at Kit with eyes of such a peculiar amber it startled the senses. She smelled of warm horseflesh and jasmine, a remarkably pleasing combination. "Yes?"

"I was told you are familiar with members of the circus, and if so, do you know where I can find a Mr. Coleman?"

"Mmm," she murmured, then went back to entwining strand over strand of the horse's mane. "Ahh. The broom pusher?"

Finally! Kit nodded even though the woman wasn't looking at her. "Yes."

"I believe he's just around the corner of the big top over there." She tipped her head. "He's cleaning the monkey cage."

"Thank you." Kit turned away, puzzling over why the monkeys were separated from the other animals yet excessively happy Mr. Coleman wasn't mucking out the tiger's pen or something else that could kill her.

"But mind you speak to him from outside the bars," Rimma called after her. "Those monkeys, while cute, are new and not yet trained. They're not accustomed to strangers. They've barely gotten used to Mr. Coleman these past few days, and he's got the scratches to prove it."

Kit charged ahead. As she rounded the tent, a man perfectly matching Mr. Coleman's description was pushing a wheelbarrow through the cage door. A white-haired man who was quite long in the tooth stood prepared to shut that door the instant he passed through.

Mr. Coleman didn't look particularly dangerous with his pasty skin and thin frame, but even so, Kit made sure to stand with the wheelbarrow between them. "Hold it right there, Mr. Coleman."

He paused, barely leaving enough room for the old man to shut the monkey door. Both eyed her. Mr. Coleman's gaze assessed her as if she were a ledger sheet with a few numbers missing. "Who are you?"

"No one of consequence. I came to warn you about your wife. Where is your daughter?"

"My. . . ?" He shook his head, the monkeys behind him scampering closer to bars. "*Who* sent you?"

"Your wife, but that's beside the point now. I must get you and Lillibeth to safety."

Monkey chatter pitched up an octave as most of the little beasts congregated in the corner closest to her. Kit spied a fresh scratch on the back of Mr. Coleman's hand. Apparently the monkeys still weren't completely used to him.

Sweat trickled down his temples. "I have no idea what you're talking about, lady."

Irritation flared in her belly. They didn't have time for this. "Come, Mr. Coleman. You've got to get out of here. Your wife is—"

"Listen, lady." A monkey made a swipe for his hat through the bars, and he jerked sideways. "You've got the wrong man. I don't know how you know my name, but I haven't got a wife or a child. Tell her, Caleb."

The old man opened his mouth just as Mrs. Coleman rounded the far side of the monkey cage, marching in a straight line towards them.

Kit swiped for his arm. "It's too late. She's here."

Mr. Coleman wrenched away.

Mrs. Coleman smiled.

Then pulled a gun, her presence and the cock of the hammer setting the monkeys into a frenzy.

Darting around the wheelbarrow, Kit jumped in front of Mr. Coleman, spreading her arms. "Put that away, Mrs. Coleman! I know you're upset, but you're taking things too far."

"Actually," she drawled. "Not quite far enough, but thanks to you, pet, that will soon be remedied. Get out of the way."

Pet? The nickname howled across time like a banshee.

"I told you I don't have a wife," Mr. Coleman growled in her ear.

The first inkling of true panic flashed like a lightning strike from head to toe. Kit stiffened. She narrowed her eyes at the woman. "Who are you?"

As she neared, Mrs. Coleman used her free hand to pull off a wig and toss it aside, shaking out chopped hair the colour of straw. The mole near her mouth disappeared next, and with the same sleight of hand Mr.

Lorenzo had employed, Mrs. Coleman's nose instantly became more slender and much longer. Her cat eyes gleamed.

Kit's head swam as a long-forgotten memory surfaced. She'd been but a lass when she'd last encountered those eyes on a bully of a girl who had no right to threaten anyone so fiercely. Kit reached for her earlobe, feeling the old scar, reliving the pain of a jabbed pencil lead just before she'd gone feral and tackled her attacker.

The same attacker now full grown.

Coarse laughter grated out of the woman. "I see ye recognize me, aye, pet?" No more silky voice passed those lips. It was street twang, bold and hardened. "Ye've no idea how satisfying it is to finally best ye."

Kit planted her feet to keep from toppling. No wonder Mrs. Coleman had seemed so familiar. She *did* know the woman. Only she wasn't a missus nor a Coleman.

She was Carky Smathers.

Chapter Sixteen

Stupid. Not mistaken, confused, or wrong. She'd been unmistakably, undeniably stupid. Why hadn't she listened to her gut sooner when things didn't seem quite right? Kit clenched her hands into fists so tightly her nails cut little crescents into the fleshy part of her palms. Stupidity such as this was what got people killed.

Carky sighted down the barrel of her gun, straight at her. "Move, pet, or I'll pop ye both."

She would. No doubt about it. As a slum girl, Carky had dismembered rats bit by bit, swinging each bloody piece around to frighten the younger orphans until they screamed for mercy. That sort of child didn't grow into a woman of idle threats.

But neither had Kit grown into a fainting flower, and she'd be hanged if she'd let this woman get the best of her again.

She flung herself sideways to the ground and rolled like a cannonball into Carky's legs. Carky flew backwards, the gun cracking into the air. Hopefully.

Before Carky could react, Kit scrambled to her feet and tore back to Mr. Coleman, shouting as she ran, "Open the door! Let those monkeys out!"

She hooked Mr. Coleman's arm and yanked him into motion as the old man nearby did as she'd said. . .only, releasing so many monkeys at one time might have been a slight miscalculation. The little beasts scattered everywhere, one of them leaping onto her skirts and slowing her down. Mr. Coleman kicked it off, the screech of the thing as loud as the curses streaming out of Carky behind them.

"Thanks," Kit said as she hauled Mr. Coleman into the big top.

"My pleasure. I hate the hairy devils." His words huffed out between gasps for air.

Kit glanced wildly about while dodging coils of rope, rigging equipment, and the long tails of tightropes dangling from the ceiling. It seemed that on this side of the tent, everything wanted to trip her, snag her, or brain her with a whap to the head.

And all the while, Carky's footsteps pounded closer.

"Hear now!" A muscleman in purple hose stepped into their path, thighs bulging, biceps swollen, and his eyes narrowed to slits. "This is no place for a chase. You're scarin' my ponies."

Sure enough, just to his left, three small Arabians tossed their heads in the air. One of them reared.

"Out with you." The man's lumber beam of an arm stretched long, indicating the door behind them.

Right where Carky yelled, "Stop those two thieves! They were trying to steal a monkey!"

The man glowered at them. "Light fingers, are you? Not if I can help it."

He reached.

Kit ducked—jerking Mr. Coleman down with her and practically ripping his arm from the socket. She skittered past the muscleman like a barmy field mouse, dragging Mr. Coleman along for the ride. Thank heavens the man didn't weigh much.

Racing ahead, she skirted the center ring. Carky or not, there was no way she'd risk the wrath of that bear on a rope. At the next available aisle, she darted sideways, more desperate than ever. Now two sets of pounding feet trailed them, for the duped muscleman had joined Carky.

"Ringo, stop them!" he bellowed.

Ahead, an orange-haired man in a clown costume looked up from the barrel he'd been about to climb into. Hardly a breath later, he reared back then kicked the big tub. Kit zipped sideways.

Too late.

Leastwise for Mr. Coleman.

The rolling barrel took him out at the knees and he face-planted.

Well, then. What couldn't be beat ought always to be joined.

Kit dropped, once again grabbing hold of the man and pulling him sideways. "This way," she hissed, and though it raised the hairs at the nape of her neck to do so, she led them into the thin space between the tiger cage and some dog kennels. As long as the tiger stayed on his own side of the cage, this wouldn't be so bad.

The dogs barked.

The tiger growled.

A spray of sawdust flew up in front of her face.

Kit froze, her very bones jarring from the tiger's unbelievably loud rumble. She slid her gaze to the left, only to stare deeply into golden eyes offset by streaks of green. A puff of meat-tinged breath landed hot on her cheek. She'd known fear in her time—and plenty of it—but nothing came close to this.

Behind her, Mr. Coleman stuttered a terror-filled whisper. "T–t–t–tiger."

"They're down there!" The clown squealed like the rat he was.

God, please, Kit silently prayed. *I got us into this mess, but I cannot get us out. Help!*

Without waiting for an answer, she crawled at top speed towards the wall of the tent. Hopefully Mr. Coleman kept time at her heels, though he probably did, judging by the next tiger roar. No doubt they looked like tasty treats to the big cat, or maybe something to play with. Surely that cage was constructed to prevent the swipe of one of those great paws. . .wasn't it?

Ahead, light seeped through a gap between canvas and ground. Flattening to her belly, Kit shimmied onward, once again grateful the man at her back was hardly any larger than she. At this end of the tent, mud coated the ground, sticking to her chin, hands, sleeves, gown, making it hard to slither fast.

At last, she cleared the tent and pushed up to all fours, then staggered to her feet. Mr. Coleman did the same as she tried to bat away a bit of the muck—until a trumpeting blast made her immediately cover her ears. She spun.

And faced an elephant rearing its great trunk in the air.

The trainer tapped the beast on the side with a rod, glaring at her.

"What do ye ken ye're doing, muddy lassie?"

She spread her hands, backing away. "Sorry! We were just leaving."

Grabbing hold of Mr. Coleman's hand, his skin just as grimy as hers, she retreated, one eye on the elephant while regaining her wits. If they just followed the side of the big top to the front, they could disappear into the crowd that was surely pouring in by now. A good plan. Solid. And most importantly, the only one she had at the moment.

She set off, cutting Mr. Coleman a sideways glance. "Why is Carky trying to kill you? What is going on?"

He shook his head. "That is a long—"

"Save it!" She spotted Carky from the corner of her eye. The woman stood in one of the big top's doorways, shading her eyes as she scanned the grounds, gun in her other hand, looking their way. Surely she wouldn't take a shot in this mob and risk hitting an innocent.

Then again. . .

"Faster, Mr. Coleman." Kit skirted a woman pushing a trolley of chickens stacked in crates.

Sure enough, a shot cracked through the air.

Mr. Coleman stumbled, a painful grunt competing with the scream of the chicken woman.

Oh God, no!

He wrenched from her grip, slapping his hand against his opposite upper arm.

Just as another shot rang out.

Kit tackled him an instant before a bullet whizzed over their heads.

More screams. Running feet. Chaos.

Was this it? Were they to be taken out here on a dirt path in a circus? Jackson would be furious, and Bella. . .sweet innocent girl. . .would have no mother. The same awful fate Kit had lived out her whole life.

Fury pushed her to her feet. If she were to die, then she'd meet the next bullet head-on. At least Bella would know her mother hadn't died on her belly, face down in the dirt.

"Let's have it, then, Carky!" she shouted. "Let everyone see. . ."

Her words died as her gaze skimmed the melee around her. Monkeys scampered by. Circus performers in various states of dress rushed about, voices raised, some calming animals, most heads turning to ascertain where the shots came from.

But there was no crazed woman aiming a revolver.

There was no Carky whatsoever.

Kit wheeled about at the pounding of boots. At least a dozen bluecoats ran her way— Charles Baggett leading the charge. No wonder the woman had vanished.

A moan from the ground dropped her to her knees where Mr. Coleman sat, face white as a January sky, clutching his arm. Red blossomed into a splotch on the fabric of his sleeve, but the rest of him appeared to be whole and hale.

"Here, let me have a look." Gently, she pried away his fingers. The sleeve of his suit coat was torn wide open in a line, as was the shirtsleeve beneath. A grazing wound, then, albeit bloody and painful. She blew out a long breath. Mr. Coleman had escaped the clutches of the grim reaper for now, but Carky was still out there.

And she'd still be gunning for him.

Jackson really shouldn't be here. Should definitely not be unlocking his own front door while the sun still whispered its final goodbye in the sky. Shouldn't even be thinking about relaxing on the sofa with his wife in his arms once Bella had gone to bed—not when he hadn't so much as touched the mountain of paperwork on his desk all day. But oh, what a day it had been.

And he just couldn't take one more problem to solve.

He hung his hat on the coat tree then cracked his neck one way and the other. Brooks snuffled down the corridor, snout to the baseboards, sniffing out bugs for dinner. Now that they had Bella, why Kit insisted on keeping the armadillo for a pet was beyond him, but it did manage to keep away the creepy crawlies.

Light glowed from the sitting room. Odd. Kit should be in the kitchen feeding Bella, not already lounging on the sofa without him.

"Kit?" He swung into the front room only to be met with the startled stare of a hump-nosed man with a square jaw sitting in his shirtsleeves—and one of them was rolled up with a bandage wrapped around his bicep. Jackson frowned. "Who are you? And why are you bleeding on my sofa?"

The fellow shifted nervously on the cushion. "I am Mr. Coleman."

Jackson's brows shot up. "The man my wife—"

"Was looking for. That's right. Welcome home, love." Skirts swished in and Kit pecked him on the cheek without missing a step on her way to the tea table, where she set down a tray, porcelain cups rattling. "We've only just got back from the doctor's office, and I thought some tea would be in order before dinner. Would you like some?"

He blinked. Did she really think a cup of tea would distract him?

"A word, please, Wife." He swept out his arm, allowing her to precede him into the corridor, but the second they cleared the door, he pulled her close and lowered his voice. "What is Mr. Coleman doing here?"

"I couldn't very well leave him bleeding on the ground in the middle of a circus. You would have done the same."

He ground his teeth, frustrated beyond measure. "When have I ever brought home a strange man and parked him on our sofa?"

"Never, but you did have a strange man in your office this morning. What's the difference?" She shrugged.

"You know very well there is a huge difference. I will not be distracted with your bait-and-switch tactics. I thought this Mr. Coleman was a brigand who stole his own daughter and beat his wife, and yet you have the audacity to bring him into our home?"

"Calm down. It's not like that." She smoothed her hands along his waistcoat. "Turns out I was wrong."

"You?" He snorted. "Wrong?"

She dropped her hands, a frown bending her brow. "Gloating ill becomes you, Husband."

He blew out a long breath. He was getting nowhere—and fast—so he backed up a bit. "By your own admission, you went to the circus, which I expressly told you not to. And not only did you disobey that directive, you actively rescued the man and his child, which you promised you would not do. Say." He narrowed his eyes. "Where is that baby, anyway?"

"Turns out there wasn't one. It was all a lie intended to pull on my heartstrings and blind me to the truth."

She looked so mournful, he almost felt sorry for her. . .but not quite.

Jackson heaved a disgusted sigh. "Why did Charles not tell me you were there? Surely he must have seen you if the picture you just painted is correct. A bleeding man laid out on the ground isn't something he would have missed."

"He didn't miss it. In fact, I was quite glad to see him, but I was compelled to swear him to secrecy. No one is to know Mr. Coleman is here." Her teeth worried her lower lip. "Though it won't be long until Carky finds out."

His ears perked up at the name—the very same as Gruver had squawked, leastwise part of it. "Carky Smathers?"

"*You* know her?" Kit's eyes widened.

"Not personally, but she's the one who hired those cutthroats that chased you and Baggett."

"Of course she was." Kit slung her arms wide, fingers brushing against the coat-tree and sending it wobbling.

In one swift movement, Jackson stilled the thing before it tipped. "But who hired her and why does she wish Mr. Coleman dead?"

"I was just about to ask the man that myself, hence the tea. I was trying to calm him." Rising to her toes, she nuzzled her nose against his ear. "Would you like to help me?"

Thunder and turf! He'd like to do more than that, and the wily little minx knew it, judging by the knowing look sparking blue in her eyes.

He pulled away from her. "I'd like nothing better."

Striding into the sitting room, Jackson took up a post at the hearth, facing the wounded man. "I am Chief Inspector Jackson Forge, Mr. Coleman, so you need not fear any harm while you are under my roof. How about you tell us your story? We would like to help you, but we must have all the facts in order to do so."

Mr. Coleman bobbed his head, the cup that Kit'd offered him clinking against the saucer. "It all started a few months back, when I looked into some numbers that didn't add up. I'm an accountant, you see, at Willis, Percival & Company."

"At least that part of Carky's story was correct." Kit smirked. "Go on, Mr. Coleman."

"Like I said, numbers weren't adding up, so I went to my superior, Mr. Blade, who told me not to pay such matters any mind. He had things under control. So, I trusted him—which was my mistake." His head dropped, and for a moment nothing but the tick of the clock and clap of horse hooves outside filled the air.

"What happened?" Jackson prodded.

Mr. Coleman inhaled deeply. "In my spare time—before and after hours, mind, for I am no shirker—I came in early and stayed late in my office. I'm working on a number puzzle I intend to sell to newspapers once I perfect it, a weekly or even daily feature. It's sure to be a most challenging diversion for those who enjoy enigmas."

A number puzzle? Jackson retrieved the paper Kit had given him from his pocket. As busy as he'd been, he'd not had a spare moment to run it over to the Foreign Office or the cryptologists, which may have been a blessing of Providence. "Is that what this is about?"

Coleman pulled the torn slip from his fingers, brows furrowing as he studied it. "Yes. Yes, indeed. This is mine." He glanced up. "Where did you find it?"

"I found it," Kit said. "At your flat."

"Ahh. Deuced careless of me." He crumpled the paper into a ball. "At any rate, I was working on this puzzle late one evening when I ran out of ledger paper. Normally I ask Mr. Blade for a fresh pad from the cabinet in his office, but he'd already gone. So, I...well." His wide mouth flattened, and he gave a little shake of his head. "I ought not admit it, but I am rather handy with a letter opener and a piece of wire."

Jackson cocked his head. What other secrets did this man have squirreled away? "You are a picklock, sir?"

"An amateur, of sorts." He took a great gulp of his tea. "But that is neither here nor there. The point is, while rummaging about for fresh paper, I discovered a ledger tucked away where it ought not to have been. Naturally, I glanced into it, and what I saw surprised me. The numbers on the pages were the exact figures missing from the book I'd been working on. Had Mr. Blade given me the wrong book? I couldn't imagine it would be anything else, so I confronted him about it the next day."

Jackson whistled low as he strolled over to where Kit sat and perched on the arm of her chair. "That didn't go well, I imagine."

"It did not. Mr. Blade threatened that if I didn't keep quiet about the whole thing, he'd terminate me immediately and make sure I didn't work as an accountant ever again. I did as he said, for a while; but then it dawned on me that should Mr. Percival or Mr. Willis find out about the phantom ledger, I could be blamed as an accomplice, or worse, Mr. Blade might blame me altogether." He set down his teacup, still half-full, wincing from the movement to his arm. "I didn't want any trouble, and I most certainly did not want to go to gaol, so I thought to get the jump on the situation and copy that ledger. That way Mr. Blade wouldn't notice anything missing and I would have hard evidence to bring to Mr. Percival and Mr. Willis."

Kit set down her own cup and whumped back to the chair, brushing against Jackson in the process. "How did you manage that? Surely Mr. Blade didn't hide the ledger in the same place."

"He didn't. And it took quite some skill to crack the code on that safe—er—I mean, well, you see, numbers are my thing. I hope you won't think ill of me."

Jackson stifled a guffaw. "My wife and I have discovered, Mr. Coleman, that in the pursuit of justice, sometimes one must wade into the murky waters that separate right from wrong." He glanced down at Kit—only to find her big blue eyes smiling up at his.

"I'm afraid," Mr. Coleman murmured, "Mr. Blade didn't merely wade, but dove headfirst into the wrong side of the criminal ocean."

Jackson jerked his head towards the man, senses heightened. Clearly there was more to the story than a simple skimming operation. "How so?"

Lifting his good arm, Mr. Coleman rubbed the back of his neck. "Late one night I was returning the ledger when I heard a key in the lock of Mr. Blade's door. I slammed the safe shut and secreted myself in the paper cabinet—which was quite a feat of contortion, I tell you. But while there, I overheard Mr. Blade conversing with some rough sort of men, or more like they were conversing with him. . .and they threatened him with more than the loss of his job. They threatened his very life if he didn't *pay up*, whatever that meant." Dropping his hand, he shrugged one shoulder. "They promised him a death of a most horrible kind. That's when I decided it might be best if I disappeared for a while. Come back later when Mr. Blade had paid whatever debt he owed. So, I took what I had and ran."

Jackson ground his teeth. This little job Kit had taken on was turning into quite the monster.

"What are you thinking?" Kit rubbed his arm.

Ignoring her touch, he rose and paced in front of the tea table. "Do you still have that copy of the ledger, Mr. Coleman?"

He patted the pocket on his waistcoat. "I keep it on me at all times. I still don't wish to answer for Mr. Blade's wrongdoings."

"You needn't worry about that anymore," Kit cut in. "Mr. Blade is dead."

"What?" Mr. Coleman deflated against the cushions, face draining of colour. "I can scarce believe it."

"It appears your Mr. Blade was in league with someone else." Stopping his pacing, Jackson faced Kit. "Carky Smathers?"

She shook her head. "If I still know anything of Carky, she is a gun for hire, nothing more."

"Then what deep pockets hired her?" He turned back to the skinny man on the sofa. "Think hard, Mr. Coleman. Were any names mentioned that night you listened in?"

"I. . .I can't recall if I caught a man's name or not."

"Think, Mr. Coleman!" Kit jumped to her feet. "The sooner you give us a name, the sooner we can put a stop to anyone else getting killed—namely you."

Mr. Coleman paled even more.

Jackson sighed. *Strongheaded, loose-tongued woman.* He tucked Kit's hand into the crook of his arm. "The man's been through a lot, Wife. Let's give him a breather." He glanced at Mr. Coleman. "Finish your tea, sir. We'll give you a few minutes to collect yourself."

He guided Kit to the corner of the room but had hardly stopped moving when she hissed into his ear, "We have got to find out who Mr. Blade—and Carky—work for before anyone discovers Mr. Coleman is here."

"You're the detective," he whispered back.

Her lips twisted, a sure sign that mind of hers was running laps behind her pretty face. "No," she said at length. "I am only half of a detective agency." She peered up at him. "And I think my father may be of some help."

"In what way?"

She glanced over her shoulder at Mr. Coleman, then lowered her voice. "The case my father has been working is related to this whole thing. He was hired to find an employee of Willis & Percival, one who had information on an embezzlement scandal or was maybe even in on the embezzling himself. That sounds an awful lot like Mr. Coleman, for the other man my father was investigating was suddenly killed—Mr. Blade. Just this morning my father said he was looking into who the murderer might be."

Jackson reared back his head. "Smathers?"

Kit angled her jaw. "I wouldn't be surprised."

A rap on the front door broke his train of thought. He ran his hands along Kit's arms. "Wait for any further questioning until I see who is here."

He strode from the room and swung open the front door—only to see his big bear of a father-in-law with a glower on his face and what appeared to be dried milk on his shoulder. Bella bounced in his arms.

"Ba-ba!" she shrieked and lunged towards him.

Jackson laughed at Kit's father as he collected her. "Papa," he corrected, then faced Graybone. "Taken up nannying, have you?"

"Don't start," Graybone rumbled. "Where's that daughter of mine?"

Jackson stepped aside, allowing the man plenty of space to stomp by. "Don't be too hard on her," he called after him. "Kit may have found the murderer you're looking for."

Chapter Seventeen

Early mornings were meant for coffee—especially Mondays—though Charles knew a handful of dandies and a woman or two who would shout him down for such a blunt affront to tea. Jackson wouldn't, though. And as Charles slapped his money onto the street stall counter and snatched up a full mug, he sincerely hoped this offering would not only mend a fence but soften the blow he must deliver to his friend.

Two blows, actually.

"Thanks, Miffy." Charles tipped his head at the frizzle-haired seller, a man with skin as dark as the roasted beans he served.

"Think naught o' it, guv'nor." The old fellow tipped his hat, the flourish of it nearly banging into the great metal urn employing more than half the space on the small cart. "I'll have it hot and ready same time tomorrow for ye."

Charles turned on his heel, leaving behind the somewhat nutty, burnt scent of roasting coffee beans. Clutching his old mug in both hands, he stepped into the fray of foot traffic that never failed to surround the Royal Exchange. The moment he turned from Cornhill onto Leadenhall Street, he spied a pair of broad shoulders bobbing a handspan above most of the other pedestrians. Charles upped his pace, gaining Jackson's side with only a few drops of liquid sloshing over the rim.

"Here." He handed Jackson the coffee.

Jackson didn't miss a step, as if someone matching his pace with a steaming morning brew was an everyday occurrence. He did, however, slip him a narrow-eyed glance as he took a sip. "Mmm. That hits the spot. Why so accommodating this morning?"

"Several reasons. One to gauge how gammy you are about the whole Coleman thing." He studied Jackson's face.

And as he expected, those dark brows of his lowered into a squall line. "You should have told me, no matter what Kit said."

Hah! As if that wife of his had given him any choice. Charles dodged a clerk running full bore down the center of the pavement, spreading his hands as he once again joined Jackson's side. "She was very persuasive. I had no choice but to swear to secrecy."

"Bested by a skirt?" Jackson snorted. "That's a pathetic excuse."

"You ought to know," he quipped right back. "You're the one who married her."

"Speaking of which. . ." His friend arched a brow at him.

"Trouble with Kit?" If so, not surprising. That woman was more wild horse than he'd wish to tame, the opposite of domestic Martha.

"I shall always have trouble with Kit, God love her, but that is not what I meant. I am referring to a certain lady who runs the soup kitchen and a certain man who has eyes for no one but her." Jackson chugged the rest of his coffee, then handed back the mug. "When are you going to make your move, man?"

"I'm not." He hooked the tin mug to a leather loop on his belt. "And that's the end of it."

With a great tug on his arm, Jackson pulled him into the less traveled Bell Alley Mews, stopping but a few paces inside the cobblestoned lane. A huge horse clip-clopped by, and Jackson shored them closer to the brick wall, allowing the animal and rider to pass.

"Listen, Baggett. Remember when you carped on me about Kit, that I'd be a fool to let her slip from my grasp? It's my turn to return that favour. Martha Jones is the woman for you." He poked his finger into Charles' chest. "Don't wait until it's too late to tell her that."

The coffee in his gut churned. Counseling Jackson was one thing, but listening to the same exposition on his own love life was quite a different matter. . .one he didn't like. "I'll not argue the point. I've never loved a woman so greatly in all my life." There. He'd finally said it aloud, and the taste of it was far more bitter than sweet on his tongue. He clenched his jaw. "But as much as Martha may be the *woman for me*, as you put it, I am most definitely not the man for her."

"Poppycock!" The word bounced from wall to wall in the narrow lane. "Any woman would be proud to be your wife."

"Edwina Draper wasn't." He regretted the admission the second it flew past his lips.

Jackson cocked his head, the blue of his eyes flashing with surprise. "Who?"

"No one. Forget I said anything." He turned away.

Jackson yanked him back, teeth shining white in a huge smile beneath his moustache. "Not a chance."

"You are as stubborn as your wife! You deserve each other."

"Indeed. Now, about this Edwina Draper. . . ?" That infernal brow lifted to the sky again.

Charles huffed a long breath. Would to heavens he'd never said the name! But there was no shoving that feral cat back into the bag now, blast it. He skewered Jackson with a sharp stare. "Promise you'll not breathe a word of this to Kit, nor anyone else?"

"Upon my honour."

"Very well. But let's keep walking." He stalked back onto Houndsditch, preferring the bustle and the fact that he wouldn't have to make eye contact with Jackson. "I nearly proposed once, years ago."

"Let me guess. To Edwina Draper?"

"The very same." He paused to ferret out a penny from his pocket, then clinked it into the metal cup held by a beggar in a faded military coat, legs wrapped in rags—what was left of them at any rate. Both ended at the knee.

"And?"

Charles chewed the inside of his cheek for a moment. "On the night I intended to pledge my troth, I arrived at the hotel restaurant a little early, only to see Edwina was already seated at a table. . .with another man."

"That is rough. Quite the scene, I imagine."

"Not what you'd expect. I hid behind some potted plants, and the man passed right by me on his way out, smelling of lemon verbena. Lemon, of all things! What sort of dandy douses himself with such a girly perfume?"

"The sort that aren't man enough to face the woman's beau and duke it out honourably." Jackson chuckled. "So, I assume you taught him some manners?"

In hindsight, he should have, but would things have really turned out any differently? "I did not school the man. Instead, I confronted Edwina about the fellow. She laughed it off, saying she'd arrived early and had merely bumped into an old family friend. A chance meeting, nothing more. My gut told me she was lying, but sap that I am, I gave her the benefit of the doubt. Dinner went on as normal, until the plates were cleared. I had just reached into my pocket for the ring box when Edwina made a completely different proposal."

They swung north onto Bevis Marks, his feet hitting the ground harder than necessary. A visceral response, and Charles knew it, but he could no more stop the angry pounding than he could dim the shaft of morning sun hitting his eyes. He tugged his hat lower.

"What was her proposal?" Jackson asked.

"Edwina wished to put our relationship on hold, saying that things were moving much too quickly for her."

"How long had you been courting?"

"Two years."

Air hissed through Jackson's teeth.

"Indeed." Charles smirked. "There was nothing quick about it, so I argued the point and she. . .em. . .let's just say it didn't end well. She stomped out the door. I stormed into the bar, where I intended to nurse my fury for the rest of the night. But after a single drink, I knew regardless of my feelings that I ought to see her home. Night had fallen by then, and you know how these streets are."

"Hey! Have a care, boy." Jackson sidestepped a demon of a street sweeper as they crossed the road. "Even in broad daylight one must keep on his toes. So, what happened when you caught up to her?"

His gut clenched tight as a vise screwed all the way shut. He'd relived that moment too many times to count, all of them waking him up in a lather of sweat. Slowly he shook his head. "God, have mercy on us all."

"Come on, old man. It couldn't have been as dire as the look on your face. I've suffered many a tongue-lashing from Kit and I'm still standing."

"Would that had been the case. But no." His throat closed, and it took several gruff clearings to get any words to pass. "I found Edwina bleeding out on the pavement from a brutal mugging. The murderer was never found."

Jackson's step faltered. "Oh Charles. . .I am so sorry. That is a bitter pill, the bitterest."

He gritted his teeth, glad for the sudden uptick in pedestrians to bind his frayed emotions into a solid rope to hang on to. He didn't even have an opportunity to speak again until they passed a trinket seller pushing a cart laden with jingling bells. "I suppose some good came out of it." He shrugged. "I vowed then and there to become a police officer."

"And a fine officer you are." Jackson clapped him on the back. "A regular brick."

"Thanks, but that's not the only vow I made that night. I promised myself I'd never get close to a woman again. Edwina was killed because of me—because I let my anger rule. I won't endanger another woman, especially not Martha. I cannot risk failing her." He cut Jackson a challenging stare. "I *will* not."

Jackson merely shook his head. "Look, Charles, what happened to Edwina is tragic. There's no doubt about that. But it's God who brings beauty from ashes. Don't push away that gift. It is never prudent or wise to stiff-arm God."

"I hardly think that is what I'm doing."

"Then what are you doing?"

He scowled. Was it not apparent? "I'm protecting Martha, that's what."

"What a load of rubbish!" Jackson stopped in the middle of the pavement and folded his arms, a rock not to be moved, forcing pedestrians to flow around them. His stance left no choice but to hunker down and weather his storm.

"Martha Jones is a strong woman, capable of protecting herself; but even were she not, God alone is her keeper. You, my misguided friend, are called to love her, to fend for her as best you can, but hear me, and hear me well." He jabbed Charles in the shoulder with his finger. "You are not now—nor ever will be—her ultimate protector. I know that is a hard lesson, one I've had several chances to learn with Kit. God knows I've failed that woman a hundred times over, but even so, I'd not trade the time I've had with her for anything in the world. I love her, as I believe you love Martha, and love covers a multitude of sins. So, pursue that. Pursue love instead of dwelling in past failure. That path can only lead to a denial of the present and a forfeiture of the future."

Jackson's words washed over him like a bucket of ice water, raising gooseflesh on his arms. Was that what he'd been doing? Living so much in the past that he couldn't dwell in the present? Had he truly been ruining his chance at any sort of a happy future? Ruining Martha's chance as well? Was holding on to fear and disgrace making him into a selfish monster?

He stumbled sideways as a burly man bumped into him, but he hardly noticed; and for a brief moment right there on a busy London street, he dipped his head.

Oh God, give me wisdom to know if I am living a lie.

A big hand squeezed his shoulder, Jackson's voice lowered to a healing balm. "If there's one thing I've learned, my friend, it is that God's love and grace is sufficient no matter what. Trust in that. Trust in Him. And for heaven's sake, tell Martha. She's of a keen enough mind to decide for herself if she wants to take on a scoundrel such as you." With a final squeeze, Jackson released him.

"I will think on what you've said." And he would, because suddenly a whole new world of hope had opened up before him.

"Good." Jackson angled his head towards a frowning stationer in a doorway who was flipping his CLOSED sign to OPEN. "Because if we don't get moving, that owner might nudge us along with a letter opener to the backside."

Charles set off with a snicker. "So, back to the Coleman thing. . .are we square?"

"We are, though I'm not sure Graybone will thank you for his new housemate."

"Is that where you've stashed him?"

"For now, and hopefully not for long. But you said that"—he aimed a finger towards the coffee mug swinging on Charles' hip—"was for several reasons. What else have you got?"

"Something I think you'll like even less than the Coleman situation." He tugged his hat towards a blue-coated constable passing by, as did

Jackson, and once a "good morning" was exchanged by all, he faced his friend. "I've already been to the station for an early morning questioning session with Mr. Gilliam, only to find a bit of an uproar in the holding cells. One of the inmates died during the night."

"Who?"

"Blackjack."

"Blast it!" At the "Oh my!" of a lady in a hat so bedecked with feathers the thing might actually take flight, Jackson lowered his tone. "How did he die?"

"Not sure. When Barrycloth did his round at the beginning of his shift, he found Blackjack stiff as his pallet, so he'd been dead for some time. Barrycloth thought he must've suffered a heart seizure during the night. The coroner's looking into it now. Personally, though, I suspect foul play, though I haven't an explanation in all the world for it. Gibbons worked the night shift and swears no one was down in the cellblock all evening."

Jackson cut him a sharp glance. "So why the suspicion?"

"Because word on the street is that in the wee hours of the morning, Gruver died as well. He choked to death at a pub over by Wapping. Only the thing is he wasn't eating anything at the time. Just drinking."

"That is odd." The lines on Jackson's face hardened. "Which gives me suspicions of my own."

Charles gazed intently into Jackson's eyes. "You thinking what I'm thinking?"

"Are the initials C.S.?"

A grin stretched his lips. "Great minds think alike, my friend. Which brings me to my last reason for accosting you this morning."

Jackson cocked his head. "And that is?"

"Watch your back, old man. This Carky Smathers is a dangerous animal."

Kit's pen flew, her thoughts moving faster than the nib. But were those thoughts any good? Her office chair creaked as she leaned closer to study her hasty scrawl. Of all the words she'd gleaned from Mr. Coleman yesterday after church, it seemed no matter how she strung them together, they didn't teach her anything new. Though she'd been at it since sunrise, she was no closer to figuring out who hired Carky Smathers.

The bell above the door jingled and in walked her father, suit coat flapping wide open, a slip of white shirttail hanging out between waistband and waistcoat, his trousers a wrinkly mess. He clutched a cup of tea in one hand and a satchel in the other, papers peeping out where they'd obviously been caught in a hasty closing. What a wreck. If she didn't know any better, she'd suspect he'd spent the last two nights with Bella instead of Mr. Coleman.

Kit set down her pen. "Oh dear. Not a good evening?"

Glowering, her father plunked down his satchel and removed his hat. "Not a good *two* evenings. That Coleman snores louder than the ripsaw over at the lumberyard. I'm surprised he hasn't blown apart his whole set of bones what with those nocturnal explosions."

"Sorry, Father."

"Sorry doesn't clear the fog from my mind. Hopefully this will." He toasted his cup in the air as he reclaimed his satchel and strode to his desk. "The man's got quite a mind on him, though, I'll give him that. Numbers-wise, that is. Straightened out my banking snarl in no time."

Kit frowned. Was her father in financial trouble? "I didn't know you had a snarl."

"I don't anymore. Turns out it was an accounting error on the bank's part, not mine." Whumping his satchel onto his desk, he unclasped the latch and began pulling out papers.

Kit shoved her own papers aside and planted her elbow on the tabletop, her chin in her palm, mulling over her father's information. There was no doubt about it. Mr. Coleman did have a flair for ledgers, but that sort of intelligence was no match for an assassin on the prowl. "Do you really think Mr. Coleman is safe at your house alone? I mean, it wouldn't be a stretch for Carky to look for him there. She knows you're my partner."

"He's fine. I left him with a loaded Webley .455 and a Colt single action within reach, and after a short tutorial on how to fire the thing, I also left a bolt-action rifle in his lap. If Carky does show her face, I told him to blow it off."

Kit shook her head. Leave it to a former police sergeant to overarm a fellow. "I hardly think Mr. Coleman is the type for such violence."

"He's not." Her father puffed air past his lips. "Which is why I also paid some of my old night-watch fellows to keep an eye on the place." Setting the satchel on the floor, he gathered the mess of papers and tapped them on the desk into a neat stack. "Now, would you like to hear all I've collected on Mr. Blade? I managed to catch a few people at home yesterday after Sunday services."

"I would." She dragged her chair over to his desk and scooted up close to his side.

"As it turns out, the gent led quite the double life. On one hand, he was the picture of an upstanding family man." He stabbed his finger onto a newspaper clipping that sported a photograph of Mr. Blade, his wife, and their two sons. "On the other hand, he was an opium addict and a gambler with ties to the Old Pye Rat Pit, just as you'd suggested. Nice to see that you don't have to be chasing a criminal to use that mind of yours. But get this. . .he wasn't merely slapping down wagers. Mr. Blade was the manager."

"I can't say I'm surprised. It is a very lucrative business. Still, in my experience, there isn't just one manager running the show. Usually there's someone in the shadows he must answer to, and if I don't miss my mark, that someone could very well be the one who supplied Mr. Blade with his opium. A higher-level criminal sticking his dirty hands into several pies." She met her father's gaze. "I've seen it before."

"As have I. Which is why I've got a meeting with—"

The merry ringing of the doorbell turned both their heads. In raced a red-capped lad, a paper flapping in his fist. He stopped in front of her, a chip-toothed grin spreading on his face. "Mornin', miss."

Kit returned his smile. "Good morning. Toffy, wasn't it?"

His grin grew and he dipped a little bow. "One and the same, at yer service, miss. And this is fer you."

She pulled the wrinkled missive from his fingers. Whoever sent it would probably frown at the state of the note. "Are you to wait for a reply?"

He shook his head so vehemently, his flat cap smeared into a red blur. "I were tol' to just drop it off."

"And a very fine job you've done of it, Toffy. Follow me." She crossed to her desk and pulled out her reticule from the top drawer, then fished out a coin.

He stared at the offering, the whites of his eyes growing two sizes. "Kipes! Another bob?" He peered up at her. "Thank ye, miss! Ye're an angel!" He scrambled out the door as quickly as he'd torn in, the bang of the wood against the frame reverberating off the office walls.

"You know that boy is just going to waste that money on Lord knows what," her father grumbled behind her.

"Maybe." She strolled back to her seat. "But maybe not. Remember, he said he had a sister to care for. Besides, I distinctly remember a wise man once telling me to have a little faith." She winked.

He rolled his eyes.

Chuckling, she unfolded the note.

> I call a truce, Pet, until we meet one-on-one.
> Today. Four o'clock. The Brasserie at Covent Garden.
> No weapons—and do not think to cross me. I know
> where you live.

Needle pricks traveled from the nape of her neck to her very feet. It was no surprise Carky had discovered her address, but seeing it in black and white was a brick to the head. Thank God they'd had foresight enough to move Mr. Coleman. She slumped back in her chair, fanning herself with Carky's note. A truce—while welcome—would only last for so long. Still, she honestly hadn't seen that coming.

"Well?" He reached for the note, putting an end to her fanning. "May I?"

"Be my guest."

His dark eyes scanned back and forth, until finally he slapped the paper onto his desktop, ruffling the top page of his stack. "Don't be daft. It's a trap."

"Probably, but this will be our best chance to question her, get information." She grabbed his hand and stood. "Come on. You can keep me safe."

"I can't." He pulled from her grasp. "As I was saying, I have a meeting with an informant of mine who might have some intelligence on the situation. But listen to me clearly, Daughter." Shoving back his chair, he rose, looming over her like a bear about to attack. "I most expressly forbid you to go alone. Do you hear me? I will not have it!"

Kit swallowed, retreating a step. Sweet heavens. She'd never seen him so animated. "Calm down, Father. I may be a risk taker, but I'm not mad. I know more than anyone that Carky is not one to face without some sort of backup waiting in the wings. I will ask Jackson."

Her father set his jaw. "And if he's busy?"

She lifted her palm. Hopefully the visual vow would help to ease his mind. "I promise I will not go to this meeting without Jackson or Mr. Baggett. There. Happy?"

A growl rumbled in his chest. "As long as you keep your word, then yes."

"Good. But what about you?" She angled her head. "Is this informant you're meeting with to be trusted? How do you know you're not the one walking headlong into a snare?"

"I don't." He sniffed. "But if I can find out where Blade got his opium, it'll be worth it, for that just might be the missing piece to our puzzle."

Chapter Eighteen

Man could not live by a bite of burnt porridge and a mug of coffee alone, no matter how much Jackson wished it were so. Lacing his fingers behind his head, he leaned back in his chair, stomach growling loud and urgent. Snubbing the paperwork on his desk for the moment, he slid his gaze to the wall clock. Was eleven too early to nab a sausage roll from the vendor down on the corner? Then again, ought he really take time away from the mountains of folders before him?

The next rumble made the decision for him.

He straightened just as a knock rapped at the door. Of all the inconvenient timing, but it wasn't as if he could ignore it. He pressed his fist to his belly, hopefully calming the thing long enough for a short conversation. "Come in."

A round ball with thick spectacles rolled in, the requisite sweat stains already darkening the fabric beneath Mr. Harvey's arms. "Good morning, sir, what is left of it at any rate."

"Morning, Harvey." Jackson gave him a sharp nod. So help him, if this man was going to shirk that insurance case, he just might explode. But though he tried, Jackson couldn't think of a single reason other than that for why the lazy inspector was in his office, especially since he carried a fat binder in his hand. "I assume your visit pertains to the insurance fraud case."

"Why yes, sir!" A smile spread on his face. "Indeed, it does, sir. How perceptive."

Oh brother. Jackson pinched the bridge of his nose. "Listen, Mr.

Harvey, I cannot help you with your investigation. As you see here"—he swept his hand towards the endless stacks atop his desk—"I have my own disaster with which to contend. Neither will I accept a refusal on your part to finish the job I've given you. It is called work for a reason, Inspector, and I expect you to roll up your sleeves and do the hard labour."

"That's just it, sir. I have done so." He approached the desk, his moustache practically crawling up his nose at the obvious distaste he felt for such chaos, then set his own thick folder atop the shortest pile.

Eyeing it, Jackson frowned. Of all the things he needed in the world, another collection of paperwork was not it. "What exactly is it that you have done, Mr. Harvey?"

"Why, I have worked, sir." He tossed back his shoulders, the movement jiggling his jowls. "My labours are now at an end."

By all the saints! Did the man seriously think he could simply back out of a tough case by depositing it here for Jackson to finish? His stomach let out a growl as furious as the one he fought to suppress in his throat. "Mr. Harvey, I find I can no longer cut you any slack based solely on the merit that you are the commissioner's nephew. If you refuse to work, then I will have to let you go."

Harvey's big eyes blinked rapidly behind his glasses. "I offer no refusal, sir. May I?" He tipped his head towards the chair. "My sciatica, you know."

He dragged the chair close to his folder at the desk before Jackson could naysay him, then proceeded to flip open the cover. "As you can see, sir. . ." He ran a podgy finger down one column and another, carefully turned the page, then did so again. And again. And—

Leaning forward, Jackson stilled the man's hand. "I see clearly that the numbers are different, Mr. Harvey. What is your point?"

The man eased back in his chair, a supremely pleased tilt to his head. "That is the point, sir."

Count to ten, man. Just count to ten. Several times over if need be.

And he did need to. In fact, the wall clock ticked a full minute and a half before he could force calm words past his lips. "For the sake of argument, Mr. Harvey, pretend I don't know what you are talking about."

The man's head jerked back, astonishment rife on his face. He pulled out an already-damp handkerchief and ran it over his shiny brow before tucking it into his pocket. "Well, I suppose if that were the case, which I highly doubt it is, then I would explain the invoices from Wentworth & Sons, Importers, did not match up with the actual worth of the goods which were supposedly damaged in a fire. Namely, the submitted documents were inflated to a most egregious degree. After comparison to fair market values—and as luck would have it, the discovery of the actual goods which were most decidedly *not* destroyed in an inferno—I propose that Mr. Vincent Wentworth, son to Mr. Robert Wentworth, ought to be issued a warrant for arrest at your earliest convenience."

A bludgeon to the kidneys couldn't have stunned him more. He gripped the arms of his chair. "Are you telling me you solved the Imperial Insurance Company's case?"

Mr. Harvey gently closed the folder and straightened it—along with a few other stacks—before lifting his face. "I did, sir."

"In two days?"

"Yes, sir."

No. No way. It wasn't humanly possible. Jackson shook his head. "How many boxes of records did you plow through?"

Both the man's bulgy eyes shifted upwards to the corner of the ceiling. "Twenty-four," he mumbled, then grew louder as he returned his gaze to Jackson. "No, twenty five, now that I think on it."

Jackson gaped. "You could not have done so in such a short amount of time."

"At the risk of sounding overly prideful, sir, I own that paperwork is not only my passion but my gifting."

"You don't say?" And yet, there might be some truth to it, for there lay the insurance case, solved in record time. There were also Smitty's orderly records to reckon with.

Harvey shifted in his chair, wincing from his sciatica. "Oh, but I do say so, sir."

Another knock rapped on the door, followed by a twist of the knob. In popped Kit's head. "Pardon my interruption, but I need to speak with you." Her gaze darted to Mr. Harvey then back to him, fire in her gaze. "Urgently."

Jackson couldn't help but smile. Everything was urgent where Kit was concerned. Though considering the whole Coleman and Carky affair, she probably did have good reason this time.

He rose, murmuring to the sweaty fellow in the chair as he rounded the desk, "Excuse me a moment, Mr. Harvey."

"Think nothing of it," Harvey answered as he once again produced his handkerchief.

The moment Jackson drew close to his wife, she handed over a folded paper, somewhat wrinkled. He shook it out, brows rising as the words sank in.

"Well?" Kit's blue-eyed stare met his.

A sigh ripped out of him. He didn't have time for this. And yet…well, it was completely out of the question to allow this fiery wife of his to meet alone with a known assassin. And she would. He had no doubt whatsoever about that.

He turned to Mr. Harvey. "Your work on the fraud case was exemplary, Harvey, so how about you tackle that?" He swept his hand towards his desk.

Mr. Harvey's thick lips pursed as he glanced from the paperwork mounds back to Jackson. "What exactly is that, sir?"

Jackson grabbed his hat off a peg, ruffling a few of the WANTED posters on the board nearby. "I'm not sure, Mr. Harvey. I am hoping you will be able to tell me that when I return."

Kit scanned the street for any sign of danger as she crossed over to meet Carky. Covent Garden had been a shrewd choice. Vendors sold everything from pickled whelks to bottles of cloudy water supposedly drawn from the baths of Jerusalem. Several street performers drew huddles of crowds, the most exciting of which was a group of fire eaters who spat cascades of sparks and flames. Children ran wild everywhere. Chickens did too. Yes, indeed. This was the perfect public place for an assassin to set up a meeting.

Or a kill.

Heart pounding, Kit stepped onto the pavement, her eyes flicking across the road where Jackson stationed himself as a newspaper seller in front of an eel pie shop. Most wouldn't detect anything unusual in his relaxed stance and may even write him off as too blasé to make a sale, but the cut of his jaw spoke volumes to her. As did the sudden lock of his gaze onto hers. In the space of a few breaths, he poured out concern for her safety with a small nod, which she returned in a slight tilt of her head. Hardly a romantic tryst, but even so, heat flared in her belly, for there could be no better assurance of his love and protection. He was in her corner, this man, looking out for her, a stalwart defense in the midst of a situation that could turn sideways in the single blink of an eye. Ahh, but she loved him.

Fiercely.

With a final shared wink—a communal reminder that vigilance was of utmost importance for them both—she faced the task at hand. Winding through the bustle, Kit bounced her gaze from one bistro table to the next, finally landing on a petite woman in a brilliant red silk gown on the far side of the outdoor restaurant. Carky sat sipping a glass of wine, as nonchalant as you please, the afternoon breeze teasing the straw-coloured ends of her hair that peeked out from beneath her jaunty hat. For all the world she appeared to be a bored lover awaiting her man.

But Kit knew better. On edge, she covered her hand over the blade on her hip, which was concealed in the fabric of her skirt. If Carky so much as twitched, she'd snap into killer mode herself.

Carky's cat-like eyes followed her every step. "Yer as skittish as a trollop at Sunday meetin', pet. Sit yer bones down and relax. I said this were a truce, din't I? I ain't gonna shoot ye here. Besides, guns are so barbaric."

"That's right. You prefer poison darts." Kit angled a wooden chair so her back faced the brick wall.

"Figured out how barmy ol' Blade died, eh? Too bad Gruver and Blackjack didn't have a brain between 'em, either." She sipped her wine, cutting a glance over the rim. "Oh well, their loss. . .of life, that is."

Kit frowned at the woman's carefree dismissal of men who had once lived and breathed and loved. . .even if they were scoundrels. "So, old friend, what made you surface here and now? Last I heard you'd been transported to Australia, one of the last ships to sail back in '68. You couldn't have been more than twelve at the time. I didn't expect to ever see you again."

"Aww. Ye missed me!" She clapped her hands. "I always knew we were kindred spirits. Yer right, though. I did skip clear across the world, but now I'm back, full grown and all the wiser, ready to take on this town. Just need me a little coin to get established, and then there'll be no stoppin' what I can do. This Coleman job oughtta get me up and runnin'." She pushed an empty glass towards Kit then picked up the wine bottle. "Take a nip, pet?"

Kit waved away her offering. "Thanks, but no."

She topped off her own glass. "Even as a girl, ye were always a bit too tight in the laces, weren't ye?"

My, how odd street twang sounded coming from lips that were once painted as a prim and proper lady's. If she blurred her vision just a bit, she could see the face of Mrs. Coleman superimposed over Carky's. The cut on the upper right side of her mouth was healing nicely, as was the purple on her eye, fading now to more of a bluish shade. Those wounds had been real enough, but Kit still marveled at how thoroughly Carky had hoodwinked her. "So," she drawled, "how did you do it?"

Carky's nose crinkled as she set down her glass. "Do what, pet?"

"Fool me."

"Zounds! 'Twere easy enough." She slapped the table, a cunning smile slashing across her elvish face. "I showed ye what ye wanted to believe, tha's all. A flifty-floo lady, all tucked and pinned in the right places. A little sleight of hand on me face, and oh, the best part?" She leaned close, her voice dropping an octave to a silky-smooth tone. "Mrs. Forge, my baby! Poor Lillibeth, my darling, my love. You must save my innocent little girl from her beast of a father, for there is no telling what he might do. Help me, please. You must help me!"

Carky laughed long and loud, igniting white-hot fury in Kit's gut. She knew better than to let emotion rule, and yet those words even now gave a slight flutter to her heart. Had motherhood changed her so much?

Carky slugged back the rest of her drink, then banged the empty vessel to the table. "Likely I needn't have spent such coin on makeup and add-ons, so taken were ye by the story. Hit ye where it hurt, din't I?"

Flit. As if she'd admit such a thing to this snake. Kit angled her head. "I am curious as to why you singled out me. Of all the charlatans and swindlers in this town, how did you decide which mark to target?"

"Why, everyone in Blackfriars knows yer the best, pet. A little soft fer my tastes, but. . ." She wiggled her fingers in the air. "Yer the most honest trickster I knows, and that's the heart o' the matter. Yer morals, ye see. Not that I agree with 'em, mind. I knew if I were to fluff ye up a bit about a babe, yank hard on those motherly heartstrings o' yers, ye'd move heaven an' earth to find the child—to find the man. Ye always could sniff out a double-dealer, so that's how I fashioned Coleman and got ye to do the hard work o' trackin' him down fer me."

Kit barked a laugh. "I'm flattered."

"I always admired yer ways, pet. Before I despised 'em, that is." The feather on her hat fluttered in the breeze, as did a loose piece of hair, which Carky made short work of with a few tucks. "But enough o' the past. It's the man I'm after. Coleman. Where is he, luv?"

"Ahh, yes. . .your recent *husband*." She swept the area with a keen gaze, alert for any sign of Carky's hired thugs, and when satisfied none were lurking, she once again faced the woman. "If you know me so well, old friend, then you ought to know where I stashed the man."

"Tha's just it. Yer a varied operator. A real creative corker. Wouldn't raise my brow a tetch if ye glued leaves on the man and planted him at Kew Gardens. The thing is, pet, I ain't got time fer such larks. So, whyn't ye just tell me? Pays good." She shrugged. "I'll split the coin fifty-fifty. 'Tis easy enough money now that ye've done the legwork."

"I don't care how much you're offering. Taking money for a man's life is a slap in God's face. I'll never tell you where Mr. Coleman is, so why not call it quits? Walk away. There's no shame in it. We both know sometimes jobs don't work out as planned."

"Come now, pet." Carky tapped her finger on the table, rattling the empty glasses. "The salary of a chief inspector surely leaves ye in want of some finery in yer life."

She shook her head. "I want for nothing."

Carky's cat eyes narrowed to slits. "Is there naught I can do to persuade ye?"

"Nothing comes to mind."

"Tha's too bad." Leaning back in her seat, Carky folded her arms over her chest, a sulky pout to her lips. "I were hopin' we could settle this without blood."

Kit narrowed her own eyes. "Are you threatening me?"

A half grin tilted the woman's mouth. "Is it working?"

Pah! She'd be a fool not to take this lioness in a skirt seriously, but she'd be an even bigger fool if she admitted aloud the unease creeping up her spine.

Kit grabbed the wine bottle and broke it on the edge of the table, the sharp sound of shattered glass jagged on the air. Holding it up to eye level, she admired the serrated edges.

"I'm not afraid of you, Carky," she murmured without pulling her gaze from the makeshift weapon. "The other girls were, but never me."

"I suspected as much. But I reckon ye'll change yer mind real fast about Coleman once those dear to ye start to bleed."

A very real and present fear crept in like a burglar in the night, silent, dark, dangerous. But she'd be hog-tied if she'd show it. Lightly, she tapped her fingertip against a sharp spire of the glass, piercing a pinhole prick in her skin. Slowly she licked off the resultant red drop without once glancing at Carky. "So, the truce is over, I take it?"

"Unless yer handin' me the man I want."

Her sole reply was a steely look.

Carky's jaw quivered for a moment, then hardened. "Ye know what I love about this grand city? The little urchins who'll do just about anythin' fer a crust o' bread. Shine yer shoes. Sweep yer way clean to cross a street." She dipped her chin, a bull about to charge. "Plant a bomb when no one's lookin'. Oh, what's that?" She craned her neck to look across the street and down a ways. "Could it be yer man is in danger, pet?"

Kit jerked her head to where Jackson stood, dread twisting her heart. He appeared whole and hale, newspapers in hand, angled for a good view of her—with a small keg a pace away, leaned up against the eel shop.

God, no!

Kit flew, chair banging to the ground behind her, sprinting as fast as her legs would pump. Dodging vendors. Skirting shoppers.

Instantly alert, Jackson pulled his gun. Women near him screamed, drowning out Kit's own mad cries.

She pulled up in front of him, panting, shaking, stabbing her finger towards the keg so wickedly close to his legs. "There's a bomb."

"What?"

She sucked in a breath and yelled, "A bomb!"

He wheeled about, then flapped his hand back at her. "Get out of here," he bellowed. "Get everyone out of the area!"

Kit snapped into action, flailing her arms like a crazed mother hen as she tore back and forth in front of the eel pie shop. "Move, people! Run to safety!"

More screaming. Some wailing. A few manly curses joined in as feet pounded and people scrambled. Kit shoved her head inside the pie shop, nearly choking on the fishy stink of brine and her own fear. "Everyone out! There's a bomb outside."

The bald man in an apron sullied with black and red smears shook a knife at her from behind the counter. "Ye can't go scarin' off my customers, missy!"

"This is no scare. This is real. Get out!"

The few women inside dropped their packages and scurried past her, shrieking all the way. Who knew if the owner left? Kit didn't stick around to find out.

She whipped back to Jackson, now crouched on the pavement. "I've done what I can. Let's go!"

"Get yourself out of here," he growled.

She retreated a few steps as commanded but then stopped. There was no way she could flee only to hear a horrific explosion split the air at her back. She couldn't live without this man, couldn't live with the knowledge she'd left him behind.

But what about Bella? Was it fair for her little lamb to grow up without a mother and a father? She gritted her teeth, fearing to stay, hating to leave.

Oh, God, what should I do? I cannot live without Jackson. You know this! But Bella. . .sweet, sweet Bella. Please, God, have mercy.

Jackson reached for the keg, and still she stood immobile. His fingers trembled, and he flexed them to still his jitters. She should run now. Get out of here far and fast.

But her heart stopped when he picked the thing up.

Bracing herself for an earth-shattering boom, she plugged her ears, face scrunching.

And—

Jackson pivoted, sweat dripping down his brow, relief on his face. Even so, he boomed at her with his very next breath. "Blast it, Kit! I told you to get out of here."

"I—never mind me! What of that bomb?" She tipped her head towards the keg now cradled in his arm.

Slowly he shook his head. "It's not real. It's only a distraction."

She whirled.

Sure enough, down the lane and across the road, Carky's chair was empty.

Chapter Nineteen

Horse hooves clattered sharp on the ear, an annoying accompaniment to the continual *skritch-skritch-skritch* of the seat springs as the cab bounced along. The combination was enough to drive a grown man to stop up his ears, but while Jackson acknowledged the noises, the clamour failed to grate on him as it usually did. He stared out the window at the foggy streets, gaslights lending an eerie glow at intervals in the darkness, trying desperately to ignore the dread lodged in his craw for what must take place this night. The day, with its faux bomb, had been stressful enough.

His gaze drifted back inside the carriage, skimming over the shadowy image of Bella chewing on the foot of a rag doll in her mother's lap and landing on Kit's face in the dim light. Judging by the grim set of his wife's jaw and her refusal to make eye contact, her belly was every bit as knotted up about the evening's imminent events—which grieved him to no end. He'd do anything to ease her pain.

But like a canker of the foot while on march, their only recourse was to chin up and suffer through it.

"Ay-oh!" the driver called, and the cab lurched to a stop. "'Ere we are then, guv'nor."

Jackson shoved open the door and alighted, taking a moment to sweep his gaze around the dark street in all directions. He even cast a glance at the rooftops before digging out a coin to plant in the jarvey's outstretched palm. Then he grabbed the travel satchel, set it on the ground, and held out both arms for Bella.

"Ba-ba!" Bella flung her little body against his.

"Pa-pa," he whispered in her ear before cradling her against one hip. Crooking his other arm, he offered his elbow to Kit to anchor herself until she landed on the pavement.

As soon as her feet touched ground, she straightened her skirts then reached for Bella. "I'll take her."

"No, I—" His voice broke, and he turned away. Too much emotion clogged his throat and likely played out on his face as well. These moments with his daughter were far too precious to so easily let her go. . .even to her mother. Clutching the sweet girl tightly to his side, he swiped up the satchel with his free hand and strode the few steps to bang on his father-in-law's door.

Graybone opened with a forbidding tilt to his head. Was everyone cursed to such angst on this foggy August eve?

Not trusting his voice quite yet, Jackson offered him a sharp nod.

Graybone craned his neck, surveilling up and down the street before opening the door wider and allowing them to pass. The instant they did, he slammed the thing shut and threw the bolt.

"Really, Father." Kit rolled her eyes. "Such dramatics. Do you think we would have attempted to approach your house if we had the slightest inkling Carky may have followed?"

He grunted as he buffed a light kiss to her cheek. "It always pays to be vigilant, Daughter."

Yet all his gruffness melted as he bent to poke a finger in Bella's belly and tickle her with his whiskers. "How's grandpa's girl?"

"Ba-ba!" She giggled.

Jackson's heart wrenched to see such tenderness softening the big man's face as he straightened. What a transformation the past two years had wrought in him. . .in all of them, truth be told.

Graybone rubbed his hands together. "Let's have at it, then, shall we?"

Jackson hung his hat on the coat-tree then followed his father-in-law and Kit into the parlour, where Mr. Coleman perched on the edge of the sofa like a nervous hen atop an egg. His fingers fluttered an uneasy rhythm on the cushions. Kit sat next to him, leaning over to lightly pat his shoulder. A valiant effort to put him at ease that did nothing to lessen his stiff posture.

"I am happy to see Carky has not yet found you, Mr. Coleman."

She winked then held out her arms for Bella. "Come to Mama, darling."

"I'm happy she hasn't found me either." Mr. Coleman's voice shook. Not surprising. He'd been through a lot.

With a last little squeeze of love for Bella, Jackson handed her over to Kit, then faced Mr. Coleman. "Which is another matter for us to discuss tonight. It's best we get you to safety. It won't be long before that woman tracks you here."

"Unless we eliminate her altogether by taking out her employer." Graybone whumped his big body into a chair near the hearth. "And I believe we are one step closer to that. I met with an informant today who was willing to talk as long as I greased the skids for his tongue to keep wagging."

Jackson lowered to an ottoman and stretched out his legs. "You know if we catch this criminal, I will see you fully reimbursed. Somehow, that is. Might take a bit of creative paperwork."

Graybone's bushy brows lowered to a thick line. "I hope I shall be reimbursed regardless. I am, after all, doing the job of one of your inspectors."

"You of all people know how short-staffed we are."

"What I know is that Hammerhead is the most tightfisted super-intendent on the face of the—"

"Boys!" Kit bounced Bella on her knee, fire in her eyes. "Blaming and budgets are not the purpose for tonight's discussion."

Jackson glanced from her back to Graybone. "She's right. How about you fill us in on what you discovered today?"

"Quite a lot, actually." His father-in-law laced his fingers over his belly. "Turns out our Mr. Blade had an opium addiction."

"I knew something wasn't right!" Mr. Coleman slapped his knee. "He'd lost a considerable amount of weight these past several months. Looked a bit yellow about the gills. I remarked on it several times, only to be reprimanded to mind my own business. Come to think of it, he grew progressively tetchy as well."

"Regardless," Jackson said, "there is nothing illegal about consuming opium."

"True, but. . ." Graybone strolled to the mantel and reached for the cigar box. Despite the shake of Kit's head, he retrieved one with a slight grin. "Don't fret, Daughter. I won't light it. Merely gives my hands something to do. Now, as I was saying"—he stabbed the cigar in the air towards Jackson—"purchasing opium from an unlicensed vendor is grounds to arrest the seller, and Mr. Bellow not only sells the drug without a permit but supposedly smuggles it in as well."

Jackson jerked up his head. "Bellow of Bellow's Glassworks?"

"One and the same."

Kit swiped up Bella's dolly from the rug where she'd thrown it and handed it to her. "Do you think Mr. Blade was involved in smuggling?"

"Good heavens!" Mr. Coleman cried. "What else was going on under my nose that I didn't know about?" He cast a worried gaze Jackson's way. "I won't be tied into this, will I? I swear I had no idea that the man was into such devilries."

"Don't worry, Mr. Coleman. All you need do is testify about the two ledgers." Jackson swiveled his head back to Graybone. "I'll have Baggett form a squad and shut down Bellow tomorrow."

"No." Once again Kit nabbed the dolly from the floor, Bella laughing at the game. "I don't think it's that simple. For one, we don't actually know if he was the man who hired Carky to assassinate Mr. Blade and Mr. Coleman, nor do we know if he is a solo operator or in league with a bigger fish. You shut him down and we may never discover the answer."

Graybone tromped back to his chair, rolling the cigar in his big fingers. "She's right again."

Blast it. Rubbing the back of his neck, Jackson circled the room. "We need reconnaissance. Someone on the inside to. . ." He stopped abruptly. "Frankie. No one would suspect a lad, and he's always up for an adventure."

"Bella, please!" Kit snatched the dolly once more from the floor—and apparently for the last time, judging by the tone of her voice. "Frankie's arm is still bandaged, and I doubt very much Martha will ever allow Frankie to set foot in that place again. I'm not convinced Frankie would wish to go, either."

Her father chuckled. "Your quick tongue could talk the two of them into it."

Jackson grinned as he resumed his seat on the ottoman. "This time your father is right."

"I am flattered at your confidence in me, gentlemen, but even if Martha and Frankie agree, that doesn't solve our problem of what to do with Mr. Coleman. Carky is still out there, and she won't give up looking for him."

Mr. Coleman tugged at his collar. "That is not a very hopeful prospect, Mrs. Forge."

"I wish I could offer you something better." She sighed.

This time when the dolly landed on the floor, Kit set Bella on the rug as well. For a moment, her little lip quivered, but then she started her own game of throwing the toy and scooting on her knees at high-speed after it.

The sight stabbed Jackson in the heart. Oh, how he'd miss the antics of this little one. . .which immediately kindled a rage deep in his belly. This whole affair wouldn't be settled quick enough for his liking.

"We can offer something better, Mr. Coleman." He flung out his arms. "We will get you somewhere safer, a place that is more fortified than a four-room flat with a handful of guns."

"Watch it, Forge," Graybone grumbled. "This is my home you're talking about."

"No offense intended, sir. Yet surely you must agree there are easier places to defend."

"Such as?" Kit scrambled after Bella before she crawled out the sitting room door. "Even the station didn't prove too hard for Carky to breach."

Oof. That truth smarted. As chief inspector, he needed to do something about station security—once his infernal paperwork was finished.

If it ever was.

Graybone waved his cigar at Coleman. "Seems to me we ultimately need to get Coleman here in the hands of the court so he can testify against Mr. Blade's embezzling scheme—which I suspect could be tied in with Bellow. So, if the court is our aim, then why not house him with a barrister? I know of one who's willing to take in high-risk witnesses, least he was that one time. . ." He went back to rolling the cigar in his fingers. "Quite the layout, though. Inner rooms. Armed guards."

Interesting. Usually barristers were puffed-up old shirts, unwilling to so much as share a breadcrumb let alone their home. Jackson cocked his head. "Who is it?"

"Barrister Muddlethorpe."

Muddlethorpe! Old soft lips? The squeaker? The timid titmouse rumoured to have once fainted dead away when approaching the bar? Jackson scrubbed his knuckles along his chin. "I never would have suspected."

"No one would, which is exactly why it will work." Graybone returned his cigar to the box. "As long as he agrees, that is."

"Excuse me, everyone." Mr. Coleman cleared his throat. "Not that I am ungrateful for the thought you are putting into moving me to a safer location, but therein lies a danger no one has yet mentioned. The move. What's to keep me safe while traveling from here to there?"

Jackson faced the man. "Though we may not look it at the moment, the three of us are a formidable foe with which to reckon, not to mention we shall have all the backing of the Old Jewry station."

Mr. Coleman narrowed his eyes. "Weren't you just complaining about staff shortages a moment ago?"

"Short-staffed or not"—Graybone slapped down the lid of the cigar box—"there are no finer officers in all of London."

Jackson's chest swelled at the praise. "Then we are agreed. We'll meet tomorrow to draw up a course of action—probably at the station, though. I don't think we ought to attract any further attention to this place by meeting here. Until then, Mr. Coleman, you're in good hands with my father-in-law, and I have no doubt he'll keep you well armed when he must leave you."

"I didn't say I agreed to the plan." Mr. Coleman rubbed his hands along his thighs, back and forth, his voice twitchy.

Kit frowned at him. "Have you a better plan in mind, sir?"

His lips pinched. "No."

Jackson stood. "Then with that, my family and I bid you gentlemen a good night." He tipped his head at Coleman and Graybone, then swung Bella—and her dolly—up into his arms. "Come along, Wife."

As Kit said her goodbyes, he strode from the room, whispering into Bella's ear as he went. "Papa."

"Ba-ba!" she squealed, then popped her thumb in her mouth as she laid her head against his shoulder.

He kissed her curly crown, her hair soft as dandelion fluff against his lips, then grabbed his hat and opened the door for his wife. When she was out of hearing range, a ragged sigh deflated him. As hard as it would be for them to get Coleman to the barrister's home, what he and Kit were about to do next would be even harder.

Hugging Bella tight, Kit laid her free hand on Jackson's arm, stopping him from pushing open the soup kitchen door. Not much light from the streetlamp stretched its arm this far away from the pavement, but the thin illumination was enough to see the anguish deepening a storm in his eyes.

"Is there no other way?" She already knew the answer, felt it like a lump of hardening plaster in her belly.

Jackson's jaw tensed. "Have you thought of any?"

"If I had, we wouldn't be standing here now." Which meant there was no other way, or perhaps motherhood had drained her to the dregs of her mental capabilities.

"I am sorry, my love." He ran his thumb over the curve of her cheek, his touch shivering along her skin with a distinct tremble. "I wish I could make this easier for you."

"I know." And though she said so, sweet heavens, how she wished she'd never have to experience the depth of this despair.

Jackson pushed open the door.

Kit hesitated, whispering all the love that threatened to choke her into Bella's ear. "Mama—" She swallowed, the world turning blurry. "Mama loves you, little one. Very much."

Strangling a sob, she followed the broad back of her husband into the soup kitchen, steeling herself for what lay ahead.

Inside, girls were busy sweeping, wiping, and stowing away pots from the evening meal. Martha stood tiptoe on a chair, shoving a crock onto the top shelf of a cupboard.

"Mrs. Kit!" Six-year-old Mary dropped her dustpan and plowed into her, wrapping her arms about her legs while peering up with sparkling blue eyes. "I bin waitin' all night fer ye to get 'ere. Bella gets to share me room!"

Despite the sorrow thick in her chest, Kit gave the girl a smile.

"You may not be so excited when you find out she babbles all hours."

"Ahh, there ye be. Mary, give 'em some space." Martha closed the cupboard door, and before she could hop to the floor, Jackson set down Bella's travel satchel and lent her a hand.

"Thank ye, Mr. Jackson." She dipped her head at Jackson then fired off a round of instructions to her girls. "'Tis clean enough now, ladies. Off with ye, save fer ye, Harriet, who can bide by the stairs a moment. Jane, see that Mary washes behind her ears. Alice, check on yer brother. Make sure he got little Hazel to bed 'stead o' lettin' her horseplay on the sofa till she dropped to pieces. Oh, and Anna, grab Bella's satchel there and no readin' till yer eyes are blurry, ye hear?"

"Yes, Mum," they said in unison, scampering off to do as she bid.

In one sweeping movement, Martha bent and gently tickled Bella's cheek. "Here now, how's my dandy girl? All ready to stay with yer Auntie May-may?" Straightening, she faced Kit, lips pinching with concern. "Though I s'pose yer not ready for it, aye?"

Flit! What an understatement. "Is a mother ever prepared to part with her child?" Leaving Bella in Martha's care during the day was one thing, but all night? And who knew how many nights until Carky was apprehended? Kit's belly cramped. This was so hard!

Jackson wrapped his arm around her shoulders. "It's only for a few days, Kit. Bella's safety is more important than the pain it causes us to leave her."

Kit leaned into him, squirmy baby and all, drawing from his strength. "I know. It's just. . .well." She peered up at him. "I know she'll be safer here than at our place, but I'd rather face a baited bear on the loose than not have our Bella with us."

The agony of agreement flashed in his eyes an instant before he closed them. His big hand rested lightly on Bella's head as he bowed his own. "God, we leave our little one in Your capable hands and those of Mrs. Jones. Bless this child, Lord. Bless this house. And may our efforts to save a man's life be swift and successful." Jackson's prayer rumbled to a stop.

Kit picked up where he left off. "Aye, God, keep watch over our little lamb." She pressed a kiss against Bella's head. "And should anyone try to harm our sweet Bella, may You unleash brimstone, hellfire, rounds from a twelve-pounder Armstrong or maybe a Nordenfelt gun, then—"

"Amen and pass me that child." Martha pulled Bella from her arms. "I think the good Lord gets the idea, luv."

"Ba-ba!" Bella nuzzled her face against Martha's chest then reached back to Kit.

Heart wrenching, Kit laid the rag doll on Bella's outstretched palm, whereupon the girl immediately stuffed the dolly's foot into her mouth. Kit pressed the back of her hand to her own lips, stifling a cry as Martha whisked her only daughter over to Harriet, who yet stood patiently at the bottom of the stairs.

Kit took a step towards them, but Jackson held her back with a firm grip to her arm just as the kitchen door flew open.

Charles Baggett trotted in, face flushed, hat askew. "Sorry I'm late. Dickens of a traffic jam over on Wentworth. Cart tipped. Quite the snarl."

"We've only just gotten here ourselves. Oh, Mrs. Jones," Jackson called across the room, "would you mind calling for Frankie? There's a matter we need to discuss before we leave you in the good care of Mr. Baggett."

"Ye heard the man, Harriet. Settle in Bella and send me yer brother." The moment she handed off Bella, she whirled with her fists on her hips. "What's the blighter done now?"

Jackson chuckled. "For once, nothing."

Pulling from Jackson's hold, Kit craned her neck to watch the last of Harriet's skirts swishing up the stairs. "Maybe I should tuck Bella in?"

"That will only make it harder, Wife." Bending, Jackson whispered, his breath warm in her ear, "Focus on the matter at hand. The sooner we solve this problem, the sooner we get back our girl."

Giving herself a last moment to wallow in misery, she embraced the hollow left behind where her heart once had been.

Then she tossed back her shoulders. Jackson was right. There was much to be done. Inhaling long and deep, she stored away all the tears pushing against her eyes for later.

"'Tis not much, Mr. Baggett, but I've set ye up a pallet o'er there behind the curtain." Martha pointed to a bed linen hung on a line in one corner of the big kitchen. "Set down yer load then join us in the dinin' room. I've laid by a bite o' cake fer us all."

"Cake? Oh boy!" Frankie, arm swathed in a cloth bandage, jumped down the last two stairs and dashed past everyone.

A small smile tugged Kit's lips as Martha collared the lad. How thoughtful of the woman to have prepared a sweet treat for them when she was the one being put out to take on another child. Not to mention having a man underfoot in the kitchen. Then again, judging by the fire in Martha's cheeks whenever Charles caught her glance, having him around would be no trouble whatsoever.

They settled in the dining room, Martha already cutting slices of pound cake. She passed around the plates, making sure the one with the largest slab landed in front of Charles.

"Hey!" Frankie scowled. "Why did Mr. Baggett get the biggest—"

"Hush yer mouth." Martha aimed the knife at him. "Mr. Jackson's to do the talkin', not ye."

Jackson exchanged a glance with Kit, and when she nodded, he began. "I suspect my wife will have a fair amount to say as well, but yes, there is a matter we wish to discuss. It was recently brought to our attention that the man who was murdered, Mr. Blade, had an opium addiction, one that was fed by your employer, Frankie."

"Caw!" The boy's eyes widened, the whites stark in the glow of lamplight. "Mr. Bellow?"

"One and the same." Kit swallowed a requisite bite of Martha's cake. Oh, it tasted fine enough, but her appetite had fled for missing Bella. "You weren't there very long, but did you notice any unusual activity at the glassworks?"

One of his thin shoulders shrugged as he shoveled in a huge mouthful. "Din't notice no runners." Crumbs flew out his mouth.

Martha cuffed him on the head. "Mind yer manners, boy."

Charles shifted in his chair. "It seemed on the up and up when I was there, albeit a chancy hellhole to toil in ten hours a day. Do you think Bellow is personally involved, or is someone else running an operation from the facility behind his back?"

Having made short work of his cake, Jackson set down his fork. Men. Apparently his appetite wasn't connected to his emotions. "Graybone's got an informant pegging Bellow specifically. And if he's selling opium, no doubt he's storing it."

"Mebbe." Frankie held out his empty plate to Martha, who shook her head. He set it down with a frown. "There were one building I weren't allowed in. Which o' course got me to itchin' 'bout it. I tried to get me a look-see, but a great jollocks of a coal shuffler shooed me off. Said if I tried pokin' 'round there again, he'd feed me to the fires."

"Beast!" Martha rapped her fist on the table "I'd like to give that bully a piece o' my mind!"

"The thing is," Jackson said, "we won't really know exactly what or all that Mr. Bellow is involved in unless we get eyes inside his glassworks."

"Tha's easy enough." Frankie jutted his jaw. "I can talk my way back in."

Martha cut her boy an evil eye. "Don't be daft. I'll not let ye risk gettin' burnt any more than ye already are."

"I'm afraid I agree with your mother," Charles rumbled. "You've taken a big enough hit with your injury as is."

Defeat mopped up what sweetness was left in Kit's mouth. If Frankie didn't sniff out any information, then who would? She leaned forward, planting both elbows on the scarred wood. "This is the best lead we have, and if it shakes out, we could land a far bigger quarry than an opium addict and an assassin for hire. If we discover who Mr. Bellow is working for or with, we just may be lifting a huge rock off lots of creepy crawlies that ought to be crushed. And the sooner we make a move, the sooner the threat of Carky harming us—or Bella—will be ended."

Martha angled her head. "So ye're saying if my boy goes nosin' about, ye could stop a smugglin' ring and slap away the danger hanging o'er all yer heads?"

"That's right."

"Then send me." Charles swept his hand towards Frankie. "I'll throw on a disguise and Bellow will never know we've met before."

Jackson shook his head. "Valiant of you, but I'm afraid not. We need you here on the off chance Carky makes a strike against Bella."

"Then you go." Charles stabbed his finger at Jackson.

Kit started stacking the empty plates, placing hers on top. "Jackson and I are tied up with moving Mr. Coleman in an effort to draw out Carky." Which was a dangerous proposition, but at least she and Jackson worked well together. Still, the chance of leaving Bella orphaned nagged at her. Once this caper was over, never again would she choose a case that involved both her and Jackson.

"It's a'right, Mr. Baggett, Mum." Frankie glanced from one to the other. "Miss Kit trained me real good. And now I know better than to bump into the wrong end o' a blowpipe."

Martha pressed her lips tight, her blue eyes searching out Charles'. Why they didn't just marry was beyond her, for clearly they were already of one accord.

"I don't like it," Martha said at length, then wagged her finger at her boy. "But see that ye keep away from that coal heaver, and don't ye dare take another tumble into anythin' hot."

"Kipes, Mum! I won't be doin' any such thing. Learned me lesson, I did."

"Then it is settled." Jackson pushed back his chair. "The moment you find out something—anything at all—you report to me. Understood?"

"Aye, sir." Frankie nodded solemnly.

"Thank you, Frankie." Kit smiled at the lad—the youngest member of her crew back in the day—then reached across the table to pat Martha's hand. "And you, Martha. I could not find a truer friend."

"Bish bosh." She fluttered her fingers in the air as she rose. "Now, if ye'll excuse me, I'd best tend to yer wee one. Like as not she'll be wantin' the milk I got warmin' on the range. Step sharp, Frankie. I won't have ye sleepy eyed if ye're to set foot in that factory in the morn. G'night to ye all. Mr. Baggett, ye'll find a plate o' bread and cheese on the counter should ye need anythin' more a'fore breakfast."

Charles dipped his head. "Thank you, Mrs. Jones."

"And thanks to you as well, Baggett." Jackson slapped the man on the back. "Though I doubt I shall sleep this night, it will not be for worrying about the safety of my little girl."

"Indeed." Kit squeezed Charles' arm. "God bless you."

"The two of you would do the same for me if I had need. Don't worry. I'll keep everyone under this roof safe, so sleep soundly—as soundly as you can, that is."

Jackson ushered her out, and once the cool air of night hit her cheeks, Kit wrapped her arms tight around her middle to give herself something to hold, for she ought to be cuddling her little girl right now. . .and it was all because of Carky she wasn't.

Blast the woman!

Kit stomped ahead of Jackson, ignoring his "Hey! Hold up!" She'd use all this sorrow, this grief, this emptiness, to fuel her rage at a woman who never should have messed with her. Carky had better watch her back.

Because Kit was out for blood.

Chapter Twenty

Jackson strode the pavement leading up to the station, Kit at his side, the early morning air around them crackling with a sense of purpose. Dark clouds scudded overhead, matching his mood. A storm would soon break—and he welcomed it.

He cut Kit a sideways glance. "How are you holding up?"

She peered at him, hat askew, hair trailing down her back. "Judging by the bags under your eyes, about the same as you."

True. Neither of them had slept, not with Bella's empty crib staring them in the face all night. Wrapping his arm about her shoulder, he gave her a little squeeze. "If all goes well, we'll have Bella back by tomorrow. I promise." He tipped his head down the block. "There is your father now. This will all be over soon, and life will be back to normal. Well, at least as normal as it can be with you." He winked.

She kicked him in the shin with her heel.

"Daughter. Jackson." Graybone nodded as he drew close.

"Good morning, Father." Rising to her toes, Kit brushed a light kiss to his whiskery cheek.

Jackson trotted up the station stairs and held open the door. "I wager you thought you'd seen the last of this place when you retired in April."

"Indeed." His father-in-law paused on the top step. "It seems you can take the man out of the station, but the station never quite lets go of the man."

"You mean I'm doomed?"

"From the day you crossed that threshold as a rookie constable, my boy." Graybone sailed inside.

Kit hooked her arm through Jackson's. "Well I, for one, am happy you did so, else we'd never have met."

"That was a fateful day, was it not?" He gazed down at his wife's lovely face, and the spark in her eyes sent a charge through him like it always did. One day such feelings might wear off, yet until then, he'd cherish every moment of reveling in her affection. He sighed. "But for now, we have work to do. After you, Wife."

He followed her inside the busy station, dodging constables and civilians alike as he and Kit caught up to his father-in-law at the front counter, chatting with Smitty.

"Not the same without ye, Sarge, and that's God's truth." Smitty slapped the counter.

Jackson narrowed his eyes. "Have you any complaints, man?"

Smitty glanced away from Graybone, his eyes widening as they landed on Jackson. "Em— Er— Why, none a'tall, Chief. I were jes' ramblin'."

"Perhaps you need more work? Because if that is the case, I'll be happy to fill your time."

"No, no. Nothin' o' the sort, sir."

"Well then, carry on." Jackson gave him a sharp nod.

Graybone chuckled as they strode towards the stairs. "I can hardly believe you're the same green recruit who stumbled in here a few years ago."

In truth, he could hardly believe it himself, especially every morning when he woke up next to a woman he still could scarce imagine was his.

Several more greetings and cuffs on Graybone's back followed them all the way up to Jackson's office, where he opened the door.

And all three of them gaped.

Papers were everywhere. The floor. The cabinets. The bookshelves. The desk. Hounds and heather! There were even papers balanced atop the windowsills, and Lord knows how it was managed, but a few dangled at intervals from the ceiling along one entire wall. In the midst of this great blizzard of documents sat a rotund toad of a man, back towards them, sweat stains bleeding damp and dark the length of his spine and hanging like black crescents from his armpits.

"What the blazes?" Graybone grumbled.

Kit eyed Jackson, a twist to her lips. "I love what you've done with the decor in here. Early-century hand grenade, is it?"

Jackson seethed, gut bubbling. "Mr. Harvey." He ground out the name like a mouthful of nails. "What have you done?"

Harvey craned his head over his shoulder, and when it registered just who had entered, he rose with a smile. "Why, good morning, Chief Inspector. You should be happy to know the wheels of progress are turning very nicely in here."

"Progress in what?" Kit whispered in Jackson's ear. "A slapdash mess?"

He shook his head, lungs deflating. "I don't have the time or energy to waste dealing with this chaos."

And like the flipping of a great switch, all the anger he desperately wished to keep a lid on could be contained no more. He raised his voice to the rafters. "Clean this up and be quick about it!"

Harvey's big eyes blinked behind his spectacles, yet other than that, the man stood there completely nonplussed. "Absolutely, sir. That is exactly what I am about."

"See that you are! Immediately and impeccably. I need my office in order, not in a shambles, man! And if you fail to comply this instant, I shall—"

A big hand landed on his shoulder, the deep voice of Graybone rumbling in his ear. "We've a bigger fish to fry than this gudgeon. You can fillet the fellow later."

Though fury still prickled like a rash, Jackson sucked in a few calming breaths. His father-in-law was unfortunately right.

"Carry on, Harvey." Jackson aimed a finger at him. "But mind you heed my words."

"Oh, indubitably, sir. Shouldn't be a problem whatsoever. As I said"—the round man rose to his toes—"the wheels are turning quite smoothly now."

Clamping his mouth against a rather unsavoury oath, Jackson ushered out Kit and Graybone before closing the door.

The second they were in the corridor, Kit opened her mouth, mischief flashing in her eyes.

Jackson shot up his hand. "Don't even think about saying another word on this matter." He stalked towards the stairs. "Since my office is occupied, we'll take the interview room."

Graybone suffered a few more good-natured fists to the arm along with several gruff "Bully to see ye" comments as they made their way to a small room at the end of the passageway. Once Kit and Graybone grabbed the only available chairs, Jackson ducked his head back out the door and hollered down the passage, "Smitty! Another chair, please."

"Righto, Chief."

Until the man could comply, Jackson leaned his back against a wall and folded his arms across his chest. "To the matter at hand, as I see it, we've got several issues to deal with. What route to take in moving Coleman, how to keep him safe while doing so, how to let Carky know in order to lure her to strike on our terms, and lastly, what role we each play in this undertaking."

"Agreed. . .mostly." Kit removed her hat and began repinning her loose hair, mumbling a bit as she stored some hairpins between her lips. "Clueing in Carky isn't an issue at all. A few well-placed words in the right ear and half of London will know within an hour. And"—hair recoiled, she pulled the last pin from her mouth and poked it into the mass—"I know just the ear to get the job done. One of my old contacts, Skivvy McGrueder. Loosest lips in town."

"Good. Now, to keep Coleman safe." Graybone planted his big palms on the tabletop. "I propose we plan three routes, one for transporting Coleman and the other two as decoys. If Carky strikes one of the fakes, she'll get a rude surprise from some armed constables. If she targets the real carriage, the three of us ought to manage the woman very nicely."

Jackson shook his head. "You forget we are short-staffed. I'm not certain Sergeant Doyle can part with enough men to fill two carriages."

"How about a few constables and some of my old crew?" Kit reset her hat.

"That should do it." Jackson nodded. "Now, for routes. I'm thinking one decoy could wind through the busy streets of the West End, maybe pass through Piccadilly Circus or Oxford and Regent Street."

Graybone grunted. "Too many civilians."

"But that's the beauty of it." Kit cut her hand through the air. "Carky won't waste her time on anything other than a direct attack on her prey."

"What about the bomb she planted by my leg? Oh, thank you, Smitty." Jackson grabbed the chair from the clerk's hand then closed the door and sat, facing Kit. "That explosive would've taken out innocent bystanders."

"It was fake, remember?" One of Kit's slim shoulders shrugged. "Her aim is true, and right now she's after Coleman or anyone that's attached to me in order to force my hand."

And that, right there, lodged under Jackson's skin like splinters. God help the woman if she moved against Bella or Kit.

Kit folded her arms. "I think it best if we split up. Divide and conquer, so to speak. Other than Mr. Coleman, there's no better decoy than me to tempt Carky."

Jackson eyed her. What was the little sphinx up to? Whatever, he'd have none of it. "No. Our best chance is to stick together, deliver Coleman as a threesome."

"If that's the case. . ." Graybone scratched his jaw, fingernails rasping against his beard. "As for the second decoy, send it through the financial district, say Lombard Street to Cannon, then on to Queen Victoria Street. With all the traffic around there, she'll have a hard enough time just keeping an eye on the thing."

Jackson pictured the route in his mind's eye. "Excellent," he murmured, then louder, "And I propose Coleman's carriage—ours, if you will—take a more direct route on quieter streets. I think Eaton Place to Cadogan then on to Wilton Crescent ought to do very nicely. Passes through areas of higher police presence as well."

Kit smiled. "So, there we have it, gentlemen. You know, you both would've been fine members of my crew back in the day." She waggled her eyebrows. "I'll take the afternoon to surveil the area around Barrister Muddlethorpe's home, see if there are any possible breaches of security and such."

"I'll go with you, Daughter." Graybone pushed back his chair. "I am to meet with the man and let him know of our discussion here this morning."

"And I'll pull together the needed men and carriages. If all goes well, we can make our move tomorrow morning." Jackson rose.

Kit's grin grew. "Then I think we have a solid plan."

"The plan may be solid, but Carky's intentions and potential accomplices are an unknown. And. . ." Jackson scrubbed his face, desperately trying to identify the root of why his gut suddenly clenched. There was no reason. They were on the offense, taking Carky on their own terms, but still. . .

"And what?" Graybone prodded.

He dropped his hand. "I don't know. I just have a feeling that even if we are successful—and I pray God we are—that somehow, this is only the beginning. And while I hope I am wrong, the stakes may be much higher than we realize."

This was far more torture than he ever imagined. Charles punched his pillow and flipped over on the pallet, blankets smelling of the savoury stew from dinner that yet permeated the air—and it'd been several hours since that had been served. Still, he couldn't escape the delicious scent any more than he could escape the maddening thought of Martha. Was she even now laying her head against her pillow? Or was she sipping some tea by lamplight, curled up in a chair, her hair loose and cascading over her shapely shoulders?

He threw off his bedcover and shot to his feet. Hastily, he shoved his legs into his trousers and tucked in his wrinkled shirt, then grabbed his waistcoat and shrugged it on. Two nights beneath the same roof as Martha and he could barely think straight! Yanking back the curtain, he stomped into the kitchen proper and paced in front of the range. At the most unexpected times, Jackson's words whacked him over the head.

"Pursue love instead of dwelling in past failure."

It'd been easy enough to shove that thought aside during the day when he'd been so concentrated on protecting Martha and the children, but now in the dark, in the quiet, there was no escape. And he couldn't afford to suffer a lapse of attention. No, if he truly wished to protect Martha, he needed to speak with her and do it now while the children were a'bed and the doors were locked against invaders. He'd pushed away God's good gift of this woman long enough. It was more than time to man up and take another chance on love.

He strode to the stairwell leading to her flat, took the steps two at a time, then stopped dead cold in front of the door. Life would never be the same once he bared his heart to this woman. Could he do this? *Should* he do this? Yet he wouldn't be able to focus until he did. For the safeguard of all—even if it resulted in his heart being trampled—he had to do this.

He raised his hand, knuckles hard as steel, then paused just before flesh met wood. What if she were already asleep and he woke her? No doubt she'd be cross and rightly so, especially if he woke the children as well. Perhaps he ought to give it a fresh try again in the morning instead.

"Pursue love."

Blast that Jackson! Charles let out a long breath then rapped on the door.

Moments later, it swung open. Martha held an oil lamp in her hand, the warm glow bathing her face. She'd shed her work apron and gown for a simple, breezy white cotton blouse and grey skirt. Not the garb of a fine lady, but no finer woman walked the face of this earth. And that dark golden braid cascading loosely over her shoulder just begged to be undone.

He tugged at his collar, suddenly finding it hard to breathe.

"Mr. Baggett?" The warmth of her smile and hint of confusion in her gaze was unutterably charming.

He ought to answer now. Speak his piece and be on his way. But every last word fled like criminals in a dark alley.

She tipped her head, studying him. "What can I do for ye? Another blanket? A bite to eat? Maybe a mug o' small beer?"

How like her to think of serving him when she'd clearly already prepared to retire for the evening. Though he'd not thought it possible, his admiration for her grew.

He cleared his throat. "No thank you, Mrs. Jones. Rather I would have a few words with you, unless, of course, you'd rather we speak in the morning."

"La! I'd not be able to sleep a wink with wonderin' what ye've got on yer mind." She stepped aside. "Come in."

Woefully aware of his state of undress—why had he not grabbed his suit coat?—he made quick work of the buttons on his waistcoat as he strode past her. His fingers stalled, however, when he met the glower of Martha's oldest daughter, Harriet, eyeing him from the chair where she sat with needlework in hand.

"Off to bed with ye now, Harriet." Martha waved her away. "And mind ye don't sleep with sich a fouly-frackas on yer face or ye'll wake with a permanent scowl."

Despite the warning, the girl's brow didn't unpucker a whit as she tucked her sewing into a basket and approached her mother. "Do you really think it wise to allow a man in our flat?" To her credit, Harriet kept her voice to a whisper—though he could still make out the words over the ticking of the clock.

"Mr. Baggett is here for our protection, child. Besides, 'tis not yer place to naysay me."

It wasn't, but was it his place to admit he'd overheard? Would the girl not be mortified if he said anything? Still, it was to her credit she cared for her mother, a woman she'd seen wronged by other men.

"Harriet." He took a single step towards the women. "Your mother speaks truth. I mean to defend her and all of you, nothing more. Nothing less. There is no need for you to fret."

Harriet pinched her lips shut, eyes wary despite his words.

"Ye heard the man, girl. Now go." Martha gave her a gentle push, then turned to him. "Have a seat Mr. Baggett. Will ye take a cup of tea as well?"

"No, thank you. It's probably best I say what I must without anything breakable in my hands." He sank onto the sofa.

Martha bit her lip as she perched on the other end of the sofa. "Is there a problem, then? Have I or the girls angered ye in any way? Ach!" Her eyes narrowed. "'Tis Frankie, aye? What's the boy done now?"

"No, it's none of those things. It's. . .well. . ." He ran his hand along his thigh. Over and over. This was turning out to be harder than facing a band of drunk bricklayers bent on some knuckle bruising.

And still the clock ticked.

Leaning aside, Martha pressed her hand atop his, stopping his nervous movement. "Yer givin' me a fright. What ails ye, Mr. Baggett?"

"That's exactly what ails me! *Mr. Baggett.*" Unbidden, his gaze shot to her mouth. He'd pay a queen's ransom to hear his Christian name from her lips. Would to God she'd someday allow such an intimacy.

But for now, all her lips did was quirk in bewilderment. "But tha's yer name, ain't it?"

"Yes, it is. Yes, of course." Curse it! He sounded like a blathering idiot. Rising, he rubbed the back of his neck. He'd never felt this mud-fuddled when he'd been with Edwina. Then again, he'd never experienced such strong passions with her as he did when in the presence of Martha. Could it be. . . ?

Had he never truly loved Edwina?

Now that was a stunning thought.

"Mr. Baggett, yer as agitated as a landed mackerel. Ye sure yer well?"

"No, I am most certainly not." He dropped back to the sofa with a sigh, irritated at his schoolboy antics, annoyed by the incessant ticking of the wretched clock, disgusted at his lack of courage. Was he a man or a sissy-footed dandy afraid of his own shadow? Enough of this!

Squaring his shoulders, he gathered Martha's hands in his. "Mrs. Jones, if you would allow it, I would be more to you than simply Mr. Baggett."

Her eyes widened. "Such as?"

"The thing is I. . .I cannot get you out of my mind. As I go to sleep, I think of you. When I wake, you are my first thought. You, Martha Jones, are with me every breath of every day. And I find I can no longer go on pretending otherwise. In short, I love you and—" Still clutching her hands, he slid off the sofa and dropped to one knee. "I would be the most honoured man in all of England if you would—"

He cocked his head, listening hard.

"If I would. . . ?" She squeezed his hands, hope brilliant in her eyes.

But the blasted ticking, ticking, ticking!

"Did you happen to get a new clock?" He glanced around.

"I beg your pardon, Mr. Baggett?"

Not a clock in sight. None on the walls. Nothing on the mantel. *Tick. Tick. Tick.*

Untwining his fingers from Martha's, he dropped to the floor and peered beneath the couch.

And his heart quit beating altogether.

"Get out!" He rocketed to his feet, pulling Martha up with him and giving her the same push she'd only moments ago nudged Harriet with.

"Get the children out immediately and hie yourself to safety. Now. Go!"

She whirled, fists on her hips. "Mr. Baggett! What is it? What is wrong?"

"There is a bomb under your sofa, Mrs. Jones."

Chapter Twenty-One

Charles' hands shook as he dropped to the floor and peered under the sofa at the bomb. This was it. The stuff of legends. The inspector who saved the day by rescuing the fair damsel and the children.

Unless they all went up in flames.

Shoving the mad thoughts aside, he forced a steadiness to his hands that he most certainly didn't feel and reached for the shoebox-sized container sitting in the shadows.

Tick. Tick. Tick. Tick.

Sweat trickled down his temples as his fingers met metal.

Behind him all sorts of mayhem broke out. Shrieks. Cries. Frankie shouting for a look at the thing. Above it all Martha's steady voice shooing them out the door. Oh God, they had to get out that door!

Please, Lord, speed them on their way. Protect Martha and the children, and give me wisdom to disarm this explosive.

Once the metal box cleared the sofa, he carefully lifted the lid with one finger.

Tick. Tick. Tick. Tick.

Inside was a bundle of dynamite, some wires, the detonator, and a clock mechanism—its long hand clicking ever onward to meet with the shorter. Two minutes remained. A mere 120 seconds separated them all from eternity.

He clenched his jaw. Which wire to clip first? It was a one in three shot. Think. *Think!* He'd been trained for this, but years ago, and he'd never actually had to put that knowledge to use.

Until now.

He edged over to the sewing basket and pulled out a pair of shears, then crawled back to the weapon. Sweat stung his eyes.

Tick. Tick. Tick. Tick.

The sound was louder now than the last of the feet racing down the stairs.

Filling his lungs until his ribs ached, Charles leaned over the bomb and traced the wires with his eyes. The first one appeared to be attached to the timing mechanism. Hopefully. Ever so gently, he eased the blades of the shears to catch the wire. Too fast and he could cause a spark, then all would be over. Slight pressure. More.

Clip.

Nothing.

He whooshed out a breath. Seventy-five seconds to go.

Next the blasting cap. A small metal cylinder, hardly larger than a pea. God only knew what Carky—for surely she was the evil brain behind this job—had used for material inside, but most likely gunpowder. Two wires ran from it. Fifty-fifty odds. Fair enough when gambling, but now? His shirt stuck to his sweaty back like a second skin.

Tick. Tick. Tick. Tick.

The shears shook violently. Slow as a rheumy old man, he eased the blades to the wire on the left. If he triggered the charge, the game would end.

He hesitated a moment more.

Steeled himself to meet his Maker.

Then at the last minute switched the blades to the other wire and gripped the handles tight.

Nip.

Nothing happened save for the incessant ticking. Praise be! One more wire to go, and only twenty seconds to take care of it. Still, a single hasty move now could still blow his head off.

Holding his breath, he slid the blades to the last remaining wire. The shears jiggled slightly against the dynamite. Enough to set the thing off?

Tick. Tick. Tick. Tick.

Sweat dripped down his forehead, stinging his eyes. The world blurred. He swiped his free hand across his eyes, flicking away the perspiration. It was now or never.

Slice.

No explosion, but the clock kept ticking.

Strangling the timing mechanism with his fingers, he eased the hair-raising annoyance away from the dynamite then slammed it against the wall. Before the pieces hit the floorboards, he collapsed back to his haunches, heaving for air, and closed his eyes.

Thank You, merciful God. Thank You.

"Is it over?" a voice shivered behind him.

He jumped to his feet and wheeled about.

And then his blood really did drain to his boots.

Martha stood just past the threshold, face phantom pale.

"What the deuce are you doing here?" he exploded, the words booming. "I told you to leave!"

Though her skirt quivered, she jutted her jaw defiantly. "I did as you asked. I got the children to safety across the street to Mrs. Henny's. Then I came back."

"Yes, I can blasted well see that." He flailed his arms, a churlish response, yet one he could no more stop than the setting of the sun. Sweet heavenly mercy! If he'd have clipped the wrong wire, he'd have sent her to eternity. "Why the blazes did you do such a thing? You could have been killed! Did you even think about that?"

"I'm not daft, Mr. Baggett." Her nostrils flared, yet he noted she avoided making eye contact with the bundle of defused dynamite on the floor. "I very well knew the consequences."

He raked his fingers through his hair. Women! Who could understand them? "Explain it to me, for I cannot begin to comprehend why you would take such a foolish risk."

"Can ye not?" Grabbing handfuls of her skirt, she approached him. "I couldn't jes leave ye here alone."

"But that is exactly what you should have done!"

She didn't so much as flinch at his outburst. On the contrary, she rested her fingers lightly on his sleeve, her scent of warm bread and all that was good in this life so heady his fury began to fade.

"All right, Mr. Baggett," she said softly. "The truth is I couldn't bear the thought of not knowing if ye'd live or die, because. . .well, because

I love ye. Ye hear?" Tipping up her face, she stared boldly into his eyes. "I love ye more than any man I've ever known."

A club to the head couldn't have stunned him more. "But. . .you've been married before. What of your former husband?"

"Flit." She pulled her hand from his arm and shoved back her long braid. "I were a namby-headed dolt, scarce but thirteen years when my father fairly sold me to the man. It weren't fer love I wed, that's fer certain. It were for survival."

Thirteen! He gritted his teeth. No girl should have to suffer such an indecency, but knowing this one had—this beautiful, stalwart woman. . . Bile rose to his throat just thinking of the violations she'd suffered. He reached out tentatively, and with his finger, he dared to sweep away a strand of hair dangling on her brow. "It grieves me to hear how sorely you were treated. Even so, you are a strong one, Martha Jones."

"No, not really." Sudden tears shimmered in her eyes. "I were close to bucklin' watchin' ye take that wicked bomb apart."

He nearly dropped to his own knees thinking of her standing silently at the door as he held both of their lives in his hands. She hadn't cried. She hadn't whimpered. She'd merely been there for him. . .been there *with* him.

Cupping her face, he drew close, his heart thudding so loudly that half of London could hear it. "You, my love, are the bravest woman I know, and I would be the most honoured man in all of England if you would agree to be my wife."

Her lips parted, and his entire future hinged on what words may pass.

"On one condition," she murmured.

Not what he'd expected, yet fair enough. This was no untried maiden but a woman who knew her own mind.

"Very well." He pulled back, suddenly hesitant to hear what she might say. "What are your terms?"

"That ye promise to never again ask me to leave yer side."

Saints above! *That* was her only concern?

"Oh, love, I never want you to leave my side. . .unless, of course, there's a bomb involved." He winked.

"But—"

He pressed a finger to her lips. "Don't you see, Martha? I could never willingly put you in harm's way, for you are too precious to me. But I promise you this." He traced the curve of her mouth then slid his whole hand to encompass the back of her head. "I shall love you solely, fiercely, madly, till the day I die, and may God grant our years be many and long. Does that satisfy?"

For a moment she said nothing, her eyes flashing with a mystery only God could understand.

And then her mouth landed firm and warm against his. "Does this satisfy?" she whispered, then kissed him again.

A million sparks burst into flame, heating his chest, his heart, burning all caution up in smoke. Like a starving man, he pulled her to him, body to body, breath to breath. Why had he waited so long for this? She *was* his! She always had been. He knew that now, tasted it on her lips, felt it in the wild beating of their mingled hearts. Sure, he'd kissed before, but Lord have mercy, never like this.

"Charles," she whispered as his mouth trailed down her neck.

"Say it again." His lips moved against the throbbing pulse just beneath her skin. "Say my name and never stop saying it."

"Charles." She moaned. "Oh, Charles."

The willingness in her voice sent a tremor through him from head to toe. Saints above, he wanted her! And miracle of miracles, she wanted him right back.

But not yet. Not like this. Not until they were man and wife.

Pulling away, he rested his brow against hers. "I take it that's a yes?"

"Aye." She grinned. "Most assuredly."

"Good. Then I suppose we shall talk of gowns and cakes and all manner of wedding trifles, but for now—" He stepped away and offered his arm. "I think it best to get you and the children to some place more secure than Mrs. Henny's."

Wrapping her fingers around his sleeve, she peered up at him. "Where will we go?"

Now there was a great gaping hole of a question. They obviously couldn't stay here. He still had dynamite to dispose of! He blew out a long breath. Neither could he deposit this crew on Jackson's doorstep, for his friend had been the one to entrust the care of his daughter to him. There was always the station, but no. That was certainly no place for children. The church? Again, a cold pew would induce no sleep, especially for a baby. Really, there was nothing to be done save for hastening them away to the only other place he could think of. Oh, what a long and sleepless night this would be.

He patted Martha's hand as he led her to the door, hardly believing what he was about to say.

"You and the children are coming home with me."

It had been another sleepless night. A real rip-roaring tug-of-war with the sheets. And now, standing in Graybone's sitting room, the sun hardly a wood shaving above the horizon, Jackson let loose an enormous yawn—and didn't care a fig that Graybone cast him an evil eye for it.

"Are we boring you, Forge?" His father-in-law grunted as he worked to shove Mr. Coleman's arm through the bulky leather body armour. "Come on, Coleman! At least try to put this on."

"Indeed, Mr. Coleman." Opposite her father, Kit coaxed the fellow's other arm into the throat of another sleeve. "You're not making this easy."

"It's too tight! I fail to see how this wadding will help. I'll be a fat duck unable to move. Ow!" Coleman wriggled like a hare on a spit, knocking Kit backwards. "That's my sore arm!"

Jackson lunged, grabbing hold of his wife's wrist before she smacked into the side table. "Watch it, Coleman. That's my wife you're knocking about."

"And my daughter," Graybone rumbled. "Come on, man! Buck up. It's either this or we'll stuff you beneath the carriage seat. And trust me, that hole will be far more constricting than this. Now, let's give this another go, and no more whining about it."

Jackson tugged Kit aside, giving the men a wide berth. "Your father's got this under control. How about you—"

The front bell rang.

"—wait here." Releasing his hold, Jackson strode to the front hall, hand covering his sidearm in case for some odd reason Carky took a perverse thrill in ringing before killing.

But it was only a lad on the other side, holding out an envelope. "I were told to deliver this, sir."

"And so you have." Jackson fished out a coin in exchange for the missive with his name scrawled on the front. "Thank you."

"What is it?" Kit asked before he shut the front door.

"I'm about to find out." He shook open the folded paper, turning so he alone could read it.

> *Change of plans. Martha et al are at my flat. Details*
> *when you come to pick up your package.*
>
> ~ *Baggett*

His gut twisted. His friend would never have chanced moving the children and Martha unless there had been a dire need. Rage fired along every nerve. If Carky had made a swipe against Bella, so help him, he'd personally wring the woman's—

"What is it? What does it say?" Kit's big blue eyes drilled into him.

He shoved the paper into his pocket. If Kit got wind of this, there'd be no stopping her from tearing out of here and hunting down Carky in cold blood. He forced a smile and pleasant tone, neither of which he felt. "Nothing to concern you, love."

Her eyes narrowed to slits. "There's more to it than that, I think."

Dogged woman! Tipping her face, he kissed her on the nose. "Truly, just some business I must attend when we are finished delivering Coleman. Speaking of which, let's see if your father has wrangled the man into the armour."

He tromped past her, and thankfully the next several minutes of gearing themselves up with weapons and cautiously leading Coleman to the waiting carriage derailed any further questions on the matter.

Coleman paused by the carriage door. "I apologize for grousing about the armour. I know you're trying to protect me, and I appreciate it. Thank you." Coleman shoved out his hand to shake Jackson's yet managed to make a muddle of that as well, for their fingers collided awkwardly.

Kit smirked.

Graybone rolled his eyes.

Jackson switched hands, adjusting for the fellow's left-hand dominance. "You are very welcome, Mr. Coleman, but let's get you into the carriage now."

The second that Coleman was safely wedged next to Graybone—the windows on their side of the carriage tightly shuttered—Jackson took the opposite seat alongside Kit and pulled out his pocket watch. Two minutes to spare. So, they sat.

And sat.

Then sat some more.

"Should we not be on the move?" Sweat dripped down Mr. Coleman's brow. "Are we in trouble already?"

"Calm yer giblets, man." Graybone shifted, rocking the whole carriage. "If there's trouble, you won't have to ask about it."

"My husband is waiting for the appropriate time, Mr. Coleman," Kit soothed. "The route is planned so that all three carriages—ours and the decoys—begin at the exact same moment."

"Which is just. . .about. . ." Jackson rapped on the wall. "Drive on!"

Up in the driver's seat, Constable Quincy immediately roused the horses into a lively trot. They were in good hands with Quincy, for he'd proven himself time and again as the best offensive coach driver of all the squad. Lord knows how many times he'd guided the Black Maria through a riotous crowd with a wagonful of criminals.

Even so, Jackson lifted a prayer. They'd need more than Quincy's skill to get Coleman safely to the barrister's house. Kit exchanged a sideways glance with him, each of them silently reassuring the other they were ready, then they both turned to their respective windows, spying for the slightest hint of attack.

By the time they turned onto Eaton Place, stress tied knots in Jackson's shoulders, yet there was no tangible reason for it. Though the streets were as busy as a kicked anthill, nothing in the slightest smacked of danger. That is until the carriage stopped.

Quincy unfurled a high-flying flag of curses.

And then the carriage took a hard left, veering off the route they'd so carefully planned.

What the devil?

Jackson cracked open the door, hollering up at the man. "What are you doing?"

"Sorry, Chief," he yelled from his perch. "There were a funeral procession a'cloggin' up Eaton. A slight detour is in order."

"Doesn't seem right. Watch your back, man!" Jackson slammed the door shut.

All the colour drained from Coleman's face.

"Don't worry, Mr. Coleman." Kit spared him but a glance before once again looking out the window. "Funerals happen all the time."

"So early in the morning?" The man's voice squeaked. "Isn't that a bit unusual?"

"Probably just some Quakers, or no. . ." Graybone rubbed his hand over his beard. "Jews, no doubt. They bury their dead within twenty-four hours of expiration."

"Let's hope that is all it was," Jackson breathed low, the hairs at the nape of his neck sticking out like rods. Graybone might be right. Then again, this could be the work of Carky, funneling them into a pinch point of her own making. He scanned the street, more hypervigilant than ever. The carriage bumped along uneventfully, however, clearing Pimlico Road and turning onto Ebury Street.

And that's when a shot rang out, followed by two more in quick succession.

"Whoa, now," Quincy called, stopping the horses.

Jackson reached for his gun in unison with Graybone. Kit pulled her own and nodded at him. Coleman whimpered like a little girl.

"Don't fret," Kit whispered. "We'll manage just fine."

Jackson flung open the door, slamming it against the carriage with a bang. He jumped out, scanning the area with his revolver, ready for blood. Graybone's boots hit the ground a breath later, his footsteps rounding the back of the carriage lest they get flanked. Quincy covered them from up on his seat. Ahead, a crowd of men huddled with their backs to them, listening to a bellowing hawker of some sort. Hard to see exactly what the commotion was about from such a poor perspective—a perfect front for camouflaging an assassin.

"Talk to me, Quincy!" Jackson ordered, heart racing.

"Appears to be a street performer, out front of a gun shop."

Jackson strained to catch the hawker's words, hoping to glean confirmation of Quincy's assessment.

"Weren't that a beaut, gents? This Smith and Wesson Model 1 is as accurate as they come. Did ye see how smoothly that hammer fell? How quickly the cylinder rotates? This is the future, I'm tellin' ya. The newest innovation in firearms technology."

Oh, boy. They'd been stopped for nothing but an advertisement?

Jackson lifted his gun in the air and shot off a few rounds, followed by a hearty "Disperse! All of you! Crown's business. Disperse at once or be arrested!"

Graybone joined his side as men scattered, some of them none too pleased, judging by the sneers carved on their faces. "You certain about this?"

"No." Jackson widened his stance. "But I will not have us pigeonholed down a narrower lane."

"You can't do this! I've a permit!" The hawker waved a paper in the air. "Paid a proper penny fer this, I did!"

"Carry on later in the day," Jackson snapped. "Better yet, do so once the work bells sound. You'll catch more buyers on their way home instead of on their way to the factory."

He followed Graybone into the carriage and once again rapped on the wall for Quincy to roll on.

By God's grace alone, they finally turned onto Wilton Crescent, the last stretch of road to get to the barrister's mansion. And good thing. By now, Coleman had practically sweat through the thick leather body armour.

Just as the stones of Barrister Muddlethorpe's fence came into view, Kit banged on the wall, startling them all. "Stop the carriage!"

"What the devil? We're nearly there!" He swiveled his head. "What do you see?"

She pounded all the harder. "Stop!"

Jackson craned his neck to peer out her window.

And saw nothing out of the ordinary.

Before the wheels even stopped rolling, Kit barreled past him and shoved open the door, flying out in a flurry of billowing skirts. He couldn't have stopped her if he tried.

"Move on!" she hollered. "Get Coleman out of here!"

Graybone leapt to fill Kit's spot at her abandoned window, gun drawn, ready for action, and all Jackson could do was stare out at his wife as she ran madly down the empty road.

So, there they sat. A target waiting to be hit. This was not even remotely part of their plan.

Though it killed him in a hundred different ways, he pulled the door shut and hollered for Quincy to drive on, all the while keeping an eye on his wife until she disappeared inside the Imperial Hotel.

Oh, Kit.

God, save her.

And God save them.

A mere twenty yards remained until they passed through the guarded gates of the barrister's home. The last stretch. The final run.

Which—blast it all—was an assassin's favoured strike zone.

Chapter Twenty-Two

It wasn't every day a woman hell-bent on stopping an assassin tore harum-scarum past the bellman of the prestigious Imperial Hotel. Kit would've smirked if she weren't so out of breath—which concerned her. Racing about town never wore her out so much before she'd had Bella. Could she even get to Carky before she pulled off a shot?

"The—stairs!" She panted at the front desk, a few papers on the counter a'swirl from her hasty arrival. "Where are the stairs—leading to the roof?"

The attendant grabbed the papers before they fluttered to the floor. "I beg your pardon, madam?"

She slapped the desk. "The stairs, man! The roof!"

He glowered. "I don't see how it signifies, but only the servants' staircase reaches the roof."

Flit! She didn't have time for this nonsense. "And where might that be?" she ground out—barely.

"Why, down that corridor"—he pointed—"then to the left, behind an unmarked panel. But I don't see why you would—"

Hiking her skirts, she took off, ignoring the clerk's sputtering and the mutterings of several women aghast at her indecorum.

"Pardon!" She shoved past a server carrying a silver tray of goblets, then winced at the accompanying crash of glass behind her. At the end of the passageway, she dodged a maid turning the corner with a rolling cart of pastries, then dashed ahead to what appeared to be a dead end. She ran her fingers along the wainscoting and—there! A latch clicked.

The panel swung open. Hiking her skirts ever higher, she took the stairs two at a time. Her thighs burned when she reached the first landing. Her body really wasn't the same as it used to be.

No time to lament that now. She pushed onward, upward, a cramp in her side and hair flopping onto her brow. Thank the good Lord this hotel was only six floors! The revolver weighed heavy against her right leg as she climbed, the metal bouncing with each step. Despite the holster Jackson had fashioned for her, the gun chafed against her skin. She gritted her teeth and pushed on, ignoring the discomfort. She had to get to that roof. Now!

She burst through the final door, lungs heaving, and squinted into the morning light. Scanning for Carky—or any other danger—she shoved her hand beneath her skirts, grabbing for leather. She much preferred her trusty old knife, but Jackson had been adamant a gun not only took out trouble at a farther distance but also lent a psychological advantage. She'd given in, of course, but only because he'd not have let her come along if she hadn't.

Fumbling with the holster strap, she finally freed the gun. She really ought to check the chamber, but no time for that now. Off to her side, her gaze locked onto Carky, flat on her belly, stationed against a chimney for support—and sighting down the long nose of a rifle.

One squeeze of that trigger and Coleman's blood would spill. . .or possibly Jackson's or her father's.

Kit pulled her hammer back to a full cock and raced towards her. "Drop it, Carky!"

Carky didn't so much as glance back. "Ye won't snipe me," she said evenly.

Taking aim, Kit pulled the trigger. A shot cracked loud. The bullet sailed true. Brick and plaster rained down on Carky's head, the smooth line of the chimney now sporting a gouge from the blast.

Carky whipped her head over her shoulder with a curse and a scowl.

Kit recocked her revolver. "That was a warning. The next one is for you."

A laugh ripped out of Carky. "Ye've changed, pet. Toughened up. I s'pose fallin' in with a lawman'll do that to a girl." Then all her mirth died, her cat eyes narrowing to slits. "How did ye know I'd be here?"

"I didn't, not until a few minutes ago." Using her advantage, Kit advanced several steps, all the while keeping her muzzle trained on Carky. "It wasn't until I was in the carriage, replaying the events of the morning, and realized Mr. Coleman is left-handed. And then it dawned on me that you are as well. When I surveilled this area yesterday, I wrote off this perch because that chimney would have blocked a straight shot from a right-hander. But this is the best—and only—clear angle for a dominant lefty."

Carky pursed her lips. "I could still take him out an' split the profits with ye."

"I think not. Knowing Jackson, he got that carriage moving the second I flew out the door. Likely even now the barrister's guards have surrounded Coleman and are escorting him through the front gate."

Carky glanced back over the roof's edge, then threw down her gun and shot to her feet, foul oaths spewing like hot lava. "Ye always were a burr in my side, pet!"

"You're the one who brought me into this whole mess. So. . ." She dared another step closer, the morning breeze cool against her hot cheeks. "Who hired you?"

A grin slashed across the woman's elfish face. "Ye should know I ne'er kiss an' tell."

"If you won't sing now, then you can rot in a gaol cell until you do." She tipped her head towards the door. "Start moving."

Carky folded her arms, not budging a whit. "Ye think yer little threat frightens me?"

"The time behind bars, no. That's nothing you've not done before. But once word spreads you've been apprehended—and trust me, it will—then you've got a whole other demon to fear, for the man who hired you won't like it a bit. Might make him as nervous as you when we took in Gruver and Blackjack." Emboldened, Kit drew ever closer, stopping but five paces from the woman. "Tell me what man is bankrolling you, and I promise we'll see him put away. Furthermore, upon your testimony against him, maybe your sentence can be lightened a bit."

Sneering, Carky applauded with grotesquely exaggerated claps. "Bang-up performance, pet. A real Drury Lane slip-slapper!" She dropped her hands, jaw jutting. "Though I hate to disappoint ye, ol' friend, I'll hafta say no to yer offer. Even assassins have their honour, ye know."

Stubborn, prideful woman! As bullish as when they were girls. And yet. . .well. . .that could as easily be Kit standing there, all stiff-necked and flouting justice, if God had not lavished His grace upon her at a young age. Save for God's great mercy alone, she would have been no different than Carky Smathers.

"Please," Kit softened her tone. "Let me help you. If you don't give me the name of the man behind this scheme, there is no way Jackson and I can protect you."

For a moment Carky said nothing. She just stood there, the wind catching her skirt and rippling the fabric of her blouse, as ordinary as you please. Had fate been different, they might be taking morning tea in a garden instead of facing off on the roof of a London hotel.

"Ahh, but that's just it, luv. Don't ye see?" A small smile curved her lips. "I don't need yer protectin'. I don't need anythin'. I live life on me own terms. Always have. Always will." Her cat eyes hardened to jade rocks. "And I'll die on such too."

Carky whirled.

Two strides later, she plummeted over the edge.

And was gone.

Jackson could still scarce believe it. Gone. In an instant. A life snuffed out like the pinching of a candle flame. God have mercy. Though he'd been far enough away not to hear the thud of Carky's body hitting the cobbles, the screams of pedestrians would haunt him for nights to come, and no doubt would for Kit as well. Thank heavens she'd had enough wits about her not to peer over the roof's edge. Still, she'd been so shaken that she'd allowed him to usher her home and see her settled with a large cup of chamomile.

And everything inside him yearned to join her.

But first, Bella.

He followed Mrs. Crumplehorn, Charles' landlady—who was more bulldog than woman—into the sitting room where Charles paced like a madman in front of the window.

"A caller for you, Mr. Baggett." The woman snipped out the words like a sharp pair of garden shears. "And if you are planning on cramming this one in my boardinghouse with the rest of your menagerie, my fee has since doubled."

"No, Mrs. Crumplehorn." Baggett stopped in his tracks, crescents beneath his eyes, hair mussed as if he'd been tugging at it. "Mr. Forge will not be staying the night, and I suspect Mrs. Jones and her children shall be leaving posthaste." He glanced at Jackson, a hopeful lift to his brow.

Jackson nodded.

"Very good, then, Mr. Baggett." She dipped her head at Jackson, her mobcap so tight it cinched lines on her forehead. "Good day, Mr. Forge."

"To you as well, Mrs. Crumplehorn." Jackson waited for her skirt hem to swirl out the door before turning on Charles. "Quite the cryptic note you sent me. Where is my *package*, as you put it?"

"Don't worry, old man. Bella is quite safe and likely even now scattering biscuit crumbs all over my bedroom floor. Take a seat?" He gestured to the sofa.

"And the rest?" Jackson sat, glad for the soft cushion after such a harrowing morning. "Mrs. Jones? Her children? I take it they are here as well."

"Mostly." Charles sank onto the adjacent chair. "Frankie has gone to the glassworks. The older girls are at the soup kitchen letting everyone know there will be no meal served today. And Martha—er, Mrs. Jones is in my room tending the younger children."

Jackson smirked. "No wonder Mrs. Crumplehorn was so put out."

"She ought not be. The woman's purse is five pounds heavier for the inconvenience." Charles rubbed his shoulder. "And I'm the one who suffered on that sofa last night. It's fine enough to perch on but not so great a bed."

"Even so, my friend, it was a woman and her daughters that you brought to a men's boardinghouse. A bold move. Why did you not come to my—no. Scrap that." He doffed his hat and set it on the tea table. "So, what happened? I'm guessing there was some sort of danger for you to risk a nighttime crossing of the city with a gaggle of young ones in tow."

"Imminent danger, more like, and you're not going to like it." Charles blew out a long breath, shaking his head. "There was a bomb in Mrs. Jones' flat. Only by God's sheer grace did I discover it in time."

A bomb?! The very thought of innocent little Bella being near an explosive ignited a fire in his gut. "What the blazes? How did that get past your nose?"

"I've been asking myself that same question ever since I first laid eyes on the thing." Charles plowed his fingers through his hair, standing parts of it on end. "Could have been a bribed delivery boy who snuck up the back stairs. Or maybe one of the many hungry slipped in the rear door during the bustle of serving soup and planted it—though the pay would've had to have been good to destroy a meal source. But who knows? Might have even been Carky herself, scaled the wall, crawled through a window. I can't say for sure."

"Impossible." And it was. Charles was the best on the force. "You would have noticed such breaches."

"Normally, yes, but. . ." Baggett's Adam's apple bobbed. "I admit I was a bit distracted yesterday trying to get a private word in with Martha. I—em—I asked her to marry me."

A flush rose up his friend's neck. This man, this rock of a lawman, had seriously fallen victim to the whims of love when he should have been looking after those in his care—particularly Bella? Sympathy, empathy, and not just a little bit of fury ran laps in Jackson's belly. "While I am glad you took my advice, the timing of it couldn't have been worse. You should have stayed focused."

"That's what I was trying to do. I went to Martha's flat to propose, and that's when I discovered the bomb."

Jackson pressed his fingers to his temple. Yes, his friend's distraction might've made it easier for an assassin to strike—and yet this was Carky. She got into a police station manned with officers and killed a prisoner. So truly, even had Charles not been preoccupied, it may have made no difference. He blew out a long breath. In the end, God had actually used that very distraction to save them all, for if Charles hadn't been compelled to speak to Martha in hopes of clearing his mind, the bomb would not have been found in time.

Jackson scrubbed his hand over his face, releasing what remained of his pent-up anger, then met Charles' gaze head-on. "I assume Martha said yes?"

Charles nodded. "She did."

"Then congratulations, my friend. And though I can see you're still blaming yourself, the fact remains that you did keep her and the children all safe, and for that I am grateful. Thank God you—and everyone else—are unharmed, and that Carky is no longer a threat."

"You finally got her in custody, then?"

"In a sense, I suppose. . ." He swallowed, throat tight. Even now he shuddered to think of Carky's ignoble end. "She chose death over capture, saying she preferred to die on her own terms—though Kit suspects her suicide had less to do with honour and more to do with fear of failing whoever hired her."

"That's awful. I mean, I'm glad Coleman is safe, but"—he slowly shook his head—"such a price."

For a moment, neither of them spoke, the silence ushering in quiet contemplation and the landlady's cat. The patch-coloured feline—black, white, and even some ginger—pranced into the room as if it owned the place, tail flicking to and fro like a conductor's baton. Captain Clawsworthy, if Jackson remembered correctly. The animal twined around Charles' legs, and he bent to scratch the creature between the ears.

"So," Charles murmured, "Martha and her children can return home, but I suspect this isn't over?"

Would that it were! "Not until we put a stop to whoever it was who hired Carky."

"And Coleman?" Charles straightened.

"Safely ensconced inside Barrister Muddlethorpe's compound."

The front door slammed shut and footsteps raced down the corridor. A breath later, Frankie bounded in, arm still wrapped in a bandage, albeit filthy now. His entrance startled the cat so that it leapt onto the sofa next to Jackson.

Charles clamped a hand on the boy's shoulder before he crashed into the tea table. "Slow down, young man. This isn't a racetrack and you're not a horse."

"Thought ye'd wanna know, Mr. Baggett, Mr. Jackson." He panted. "Whew. Nearly got snagged, but it were worth it."

"By whom?" Jackson nudged the curious cat off his lap before the thing clawed his trousers. "And for what?"

"I were snufflin' about the glassworks, just like ye asked me to." The boy's words traveled on great puffs of air.

Charles circled over to a side table and retrieved a glass of water for Frankie. "Here, have a drink. Then tell us what you learned."

The lad gulped the entire glass, liquid dripping down his chin as he did so. "I were slinkin' around Bellow's office"—he swiped the back of his hand across his mouth, holding out the glass for a refill—"and propped open one o' the panes o' glass facing the work floor. Got out o' there just in time, too, a'fore he returned. Saw the tails o' him and another man. Small fellow who tried to make up for it with a top hat. Wore a tan carrick coat too, which were odd fer this time o' year."

Jackson snatched his hat from the tea table before the cat destroyed it with its claws. "Did you see his face?"

"No, but I caught the end o' their conversation soon as I shimmied up to the rafters and perched outside the office window."

Charles frowned at the lad as he handed him another drink. "If you reinjured your arm, there'll be the devil to pay with your mum."

"Pah! I managed all right." A lopsided smile twitched his lips an instant before he downed another full glass. "'Asides, ye'll think it worth it when I tell ye what I heard."

He was a brave one, this boy. Make a fine officer one day. But for now, Jackson clutched his hat and tipped his head. "Let's have it, then."

"Well, like I say, I din't catch it all, but that cully in a coat owns ol' Bellow. I ne'er heard Bellow's voice squeak like that a'fore, not even when that horse I made bolt—I mean, when that wild runaway nearly took him down. The man in the coat told Bellow his next shipment better be on time, or he'd have him taken care of just like Blade and Coleman."

Charles glanced at Jackson. "You thinking what I am?"

Jackson nodded. "I'd say the boy found Carky's employer." His gaze shifted back to Frankie. "Please tell me you got the man's name."

"Blimey, Mr. Jackson! Ye think I be daft as a daisy picker?"

Charles gently—yet firmly—cuffed the boy on the head. "Mind your tongue, lad. That's no way to speak to a chief inspector—or anyone else, for that matter."

"Pardon, Mr. Jackson." Frankie tucked his chin. "But aye, I did get a name, for I din't leave till ol' Bellow bid the man a good day. Goes by the name o' Mr. Child."

"Mr. Child," Charles repeated. "Never heard of him."

"Neither have I." Jackson stood and donned his hat. "Which could be to our advantage, for hopefully he's never heard of us either. Good work, Frankie." He fished a coin from his pocket and held it out.

Frankie snatched it in a flash, calling over his shoulder as he dashed from the room, "Thank ye, Mr. Jackson!"

"That boy has only one speed." Charles huffed, then faced Jackson. "So, what have you in mind?"

"Nothing yet, but I suspect if we are out to catch a bully of a smuggler, Kit will have a thing or two to say on the matter. I suggest we meet tomorrow at the enquiry agency and pool our ideas into a real wig flinger of a scheme to bring down Bellow and Child." He strode to the door and paused at the threshold. "Oh, and if you don't mind, not a word to Kit of what happened last night. She's been shaken enough. I fear that in such a state of mind, there'd be no stopping her if she found out Bella had been in such grave danger."

Charles' brows gathered. "But the danger was by Carky, and she is now out of the picture."

"True," he agreed. "Yet that would not stop her from going after Mr. Child, and we cannot afford to tip off the man before we organize a deadly strike."

Chapter Twenty-Three

Life had been topsy-turvy since the day Kit had been born. She'd seen a lot. Done a lot. But Carky's death was personal, leaving an indelible mark on Kit's heart. If not for the grace of God that had steered her life onto a new course, she could have easily been the one sailing over that ledge, lost in despair. Even now, a full day after witnessing Carky's tragic demise, Kit still reeled from the shock of watching the woman throw away her life. With shaky hands, she set down the tea tray on an upturned crate—the sorriest tea table in all of London, but not bad for an enquiry agency that'd been open a scant eleven days.

Jackson leaned aside as she joined the circle of men—him, her father, and Charles Baggett—already seated. "You all right?" he whispered.

"I am fine," she breathed back, then spoke louder for all to hear. "Help yourselves, gentlemen. Shall we begin?"

Indeed. A new beginning would be just the thing. It would be far better to put her mind on something else.

Favouring her with a last concerned glance, Jackson reached for a teacup. "I think we all know it is imperative we move with haste before Mr. Child has an inkling the law is against him."

Kit snagged her own cup and blew the steam off the hot liquid. "As he is an opium runner and murderer, I suspect he already knows which side of the law he stands on. He probably wakes up each morning with a glance about for bluecoats."

"True," her father rumbled. "But Jackson has a point. The man doesn't know that we—specifically—are gunning for him. Neither does Bellow.

But even so, we've got to be smart about how we proceed."

Charles grabbed a biscuit, waving it in the air as he spoke. "We could infiltrate, pose as customers, discover where and when the shipments arrive, then nail both Bellow and Child when money is exchanged for the opium."

Jackson shook his head. "To do that right would take too long. The sooner we squash this bug beneath our heel, the better."

"Then skip the infiltration." Kit shrugged a shoulder, taking care not to spill the hot brew onto her lap. "Have Frankie find out when the next shipment is to arrive and then go in with a gun-blazing raid."

"No good." Her father bit into a biscuit. . .or tried to. Even from across the circle Kit could hear the grind of his teeth trying to break through the rock-hard dough. Though he graciously removed the sweet from his mouth and palmed the failed baked good—no doubt to toss it in the dustbin as soon as they finished—she could still tell by the wince he unsuccessfully hid that a few choice words of condemnation had risen to his tongue.

Flit. Cooking was just not the talent for her.

"As I was saying," her father continued, "a warrant would need to be pulled before a raid, and without sufficient evidence up front, there's no way a judge or a magistrate would issue one."

"That is *if* we follow strict protocol." Jackson rubbed the back of his neck, casting her a sideways glance. "What about your contacts? If we knew the details of the next shipment, I could pull together some men just like we did several years ago when we cornered Poxley at his gun sale."

Her father stabbed his finger towards Jackson. "Which still stretched the limits of the law, if you'll recall. Had it not been for Poxley violating the trust of his high position—and some fancy talking I did with the superintendent—that case would have been kicked to the kerb."

"So. . ." Charles slumped against his seat, arms folding across his chest. "We are back to needing solid evidence."

Kit drummed her fingers on her thigh, thinking hard. Whether arranging a grand masquerade ball or a simple street-corner swindle, success always came down to the fine details. Granted, this one would be a bit more deadly than deciding which finger foods to serve, but the principle was still the same. So. . .how to pull it off? What past jobs had she worked that might serve as a template to—

She snapped to attention. "I think I know just the thing. There was a time I needed to remove a cullion who'd slunk into my territory, snatching up children to sell for profit, which of course I couldn't abide. I posed as a seller, offering him one of the younger members of my crew, and when he handed over money for the boy, I signaled for the bluecoats I'd tipped off ahead of time to bag him."

Her father wagged his head, brows gathering into a thundercloud. "My daughter operated a high-stakes confidence operation?"

"Yes." She smiled, her grin growing larger as she remembered how the villain cried like a little girl when the darbies were slapped on his wrists. "Worked like a charm. Sometimes it takes a swindler to catch one, you know."

"The idea has its merits, but"—Jackson steeled his jaw, his gaze flint hard—"I will not have you going up against a man whom even a trained assassin feared. I will pose as the seller."

"But that puts *you* in danger."

"Which is my job, remember?"

"It is." She set down her half-full cup, stomach rebelling. "Yet I cannot say I like that portion of it."

"It may not be as much danger as you fear." Charles pulled his now-soggy biscuit from his teacup and, shaking off the excess drips, dared a bite. . .and met with the same fate as her father.

Double flit. Next time she'd have to swing by Martha's for refreshments.

Charles plopped the biscuit back into his cup and set the whole mess onto the tray before continuing. "Just as in the Poxley capture, I and some fine fellows will be waiting in the wings with guns loaded, ready to fill the ol' Maria the moment the money is exchanged."

A grunt rasped in her father's throat. "A man like Child· may not be as easily deceived as that pompous Poxley was." He faced Jackson. "You'll need some substantial street credentials to make him believe you're an authentic seller."

"Pish." Kit fluttered her fingers in the air. "That's naught but child's play. With my connections, I can manage documents galore if needed, though word of mouth in the right ears ought to do very nicely." At least that was something she excelled at. No baking required.

"False identification aside," Charles said, "Jackson will still need an opium sample to entice the fellow, and some real premium product at that."

"I can get it." The words slipped past her father's lips as if he offered to do nothing more difficult than pick up a bottle of cream on his way home to dinner.

Kit arched a brow at him.

"Saints above, the look on your face, Daughter." He chuckled. "After twenty-five years of law enforcement, I've got a few connections of my own."

"Well then, it is settled." Jackson slapped his thighs. "I'll send word to Bellow that a new player is in town, one who wishes to meet with him. Charles, you have my permission to organize a squad." He rose, but concern still wrinkled his brow. Maybe to him, like her, it sounded all so easy. Almost too easy, as if were they each to perform their tasks like cogs in a machine, the trap for Child and Bellow would snap seamlessly shut. Yet in her experience, things almost never ran so smoothly.

But she wouldn't tell Jackson that. Clasping his warm grip, she allowed him to pull her to her feet. "Don't worry, Husband. I shall create a persona for you that will fool even me." She winked.

And she'd pray this time would be the exception, that all the four of them would have to do was stand clear when the hammer slammed down.

May God make it so.

Two days later, Jackson stalked into the front office of Bellow's Glassworks with all the confidence of a conqueror. Kit had truly outdone herself this time, providing him with the means to intimidate anyone in his path. Dressed in a midnight silk sherwani that draped to his knees and a flashy gem-encrusted dagger at his waist, his regal attire announced his arrival before he spoke a word. He looked every bit a maharaja, and with the Punjabi muscleman, Shivaji, at his back, he was ready to take on anyone who crossed him. The only downside to his new persona as Dominic Black—a.k.a. The Cobra—was his itchy upper lip, for he'd also shaved off his trademark moustache. A necessary irritation, however, to shed any semblance of Chief Inspector Jackson Forge.

He stopped several paces from Bellow's clerk, a spindly man who peered at him from the other side of the desk. Folding his arms, he stared down at the red-cheeked fellow.

The clerk looked from him to Shivaji, then back again. "I assume you must be Mr. Black?"

Without a word, Jackson snapped his fingers in the air.

His bodyguard strode to within inches of the man, each footstep rattling the inkwell on the desk. Shivaji's muscles flexed beneath his belted kurta as he loomed over the fellow, the turban on his head making him seem all the more imperious. And when the bodyguard bared his teeth, even Jackson's anxiety rose a notch. Thankfully this slab of a man was on his payroll.

"Assumptions are for women and fools." Shivaji's voice was kicked gravel. "My sahib has more important matters to attend than conversing with a lowly beetle such as you. It is ten o'clock, the agreed-upon time, so bring us to your master, little beetle."

The clerk visibly shrank as he shoved back his chair and bolted to his feet. "Right this way, gentlemen," he squeaked, giving Shivaji a wide berth. After a nervous rap of his knuckles on Bellow's door, he pushed it open. "Mr. Bellow? Mr. Black and his. . .em. . .associate are here."

"Yes, I can see that. Don't just stand there, man. Let them in! Pardon my clerk, gentlemen." Mr. Bellow whisked from his desk to the door as the clerk fled. The glassworks owner was just as Baggett had described: well built, sharply dressed, and eyes keen as a falcon's.

He extended his hand to Jackson. "Mr. Black, what an honour! Your reputation precedes you."

Jackson looked at the man's hand then directed a pointed stare at Shivaji.

His bodyguard immediately filled the gap between them, towering over Bellow a good several handspans. "Sahib prefers no physical contact."

"Oh. I—see." Bellow dropped his arm, left eye twitching. Clearly he didn't see at all.

"Nothing personal, Mr. Bellow." Jackson sidestepped the behemoth Shivaji and strolled to a chair. "You must understand that in my line of work, one never knows what sort of poison may be transferred by the simple show of greeting. May I?" He tipped his head towards the leather high-back.

"As you wish." Bellow closed the office door then stopped near a tea cart. "Will you take a cup? Poison-free, that is."

"Not necessary." Jackson waited for Shivaji to finish swiping the chair with a white cloth, then sat at the edge of the seat, back ramrod straight. Shivaji flanked him, on alert—and Jackson couldn't help but be impressed. The man was attentive, precise, and keen on playing his role. Perhaps when this was all finished, he might consider taking a job on the force.

Mr. Bellow stationed himself behind his desk. At his back, a massive window made up of many rectangular frames overlooked the hot shop. Anchoring his elbows atop the cherrywood, Bellow steepled his fingers. "I must admit I was surprised to receive a request from you, Mr. Black. It's not every day a dealer such as yourself makes a point of meeting with a smaller player such as me."

If the swell of the man's Adam's apple were any indication, such humility nearly choked him. Jackson hid a smile. "I find it takes players of all sizes to make an operation a success."

"A principle you obviously live by, for The Cobra's success is undeniable."

This time he let his smile run off leash across his face. "Clearly you have done your research, Mr. Bellow." And clearly Kit had done hers. Those rumours she'd spread at the local opium dens and a few well-placed words at the club Bellow frequented surely had done the trick.

"A man can never be too careful." Bellow lifted his chin defiantly. "And speaking of which, I am sure you will understand when I ask you for a sample of what you can provide before I procure a buyer. Hearing of your reputation is one thing. Seeing the goods for myself, however, is quite another."

"I would expect nothing less. Show the man, Shivaji." Jackson gestured with his index finger.

The Punjabi approached the desk and pulled a silver box from his pocket. Flipping open the lid, he then held it out on cupped palms. The distinct scent of opium—pungent, sweet, slightly fruity yet acrid—filled the air.

Barrow leaned over the desk, appreciation widening his eyes. "That is. . .oh. . .may I?" He glanced at Jackson.

"Of course."

Plucking the ornate box from Shivaji's hand, Bellow leaned back in his seat and carefully poked a finger at the dark brown ball. The stickier and more resinous, the better, or so Graybone had said, and this chunk left a dark stain on Bellow's fingertip—one that he licked off.

"I've not seen such a pure specimen," he murmured as he closed the lid and pushed it back across the desk.

Jackson held up his palm. "It is yours."

"Mmm," Bellow purred. "Very generous of you. Thank you."

And there he had it. Bait cast. Hook set. Time to reel Bellow in. "Think of it as a token of gratitude, my new friend, for your effort of arranging for me a meeting with Mr. Child."

"Child?" Bellow's face blanched to parchment. "I do not think that would be advisable."

Jackson edged forward on his seat. "Why not?"

"Mr. Child is. . ." Bellow cleared his throat while tugging on his collar. "He is. . .well, suffice it to say he is a very private man. Prefers the shadows to light and doesn't take kindly to making new connections. So, in that respect, I do not think a partnership with him would be a good fit for you. I can, however, set you up with William Jardine, a rival of his, so to speak."

"No. Jardine doesn't have the reach Child does." Hopefully he didn't, for Jackson had no idea who the man was.

"Then I am sorry, Mr. Black, but I fear I cannot help you." Rising, he rounded the desk and held out the silver opium box to Shivaji.

"Keep it." Jackson stood as well. "You may need it to aid your recovery."

"My what?"

Jackson gave a slight tilt of his head to Shivaji. In the space of a single breath, the big Punjabi swung around Bellow and pinioned the man's arms behind his back. Bellow struggled, rage sparking in his eyes, then went completely still as Jackson unsheathed his ornate dagger. Holding the weapon up to within inches of Bellow's face, he ran his finger along the flat part of the shiny blade, pausing at the end where the metal split into two prongs.

"Did you know, Mr. Bellow, that Indian cobras can be found in any habitation? Forests, plains, wetlands, dry, villages or cities, it matters not. . .which is why so many fall victim to the fangs of such a villain. You never know when one will strike." He pressed the tip to Bellow's throat. "You never know when *I* will strike. Now, about that meeting with Mr. Child?"

Bellow's nostrils flared, his chest heaving for breath. "I shall be happy to arrange it."

"Very good. I am staying in the club room at the Langham. Send word as soon as possible, emphasis on soon. I've an incoming shipment in three days. No time to spare when money is to be made. Being a businessman, I'm sure you understand, do you not?"

"Absolutely." Contempt thickened his voice.

Jackson held the blade to the man's throbbing vein a moment longer, then sheathed the knife with a smile. "Good day to you, then, Mr. Bellow. Come Shivaji."

Wheeling about, his grin grew. That hadn't been so hard. . .and yet every mountain climb began with easy steps. From here on out the road would be treacherous.

For he suspected Mr. Child would sooner shove him off a cliff than be as easily bamboozled.

Chapter Twenty-Four

Charles squinted at his pocket watch in the dark alcove of Spenlow & Jorkins' front doorway. Ten more minutes. Just ten and this part of the plan would be over. And good thing, too. Three in the morning was far too late for standing in the shadows of a tailor's shop, but such was the life he'd signed up for years ago. Once he married Martha, would she understand his erratic schedule?

Hand covering the hilt of his knife, he scanned the street for any sign of trouble, just as Kit did at his back. Between the two of them, any sort of ambush Child may have set would be snuffed out the moment they detected it.

Across the road, streetlamps flickered off several carriages waiting to haul home their inebriated owners the moment they emerged from the Palace Club, but Charles' gaze kept drifting to one in particular. Jackson sat in a black enameled barouche, his inky Indian garb stark against the white leather seats and accoutrements. His Punjabi bodyguard stood like a sentinel near the coach's door, arms folded, a veritable mountain of a man.

Charles blew out a long breath. It was a risky game they played, Jackson in particular. Once Child climbed up to that seat, a quick jab of a knife could end Jackson's life. And yet Jackson had proved time and again he could handle himself. Charles could only pray to God his friend would once again beat the odds of life and death.

The sound of approaching footsteps stumbled his way. He tensed as a drunk emerged from the darkness and staggered past them.

"What do you think?" he whispered to Kit. "One of Child's men?"

"Unlikely."

"How do you know?"

"His gait is too erratic, showing a disconnect from his brain. A sober man trying to look inebriated generally has an unconscious pattern to his steps no matter how hard he tries to do otherwise. And did you get a whiff of him? His gin stink blended with sweat, indicating the alcohol wasn't merely doused on his garments but ingested. Chances are that tosspot is legitimate, but even so, I'll keep an eye on him until he disappears."

Charles frowned. Jackson's wife knew way more of life than a lady ought to. Once he and Martha were wed, he'd do his utmost to keep her sheltered from such ugly truths. . .and that day couldn't come soon enough for his liking.

He shifted his stance, working out a cramp in his leg. "Did Jackson mention I proposed to Mrs. Jones?"

"What?" Kit whirled, blue eyes blazing in the night. "He most certainly did not!"

"Hsst!" He swept the area with a glance. "Keep it down. We're supposed to be spotting trouble, not causing it."

Kit huffed as she turned back to her surveillance position. "How did you ask her? What did she say? When is the wedding?" Though whispered, the questions peppered the air like grapeshot.

"I asked her the night I discovered the bo—" He clamped his lips tight. Jackson had asked him and Martha specifically not to mention the bomb to Kit.

"The night you discovered the what?" she pressed.

Blast it! Of course she noticed his slipup, but how to now salvage it in a believable fashion? He tugged at his collar, mind whirring.

"The night I discovered. . .that I should have brought along a box of chocolates. I was very ill prepared, you see. It's a miracle she said yes." He held his breath. Would Kit buy that explanation?

"Do you really expect me to believe that?" she whisper-scolded.

Thunderation but the woman was too keen! He opened his mouth to double down on the chocolate angle, but Kit beat him to the punch.

"You didn't need to bring Martha chocolates to get her to say yes.

It's plain enough she loves you. You are a fine man, Mr. Baggett, and Martha is the best woman I know. You're perfect for each other. But I wonder why Jackson didn't tell me." She arched a brow at him over her shoulder.

He shrugged, not really surprised his friend hadn't mentioned the news. Jackson had much more pressing items to deal with. "First Coleman, then Carky, now Child, not to mention he's only days away from the deadline of sorting through that paperwork for the superintendent. He's not even been to his office the past two days. All in all, your husband has been a bit preoccupied, I'd say."

"I suppose we all have." A sigh leaked out of her as she pivoted back to scanning her side of the street. Moments passed, as did the steady *clip-clop* of several horses trotting by with carriages in tow.

"Do you ever think about what life might be like with nothing more serious than a paper cut to fret over?" Her question floated on the air like an unmoored ghost.

"Sometimes," he murmured. "It gets old, this waiting around for bad things to happen, but then I remind myself we're fighting for something bigger than ourselves. We're keeping our loved ones safe, making the streets a better place for all. I believe that is what God has called me to do."

"Would that I were as certain that I am where I'm supposed to be." Longing strained her voice.

This time he cut a glance at her. "You were the one who was so adamant to be here tonight."

"No, I mean in a larger sense."

"Oh." He turned back, mulling on her confession. "You have regrets, then?" he asked at length.

"Don't we all?"

"Yes, but. . ." He narrowed his eyes across the road as a man in a grey suit exited the Palace. The fellow paused on the stoop, scanning the row of coaches, gaze landing on Jackson. Was this the infamous Mr. Child? Charles tensed.

The man strolled down the steps, then immediately hung left, nodded at the driver of the carriage preceding Jackson's, and disappeared inside that coach. False alarm.

The muscles in his shoulders loosened, and Charles returned to the conversation at hand. "Surely you are not unhappy with Jackson and little Bella?"

"Actually, Mr. Baggett," Kit's voice drifted low and even, "those are the two things in my life that I never question."

"Then what are you questioning?"

"Everything else, seems like." Her tone dropped even lower, and he strained to hear. "Am I doing enough or too much? Should I be at home more or the office more? Do I owe my allegiance to family first or to justice? Flit! I am being pulled in so many directions I don't know if anything I do anywhere makes a difference. It's just so hard to see the big picture and where I fit in exactly, you know?"

Pah! She could have no idea how many times he'd wrestled with that same brutal truth. He inhaled deeply, the weight of the conversation draping heavy on his shoulders. He'd been down the road Kit now traveled—several times—questioning his purpose, his impact, his very existence. It was a dark place to be, one he'd no doubt struggle with until his last breath. . .a burden he'd learned was far too cumbersome to carry alone.

"Take it from someone who's been at this awhile." He turned to her then, closing the distance between them. "It's easy to lose your way in this world, which is why it always comes back to trusting in God's plan. Rest assured that no matter what you do or don't do, you will not thwart whatever our mighty Creator is up to. The best we can accomplish is to hold tight to our faith and keep walking towards eternity a step at a time."

The streetlamp cast shadows on her jaw as she worked it. "Wise words, Mr. Baggett."

A small smile twitched his lips. "Words that were hard earned, I assure you."

Just then the deep bong of Big Ben chimed out the hour. *Gong. Gong.* Charles tensed. *Gong.*

"And so it begins," Kit whispered.

In unison, they faced the Palace. The doors opened. Men poured out, many at first, dribbling eventually to ones and twos. How long it would take to purge the place of all the guests was anyone's guess, but they needn't wait for the club to completely empty. Just one man in particular.

So, they waited.

And waited.

But none of the stragglers emerging matched Frankie's description or approached Jackson's carriage.

Charles flipped open his watch. Half past the hour.

"Perhaps he won't show," Kit murmured.

His thoughts exactly.

A skinny man passed through the door next, garbed in a bodacious red coat and a black mask. Clearly the club was about to lock its doors if the entertainment was now leaving. Perhaps Child had gotten wind of their little plan and decided to keep away.

"Oh no," Kit drawled.

Charles squinted, straining to see what may have drawn such a reaction. But the only man in sight was the red-coated stick figure who jogged down the stairs, staring at Jackson.

Odd that Jackson swiveled in his seat, facing him and Kit.

Charles reached for his gun. "Looks like we may have trouble."

"If that's who I think it is," Kit said, "then you couldn't be more right."

Here? Now? Unbelievable! Of all the men in all the city, it had to be Catchpole trotting down the stairs of the Palace Club at three in the morning? Turning his back on the peculiar fellow, Jackson lifted his eyes to the night sky.

Is this some sort of punishment, Lord? My own personal thorn in the flesh? He ground his teeth, the prayer sounding whiny even in his own head. Blowing out a low breath, he regrouped before trying again. *Forgive my irritation, God, but please, I beg You, grant that Mr. Catchpole doesn't see me. Send him away. Far, far away. And help me root out the real villain, Mr. Child.*

"Mr. Forge?" Catchpole's voice—usually squeaky—rang out surprisingly bold in the night air, his footsteps drawing closer. "Chief Inspector? Is it really you?"

Hounds a'fire! If the man kept it up, half of London would know he was here. Though perhaps—and a very big perhaps at that—if he didn't acknowledge the man, Catchpole might think he was wrong and simply go away. Gritting his teeth, Jackson held his ground, sitting rock still in the carriage seat lest the slightest movement give Catchpole any encouragement.

"Stand back, maggot." Shivaji's command was a low roll of thunder.

"I say!" Catchpole yelped. "No need to wrinkle the coat, my good fellow. I mean no harm to my dear friend. But why are you keeping guard over...oh!" The man's voice dropped. "I begin to understand. How capital! This is all a disguise, is it not? And a very good one at that. I must say you could pass for a real Punjabi. Tell me, where did you buy that turban? It's a stunning piece of fabric."

"One more word, maggot," Shivaji said, his already low voice dropping a full octave, "and I will cut out your tongue."

Blast. Ignoring Catchpole could get the man hurt. Jackson swung about and leaned over the railing, speaking for Catchpole alone. "As you can see, it is I, and I am working a clandestine meeting, so I would appreciate it if you would not draw so much attention."

"I knew it!" The skinny man gasped then immediately softened his tone. "I mean how clever. How indiscriminately brilliant. Why, you are a star in the night sky, Inspector." He slapped his hand to his mouth. "Oops," he mumbled. "Ought not to have said that."

Jackson fought against rolling his eyes. "Time for you to move along, Mr. Catchpole." His gaze flicked to the Palace door, where yet one more man emerged. "Now."

Jackson tensed. If that man was Mr. Child and Catchpole gave him away, it could set the whole investigation back indeterminately.

But the man at the door lingered with his back to the street, pulled out a set of keys from his pocket, then bent to secure the lock, officially closing the Palace. Whistling a tune, he descended the stairs, and without so much as a glance at them, he strolled off into the darkness.

A sigh whooshed the air from Jackson's lungs. Child had stood him up. And stars above, how he hated to be stood up!

"You heard the man, maggot. Leave!" Shivaji advanced towards Catchpole, making a swipe for him.

Catchpole hopped back just in time. "I assure you there is no need to be so forceful." He frowned at Jackson. "I cannot say I care for your new company, Inspect—" His eyes widened at the blunder. "At any rate, all the best to you and your endeavour. Good night."

He walked away just as Baggett and Kit drew near. Kit tipped her head at the retreating man. "Mr. Catchpole, I assume?"

"Unfortunately, yes." Jackson pinched the bridge of his nose. "Good thing Child didn't show up or this whole thing would have blown apart."

"Hmm." Kit tapped her lower lip.

Jackson dropped his hand. "I know that look. What are you thinking?"

"Clearly Mr. Catchpole has some sort of connection to the Palace. Perhaps he could be of help."

Baggett folded his arms. "I thought the fellow was an entertainer. I mean, look at that coat."

Actually, now that Jackson had a moment to think on it, what had Catchpole been doing in such a prestigious club? He studied the carefree stride of the skinny man as he strolled down the street. Surely he couldn't be a member, and likely not an entertainer. So, then what? Unless. . .

Jackson glanced once more at Baggett, the man a stark reminder that not all distractions were bad in and of themselves. Had Baggett not been preoccupied with the need to speak with Martha, he'd not have detected the bomb. Maybe—in a very convoluted way—God had put Catchpole here for a reason?

He smirked. Now there was a stretch. But still. . .in all his busyness and assumptions, had he overlooked something God wanted him to see or know? Perhaps the only way to find out was to finally stop and listen to the man—*really* listen—instead of just trying to get rid of him.

He faced the big Punjabi. "Shivaji, could you fetch that man?"

White teeth shone bright in a large smile an instant before he wheeled about. "My pleasure, sahib."

"Gently!" Jackson called after him.

A yap rang out as Shivaji collared the man and escorted him back to the carriage.

Catchpole wrenched from Shivaji's grip, glaring at the Punjabi as he tugged down his waistcoat and brushed away wrinkles. "This is highly irregular! I do not appreciate such handling."

A peahen couldn't have looked more ruffled.

Kit covered a smile with her hand.

Baggett smirked.

Jackson opened the door of the barouche. "My apologies, Mr. Catchpole. How about I drive you to wherever it is you're going? Baggett, I assume you will see Kit safely home?"

His friend gave a sharp nod.

"Until later, then." Jackson winked at Kit then once again faced Catchpole. "There is nothing to fear, Mr. Catchpole. I'd merely like a few words with you."

The skinny fellow hesitated, gaze bouncing between him and Shivaji. With a final scowl at the Punjabi, Catchpole apparently made up his mind and hopped up on the step.

Jackson moved aside to allow him space. "Where to, Mr. Catchpole?"

Catchpole clicked the door shut then sank onto the cushion beside him. "Camden Lock, if you please."

A strange time of night to visit a canal. Then again, everything about Catchpole was strange. He called to Shivaji as the big man gained the driver's seat and took the reins in hand. "Camden Lock."

The carriage glided into action, a far smoother ride than an average hack. No doubt Hammerhead would have a thing or two to say when he saw the invoice for this rental on the expense report.

Catchpole's dark eyes stared at him from behind his mask. "It is very generous of you to offer me a ride after the debacle I nearly created for you. I must say your disguise is quite well done. Better than my own, in fact." He tapped the side of the black leather near his temple.

Jackson stretched out his legs, crossing one over the other. "Tell me, Mr. Catchpole, why do you wear a mask?"

He was quiet for some time, the *clip-clop* of the horse's hooves and the yowl of an alley cat the only sound.

"Perhaps I shall tell you someday," he murmured at length.

"No one is promised another day, Mr. Catchpole, not even another breath. Now is your chance." He shifted on the seat, angling to face the man. "I think you know you can trust me."

"I most emphatically do." His stringy brown hair bounced against his collar as he nodded vigorously. "You have proven yourself to be the most steadfast man I know."

"Then tell me who you are—who you *really* are—for we both know the Palace only allows men of status and means to join their club."

Catchpole's lips pursed, twitching one way then the other until finally he spoke. "Whatever I tell you must stay inside this carriage. Have I your word, sir?"

Jackson placed his hand against his heart. "Upon my honour."

Catchpole whooshed a breath. "I was hoping you'd say that. And so. . ." He tossed back his shoulders. "I begin my tale with a young lad, a voracious reader with a flair for the artistic, and passionate about all things vulnerable: birds, rabbits, mice, even snails or slugs. He was particularly tender of heart, you see, a trait that vexed his father, for he was a man's man. Hunting parties, brandy and cigars—you know the type. And though this boy tried very hard to please him, nothing he did ever quite measured up to his older brother. Second son, second best, so they say. . .and they are correct. Oftentimes the boy wished his family were neither wealthy nor powerful."

Catchpole's head dipped, the ostrich feather in his hat bowing in sorrow as well.

Sympathy flared in Jackson's chest. There was no doubt in his mind the man spoke of himself. Even so, he'd play the game set before him. "What happened to the lad?"

"Eventually he realised, though he'd tried to be like his brother, his father simply never accepted him, not even to his dying day." The carriage veered around a corner, and Catchpole grabbed for the seat before continuing. "So the boy-turned-man purposely set out to be different. . .which landed him in gaol."

"Great heavens. What for?"

He chuckled, his crooked teeth flashing as they passed by a streetlamp. "Nothing too grotesque, I assure you. A simple matter of out-of-hand carousing that led to throwing squibs in the marketplace. The resultant bangs caused quite an uproar. One lady even swooned. Still, no one was hurt, and no property was damaged, but being hauled in by the law was enough to shame the family name. So his brother—now the head of the family—sent him packing, albeit with a monthly stipend. Put him up on the far side of town in a not-too-shabby flat." Catchpole shook his head sadly. "But I could never be a kept man, so I never did stay there."

Jackson noted the slip. On purpose or a slight? Perhaps better not to question it. . .yet. In fact, in order to get more personal information out of the man, he averted his gaze, looking out at the passing buildings instead of directly at Catchpole. "And the mask?"

"A necessary evil, one I was forced to don the day I moved to the streets. The funny thing is, though, that I soon learned street people really aren't any more virtuous than the wealthy. They are just as conniving and discriminating. No one accepted me for who I am. That is what brought me to my lowest point—the day you redeemed my life on the Blackfriars Bridge. I wasn't jesting when I said you restored my hope in mankind, and even more so in these following weeks when you never once banished me from your presence. I believe you have shown me the very grace of God."

Bah. Catchpole couldn't be more wrong. It was God who'd shown *him* grace! Guilt stuck thick in Jackson's craw. All this time he'd been wishing away the very man who needed to see God's love. . .and it was by God's restraint alone he'd kept his frustration in check and shown it to him. Jackson gripped the side of the carriage—hard—shame tugging at his heart. "I fear you credit me far too much, my friend."

"Oh, I realize it was small enough, your acceptance of the crushed bag of sweets, the fish on your desk, the many times I stopped you in the street and you gave me the time of day. But it is in the little things Christ's love is shown most. And that was all I needed. Just a glimmer, a faint flicker, of love."

They rode in silence then, mist curling on the night air the closer they drew to the canal. Catchpole had given him much to think on, and he would, but for now there was still an unanswered question dangling between them.

Jackson faced him. "I yet find it hard to understand the need for the disguise. Are you hiding from your brother?"

"No. From notoriety." Hesitant at first, then with a quicker working of his fingers, Catchpole pulled off the mask.

Jackson's jaw dropped. He knew the face. He knew the Roman nose and the thick brows unified into a single line. Why, this man was the mirror image of one of the most powerful men in Parliament. "If I didn't know any better, I'd say you were the Viscount Eldridge Suthmeer. But. . .you cannot be him. It is not possible."

Catchpole smiled widely as he once again lifted the mask and laced it behind his head. "Eldridge is my twin, born mere minutes ahead of me. I am Ezra Suthmeer."

Jackson sucked in a breath. A thunderbolt couldn't have struck any harder. "So that is your connection to Parliament."

"It is. And had you not encouraged me to seek reconciliation with him, I doubt we'd yet have said a single word to each other. I wonder if you know, Inspector, just how much a few words spoken in love can impact a man?"

He worked his jaw, once again feeling the nip of shame. In truth, his words had been spoken more in exasperation than in love, but—wonder of wonders—God had apparently seen fit to use them. He smiled at the man as the carriage rolled to a stop. "I am happy to have played a small role in your journey towards resolution with your brother. Thank you for trusting me with your story. I vow it will go no further than my ears."

"I have no doubt on the matter, and I thank you for the ride." He reached for the door latch.

"Mr. Catchpole—" The name felt strange on his tongue now that he knew the man was a mighty Suthmeer. "I hate to ask and yet there is a need. I wonder with your connections if you could do me a favour?"

"Oh!" He clasped his hands to his chest. "It would be my greatest delight!"

"I was supposed to meet with a Mr. Child tonight. I wonder if you know him?"

Catchpole dropped his hands, the corners of his mouth turning downwards as well. "Odious man."

For a moment, Jackson sat dumbfounded. Perhaps God had been working all things towards this moment, for here was a man with the contacts he desperately needed. "Could you help me find him? I should urgently like to speak with him."

"Ahh, that is why all this." Catchpole circled his fingers to include Jackson, the barouche, and even the hulking Shivaji up on the driver's seat. "But of course. I shall see what I can manage and get word to you at the station on Monday morning. Does that suit?"

Jackson gave him a sharp nod. "It does."

"Excellent. Then good night." Catchpole hopped to the ground and shut the coach door, then took several paces before doubling back.

Behind the mask his eyes were troubled. "But a word of warning, my dearest friend. Of all the wickedness I've seen in both rich and poor, there is a blackness about Mr. Child which tops it all. Be careful in your dealings. Be *very* careful indeed."

Chapter Twenty-Five

Kit always knew she was different, a fact she'd spit shined and worn like a badge of honour. But this Monday morning, pushing Bella in the pram amidst other mothers haggling at the Leadenhall Market, she wasn't so sure she wanted to wear that badge anymore. Not that she'd throw it away entirely, for to do so would erase who she was at the core, but maybe—perhaps—she didn't always have to be such a stark anomaly.

Rising to her toes, she shaded her eyes and searched for Martha. Bonnets were everywhere. Women clutching the hands of little ones. Wives bartering for the best price on melons, cheeses, bread. Good homemakers, all. She'd wager five pounds not a one of them had been out on a street corner last night with a knife in her hand looking for trouble. No, each and every one of these skirts was dutifully living out her womanly roles. . .and a small part of Kit wondered if she ought to be doing the same.

She gripped the pram handle tight and veered around a pickle barrel. Could she truly be happy shoehorned into a life of nothing but dishes and laundry? Surely there must be some way to find a balance that wouldn't forsake her individuality.

Wasn't there?

She spied Martha chatting with an apple vendor, a pleasant little laugh trilling from her lips as she handed over some coins and placed the fruit into the basket on her arm. Her friend was a shining example of what society expected from a female, and—surprisingly—a pang of jealousy stabbed Kit in the belly.

Annoyed with herself, she pasted on a smile and rolled the pram alongside Martha. "So, when were you planning on telling me?"

"Tell ye?" Her friend wrinkled her nose. "Since when do ye care a fig about a change in menu? Hungry bellies don't mind if 'tis apples or pears what's in the sweet bread." She leaned over the pram and tickled Bella. "And how is me girl today, eh sweetums?"

"Ba-ba!" Bella hooted, feet kicking, arms flailing.

Kit arched a brow at Martha. "You're right, I don't care about what you serve, but I am more than vexed I heard of your upcoming nuptials from Mr. Baggett instead of from you."

Martha straightened, fire in her cheeks. "Ahh. That. Ye've got to admit ye've been flittin' in and out so fast I scarce get a word wedged betwixt us."

"True." She sighed. "But I am here now, so give me the details."

"All right, but I still need a few dates to go along with th' apples. Old lady Spivum has the best prices on the other side o' the market."

"It'll be faster if we skirt this crowd." Kit steered the pram down the aisle towards the edge of the stalls and glanced at her friend. "Well?"

"It were quite the thing." Martha grinned. "Remember th' day Mr. Baggett were stationed at the soup kitchen to keep watch o'er us? He were a distracted mess the whole time, which ain't like him. Not a bit. So I knew somethin' weren't right. And when he rapped at my door after hours—"

"He came to your flat?" Kit's brows shot up. Bold move.

"He did, and good thing too or we might all have been blown to—" Martha clamped her lips tight and whirled to a meat seller. "I'll take a string o' those bangers, if ye please."

Kit narrowed her eyes. Martha didn't need sausages any more than she needed a hole in her head. And, come to think of it, when Charles had relayed his account of the proposal, he'd staggered over his words as well. Could be nerves, emotion, the blush of love and all that. . .but Kit doubted it very much.

She leaned towards Martha. "What exactly might have happened?"

Martha took her time fishing out coins and packing the meat into her basket. At length she faced her, shrugging one slim shoulder. "I s'pose he might not have proposed, that's all."

What a whopper!

With quick steps and a firm grip on the pram handle, she herded Martha away from the stall and pinned her against the side of a shop. Bella laughed at the wild ride.

Martha scowled. "What the skip-nippity do ye think yer doin'? I've got work to get on!"

Kit set her jaw. "I'll not let you go until you tell me exactly what Jackson and Mr. Baggett will not."

"Don't be a ninny. There's nothing to tell."

Martha's mouth always twitched on the left side when she stretched the truth, and sure enough, her lip contracted. Kit folded her arms. "Either you tell me the truth or we will be here a very long time. And do not think to try to leap over the pram and escape. Though we are friends, that would not go well for you."

Martha stiffened, jolting the apples in the basket to one side. "I'm not to say a word. I promised Mr. Jackson."

Pish. Of course she had. Jackson would make the queen perform a blood oath if he thought it would protect Kit. "Very well," she clipped, more annoyed with Jackson than her friend. When would he learn she wasn't as fragile as a porcelain teacup? "You don't have to say anything. Simply nod your head. Fair enough?"

"I dunno..." Martha leaned against the brick wall, blue eyes searching Kit's. "I tol' ye I gave Mr. Jackson me word."

"And you won't be breaking it. Now then, what I know is something awful happened the night Mr. Baggett kept guard over you, the very same night before Carky ended her life, so I suspect she was somehow involved. Is that true?"

Martha pursed her lips. "I honestly don' know."

"Even so, let's run with it." Kit paced in front of the pram, Bella reaching for her skirt every time she passed. "We moved Bella to your care for her protection in case Carky struck, which clearly she must have, or Jackson would not have sworn you to secrecy. That implies there was a danger to you and the children, wasn't there?"

She glanced at Martha—who reluctantly nodded.

"But what sort of danger?" She paced a few more times, thinking aloud. "Carky favoured poison, so it could have been that. Was there some sort of poisonous threat?"

Her friend shook her head.

"All right. Carky also knew how to use a gun. Were shots fired?"

Another shake.

Hmm. What else would Carky—

Behind her a loud crack rang out, followed by bass thuds. Tensing, she whirled. Sweet potatoes rolled everywhere, spilled by an upset cart with an axle that'd cracked, the sound of the accident jogging loose a memory in her mind.

She turned back to Martha with a smile. "A bomb. That's it, isn't it? When Mr. Baggett came to your flat to propose, he discovered a bomb. Am I right?"

Martha's lips flattened, and a breath later, she gave a hesitant nod.

"I knew it!" Kit grinned at the victory, then immediately shot her hand to her mouth, gut sinking. Sweet, blessed mercy! What sort of danger had she placed everyone in, placed her own precious little girl in, by taking on the Coleman case?

"La, Kit! Yer white as a bride's frillies." Martha cornered the pram and snagged her arm, guiding her to a nearby crate. "See? This is exactly why yer husband asked me not to say somethin'. Please, don't fret so. Mr. Baggett was more than capable to handle it. All is well."

"But if it weren't for me taking on that case. . ." She sagged against the wall. Why hadn't she listened to her father that first day? But no, she'd thought she knew better, hadn't even bothered to ask the Almighty what He might think. Flit! Would she never learn?

She peered over at Martha. "What am I doing? What by all that is holy am I doing?"

"Hear, now." Reaching out, her friend swept a piece of hair from Kit's brow. "Yer bein' Kit Forge, tha's what. 'Tis who ye are."

Kit's gaze drifted to Bella, who batted at the colourful toys hanging from the pram's canopy. Guilt and fear tasted sour on her tongue. "If being who I am involves endangering those I love, then I don't want it anymore. Don't you understand? For the safety of those around me, I cannot go on like this."

Martha shook her head slowly. "Ye cannot perfectly protect yer family any more than Mr. Jackson can you."

"But neither must I drag them straight into danger!"

"Then don't." Martha shrugged. "Ye aren't runnin' a crew no more, luv. Nothing says ye must be the one trackin' down evil, is there? T'aint that what yer husband, yer father, and even Mr. Baggett are around for?"

Kit lifted her head and blinked, once again hearing her father's chastisement about them being partners. Could it be so simple? That perhaps God didn't intend her to stop pursuing justice, but rather change the way she went about it?

Jackson hadn't thought it possible. Not that he hadn't seen things go from bad to worse, but this? He stood speechless at his office door, clutching the handle of his satchel with a death grip. Though it be a muggy August day, Harvey hunched like a toad in front of the hearth, pitching papers into a blazing fire. The very documents Jackson was supposed to be deciphering into a comprehensive report that was due on the commissioner's desk in two days.

The one that would make or break his career as chief inspector.

So much rage boiled up from his gut that he gusted out a breath as if sucker punched in the breadbasket.

Harvey glanced over his shoulder, then rose with a smile. "Why, good morning, Chief Inspector. Or nearly afternoon, I should say. At any rate, you should be happy to know I am just about finished up here."

"You are finished right now, Harvey," he ground out.

"Oh, perhaps you misheard me, sir." Harvey pounded his chest as he cleared his throat, then spoke all the louder. "Just a bit more tidying up and—"

"Out!" Jackson exploded.

Harvey's owl eyes blinked behind his thick spectacles. "I beg your pardon, sir?"

"I said—"

"Chief Inspector! Delightful!" Catchpole's voice squeaked behind him. "You're exactly where I hoped you'd be."

Gritting his teeth, Jackson wheeled about. "This is not a good time, Mr. Catchpole."

"On the contrary, it is the best of times." The string bean of a fellow lifted his chin, the feather on his hat bobbing. "And if you hurry, you just may intercept him."

Fabulous. Here he stood playing a word game while a failure of an inspector incinerated police records at his back when he ought to be tracking down a yet-to-be-found evil mastermind. But it would do no good to ignore or put off the red-coated fence post in front of him...and to be fair, hadn't his last meeting with this same man reminded him not to be quite so quick to judge? Somehow, the thought eased some of the tension and brought calmness to his voice. "What are you talking about, Mr. Catchpole?"

"Mr. Child, of course."

His heart skipped a beat. "What have you discovered?"

Catchpole hitched his thumbs around his lapels. "I apologize there wasn't time for me to copy down the evidence, but I saw with my own eyes a ledger that the president of Barclay's shared with me this morning."

Jackson sucked in a breath. Though it shouldn't be a surprise the twin brother of Suthmeer had access to such a high official, it was still hard to fathom that this peculiar little man was actually quite important himself. "What did the ledger show?"

"That Mr. Child makes a weekly deposit every Monday at the Lombard Street branch. Noon. Like clockwork."

Jackson yanked out his pocket watch and flipped open the lid. Half past eleven. No time to waste. He snapped it shut and took off at a run down the corridor, calling over his shoulder, "Thank you, Mr. Catchpole."

"My pleasure, Chief Inspect—"

Jackson swung into a storage room and slammed the door. He practically ripped the clasp off the bag in haste as he opened it. His mind whirred while he pulled out the rolled-up sherwani and salwar, then shrugged out of his clothes and donned his Dominic Black persona. He ought to send a note to Shivaji, but no time. He fished out a scrap of paper and pencil from the bag and with bold strokes wrote a cryptic message instead—one he prayed would do the trick. Pocketing the note, he reached into the bag once more and removed an identical silver box to the one he'd given Bellow, then pocketed that as well. Without another thought on the matter, he tossed his bag onto a shelf and fled the station, racing to Lombard Street like a madman.

He made it with several minutes to spare, and good thing too, for his lungs heaved like a rat catcher's on the chase. Inhaling deeply, he forced even breaths while waiting in the shadows of a nearby alcove.

Moments later, a short man in a tan carrick coat exited, two hulks flanking him. Blast. He should've at least tried to contact Shivaji. Too late now, though. He sucked in one more lungful of air, then dashed after the trio. "Pardon me, but I believe you dropped this."

They turned in unison. The henchmen were the usual bulldogs with hams for hands. But Child was another matter altogether. He wore a garishly tall top hat that merely elongated his narrow face instead of lending him height. Small scabs flaked on his ruddy skin, adding a bizarre reptilian flair to his long snout and beady eyes. Now the coat made sense, for clearly the man suffered from a skin condition.

Child tipped his head at the brute on his left, who immediately advanced and snatched the paper from Jackson's grasp. He handed it over to Child, whose lips moved silently as he read.

In the snake pit, only the strong survive.

Child crushed the paper into a wad, his dark eyes flicking to Jackson. "Who are you?"

Jackson held his stare. "Your new business partner."

A ripple of annoyance flickered on his face an instant before he jutted his jaw at the same henchman. Then he wheeled about and strode away.

The big man advanced, his mouth slashing into a sneer.

Jackson crouched, stance ready, measuring the fellow's gait, weight, and most importantly, how he raised his hands—a lesson he'd learned the hard way in the ring with Baggett. The instant the man threw his right fist, Jackson ducked. Swerved. Came around and swung a hard left hook, connecting an open-palm strike directly behind the oaf's ear.

The man's eyes rolled at the same time his body plummeted backwards. The bigger the man, the harder the fall, and this one thwumped like a dropped load of bricks.

Shaking out his hand, Jackson pivoted and caught up to Child before he could disappear into a black coach waiting at the kerb. "Do not try my patience, Mr. Child," he growled.

Child glanced at him then beyond, a single thin brow arching as he spied the big brute on the pavement. His gaze drifted back to Jackson. "I could say the same to you."

"Point taken, yet I think you'll wish to hear me out."

"I am a busy man, Mr. . . . ?"

"Black."

Child's head reared back. "Ahh. The famed Cobra?"

Once again Kit's connections had come in handy. A small smile curved his lips. "I neither confirm nor deny your allegation, but what I can tell you for certain is I have what you want."

Child's eyes narrowed. "Oh? And what is that?"

"A street corner is a rather inconvenient place to discuss such matters. Shall we?" He swept his arm to a coffee shop two doors down.

Child hesitated.

"You can bring your pet along." Jackson angled his head at the beefy man holding open the carriage door. "I assure you it will be worth your while."

"How do I know this isn't a setup?"

"How do I know you won't order your dog there to slit my throat?"

Child chuckled, a raspy, gurgly sound, as if scabs lined the inside of his throat as well. "Very well, Mr. Black. Let us convene for a hot cup. After you."

Jackson led the way, which went against his every defense instinct. He was wide open to a blow to the back of his skull or a knife to the kidney. Thankfully, though, he made it to the back corner of the coffee shop and snagged a table unscathed.

Child sat. His man didn't. The pillar merely towered over them both, glowering.

"We are busy men, Mr. Child, and so. . ." Jackson reached carefully into his pocket and pulled out the silver box, then set it on the small table.

The henchman reached for it.

Jackson gripped his wrist in a merciless hold, locking eyes with Child. "I deal with you directly or not at all."

Child shook his head, his narrow nose sniffing the air. "What is to say there isn't a poisonous powder in that little gift that could kill me on the spot?"

"There are never any guarantees in this life. But to put your mind at ease." Jackson lifted the box and flipped open the lid, inhaled deeply, and then snapped it shut and returned it to the table. "Satisfied?"

"Sir, I—" The henchman clamped his mouth tight at Child's evil eye.

Child then collected the offering and opened the small container, his tiny eyes widening as he stared at the premium opium sample. His gaze flicked to Jackson. "Impressive, but why me?"

Jackson shrugged. "I am only recently returned from India. I need connections. Word has it you are the best."

His reptilian eyes didn't so much as blink at the compliment. "How much?"

"I have a shipment of one hundred pounds arriving tomorrow night. As an introductory offer, I would be willing to sell it to you for ten on the pound, which—as you know—is a significant discount for such a prime specimen."

Child tossed back his head, nearly losing his hat. Hoarse laughter ripped out of him. "Are you trying to get me addicted to you and your supply, Mr. Black?"

Jackson spread his hands. "You know how the game is played." Not that he did, but it was a line he'd heard Kit use successfully.

All humour fled from Child's face as he pocketed the sample. "Why should I trust you? As you say, you have no connections here, no one to refer your services."

"Because you have no other choice. I have looked into your dealings and learned quite a bit about you. Let us say that if you do not avail yourself of my generous offer"—he waved away an approaching server and leaned closer to Child—"it could be dangerous for you."

Child's thin nostrils flared. "You dare threaten me?"

The henchman stepped closer, fingers wrapped around a knife shushing from its sheath.

Jackson held his position. To show weakness now was a death sentence. "What I dare, Mr. Child, is to offer you a chance to make a lot of money, more than you'll ever make with a small-time fizzer like Bellow. Bring your payment in gold coin, packed in brief bags."

"Mmm." Child grunted, his hand going to his pocket. After a final perusal of the opium chunk, he stashed it away once more and leaned back in his seat. "That can be arranged. But if this turns out to be a trap,

I will not hesitate to strike you where it hurts."

"You may strike, but I assure you, the cobra's bite is deadly." Jackson stood, ignoring the muscle scowling at him. "I shall send word where the shipment will arrive."

Child shook his head. "I expect a full-service delivery. Two a.m., East End Depot, Whitechapel."

Bah! The man had to know it would take more than two hours to unload a shipment and haul it covertly to such an address. Not that he had an actual shipment. Was that what Child was trying to fish out of him?

"Impossible, as you know." Jackson stared holes into the little reptile. "Even with my best men, I could not possibly have it to you until three at the earliest."

"Three, then." Child's eyes were dark pinpoints. "Be there with the goods, and I will be there with the money."

Jackson gave him a sharp nod and strode away without a backwards glance. Mission accomplished. The snare was set.

But it remained to be seen who would be caught. . .Child or him?

Chapter Twenty-Six

Holding the dagger's blade up to the lamp on the dining room table, Kit narrowed her eyes. Metal gleamed, the edge deadly sharp. If she ran the pad of her finger along it, blood would drip before she felt a thing. Perfect.

"Are you about done?" Jackson grumbled behind her. "I could use some help."

"Ba-ba!" Bella tugged at Kit's hem where she sat busily playing with old sharpening stones on the rug.

"Mama," Kit corrected, then handed over the stone she'd been using to Bella's outstretched hand before turning to Jackson, her stomach feeling like she had eaten the stone rather than given it to Bella. When she first heard about Jackson's meeting, she immediately had asked to join—anything to see the man taken down who'd nearly gotten her girl killed. But after her blood cooled, she'd had to admit that perhaps she ought to take Martha's advice and let the men do the chasing this time. Still... "I'd be a great pair of eyes on the back side of the warehouse—"

"That's not the help I need." He waggled a leather waistcoat in the air. "I was talking about this."

An odd mixture of anger and relief collided inside her. Jackson didn't want her. She should stay with Bella. Easy enough to understand but hard to accept. Frustrated, she added the knife to the roll pouch already containing a pair of brass knuckles, a bowie, a stiletto, and a throwing blade. Personally, she'd have stuck with the push knife, but in this situation, it probably paid to be overarmed rather than under.

Snatching the body armour from his fingers, she gave the thing a good shake then held it out, allowing him to slip his arms through the sleeve openings. Maybe she could find a compromise? "I promise to stay in the shadows, glued to Mr. Baggett's side. No risk-taking unless it is absolutely necessary. I am sure Mr. Child has prepared quite the gauntlet for you to run through this evening."

He stood deadly still. "We've been over this before, remember?"

Grabbing hold of the laces, she tugged hard, working out her frustration on the bindings. Since she'd begun this case with Coleman, it only seemed fair that she be there for the final arrest of the man responsible for it all...yet was it really worth forcing it? After all, forcing it was what landed her in this mess in the first place.

"Hey!" Jackson wheezed. "Not so tight."

"Now you know how a woman feels." She smirked as she knotted the laces, though her stomach knotted just as tightly. Admitting Jackson was right, giving this up, was monumentally difficult and yet. . .Bella's babbling plucked her heart. Staying behind wouldn't be as hard as it would be on Bella if something went wrong tonight and both she and her husband came under fire. "Jackson, about this meeting—"

He turned, his big hands grasping her shoulders and pulling her close. "I cannot do this if I am worried about your safety. Tonight, for once, your place is here with Bella."

As if on cue, Bella clunked the stones together and laughed at the thwacking noise—the same laughter as the little ones Kit had heard at Leadenhall Market—and Martha's words returned to her. *Nothing says ye must be the one trackin' down evil, is there? T'aint that what yer husband, yer father, and even Mr. Baggett are around for?* Kit nibbled her lip, then sighed. "Very well. I promise I'll not leave the house."

Jackson tipped up her chin with his knuckle. "What are you scheming now?"

Kit offered him a smile, but it felt wobbly after such an internal battle. "Nothing but wrangling Bella to bed, then a hot bath and a good book to fall asleep with."

He pressed his fingers to her forehead. "Are you ill?"

Frowning, she batted away his hand. "Is that any way to treat the woman who just agreed with you?"

His fingers flew to his own forehead. "Perhaps I'm the one who's feverish. Am I hallucinating that you just consented to remain here while I go out and do my job unhindered?"

She rolled her eyes. "Such theatrics do not become you, Chief Inspector. Oh!" She swayed as the armadillo bumped rather forcefully into her ankle. "Off with you, Brooks." Toeing the animal, she nudged it all the way to the dining room door, where it happily snuffled along the corridor baseboards.

"That creature is a menace, sure to knock over Bella once she starts toddling about. It is time to find a new home for the thing." Jackson pulled the black silk sherwani over his head and settled it over the body armour, his broad chest all the thicker.

"I've already agreed to stay home. That's enough progress for one evening, don't you think? Brooks is a topic for another night." Kit rolled the weapon apron into a tight bundle and tied it—or tried to. Jackson pulled her around and cupped her face before she finished.

"So will you truly stay here? Can I trust you this time?"

Her heart squeezed. She had no one to blame but herself for the suspicion creasing his brow. "I know in the past I have given you cause to believe otherwise, but yes, this time I vow it. I will stay here." She grabbed hold of the golden hem of his sherwani and pulled him closer. "But listen well, Husband. If you do not come home alive, I will hunt you down in the afterlife for a thorough explanation."

The left side of his mouth quirked, the naked skin above his lips still jarring to behold. "You fret like an old woman. Where is the carefree girl I married?"

"She's older, wiser, and has hopefully learned a thing or two." Stretching to tiptoes, she kissed him full on the mouth, then nuzzled her cheek in the crook of his neck. "Please come back to me," she whispered. "I couldn't bear it if you didn't."

He pressed his lips to the crown of her head. "Your father and Baggett shall be outside Child's warehouse the entire time, keeping a sharp eye for trouble. And thanks to you"—he pulled away and swiped up the bundle of freshly sharpened weapons—"I shall manage the trouble from within." He tucked the canvas under his arm. "Once the deal is done, this will all be over."

"Ba-ba!" Bella cooed from the corner.

"Papa." Jackson smiled at her, the fatherly love in his eyes so pure it hurt to witness.

Kit's belly twisted. If anything went wrong tonight, these walls would never more ring with his deep voice. This man—father—lover—may not ever grace this room again once he strode from it.

Stifling a sob, Kit reached for his arm. "I love you more than you'll ever know."

"If that is only half as much as I love you, then yes, I do know." The sultry gleam in his eyes added to the sinking feeling in her gut.

She trailed her finger to his upper lip, running over the softness where his trademark moustache used to be. Loss stole her breath. Loss of what was. Loss of what might be.

"Be careful," she murmured.

Grabbing her hand, he kissed her finger, then gave her a sharp nod. And was gone.

Kit dashed to the window and pulled aside the curtain, practically mashing her nose against the glass to catch a last glimpse of those strong shoulders, that warrior stride. He was a brawny, strapping fellow, capable of protecting himself and those around him; but even so, long after he climbed into the waiting carriage and drove off, she yet stood there.

Praying to God it wasn't the last time she'd ever see him.

"God go with you, sahib."

Jackson gave a crisp nod to the barely visible Punjabi perched on the driver's seat of the carriage. Dark had fallen hours ago, yet still they had waited in the station hours more for the clock hands to creep towards the appointed time.

Moving past the barouche, Jackson strode along the gravel lane to the wagon pulling up behind it. He would need God's intervention to carry out this swindle seamlessly. . .not to mention the burliness of the six police officers hidden beneath that wagon's canvas, and the twice as many stationed in the shadows.

Baggett pulled on the reins, halting the dray, while next to him, Graybone frowned down at Jackson. "You ready for this?"

"Your daughter made sure I am." He patted his hip where one of the many knives Kit insisted he bring rested in a slim sheath.

Graybone's moustache twitched. "That girl," he grumbled. "Please tell me you slapped a pair of darbies on her to keep her at home tonight."

Pah! As if that would work. "That same girl can pick a cuff lock before either of us could blink."

Charles snorted. "Let's be about it, then, before she shows up." He glanced at the soot-blackened warehouse. "Unless she's already in there making a deal with the devil."

She very well could be, and the thought of it hardened Jackson's gut. "Let us hope she is not. Now, to reiterate, the moment Child hands over money for the crate of opium at the back, I'll give a shrill whistle. I assume the rest of the men are posted to flank the villain and whatever henchmen he may have with him?"

"All is set." Charles nodded.

"Good. Then converge on Child and his cronies as planned." Jackson turned on his heel and approached the old warehouse. A torch in a medieval-era sconce sizzled and flickered on one side of the big front door, making the place seem more like a castle fortress than a quayside storage building. He tried the handle, which gave, then sucked in a breath and charged ahead, ready for anything.

Anything but nothing, that is. No Child. No henchmen. The only movements were the macabre shadows he'd induced by the waft of air that came in with him, flickering the flame of a nearby lantern—which didn't do a thing to dispel the darkness of such an abyss. He snatched the light off the hook and held it out, scanning the area. The front ends of long rows of shelving mocked him in their resolve to be hiding any number of assassins. One could be training a muzzle on his head right now.

Banishing the thought, he advanced several steps then stopped, nerves on high alert. The faint scent of cigarette smoke wafted down a wooden staircase to his right. Craning his neck, he peered up the length of it. Dim light glowed at the top.

He took the stairs two at a time, lamp in one hand, the other poised to snatch his revolver from a hidden holster. As much as Kit loved a blade in her hand, he'd take a six-shot Webley any day.

There wasn't much to the upstairs but a short passageway with a few doors. Only one of them stood open, golden light cutting a triangle on the dusty floorboards. Keeping a sharp eye lest this be a trap, Jackson approached, with each step calculating how to react should he get jumped the moment his foot crossed the threshold. Heart beating hard, he swung into the room.

One man sat behind a paper-strewn desk, feet kicked up and crossed at the ankle, the red glow of a cigarette sticking out of his mouth. He was a middle-aged fellow, thick of waist and thin of hair. He wore a fashionable woolen coat, a crisp white dress shirt with a neatly knotted bow tie, and a pair of dark trousers. He could be the manager of this place or any number of other businesses. But that cold blue gaze belonged to a man who knew how to handle himself in a back-alley deal. He craned his neck, peering beyond Jackson before finally settling back on him. "Alone, are you?"

"Unlike your boss, I can manage on my own. Speaking of which, where is he?"

He took a final drag on his cigarette, the red tip flaring like a demon's eye, then abruptly sat up and ground the thing out in a glass dish overflowing with spent butts. He produced a card from inside his coat and held it out between two fingers.

What sort of game was this?

Wary, Jackson pinched the thing and retreated a step, positioning his back to the wall before flicking his gaze to the paper.

> *Unforeseen circumstance. Must reschedule.*
> *8:00 P.M. tomorrow.*
> *Bellow's Glassworks*

Jackson stifled a growl. Stood up. Again. Unless this were some sort of trick and even now Baggett and Graybone were outside fighting for their lives. He slammed the paper down on the desk. "Tell your boss I'm finished with his games."

"Tell him yourself." The man's gaze shifted slightly.

Jackson wheeled about.

No one was there.

Ugly laughter spilled out of the man in great peals. Snatching the throwing knife from the front slit in his sherwani, Jackson hurled the blade through the air. The man's hair riffled just above his ear as it passed and thwacked into the wall behind him.

The laughter instantly stopped.

"Next time I won't miss," Jackson called over his shoulder as he stalked from the room. His feet pounded hard on the stairs while he braced himself for what he might find outside. If an ambush were taking place, it was certainly a silent maneuver, for not a single sound of fists, grunts, curses, or gunfire leached through the warehouse walls. Even so, Jackson pulled his gun as he swung open the door.

But not one blessed thing smacked of danger. Baggett and Graybone yet perched on the wagon seat, the back of which remained covered with canvas. The street was eerily empty—as it should be after three in the morning. The only thing different was Shivaji now stood with arms folded near the front of the carriage instead of occupying the driver's seat.

Huh.

It appeared Child really did have something come up.

Both Baggett and Graybone eyed him as he drew near, and he lowered his voice for them alone. "It's a bust. Child rescheduled to tomorrow night at Bellow's."

Charles puffed out some air. "That doesn't bode well."

"No, it does not, but there's nothing to do about it other than regroup and give it a go tomorrow." Jackson tucked away his gun. "Maybe send in Frankie ahead of time for reconnaissance."

"Right." Charles tipped his head towards Graybone. "We'll see these men back to the station, then. Get yourself some sleep. Could be a rough one tomorrow evening."

Jackson nodded, the stone in his gut confirming the truth of Baggett's prophecy. Child was up to something, all right.

And only God knew what that might be.

Chapter Twenty-Seven

Kit jerked awake, groggy as a drunken sailor. Flit. She hadn't meant to doze off, but with her book fallen to her lap and the now-guttering lamp on the nightstand spitting remnants of light, clearly she had. Downstairs a floorboard creaked, and her gaze shot to the mantel clock. The minute hand crawled towards half past three. Oh dear. Yawning, she shoved the hair out of her face. Something must have gone wrong for Jackson to have returned so soon.

Kicking the blanket off her feet, she rose and frowned down at her skirt. She also hadn't meant to sleep in her day dress, but there was nothing to be done for it now except brush out a few of the wrinkles. Another floorboard groaned, this time closer to the bottom of the stairs. La! Why bother with wrinkles when her husband would likely have the gown off the moment he climbed those stairs and entered their bedroom?

And then she'd not find out what had happened until morning.

She adjusted the wick, filling the room with light, just as a shriek from the nursery traveled down the corridor. Crying followed. Kit smirked. Guess she *and* Bella would hear how Jackson's night went. She strode to the door, flung it open—

And stood face-to-face with a scar-faced man who stunk of burnt cabbage.

She reached for her knife.

Gone.

Blast!

She'd given it to Jackson.

Fingers bit into her upper arm, a sneer twisting the man's lips. "Gimme any trouble and there'll be the devil to pay."

She sized him up as he yanked her out of the doorway. The hulk outweighed her by at least ten or twelve stone, and those shoulders were as broad as a Devon bull's. Fist to fist was out of the question.

So she feigned a stumble. When his grip shifted, she wrenched free and lunged for the heavy crystal vase on the console table. The instant her fingers made purchase, she swung with all her might towards the brute's head. Flowers flew. But her reach wasn't quite high enough. The vase struck him in the shoulder, not a wounding blow, but enough to make him stagger.

Whirling about, she sprinted a few steps, then stopped dead cold. Another dark figure stepped from the nursery, Bella tucked beneath his arm. His other hand gripped a knife.

Bella wailed.

Kit stiffened.

They'd picked the wrong mama bear to cross.

She charged, head bent. If she rammed him in the gut, Bella would fall but so would the blade. And once her fingers met steel, by all that was holy she would—

Kit whumped to the floor, chin hitting hard. Teeth puncturing tongue. Blood filled her mouth. The next instant she was yanked to her feet, an iron bar of an arm across her chest, pinning her tight against a thick body.

And a blade at her throat.

Hot breath hit her ear. "Another move like that, and my partner there'll bash that baby's skull with his hilt. Understand?"

The other man raised his knife, ready to strike.

Cold terror prickled down her spine.

Oh God, please, spare my sweet girl.

Bella raged all the more.

Kit forced her body to slacken as if the life had been sucked from her bones, which it would be if anything happened to her baby. "No more trouble from me."

She felt more than saw the thug behind her nod at the other man. That brute carried Bella like a bundle of kindling beneath his arm as he tromped down the stairs. The beast behind her withdrew the knife from her throat then wrenched her arm behind her back, forcing her to follow or suffer a dislocation of the shoulder.

It was the longest walk of her life. From upstairs to sitting room, each of Bella's sobs pierced her heart afresh. The man jerked her to a stop in the center of the room, where she faced a scabby-skinned fellow with a pointy nose and dark buttons for eyes. She suspected the top hat on his head was more a power statement than for fashion, as was the black cane on which he languidly propped his forearm.

By now, Bella was red-faced bawling.

Kit scowled yet forced an even tone to her voice. "Do as you will with me but let my baby go."

"What's this? No tears? No hysterics? How singular." The man on the sofa twitched his head sideways, studying her. "I think I like you, Mrs. Forge."

"I do not share the sentiment," she snapped. "Who are you?"

His thin lips pinched. "I am disappointed you feel the need to ask. Carky esteemed your intelligence much higher than appears warranted."

Ahh. This was the man Carky had preferred to die for instead of disappoint...the man who'd clearly double-crossed Jackson. Gooseflesh lifted on Kit's arms. "What are you doing here, Mr. Child?"

"That's more like it." He grinned, exposing yellowed teeth. "Just thought I'd see for myself where Dominic Black lives. A bit shabbier than I expected. . ." He glanced from wall to wall. "For a chief inspector, that is. Have a seat, Mrs. Forge, before the shock weakens your knees. Can't have you swooning on me now."

The man behind her shoved her into the wingback adjacent the sofa, but the rough handling barely registered. He knew. Child knew! When had Jackson's cover been blown? How? Was there a mole somewhere or—

Bella's screeches cut into her thoughts, and she pushed to the edge of the cushion. "Please let me hold my baby."

"I am afraid that is out of the question." Child's head swiveled on his scaly neck, his dark eyes narrowing on the heavyweight holding her sweet girl. "Shut the brat up."

Kit grabbed hold of the chair arms. If that man dared strike Bella, she'd fly at him and die satisfied knowing she'd gouged out his eyes.

He reached into his pocket. Kit held her breath, praying so hard that sweat popped on her brow.

A dirty white cloth unfurled, and he shoved it into Bella's mouth. She kicked and squirmed, cries muffled, but was no match for a grown man.

Kit skewered Child with a sharp glare. "You won't get away with this."

Half a smile lifted one side of his mouth as he leaned back on the sofa, rubbing his thumb and forefinger along the length of the cane. "My dear, I get away with anything I please."

"No. Not always. Coleman is still alive and able to testify against you."

"A trifle." His gaze followed the movement of his fingers. "Coleman's knowledge goes only so far as the former Mr. Blade and the bumbling Mr. Bellow, for it was Bellow who oversaw the embezzling scheme, leaving me totally out of the picture. Coleman has no knowledge of who I am."

That didn't add up. "Then why hire Carky to kill him?"

"Because Coleman's testimony will ruin the beautiful downfall of Willis and Percival." His eyes hardened as he laid the cane in his lap. "A shame that plan got foiled, but it does give me a chance to devise a new and possibly more deadly way to shut them down."

A vendetta? That's what this was about? But try as she might, there was no way to figure out the gist of all he'd said with Bella's pathetic mewling breaking her heart. Fisting her hands to her belly, she eyed Mr. Child. "Did they shortchange you? Renege on a loan? Or, no, I know. . .Willis or Percival—both, perhaps—stumbled upon one of your dealings and cut in on it."

"Clever." Admiration sparked in his eyes. "But wrong on all accounts. Family honour runs deeper than money, you know."

"So your family was somehow slighted by Willis and Percival," she thought aloud. "They refused some funding or closed an account. Yet if so, that is hardly grounds to ruin the livelihood of two men, not to mention those who work beneath them."

"Do not think to lecture me, missy!" He rapped the cane sharply against the rug. "You have no idea what it is to grow up in a workhouse."

"You're right, I don't." Lifting her chin, she stared down her nose at him. "I didn't have the luxury of a roof while living on the streets."

Air hissed through his teeth. "The chief inspector married a guttersnipe?"

"Clearly you didn't do your research." She smiled, a nearly impossible feat when everything inside her ached to gather Bella in her arms.

Child shrugged. "You have to admit I was pressed for time."

Pah! She'd sooner take a brick to the head than sympathize with this villain. "Tell me, Mr. Child, how did Mr. Willis and Mr. Percival exile your family to such a harsh existence?"

"Mmm. Well. I suppose we have time." He wrapped his hands around the cane as if it were a neck to be choked. "I was a healthy, strapping boy until the current Mr. Percival's father ousted my own father from a partnership position with old man Willis, and the only way he could do it was through slander. Percival senior smeared my father's name with so much excrement, no one would hire him for the stink of his reputation. My father lost everything, our home, my mother—God rest her—and the health of his only son. . .me."

Well. That explained a lot. She might actually be inclined to extend him some grace were Bella not dampening the rug with the tears raining from her face. "I am sorry," she ground out, "but you are not the only one who has ever suffered so unjustly. I am living proof that mean childhood circumstances do not have to define who you are now."

"A pretty speech, Mrs. Forge, but it falls on deaf ears." His jaw stiffened.

So did Kit's. Trying to reason with the man would get her nowhere. Quickly, she shuffled through a dozen escape scenarios—bolt for the window, the door, the blackguard's neck who held Bella—yet each one fell flat. There was no simple way to make sure Bella didn't get hurt.

She looked daggers at the man defiling her sofa. "What do you intend to do with me and my baby?"

"The answer to that, my dear, hinges entirely on what your husband decides."

Jackson exited the carriage, annoyed with Child for rescheduling, with Shivaji for demanding to be paid at such a ridiculous hour instead of waiting till later, and especially with the sleek carriage parked in front of his house so that he'd have to walk extra steps to get to his door. Deep down he knew he was being petty, and yet he nursed the irritation with some satisfaction. It was always hard to be primed for a fight only to have the thing postponed. Blast that Child!

He tipped his head up at the big Punjabi hunched on the driver's seat. "Give me a moment."

Then he strode down the pavement and paused at the next carriage. "You there!" he hollered up at the driver. "Park this rig across the road in front of the pub instead of loitering in front of a residence. . .*my* residence."

The man nodded, his face hidden by the wide brim of a black hat.

That settled, Jackson turned to his home, not really surprised to see the sitting room light glowing behind the curtains. Though the little sprite had said otherwise, Kit was clearly waiting up for him instead of snuggled in bed with a book. He set his key in the lock but a click didn't follow. And his annoyance once again flared. He shoved open the door with a frown. "Kit! You should have bolted the door."

He pulled off his hat, which admittedly was quite the oddity in his Indian garb, but hanged if he didn't feel naked without his trusty old bowler atop his head. Pitiful wails—albeit muffled—pealed out from the sitting room. "Kit?" he hollered as he hung up his hat. "What's wrong with Bella?"

Down the corridor, Kit stepped one foot past the threshold, half in and half out of the sitting room. "I—em—I actually could use your help in here."

"Give me a moment. I first must pay—" He narrowed his eyes as he strode towards her. "Why is there blood on your mouth? What happened?"

"I. . .took a tumble."

The hairs at the back of his neck stood out like wires. This cat always landed on her feet. He pulled his gun from the holster.

Kit stiffened, a slight wince tightening her lips. "I'm fine, really. Come into the sitting room, darling, and I shall tell you all about the silly little mishap."

He paused, straining to decipher such mixed messages. Was something wrong, or had she truly taken a tumble and was trying to hide her hurt?

And suddenly she was yanked backwards.

He cocked the hammer as he stormed into the room, his heart stopping before his feet did. Child sat like a smug son-of-a-bullfrog on the sofa. To his left, a muscleman clutched Kit to his chest with an arm around her throat and a knifepoint to the side of her belly. And to his right—dear God! To Child's right stood the man he'd bested on the pavement in front of the bank, gripping Bella beneath his arm, a cloth poking out of her mouth. White-hot rage burned through Jackson's veins.

Child picked at one of the scabs on his cheek. "About time you arrived, Chief Inspector."

Thunderation! He knew. Half-blind with fury, Jackson sighted down the muzzle straight at Child's heart.

"Tut, tut." Child waggled his finger in the air. "Is my life worth that of your wife and daughter?"

"Do what you must to save Bella," Kit whispered.

Child chuckled. "Your wife is highly entertaining. I almost wish I didn't have to kill her." His eyes hardened to coal. "Put the gun on the floor, Chief."

Oh, God. . .

With each pound of Jackson's heart, he devised a different tactical maneuver. None would work, not without at least one of them getting killed. If he could be sure it would be him, then so be it, but were he to be taken out, that wouldn't completely rid Kit and Bella from Child's threat. How on earth had these knuckle bruisers gotten the jump on Kit?

"The gun!" Child barked.

Dread dried his mouth to ash. He was powerless—and there wasn't a blessed thing he could do about it. He released the hammer and slowly set the gun on the rug.

"Now kick it to me." Child rapped the tip of his black cane against the floor.

Sweat trickled down Jackson's spine.

"Do it!" Child roared.

Jackson kicked, hating his impotence, hating even more the scaly-faced man in front of him. Bella whimpered pathetically, each cry boiling his blood.

"Very good, Chief Inspector." Child swiped up the gun and trained it on him. "I see you are a reasonable man, which will make working out a deal with you all the easier."

"I don't make deals with criminals," he growled.

"You do if you want your baby to live." He snapped his fingers and the brute holding Bella immediately tipped her upside down. Her little body dangled, all the blood rushing to her head. A fall from that height would crack her skull.

"Jackson," Kit snarled. "Save Bella!"

She grunted. Blood bloomed a small circle at her waist where the knife bit deeper.

"That's enough!" Jackson shouted. "What do you want, Child? I've done as you asked."

"I want many things, Chief, but for now?" A smile slashed across his face. "For now, I think leverage will work just fine."

Bella's cries weakened. Kit sucked air audibly.

Jackson shook. "Either talk faster or call off your dogs!"

"I will take no commands from you, pig." Child cocked the hammer.

"Fine," he spit out the word, barely able to breathe. "What's your angle?"

"I could kill you all here and now, but like you, I am a reasonable man. And so, I have a proposition for you."

Terrorising an innocent child and woman, aiming a revolver at Jackson's heart—these were the acts of a reasonable man? Jackson seethed, the world turning a murderous red. "Get to it."

"Impatience ill becomes you, Chief. And yet I suppose we should get down to business." He inhaled, his chest puffing out a full two inches. "Instead of taking three lives, I will take the life of your wife alone. You shall live, as will your daughter, and in return you shall keep the law off my tail as I continue to do business as usual in this magnificent city of opportunity."

Hah! The man was mad if he thought he'd agree to any such thing. "I will hunt you down, Child, you and your men, and gut you like the animals you are."

"I think not." Child shook his head. "For you see, your darling little Bella will be coming with me. This is who she will call papa"—he circled his hand around his face—"and I shall raise her to be twice the mastermind I am. She will own this city, my little protégée. . .Miss Isabella *Child*."

"Over my dead body!" Kit bellowed.

"Yes, that has already been established. She's all yours, Gower, only do the deed elsewhere. I do not wish her husband to be distracted, as I am not yet finished negotiating. No, that's not the right word." He sneered at Jackson. "Commanding, more like."

The taunting words cut through Jackson's resolve like a knife. Just the thought of losing Bella to this monster drained the very blood from his body.

The big man—Gower—lugged Kit from the room. Or tried to. Kit was a wild, snarling animal. . .and Jackson prayed to God she could hold her own until he could get to her.

If he could get to her.

Fury and fear rose like bile to his throat.

"The conflict on your face is priceless, Chief Inspector. So, what's it to be? A quick slice of your child's throat and a bullet to your heart, or live with the knowledge that Bella is alive and well, safely in my care?" Child poked out his lower lip. "You can always marry again, you know."

Sweat rained down his back. Bella didn't cry anymore. Her whole head was red. Jackson's hands balled into tight fists, his jaw clenched even tighter. He couldn't bear the thought of Bella being raised by this demon, but what choice did he have? To say or do anything other would kill her on the spot.

A man roared from the dining room, followed by a bone-chilling scream. Then silence.

Jackson's bowels turned to water. Had he lost her? After all they'd been through? No! He wouldn't—*couldn't*—believe it. Not now. Not like this. He had to get to her. Had to see if she was bleeding out on the floor. Do something to save her!

But Bella. . .

Oh, God, what a choice!

Though it killed him in a thousand different ways, he looked Child square in the eyes. "Take the girl and go," he growled, voice so thick with emotion it was more of a rasp. "Just promise me she'll be safe."

Child's smirk widened, a sickening glint flashing in his dark eyes.

"Oh, she'll be safe, Chief. . .as safe as I want her to be."

As Child signaled for the man to haul Bella away, Jackson stood ramrod straight. Timing was everything, and at the right time, for Kit and Bella's sake, he would become a monster himself.

Chapter Twenty-Eight

Too fast! Her heartbeats. Her breath. The all-too-short time she'd been Bella's mother and Jackson's wife. She couldn't die. Not yet. Hot blood glued Kit's blouse to her waist. A flesh wound, she suspected, but once the brute dragged her into the dining room, he'd give her more than that.

Unless she gave it to him first.

She writhed. Wiggled. Wrenched. The knife blade scraped the skin along her ribs. The brute spat vile curses. Off balance, they stumbled into the dining room, the man's hip hitting a chair and tipping it over with a jarring crash.

Instead of pulling away, she leaned against him. Hard. He teetered, and the instant he did so, she jerked free. Backing away, she crouched to fight.

"Now ye've gone and done it." A cold smile broke on his face, lamplight from the dining room spilling in to glint off his upraised knife blade. "This'll be a pleasure."

Kit swallowed the fear clogging her throat. What she wouldn't give for the feel of a carved bone hilt clutched in her hand right about now.

Trying to ignore the pain in her side, she glanced wildly about for a weapon—*any* weapon. A chair? Possibly. Though by the time she grabbed the nearest she'd likely already have a blade planted in her back. Across the other side of the room the silver teapot on the sideboard tempted her. She could whale that against the man's skull if she could get to it.

But already he advanced.

Think. Think!

Angry voices boomed in from the sitting room. How much longer would Jackson and Bella have? She had to get to them. Had to do something!

Claws scratched along the baseboard to her right. Of all the times for Brooks to search for food, he had to pick now? Here?

She gasped.

Of course!

She lunged for the animal and flung it at her attacker with all her might.

The armadillo hit with a *thwack* against the man's face—and held, Brooks' claws making purchase. The man screamed. The knife fell.

Kit scrambled for it, barely snatching it up as Brooks once again flew through the air. Clutching the handle, she put all her weight into swinging her arm wide, praying for success.

If she failed now, she'd have only succeeded at enflaming the thug even more.

God, please.

The hilt hit the man's skull. A sickening thud. And yet as his eyes rolled back and he dropped like a felled log, never had she been so grateful.

But that didn't mean the war had been won.

She opened her mouth wide and screamed.

Then waited in silence.

Let them think she'd been bested. Killed. Because all she had now to help Jackson and Bella was the element of surprise.

Gripping the knife all the tighter, she crept towards the corridor as footsteps rushed out the front door.

No, no, no! Surely the villains weren't getting away. Surely she'd not find her husband and child dead on the sitting room floor. . .would she?

Her heart stopped, and it took everything inside her to keep edging onward, blade ready for retribution.

Jackson swung into the dining room, murder pumping through his veins. A lightning flash of steel arced towards his face. He lurched back just in time to feel a whoosh of air against his cheek.

A sharp intake of breath cut the silence—Kit's.

"Jackson?" His name was a shiver, her blue eyes blazing in the shadows. And he'd never loved her more in all his life.

Thank You, God! Thank You for sparing my wife.

But then his gaze fixed on where her hand pressed against her side. Shredded fabric and blood mingled together in an ugly mess. "You're hurt!"

"Never mind me. Where is Bella?"

Thunderation! That bleeding needed to be stopped—but Child was getting away.

Kit shoved past him. "Where is she!"

He grabbed her arm. Clearly Kit wasn't quite at death's door yet. "Tend to your wound. I'll go after her."

He charged into the front hall and yanked open the top drawer of the entry table, snatching out his Colt single action.

"Don't you dare think you're leaving me here," Kit hissed as he shoved open the door.

There was no time to argue the point. Child's carriage was already a dark spot in the night, the cad leaving behind one of his own men. Jackson raced to the barouche and hollered at Shivaji as he swung up to the seat. "Follow that hack!"

Twisting, the big Punjabi held out his hand. "Money first."

"You'll get your blasted money when we return. Go!"

Shivaji's hand didn't waver. "Now, sahib, or I walk."

"Then have a nice stroll." Kit leapt up to the driver's seat with a groan and snatched the reins from where they looped over the whip socket.

"Kit, you cannot seriously—" Jackson smacked against the seat as she cracked the horses into action.

Shivaji jumped ship.

And the chase was on.

Fighting for balance, Jackson worked his way to the front of the carriage and grabbed hold of the side rail—barely. At this speed, if she took a corner, he'd fly off. A grunt and a heave later, he climbed to the driver's seat next to Kit. "Give me those ribbons!"

She shook her head, gaze pinned sharply on Child's carriage in the distance. "You're a better shot than I am. I'll get us in range, then you take out the driver."

"Are you insane? I could hit Bella." He clutched the dash as they veered around a monstrous pothole.

"Do you have a better idea?" Kit hollered above the rumble of the wheels.

Hang it all! No, he didn't. But he'd have to come up with something fast. The blood on Kit's blouse bloomed all the larger. Grabbing hold of the hem of his sherwani, he ripped the fabric in a long strip then held it out in one hand. "At least bind that bleeding until we catch up. I'll take the reins."

She didn't spare him a glance, but she did comply. Leather firmly in his grip, he urged the horses onward. Much too slowly for his liking, he edged closer to Child's coupé, though the brigand was still several streets ahead. It didn't help that at this hour the city was slowly waking. Jackson narrowly missed a boy on a bicycle towing a cart of newspapers, and curses rang from the delivery man he'd cut off.

Yanking hard on the reins, he wheeled them around a corner.

"Oof!" Kit grunted. "I'm nearly done but take it easy."

"I'm gaining on him. His carriage is lighter, prone to swaying and skidding as he takes a corner, so we have the advantage."

Ahead, the coupé turned yet again. Good! For once the maze of London streets worked in his favour. But this time when he reached the next turning point, Jackson yanked on the reins, stopping them flat. "Blast!"

He stared down the darkened passage at the fleeing villain, his own barouche too wide to fit through such a thin throat. Anger boiled in his gut. Hot. Fierce. That blackguard was getting away with his daughter, his flesh, his blood, his heart. He angled, poising to leap and chase them down like the dogs they were.

But Kit's hand on his arm held him back.

"Let me." She grabbed the ribbons. "That passage ends in a T, and I know where he'll spit back out on the road."

The horses bolted. He once again grabbed the dash. "There are two sides to that T," he hollered. "How do you know he won't turn the other way?"

"Because the Limehouse Lashers blocked one end up years ago as a way to control their territory."

Years ago? Bah! Any number of things might've changed since then. "I hope you're right."

"I hope so too." Fear tightened her voice.

The same fear that stole the air from his lungs. Even if they did catch up—no, when!—there was no telling what sort of state Bella might be in after such a harrowing ride. Squinting, he strained to see ahead as Kit rounded the next corner on what felt like only two wheels.

"There he is!" Jackson pointed at the dark blob of a carriage many streets ahead.

"Are you sure that's a coupé and not a cab?"

"As sure as you were about that T."

She urged the horses to a lather. They wouldn't last much longer at this rate, but. . .yes. . .that was Child's coupé. He'd bet his life on it—and just may lose it if things didn't go as planned. "It's him all right."

Holding a steady course, Kit gained on them. Jackson pulled his gun and cocked the hammer. Timing and precision would be everything now. As much as he wanted to take out the brute holding the reins, a driverless carriage would crash, with Bella inside. He just couldn't take the chance. It would be tough, but with God's help, the moment Kit pulled alongside them, he'd aim for the horses' legs.

"Steady," he warned as Kit closed in on them, their horses' noses practically kissing the back bumper of Child's coupé.

But then the coupé turned again, this time onto London Bridge. Child surged ahead, their heavier barouche no match on the straightaway.

"Come on. Come on!" Kit snapped the reins like a whip.

Jackson released the hammer, frustrated beyond measure. Would this cat-and-mouse game never end? Child's coupé reached the end of the bridge deck before they made it even halfway. But then—what was this? Jackson narrowed his eyes.

"Looks like he's, no. . .can't be." He leaned ahead, straining to see. "He's turning around." His eyes widened. "He's coming right for us!"

"Well, we'll just see who flinches first."

Pulling his gaze from Child's coupé, he glanced at his wife, heart clenching at the determined set of her jaw. "Kit, that's our child in there. Do not think to crash into him."

"Just have your gun ready. You ought to be able to take out that driver with one shot."

"You're mad!" He shoved the gun back into his holster. "I'm not going to shoot here on the bridge. Those horses go out of control and Bella will be plunged into the Thames."

She spared him a dark scowl. "We have to do something!"

Indeed. But what?

Horse hooves pounded. Theirs. Child's. Closer. Closer. The coupé's light shone on the monster's face driving the thing. No doubt that villain was counting on them to swerve, lose command of the horses, and plummet—

Hold on. *Swerve?*

"Plan this well, Wife. Veer off at the last minute but stay close to the coupé. The instant we are parallel, I'll jump."

She glanced at him, a horrified twist to her lips. "Now who's the mad one?"

"Have *you* a better idea?"

Cheeks pale, she faced forward. Hopefully she had enough stamina left in her to pull this off.

Wheels rumbled. Jackson's heart thundered against his ribs as he once again poised to leap. . .but this time onto a carriage speeding pell-mell. One slip and he'd easily go under the wheels, crushed like a beetle.

They drew closer, so near, the whites of the driver's eyes flashed in the darkness. Hold. Hold. And. . .

"Now!" Jackson growled.

Kit yanked the left rein. The horses swerved. The barouche juddered. But Kit held course, thank God! Child's horses pounded past. A breath more and he'd be even with the carriage. He'd spring and—

Child's driver swung his arm, a fireball hurtling towards Jackson like a thrown grenade. Jackson raised his hand to ward it off. Too late. Glass and metal cracked into his shoulder. He jerked against Kit as the lantern that'd hit him bounced to the ground and smashed beneath the wheels in a sickening grind.

She pulled on the reins, slowing the barouche enough to turn in a tight circle. "Are you all right?"

A growl rumbled low in his throat, words impossible, so much fury choked him.

They raced ahead, but by the time they cleared the bridge deck and peered down the possible avenues of choice, no coupé was in sight.

Kit pulled the heaving horses to a halt. "Which way?"

His gaze swept from one street to the next. "I don't know."

"We can't have lost them!"

He'd never heard her so hysterical—and the sound chilled him to the marrow of his bones. After all this, they couldn't lose Bella. Not now. Heart sinking clear to his boots, he once again studied the roads, three in all. Roughly a thirty percent chance, a wager so dismal he'd not take it at a horse race. He jumped to the cobbles, pacing to keep from exploding.

And then he spied it. A broken cobble. Fresh. Not much to go on, but it was all they had.

Tearing back to the carriage, he leapt to the seat and pointed. "There. That way."

It didn't take any further encouragement for Kit to get them rolling, though by now the horses were spent. Then again, Child's had to be too…and thankfully, they must've been. When the road curved, Jackson once again sighted the coupé. This time, though, something banged about beneath it. A wheel chock, if he didn't miss his mark, jerking like a crazed cannonball tethered to a chain. If that thing hit a wheel, a spoke would break and—

Crack!

The carriage listed. The driver bailed. The horses took off at the sound.

"Jackson," Kit moaned, desperation thick in her tone.

And there wasn't a blasted thing he could do about it but watch, horrified, as Child's coupé flipped and skidded to a stop at the base of a streetlamp.

Chapter Twenty-Nine

More paperwork. Wouldn't Jackson love that? Charles smirked as he shoved the pile across the counter to Breakhouse, the night-shift clerk. And the kicker of it all was that he'd have to fill out the same forms all over again tomorrow—no, make that later today. Yawning, he scrubbed a hand over his face. He honestly didn't know what was worse, sitting wired up for a fight to begin or filling out the report afterwards. Ludicrous, though, that success or not, he must sign off on duplicates and triplicates for the equipment used, even if it was only a wagon and some horses.

Breakhouse tapped the papers on the counter, straightening them to an orderly stack. "That oughtta do it, Baggett. See ya in"—he swung his head over his shoulder to glance at the clock—"four hours. Well, I won't, but Smitty will."

"Thanks, Break—"

The front doors crashed open. In ran a man in a tattered coat, sleeves frayed, his trousers patched at the knees and stained with dirt and grime. The smell of human waste wafted about him like a noxious cloud. A night-soil man. He'd bet on it.

"There's been a terrible accident!" The fellow rapped the counter with his fist. "Someone's bound to be hurt or worse."

Charles glowered. "And you didn't stay to help?"

"Oh no." He shook his head, his greasy beard swinging in an arc against his coat. "The sight of blood makes me positively green."

Pah! The man's stench was enough to make Charles vomit.

"Where at?" Breakhouse asked.

"Over on Poultry and Queen Victoria."

Breakhouse faced Charles. "I know you're supposed to be off duty, but could you? We're a bit short-staffed at the moment."

Well. So much for four hours of shut-eye.

"I'm on it." He sighed. "Summon a doctor for now and pray we won't need the coroner."

Fortunately the intersection wasn't far away. Fortunate as well that the sky hadn't broken yet, for the scent of rain hung thick on the air. But if the weather held, and depending on how long this incident took, he just might swing by Martha's on his way home for a cup of coffee.

Several streets later, he turned onto Poultry. In the distance he spied the dark hulk of an overturned carriage beneath a streetlamp, another carriage behind it yet upright. As he drew closer, he also made out the silhouette of what appeared to be two people huddled together, sitting on the kerb away from the crash. Apparently the night-soil man needn't have worried about tossing his accounts, for clearly they'd made it out alive.

But the closer he drew, the more a cold sweat formed on his brow. He couldn't identify the crashed coupé, but that barouche parked behind it looked suspiciously like the one Jackson had requisitioned. He upped his pace.

And then his step hitched.

Jackson sat on that kerb, his arm around his wife. Kit bent so that her face wasn't visible, curled over the still form of a child. Blood darkened the side of her blouse and skirt.

He ran the last few steps, barely breathing, eyes pinned on little Bella. "Great heavens! Is she. . . ?" His throat closed tight, refusing to voice the abominable thought.

Jackson glanced up, eyes glassy, face haggard. "Charles? What are you doing here?"

Clearly the shock of what had happened was too much for Jackson. It would've been for any man. Though he hated to part them, Charles offered his friend a hand. He wasn't a husband yet, but instinct told him Jackson wouldn't speak candidly in front of a grieving wife and mother. "A word, Jackson, if you are able. We won't be but a moment, Mrs. Forge."

Kit didn't acknowledge him.

Jackson took his hand, allowing him to pull him to his feet. The contact lasted less than a breath, but long enough to note the clamminess of Jackson's skin. Charles strode a few steps then turned to him. "What happened?"

Jackson rubbed the back of his neck as he stared up at the night sky. In the glow of the streetlamp, he looked years older. "Child double-crossed me. He didn't show at the warehouse because he was at my home. He and his hired dogs held Kit at knifepoint and then. . ." He dropped his hand, his gaze now burning into Charles'. "He took her, Charles. Child took my girl, and I—Kit and I gave chase. I thought. . .oh, I thought—" Jackson's Adam's apple bobbled, his eyes turning red.

Charles struggled to maintain his own composure. There was a time once when he'd been a lad and came across a boy several years his junior. The boy wept great tears over his pet bunny that lay in the gutter with a twisted neck, bullies mocking behind him. And the same awful mix of horror, fury, and gut-wrenching sorrow clenched his hands as tightly now as it had then.

"We'll need a coroner," Jackson murmured.

"Yes, of course."

"And a doctor."

Charles studied his friend. He appeared to be whole apart from some blood smeared on his sherwani, blood which Charles suspected was not his own. But on the off chance, he asked, "Are you hurt?"

Jackson shook his head. "Kit needs a doctor. She's lost a lot of blood. Oh, and send a constable to my house. She took down another man there."

"What about Child? He inside that carriage?" He tipped his head towards the wreckage.

Jackson's face hardened to granite. "He is. Ironic, is it not, that the very monster who wished to harm my daughter ended up saving her."

Saving? Was this some sort of denial? Some clinging to false hope to avoid reality?

Charles glanced over at Kit and the still form of Bella. A heart-breaking sight if ever there was one, enough to crack a strong mind like Jackson's right in half. Out of respect, though, he ought to at least offer a modicum of respect and give his old friend the benefit of the doubt. "Feel up to explaining that?"

Jackson inhaled deeply. "I don't know how it happened exactly, other than by the grace of God. When that coupé crashed, it landed in such a way that Child's neck was snapped, but his body shielded Bella's. The law of physics, momentum and whatnot, I suppose, though I prefer to think of it as a miracle."

Charles blinked. Try as he might, Jackson's words made no sense whatsoever. "Are you saying Bella is alive?"

Jackson's brow bunched, mirroring his own look of bewilderment. "She is, though she's been banged up and given in to exhaustion. As soon as the doctor stitches up Kit, I shall have him give Bella a thorough examination. It's been a harrowing experience for us all."

Charles' jaw dropped, the world beneath his feet tilting off its axis. Life was fleeting and fragile, and yet little Bella had survived. "That is good news. I mean that's wonderful news!"

Half a smirk twitched Jackson's mouth. "Sorry if I led you to believe otherwise."

"Think nothing of it." He cuffed Jackson on the arm. "You've been through a lot. Go sit by your wife. I'll manage what's to be done."

"I appreciate that. This whole thing has hit me harder than you can imagine." He squeezed Charles' shoulder. "You're a good friend, Baggett."

"Just doing my job, Chief."

Giving his old friend plenty of space to continue comforting his wife, Charles strode towards the downed coupé. A glance of the area showed no bodies thrown from the crash. "Forgot to ask about the driver," he called over his shoulder. "What happened to him?"

"He ran off, but trust me when I say he will be found." A murderous tone sharpened Jackson's voice. "If I have to tear this city apart brick by brick, he *will* be found."

Rain pelted the nursery windows. A dismal start to a dismal day. . .and yet there was so much to be thankful for. Kit leaned over Bella's crib, mourning the bruise on her sweet baby's brow and the scrape on her little chin. But Isabella Jane Forge was a scrapper, all right, sleeping soundly as if she'd not narrowly missed death a few hours ago. Just thinking of pulling the bawling child from the mangled carriage weakened Kit's knees, and she shuddered with the aftershock.

Beside her, Jackson squeezed her hand. "All is well now, Wife. Come, you need rest yourself. Doctor's orders, remember?"

Though her husband said otherwise, worry pinched the sides of his mouth, evidence of the tension and stress that'd taken a toll on him. In truth, her side did ache something fierce and she was weary. Yet despite all that, deep down she knew rest would not come easy, not until her nervous energy subsided. She squeezed his fingers back. "What I need first is a cup of tea."

"I think I can manage that." He winked.

Her knees wobbled again, but for a very different reason. Oh, how she loved this man, this child they'd made, this home, this life. And she'd come so close to losing it all. She leaned heavily on the railing as she followed Jackson downstairs. Of course such weakness could be blamed on the stitches in her side—and naturally that played into it—but more likely it was the battle raging inside her that drained her vigour. All this time she'd been wishing away the dirty dishes and soiled nappies, the laundry and the cooking, counting such tasks as less important than bringing justice to those in need. Yet were the seemingly small details of life really less significant than her grandiose ambitions? Was being a detective worth sacrificing the simple, mundane joys that made life worth living?

She eased into the kitchen chair that Jackson held out for her. "I'm going to quit the agency."

He frowned as he reached for the kettle. "That's a bit rash, don't you think?"

Hardly. She'd been pondering this for some time now, but how to explain the angst she barely understood herself? She shifted on the chair, wincing as she did so. "Bella was almost killed today."

"I know, love." Sorrow ran thick in his voice. He finished filling the kettle and set it on the fire before turning to her. "But the fact remains she wasn't. It is God who numbers our days, not you or I or anyone else. You're weary. You're hurt. It's the worst possible time for you to make any snap decisions."

"But Jackson, I do not say this in haste. I've given this a great deal of thought." Heaving a sigh, she glanced down at her ripped blouse and stained skirt. Oh, but she was tired of blood. "I want to be a good wife, a good mother. I want to make a good home for you and Bella, a shelter, a refuge."

"I know you do, yet that doesn't mean you must go about those roles in the same way as other women." He set two cups on the table, his eyes narrowing. "Wait a minute, you're not blaming yourself for this whole mess, are you?"

Though the cup was empty, she clutched it, seeking warmth as a sudden chill shivered across her shoulders. "If I'd never taken the Coleman case, none of this would have happened. I shouldn't be running around on the streets pegging for trouble. I'm not a girl anymore. I'm not *that* girl anymore, and I should stop trying to be."

"Yet you weren't on the streets. You were home when this happened. Isolating yourself is no guarantee of safety because there are no guarantees. You of all people should know this."

"I don't get it." She shook her head slowly. "I thought you'd be pleased if I became a homemaker."

"Of all the absurd ideas." He pulled a chair close to her and reached for both her hands, the touch of him warm and soothing as he rubbed circles on her wrists with his thumbs. "Listen to me, Kit. I don't want a housewife. What I want is you just exactly as God has made you. That's all I've ever wanted. . .*you're* all I've ever wanted."

The huskiness of his voice, the naked love flaring in his eyes, the words—all of it went down deep and comforted like a soothing balm. She closed her eyes, memorising the feel of his big hands pressed against hers, desperately trying to ignore the burn of tears.

Because despite his affirming sentiment, something had to change. She couldn't keep putting herself in danger and neglecting her family. A balance must be found.

But how?

Chapter Thirty

The rain had stopped, but the puddles left behind were many and massive. Jackson sidestepped a wide pool as he closed in on the Old Jewry station, attention snagged by a black-lacquered landau with gold trim parked out front. Not a speck of mud marred the shiny coach, for the driver even now was buffing a fender. Quite the eye-catcher for this neighbourhood. Some toff either had gotten lost and needed directions or was filing a complaint of some sort. Hopefully not the latter, for he had other matters to attend. . .namely slapping irons on Child's thug who'd bailed from the carriage.

And once again he thanked God for sparing little Bella.

Inside the station, the usual afternoon hubbub filled the corridors. Smitty hailed him before he could make it to the stairs. "Oy, Chief! Two men up in yer office. Might wanna brace yerself."

The clerk's warning juddered through him. Sweet heavens. "What day is it?"

"'Tis the seventeenth all day, Chief."

His heart sank clear to his muddy shoes. Hammerhead expected his report today. . .a report he'd last seen going up in flames thanks to Harvey. If the fancy carriage outside were any indication, not only was the superintendent tapping his toes up in his office but so was the commissioner. Jackson took the steps two at a time, heart pounding. He may as well box up his personal belongings and call it quits right now.

Pausing before shoving open the door, he inhaled deeply, lifted a prayer, then strode in to his own execution. Two steps later, he stopped, blinking. Not only was his office immaculate, but neither of the two finely dressed gents rising to their feet were the superintendent or the commissioner.

They were mirror images of each other.

"Come in, come in, my dearest of friends." The squeaky voice was Catchpole's. The rest of him was not. His hair had been trimmed and neatly slicked back. The bodacious red coat was replaced with a modest navy-blue suit of worsted wool. And most surprisingly, his clean-shaven face was not hidden by a masquerade mask. Though still woefully thin, Ezra Catchpole looked every bit the nobleman as the man standing next to him.

"Please"—Ezra motioned him in—"allow me to introduce you to my brother, the Viscount Eldridge Suthmeer. Brother, this is the man who saved my life, Chief Inspector Jackson Forge."

"Pleased to meet you, Lord Suthmeer." Jackson dipped a formal bow.

"The pleasure is mine, Chief Inspector." The viscount gave a sharp nod.

Jackson looked beyond them, still stunned to see the chairs were cleared of papers. "Do have a seat, gentlemen." He rounded his desk and took his own.

The viscount settled deeply into the wingback while Ezra perched on the edge of his. Jackson hid a smile. He may be spit shined outwardly, but it was oddly good to see he yet retained some of his eccentricity.

"We will not keep you long. You are surely as busy a man as I." The viscount sniffed, his Roman nose bunching with the movement. "Yet I wished to extend a personal thank-you for taking my wayward brother under your wing."

Under his wing? Hah. More like he'd been trying to bat the man away, or at the very least avoid him. "I wouldn't be so generous as to say that, my lord. Nonetheless, I am happy to be of service."

"Such modesty is commendable yet misplaced. Because of you not only has our relationship been restored but so has our family honour." He swiveled his head towards Ezra. "Would you like to tell him, Brother?"

"Indeed." The same crooked teeth flashed full force in a huge smile cracking across Ezra's face. "You, Chief Inspector Forge, have been such an excellent example to follow that I have decided to leave behind my vagabond ways and pursue the law."

He swallowed lest he choke. Stars and wonder! Pursue law? A terrible picture formed in his mind, that of trying to make an officer out of Ezra Catchpole. . .and his viscount brother had all the clout to make that happen. "Mr. Catch—er—Suthmeer, it is in your best interest when I say that I really don't think you are well suited for the rough-and-tumble life of an officer."

"Oh!" Ezra chuckled, slapping the arm of the chair. "As always, you could not be more correct. No, no, I intend to become a solicitor. When you asked me to check into that criminal Mr. Child, I acquired quite the taste for rooting out injustice. I hope to help others right the wrongs committed against them, and as a solicitor, I can do just that."

Relief shot him to his feet, and he rounded the desk to shake Ezra's hand. "That is brilliant news! I wish you all the best."

The viscount stood as well. "Thank you, Chief Inspector, and on that note, we shall bid you good day. Come along, Ezra."

Ezra gave his hand an extra shake before releasing his hold. "Goodbye, my friend. Perhaps I shall see you in court someday."

Jackson grinned. "Perhaps you will."

But as the door shut behind them, that grin faded and he plopped into the recently vacated wingback, face in his hands. That report was due today and he had nothing to show for it. Nothing! He'd be dismissed before he could muster enough resources to track down that villainous driver who'd nearly killed Bella.

Huffing a sigh, he dropped his hands, and then his gaze focused on a thick but neat folder atop his desk, one he hadn't noticed before. He reached for it and paged through, his jaw dropping lower with each swipe. Smart penmanship filled row upon row, each one stating concisely an offender's name, date of apprehension and charges, time of hearing and sentence, and the accompanying prison information if applicable. Closing the cover in disbelief, he stalked to the file cabinets. Yet he didn't need to rummage through drawer after drawer, for each one bore a clear label for what could be found inside. . .and not a blessed one of them was in code. All made sense, were alphabetized, and were even ranked in chronological order. Harvey had done it. The rotund little meatball in a suit had made order out of chaos. The man was a miracle worker. A genius of administration. A valuable asset that he ought to have employed sooner as his own personal assistant.

And yet he'd dismissed him. Blast! What a mistake. Worse still, he could almost hear the Almighty chuckling at his realisation. Hadn't He warned Jackson not to be so quick about judging someone's appearance but to actually stop to listen? For Harvey had told him— repeatedly if memory served right—that his gift was paperwork. Jackson cast a glance heavenward.

I get it, Lord. Don't judge. Listen.

Snatching the report off the desk, he dashed out of the office and jogged down the stairs to the front counter. "Smitty, I need this sent by courier to Superintendent Hammerhead's office immediately." He set down the folder and glanced at the clock. An hour to spare before Hammerhead would call it a day. He tapped his finger on top of the pile. "Make it top priority."

"I'm on it, Chief." Smitty pulled the report across the counter.

"Also, send word at once to Ira Harvey that I wish him to return to work here at the station posthaste. Tomorrow morning, if possible. Inform him he is to be my new personal assistant."

Smitty's face twisted, his side-whiskers skipping along for the ride. "I don't follow, sir. How can ye rehire someone who wasn't dismissed in the first place?"

"But I did dismiss him."

"Must not have been clear to him, then." Smitty wagged his big head. "Why, this very moment he's poking about the supply room, planning how to reorganize that mess."

What a kicker—but a good one for a change.

"Ahh, you're here." Baggett's voice boomed down the hall as he approached. "I've got good news and bad. Which do you prefer first?"

Jackson held up a finger and faced the clerk. "See to that report immediately, Smitty. There's a lot depending upon it."

"Aye, Chief."

Jackson tipped his head, signaling for Baggett to follow him to a nearby bench. In all his years of service, he'd learned that good news was often elusive and bad news all too abundant. If he were to shoulder ill tidings, best to do so sitting down. "Let's have the worst over with." He held his voice steady despite the trepidation settling in his left temple like a big headache.

Charles dropped beside him, weary crescents smudged beneath his eyes. The man deserved a leave of absence for the nonstop service he'd performed these past several weeks.

"That driver whose head you want on a platter?" He waited until Jackson nodded. "Too late. Someone else got to him first. His body's over at the city morgue right now."

Mixed emotions roiled in his gut, one of which he was ashamed to admit was a slight amount of perverse pleasure in seeing justice—albeit harsh—served, even if he had not been the one to deliver it. "Do you know who did it?"

Charles nodded. "Bellow. Not directly, mind. He hired a killer."

"But why? It was my understanding that cully worked for Child, not Bellow."

"Apparently he worked for both." Charles shrugged. "And with Child gone, Bellow made a move to have him put down, along with any others who held split allegiance."

"Bold move for such a weasel." He stretched out his legs, then pulled them back as several officers lugged a man towards the stairs. Did Bellow seriously think to claim the criminal dynasty left behind by Child?

"What's the good news?" He studied Charles' face.

A smile lifted Baggett's moustache. "Bellow is locked up downstairs. Frankie found a cache of crates packed with blown-glass figurines, each one filled with a ball of opium. And if Coleman's testimony can tie him into the embezzlement scheme against Percival and Willis, Mr. Bellow is looking at a very, very long time in gaol."

Baggett's smile was infectious, and for the first time in weeks, hope buoyed Jackson's soul. "Then I'd say justice has been served on all accounts."

"Which is cause for celebration, eh?" Charles clapped him on the back.

Jackson eyed him. "What have you in mind?"

"First, a pint at the pub." He winked. "And then a wedding."

He'd known this day was coming. Had even told Jackson so on a day that seemed like forever ago instead of only a week. But now that Charles stood at the altar, he could hardly believe the time had arrived. Yet here it was. Any moment now, Martha would sweep down that aisle. Unless she didn't. A lifetime commitment was a big decision after all. What if she harboured second thoughts? Had changed her mind completely? He tugged at his collar, the infernal thing suddenly a noose.

Beside him, Jackson leaned close and spoke low. "Steady on, old man. She'll be here. She's not Kit."

He hid a shudder. What horror Jackson had suffered when he'd stood in this very place and his bride hadn't shown. "I don't know how you did it," he whispered. "You're made of sterner stuff than I."

A rogue smile curved Jackson's mouth. "You wouldn't have said that a few years ago to a certain bubble-headed rookie."

"I didn't say you were bubble-headed." He smirked. "I said your ideas were."

"Well, this one isn't. Marrying Martha is the right thing to do. You were made for each other."

Some of the tension eased in his shoulders. Jackson was right. From the moment he'd met Martha, he'd felt she was a kindred spirit, something he'd never experienced with any other woman. He was making the right choice. Besides, it wasn't as if he hadn't given this any thought whatsoever. He'd agonized over it the past year and a half.

He exhaled long and slow, his gaze drifting to the few friends and family seated in the pews...and then his muscles knotted up again. Seven pairs of eyes locked on to him from the front row, ranging in age from three to fifteen. Martha's children. Soon to be *his* children. Though he'd asked each of them, and somewhat miraculously all seven had agreed to this wedding—even Harriet—reactions had been mixed, from thrilled to coolly accepting to Frankie's "That's all right by me but—hey! Yer not goin' to kiss my mum, are ye?"

A smile twitched Charles' lips as his gaze passed from the boy to Harriet. For once she didn't have a hostile gleam in her eyes, but neither was it effervescent. This wouldn't be an easy transition for any of them. What did he know of being a father? How did one rear a small human to become a fully functioning adult? Certainly a whack with a truncheon or a slapped-on pair of darbies wouldn't do the trick, and yet that was all he knew. His palms turned slick with sweat. He'd faced down some of the worst criminals in London, but nothing—*nothing*—had prepared him for the role he was about to take on.

Great heavens. The weight of this moment was too much to bear. Maybe he should walk away. Apologize profusely for the mistake he'd committed. Repent of ever thinking he'd make a good husband and father. He shuffled his feet, gut twisting. Organ music began, the first strains of "All Creatures of Our God and King" lifting to the rafters. If he were going to bust out of here, now was the time.

Jackson elbowed him. "Here she comes."

Charles' gaze shot to the back of the sanctuary, and the moment his eyes fixed on Martha, every fear and doubt fled like a hot-footed cutpurse. With each steady step, she radiated elegance in her simple gown of soft pink, the same hue that glowed on her cheeks. Her hair was pulled back in a loose braid, uncaught tendrils framing her heart-shaped face and curling against her bare neck. Ahh, but she was a picture. Nay, a masterpiece. His pulse raced.

And when she joined his side at the altar, her gaze of adoration nearly buckled his knees.

The ceremony blurred. He'd not be able to repeat a blessed word spoken by the reverend were a gun held to his head. But one thing he knew now for certain: he was in love with this woman, and he'd give every day for the rest of his life proving that to her.

"Charles?" Martha's blue eyes looked hopefully into his.

He stiffened, aware now that he ought to be doing something. Saying something. But what? More organ music played, yet for the life of him, he couldn't think what to do. How could he? All his thoughts were filled with the beauty in front of him.

"That's your cue, old man." Jackson nudged him. "Give her a kiss and take her away."

He didn't need any further urging. Pulling Martha into his arms, he kissed her soundly to the cheers of those in the sanctuary. His heart swelled as he took her hand and led his wife—*his wife!*—down the aisle. Her children trailed behind, flower petals raining over them save for the handfuls Frankie used to pelt him in the back. They emerged into bright sunlight to a waiting carriage, the horses festooned with ribbons and flowers. He grinned. Kit's handiwork, no doubt.

He opened the door then turned to his wife with an extended hand. "May I help you up, Mrs. Baggett?"

"Oohh, I like the sound of that." Smiling, she gripped his fingers, then called over her shoulder, "Behave yerselves, children, or ye'll have Miss Kit and Mr. Jackson to answer to."

"Kipes!" Frankie bellowed.

Without missing a beat, Kit promptly cuffed the boy in the head.

Chuckling, Charles helped Martha into the carriage then took his place beside her. As the wheels lurched into motion, he wrapped his arm around his wife's shoulders. "Well, we did it."

"We did—and about time, too!" She rested her head against his chest, a contented sigh making his heart soar.

The carriage rolled onward, an uncertain future stretching before them, but one they would face together with love and determination.

"Kipes!"

"Mind your tongue, young man." Kit smacked a light yet firm warning on Frankie's head, then peered up at Jackson, a squirming Bella in his arms. "Are you ready for chaos?"

"I married you, didn't I?" He arched a brow.

She scowled. "I meant with watching Martha's children for the next few days."

"Yes, Wife." A handsome smile lit his face, the dark stubble of a newly forming moustache making him all the more attractive. "If things get out of hand, we'll just lock them up down at the station."

"You read my mind."

"Now that would be a miracle." Bending, he buffed a light kiss on her brow.

"You, sir, are a scoundrel, but speaking of miracles—" She lunged for three-year-old Hazel and snatched her back before the girl tore off into the road. How Martha had managed for so long on her own was a wonder. It truly hadn't been fair of her to add to her friend's load by asking her to care for Bella this past month.

Handing Hazel her unused bag of flower petals to play with, Kit then faced Jackson. "Speaking of miracles, I think I've finally come up with a solution to my dilemma about how to juggle being a detective and a mother."

"Oh?" He jostled Bella to his other arm, prying her little hand from his jaw. "Pray tell."

She should, and she would. . .but not quite yet. She gave him a mysterious smile. "I need to discuss it with my father—I mean, my partner, first."

His brows pulled into a dark line. "But I am your husband."

"You are." She grinned in full. "And as such, you should know I like to keep you on your toes."

Chapter Thirty-One

The streets of Blackfriars were a'swirl this morning. An old lady clucked at a chicken she chased along the gutter. A shabby-skirted girl pulling a wagon of fresh watercress to market catcalled back and forth with a group of lads lugging bags over their shoulders. Coffee sellers barked. Bread merchants one-upped them. Carriages, horses, even a penny-farthing bicycle all rolled along the streets, wheels grating against the cobbles. But after several days of tending Martha's children, this bedlam was a reprieve. Kit would much rather take her chances with dodging a loaded dray than to referee yet one more tearful argument about who'd used whose hairbrush without first asking. Not to mention Frankie's usual hijinks in harassing Brooks or hiding a mouse in his sister's bed. Despite all the hubbub, Jackson hadn't breathed another word about getting rid of Brooks. When she'd asked about it the other day, he muttered something about not dishonouring a hero.

Beside her, Jackson bought a newspaper off a seller. Tucking it beneath his arm, he glanced at her. "Remind me again why you are not taking Bella to Martha's?"

Ahh. A new tactic. Did he truly think she'd fall for such a nonchalant way of squeezing details from her? "Nice try, Chief Inspector." She smiled up at him. "But you'll not get any information out of me until we meet with my father."

"You'll have to admit I gave it a good try last night, though, didn't I?" He winked.

Her blood instantly heated with the memory. Indeed. She'd nearly told him all beneath such coercion—which made her frown. "I certainly hope you don't use that method when interrogating other women."

"Only you." He pressed a sideways kiss to her cheek. "Yet I still don't understand why I am accompanying you and Bella to the agency."

"Maybe I just enjoy your company." She shrugged.

"Or maybe you've got something up your sleeve."

"Pish." She steered around a gingerbread stall sticking out much too far on the pavement. "After minding all of Martha's—and now Charles'—children, I am fortunate to have sleeves yet on my arms."

"They were a handful." He straightened his tie, hiding the jagged edges snipped by six-year-old Mary when she'd gotten hold of the scissors. "Baggett's got his work cut out for him."

She arched a brow. "Are you saying you wouldn't like more children?"

"Would you?" He met her stare, poker face in place. Handsome but irritating.

"I think I should like very much to have a son who looks like you. Someday. But for now Miss Bella is enough." She leaned over the top of the pram. "Aren't you, sweetums? Say mama. Ma. Ma."

Jackson nosed her out of the way. "Papa, little love. Say papa."

Bella waved her rag doll in the air. "Ba-ba!"

"There you are," her father rumbled as they drew near the front door of the Blackfriars Lane Enquiry Agency. He snapped his watch shut and tucked it away. "Two minutes late. Quite an improvement for the rookie who couldn't make it to a briefing on time even if his life depended upon it." His dark eyes speared Jackson with a sharp gaze.

A smile quirked Jackson's lips. "Good thing I had such a benevolent sergeant."

Warmth spread in Kit's belly at the good-natured banter between the two men she loved most in the world. Even more gratifying was they loved each other and her. . .and that was a very good thing considering the proposal she was about to present.

"Good morning, Father." Rising to her toes, she brushed a light kiss on his whiskery cheek.

He grunted—his customary yet affectionate response. To her, at any rate. As his gaze locked on to Bella, his whole face softened. "And how is my darling little granddaughter today?" He nuzzled her with his whiskers until she shriek-laughed and threw her arms around his neck, her dolly smacking him on the back.

"That's right." He laughed as he cuddled her. "Grandpa loves you, little one."

She patted her hands on his face. "Ga-pa!"

Kit's jaw dropped. So did Jackson's. They all stared, stunned beyond belief.

"Did she just say her first word?" Kit whispered.

Jackson chuckled, nudging her with his elbow. "Looks like that daughter of yours just thwarted all our best efforts, Wife."

Kit shook her head. After all the coaxing of *mama* and *papa*, how in the world had Bella learned *ga-pa*? She narrowed her eyes—and the twinkle in her father's confirmed her suspicions. He'd been secretly coaxing her himself.

"That's my girl!" Her father shifted Bella to his other arm, chest puffing out.

"I'd be careful if I were you." Kit poked him in the waistcoat. "Pride goes before a fall, you know."

"I hate to interrupt this sermon," Jackson cut in, "but I really should be getting on to the station. Wouldn't want to be late."

"Hmph," her father blustered, his gaze drifting to hers. "But indeed, why did you wish to meet with me *and* your husband? And outside, no less?"

Kit cut her hand through the air. "I didn't intend on meeting on the street, but since Jackson is in a rush and we're already here..." She inhaled deeply, suddenly nervous. If either of them didn't like her brilliant new idea, she didn't have a backup plan. "I have a few things to say, though I very much apologize I didn't clear one of them with you first, Father, as we are business partners. I intended to, but Jackson and I have been up to our ears with managing a herd of children."

"And I've got the scars to prove it," Jackson snorted.

Her father eyed her. "Let's have it, then."

Though she'd thought on this a good long while now, doubt reared like a cobra about to strike. But no. She needed to trust these men, believe they had her—and Bella's—best interests at heart...which was still a scary thing to do after having relied on herself alone for most of her life. Yet these were the men God had given her. She would trust them—and Him—or die in the trying.

Which was kind of how she felt at the moment.

Nevertheless, she lifted her chin and forged ahead. "I have made a decision about my role here at the Blackfriars Lane Enquiry Agency. If it is agreeable to you both, I propose that Bella accompany me every day to work."

"You cannot be serious." Her father wagged his head, and Bella grabbed for his beard.

"Absolutely not!" Jackson glowered. "By all that's holy, Kit, what are you thinking? I will not have my little girl dragged about the streets while you pursue dangerous criminals."

Her hands fisted, and she popped them onto her hips. This was exactly the response she'd feared. "Allow me to finish, gentlemen, before knotting your drawers."

"Mind your tongue, Daughter." Her father scowled as fiercely as Jackson.

"Oh dear." She sighed. "I am making a muddle of this. Let me start again."

She paced a few steps, gathering her thoughts, then whirled back, ready to give it another go. "I love being a mother, and I would do nothing to endanger Bella." She skewered Jackson with a look. "But I also love being an investigator and righting wrongs that have been committed. My proposal is that I continue working here at the agency but only behind the curtain, so to speak."

She advanced towards her father. "And I really think it can be done. Have I not recently employed contacts to help instead of doing everything myself? Did I not supply you with knowledge of street life? And don't forget I helped you with your crime diagram. All these things I did without any endangerment to me or Bella. So, if you're agreeable, you would do all the legwork a case may require. We'll confer together on details, plan a course of action, and then you shall carry it out while I remain at the agency. That way I can keep Bella with me all day while pursuing justice safely. Do you think that's feasible? Please say it is."

He stroked his beard with one big hand, Bella now busy playing with his hat, yet he said nothing as he exchanged a glance with Jackson.

Kit held her breath. It would do no good to say any more, and in fact might harm the case altogether.

"I must have your word Bella would be in no danger. Ever." Though Jackson rarely used such a grave tone, it never failed to send a shiver down her spine. "I mean it, Kit."

She nodded slowly, holding his gaze. "I solemnly vow it."

"Then. . ." He blew a long breath. "How can I say no, for such a situation would keep you off the streets as well—which I very much like. So, it appears the ball is in your hands, Henry. Nay or yea?"

She whirled, facing her father. "Well?"

He picked away the dolly Bella had shoved in his face, then tickled her, speaking to Kit but with eyes for no one but the girl. "I cannot object to seeing my little Bella so often. Isn't that right, girl? Would you like to see your grandpa every day?"

"Ga-pa!" she shrieked.

Kit grinned. "I am pleased to hear it! And I can only assume you wouldn't also mind an additional younger partner joining us as well."

"Wait a minute." Her father's eyes widened on her. "What are you saying?"

"Are you. . . ?" Jackson looked as if he might swoon.

"Oh my." Kit laughed long and hard. "Your faces." She swiped at a few happy tears. "Reminds me of when I brought that tiger cub home and everyone thought I was with child."

Jackson gasped. "So, you're not—?"

"Heavens no. Not that I know of, anyway. I am referring to young Frankie, Martha's boy. With Bellow's Glassworks going under, he is in need of employ, and he's quite handy to boot. Do you not think he would be a fine addition, Husband?"

"He is a clever lad." Jackson retucked his newspaper, the edges of it rippling in the morning breeze. "Sometimes too much so."

"Father?" She turned to him.

"Perhaps we should hold off for now." He hitched his thumb over his shoulder at the agency. "We don't even have any cases on the books currently."

"Come now." She grinned. "As a wise man once told me, sometimes all it takes is a little faith."

"Between the two of you, I have no doubt you'll be busy." Jackson stepped aside as an old duffer in a dirty apron pushed a wheelbarrow of potatoes along the pavement. "But in the meanwhile, I just may hire the sprat myself."

"For what?" Kit angled her head.

"Well, I suppose now is as good a time as any to tell you, though you'll both have to keep it under your hats until it's made official later today." He tossed back his shoulders. "You're looking at the senior officer of the recently established opium-trade task force. The superintendent was impressed with the cache we uncovered at the glassworks and assigned me and Baggett to head up a crew to snuff out such smuggling."

"Congratulations!" She pecked him on the cheek, pride swelling in her chest. What a man she'd married. A capable, attractive, dependable protector if ever there was one, and with a cunning mind as well. Why, she had no doubt he'd someday make commissioner.

Even so, she tapped him on the temple. "But don't let it go to your head."

"Somehow, dear Wife, I doubt very much that you'd let it." He grabbed her wrist and pressed a kiss to her palm.

"Well," her father grumbled. "It seems we're all taking on different roles, but such is life, I suppose. Nothing ever stays the same."

"One thing does, Father." She pulled him and Bella into an embrace along with Jackson. Arms full. Heart even fuller. "We are family," she said with a grin, "and nothing can ever change that."

Historical Notes

BONNETING

In Victorian London, crime was abundant, particularly mugging. There were many ways thieves went about preying on the unsuspecting, but one way was called bonneting. This was accomplished by a handkerchief dipped in chloroform. The attacker came from behind, pressed the cloth to the victim's nose, and once the poor fellow fainted, robbed him blind.

THE VICTORIAN CIRCUS

There were several known circuses operating in 1887 London: Lord George Sanger's Circus and Hengler's Circus, to name two. Most circuses toured throughout the country and the continent and were very popular forms of entertainment. Aerial performances, animal acts, and acrobats were the most common components of a Victorian circus.

SQUIBS

A squib is an early form of a firecracker, a tiny explosive device that was used in different industries of the time. Think of a teeny-weeny stick of dynamite and you'll have a good image in mind. They were used in the mining industry for blasting purposes, in the military for training exercises, and in the theater for special effects; they were also employed as fireworks. There are actual cases on record at the Old Bailey for instances of breaking the peace by throwing squibs.

MASKERS

There were several methods used by disguise artists in the late nineteenth century. Such people were known as "maskers," those who "change their face." Common methods maskers employed were makeup; false wigs and beards; prosthetic noses, ears, and chins; actual masks; and disguise glasses that changed eye color and shape. Also, in the entertainment industry, wax prosthetics were used, painted to match skin tone and applied to face or body. They weren't as realistic as today's rubber varieties, but they did the trick.

WILLIS, PERCIVAL & CO.

This was an actual business dating back to 1787. Thomas Williams originally started a goldsmith business in the City of London in 1677. In 1698, Benjamin Tudman took over the company. By 1708 he was joined by Stephen Child, formerly of the bankers Child & Co., and at that point the company took on the new name of Tudman & Child. There were other frequent name changes as the years went on until it finally became Willis, Percival & Co. in 1814, and by then it was a bank. They financed international trade, namely sugar from the West Indies. By 1878 the company collapsed after one of their largest customers—a Greek firm of importers—went bankrupt.

ALL THE YEAR ROUND

Cove. Brick. Gammy. These are some of the Victorian slang words I incorporated into this story to give it a Dickens flavor and were taken from Dickens himself. He and his son compiled a weekly literary journal called *All the Year Round*, a periodical that was distributed throughout the UK between 1859 and 1895. And in case you're wondering exactly what those words mean, a *cove* is slang for a man or a person, to say someone is a *brick* means he is the best of fellows with a good character, and *gammy* means to be ill-tempered or ill-natured. *A gentleman of four outs* is someone who acts like or claims to be a person of high class but lacks the necessary qualities. The "four outs" means he is without wit, money, credit, or manners.

COFFEE STALLS

Vendors known as coffee-stall men worked on many streets in London during the later nineteenth century and were quite a common sight in working-class neighborhoods. They would sell cheap ceramic or metal cups of coffee, or most often people brought their own empty cups along for a fill. These stalls were more like open-air kiosks, equipped with a large metal urn for brewing coffee as well as a jug of milk or cream. Some vendors had a small table and chair for customers to sit and enjoy their coffee, but most did not.

Sudoku

As modern as we like to think we are, perhaps we are not so much. Today's fun Sudoku craze traces its roots way back to the fourth century when the Chinese mathematician Wei Dakan created a number-placement puzzle. Zoom ahead to the eighteenth century when Swiss mathematician Leonhard Euler developed a Latin square puzzle with numbers. Then late in the nineteenth century, a French newspaper featured a puzzle called The Diabolical Magic Square. It used the 9x9 grid we know today, but it didn't use the same rules as we do for modern Sudoku. That's what gave me the idea to use it as part of a side character's interest. There truly is nothing new under the sun, folks.

Eel Pie Shops

Eel pie shops were the fast food of the day in 1880's London. They were cramped establishments with a counter running along one wall. Some actually had tanks of live eels on the premises. To make an eel pie, the snakelike fish was first skinned, gutted, and chopped into small pieces, then stewed with spices, herbs, and stock. That mixture was put in a pie shell and baked till golden. Pies were often served with mashed potatoes and a parsley sauce.

Opium Trade in Britain

Believe it or not, opium use was legal in Victorian London, and it was widely available in opium dens—where most men went to smoke it. However, despite its availability, this drug was a highly controlled substance and there were strict laws in place. You couldn't sell opium to minors. You couldn't use opium in a public space or create a nuisance while under the influence. And you definitely could not sell opium without a license or a permit. There were only a few major British opium dealers who held exclusive licenses at the time.

Leadenhall Market

If you pop over to London today, you can still visit Leadenhall Market just as I did; and in fact, it was one of the filming locations for Harry Potter for the Diagon Alley scenes. But it's not just a pop-culture venue. This market dates back to 1321 and was actually in the center of what was Roman London. Originally it was a meat, poultry, and game market, but now it's a shopping mecca with lots of variety. It is located just over a mile east of Blackfriars.

NIGHT-SOIL MAN

As careers go, not many aspired to become a night-soil man. This job involved collecting human waste from privies and cesspools in the city. They worked late at night when the streets were empty to avoid being seen...and smelled. In carts they transported away waste to disposal sites where it was gathered and used as fertilizer. These men were considered among the lowest on the social ladder, and they were also at great risk of contracting cholera or typhoid fever.

ARMADILLOS AND LEPROSY

Yes, indeed, some armadillos do carry the bacteria for leprosy, which nowadays is called Hansen's disease. It is not the same dreaded leprosy as in biblical times, however. Research does confirm that a particular species of armadillo that is native to the southern United States and Mexico can carry mycobacterium leprae, but not all do.

Bibliography

A Dictionary of Victorian London, An A-Z of the Great Metropolis. Lee Jackson. 2006. Anthem Press, London.

The Circus and Victorian Society. Brenda Assael. 2005. University of Virginia Press, US.

Endangered Lives Public Health in Victorian Britain. Anthony S. Wohl. 1983. Biddles Ltd, Guildford, London.

The Industrial Revolution Explained Steam, Sparks & Massive Wheels. Stan Yorke. 2005. Countryside Books, Newbury.

Plain Clothes & Sleuths A History of Detectives in Britain. Stephen Wade. 2007. Tempus Publishing Ltd, Goucestershire.

The Secret World of the Victorian Lodging House. Joseph O'Neill. 2014. Pen & Sword Books Ltd, Barnsley.

Victorian Factory Life. Trevor May. 2011. Shire Publications Ltd, Midlands.

Walking Dickens' London. Lee Jackson. 2012. Shire Publications Ltd, Midlands.

Acknowledgments

My favorite part of writing a book is thanking those who made this book possible. Here are just a few because if I named them all, that would be a novel in and of itself.

Shout-out to my awesome editors Annie Tipton and Reagan Reed, the ladies who get my books in tip-top shape for you to read.

Kudos to Books & Such Literary Agency and my agent Wendy Lawton, the gal who holds my hand and/or corrals me in when needed.

HUGE thanks to my long-suffering critique buddies that slog through my rough drafts: Tara Johnson, Shannon McNear, Ane Mulligan, Chawna Schroeder, MaryLu Tyndall, and Julie Klassen, who keeps me on the historical straight and narrow.

Applause to Pastor Justin Nelson, who teaches me much every Sunday and also imparted his great wisdom and skill about glassmaking.

Much appreciation to my readers. You're the ones who make this whole thing possible; and to highlight several of my faithful fans, a round of applause to Erna Arnesen, Paty Hinojosa, Jennifer Kracht, Kristine Lilja Morgan, and Elodie Papon.

And last—but never least—God bless my husband, Mark, who gets me out of plot pickles more than he would like to and gives me free rein to gallop ahead with story after story.

About the Author

Michelle Griep's been writing since she first discovered blank wall space and Crayolas. She is the Christy Award–winning author of historical romances—*Man of Shadow and Mist, Lost in Darkness, The Bride of Blackfriars Lane, The Thief of Blackfriars Lane, The House at the End of the Moor, The Noble Guardian, A Tale of Two Hearts, The Captured Bride, The Innkeeper's Daughter, 12 Days at Bleakly Manor, The Captive Heart, Brentwood's Ward, A Heart Deceived,* and *Gallimore*—but also leaped the historical fence into the realm of contemporary with the zany romantic mystery *Out of the Frying Pan.* If you'd like to keep up with her escapades, find her at www.michellegriep.com or stalk her on Facebook, Instagram, and Pinterest.

And guess what? She loves to hear from readers!
Feel free to drop her a note at michellegriep@gmail.com.

OTHER BOOKS BY MICHELLE

Man of Shadow and Mist
Lost in Darkness
The House at the End of the Moor
Brentwood's Ward
The Innkeeper's Daughter
The Noble Guardian
The Captive Heart
The Captured Bride
Once Upon a Dickens Christmas

Join Kit and Jackson
on their adventures. . .

The Thief of Blackfriars Lane

Newly commissioned officer Jackson Forge intends to clean up the crime-ridden streets of Victorian London even if it kills him, and it just might when he crosses paths with the notorious swindler Kit Turner—but Kit's just trying to survive, which is a full-time occupation for a woman on her own.

Paperback / 978-1-64352-715-4

The Bride of Blackfriars Lane

Detective Jackson Forge can hardly wait to marry the street-sly swindler who's turned his life upside down. But as Kit digs into the mystery of what happened to Jackson's brother, she unwittingly tumbles into her own history and endangers her future happiness with Jackson.

Paperback / 978-1-63609-268-3